I0647592

SAVE THE DAY

by D.J. Fahl

Save the Day

Copyright © D.J. Fahl
2010

Cover and Interior Artwork by Vince Suzukawa

Published by FurPlanet Productions
Dallas, Texas
www.furplanet.com

ISBN 978-1-61450-405-4

Printed in the United States of America
Second Edition Trade Paperback 2017

All rights reserved. No portion of this work may be
reproduced in any form, in any medium, without the
expressed permission of the author.

Dedicated to my Grandfather Ed Loder,
who taught me the joy in thinking rationally
about irrational things.

And to my Grandmother Catherine,
who inspired the bravery I needed
to actually write this book.

-D.J. Fahl

TABLE OF CONTENTS

Chapter 1
The Truth

As I step through the door, I turn on the house lights, a cool breeze following as I shrug off my jacket. I plop the mail down on a desk in the hallway next to our living room. I don't have the energy to look at it right now. My name is Jay Carson, and while I love living here, Portland, Oregon can be a wet and cold place as the seasons change. Especially if you have to go looking through damp bushes just to find the newspaper. I swear that paper guy is not getting a good tip from me.

I fix my black and white fur, absentmindedly straightening a few mussed bits. The curse of thick fur is that it can be hard to manage. Being a border collie I'm used to luxurious fur. I always have it and it can be a hassle. My ruff of fur tends to make my torso bulk out a bit. Then add in a very fluffy tail, one that amused my boyfriend to no end when we first started sleeping together. He's a coyote so he's got a shorter, more bottle brush tail. It can be nice brushing all the fur, but upkeep can be hell. I'm a good looking guy by most marks. There was a time, only a few years ago but it feels like a lifetime, when I never spent a night alone. That was before I met Ted and gave that gallivanting life up. I still wear decent clothes, I spend the time to look presentable. I've gone from the young gay clubbing look to a more professional look, but I think it works for me. I wag my tail, pleasantly surprised at how little work needs to be done fixing my fur just now after a long drive and rooting around for the paper. Then my pricked up ears droop as I realize I've just come home and I'm not going out again tonight, so the effort just seems wasted.

Turning a light on in the kitchen, I glance around and grab a wine glass and pour some merlot for myself. It's funny. You would think that after moving in with your boyfriend you'd spend more nights with someone than when you were living by yourself. I at least assumed that would be the case. No such luck. It feels like I spend more nights alone, in a cold bed, than with the guy I thought I was getting all to myself.

I look at a picture on the fridge of Ted and I out on the river a few years ago. Thanks to his perpetual lateness we had missed a meeting with friends to play cards and he had treated me to a night out on a very nice river cruise ship to make up for it. It had been sweet. We're cuddling in the picture. Being pretty much the same height, if you discount those huge ears of his, the mechanics of a good cuddle are something we perfected from trial and error. I can't help a wuffing sigh as I look at the picture.

Tonight was supposed to be a fun night. Ted and I were going to meet up with our best friends Gary, Mattie, and Brandon at Somewhere Over the Java, the best coffee place in town, and spend the night having fun. We were going to hear some of Brandon's poetry and then hit a really nice pizza place Mattie had found with her latest fling, Ann Marie. Gary had been there, in another skimpy tank top that showed off the wolf's weight lifter torso. Brandon was in his usual sweater vest and slacks combination, seemingly uniform of the urban poet. Mattie was wearing jeans and a t-shirt. It had been nice being with the gang; we had a good night planned altogether. It had felt like we had begun to drift lately as friends. This was a chance to reconnect, grab dinner, talk and hang out. Ted still hadn't shown up, or even called, an hour after we had gathered. When we were just dating, before we had moved in together, he would at least call if he was going to be late.

I left soon after that. I was getting sick of how everyone kept trying to tap dance around what Ted was doing. While it was our first time all together in a while they had each been there for Ted to flake off on me like this. It was embarrassing, maddening. I choked those feelings down as best I could, though making pleasant conversation was out of the question by the end of it. I was tired of them feeling bad for me and the silent, pregnant pauses.

I turn on the radio because I want to hear the rest of the news reports I had been listening to on the way home. The airwaves were flush with the latest out of Vancouver. The city had come under assault by the supervillain Douleur, and the blade wielding boar was making some sort of terrorist attack on the city. The Quebec Separatist is a highly trained killer with tremendous finesse and skill, and he was attacking the city with some allies to make some sort of statement. I remember the boar's name and what he wants because he's in the news fairly often here in the northwest, he has a real thing against Canada, but it is hard to keep all the supercrime straight. There are a lot of villains out there and, unlike Gary or Brandon who are nuts for superheroes and villains, I don't usually pay attention.

Well, except for their hilarious 'what superhero would you sleep with' argument. They love to bicker and ask different people about it. My answer has been Star Coyote for a long time. I suppose it could be because he's saved my life a few times, or it could just be that body. Unlike Glacier or Metalyena, he has a more lithe tone to him I really find attractive. Or maybe it's because he is Portland's superhero. A lot of the heroes tend to choose a city to operate out of as a personal protectorate. Gary has an obsession with the Texan hero, Glacier; though don't ask me what city he's in, I can't keep those details straight. Which is ironic considering the numbers of times I have been put in danger by supervillains. I've had some bad luck with that. I've been rescued—nearly unscathed most times—usually by Star Coyote, but it has been troubling.

Of course my parents and others from their generation often shake their heads at that kind of talk. I doubt they'll ever be used to the world we live in now; it is very different from when they grew up. It has been twenty years since the supposed "Age of the Supers", as the media likes to call it, began. I was just a little pup when the first reports were coming out of odd occurrences, strange abilities, and impossible events. It started slowly, no one is exactly sure how it began or who was the first, but over time greater and flashier powers started showing up. Powerful physics defying effects and stuff out of science fiction: flight, strength, healing, speed, and even stranger skills.

It took a few years for the first superheroes to appear, long hard years as things got progressively worse. The crimes escalated as super beings began abusing their powers more and more, and the idea of a superbeing taking advantage of people was becoming almost normal. I was a little kid, hell Ted was a little kid, during those hard times. The worst, in my opinion, was that monster Power Puma, a racist homophobe who launched terror attacks for years. Sure his powers seemed almost banal compared to some, but it was his army of devoted followers that scared me. It was deeply frightening growing up gay and knowing there was an army of people that hated you out there and everyone was hard pressed to stop them. He still scares me, he's super strong and his followers are fanatical. He also has a skill for bringing together groups of people who should not be able to work together. He's been behind more than a few criminal cartels and super villain teams.

Then the heroes began to appear. Solarcoon in Phoenix, was the first to fight back during an attack by the mountain lion nazi, humiliating Power Puma on live TV, and soon after him others came forward. There were people willing to use their powers to help others, to protect society and the common good, and uphold the law. We finally had masked adventurers and heroes defending us instead of just villains and criminals terrifying people. Soon enough that became normal life. That is the world we live in, where fantastic costumed heroes and dastardly villains meet in the air or on the ground. People aren't as afraid as they used to be. More heroes appeared to help us, to inspire us, and the greatest among them joined forces to become the legendary superhero team the Extraordinaries.

By now the full details of the attack on Vancouver have become clear. Douleur has apparently convinced the Iron Ravers to help him assault the city. The radio personality had to give me a refresher on who they were. They're apparently a biker gang of bears who have been transformed into living metal automatons that can restructure themselves from the bits of metal and scrap around them which gives them a jagged frightening appearance. All of them are fierce, rusted, and crazed behemoths, and no one is sure if they still truly have their minds. Star Coyote showed up and used his super strength and speed to curtail all four of the Ravers, and is now helping the authorities finish containing the rioters, but Douleur has somehow gotten away. It will probably be front page news tomorrow, another bit of bragging for Portland that our superhero once again saved Vancouver. We do that whenever Seattle or Vancouver gets a surprise save from him. He might pretty much be the hero of the whole northwest but he's Portland's hero first and foremost.

I fidget slightly, hoping Ted will call or even just come home. Flipping the morning paper open I glanced around to see if there was any other major news I had missed during the day. Mayor Richard's grinning, bucktoothed beaver face is on the front page. He had scored some major event from the city council and the Governor's office. Portland was looking at a big fat check. I have to admit he is a capable mayor even though neither of us had voted for him. Shrugging a bit I look under the fold and suppress a shudder. El Esclavador made the headlines. He apparently wasn't dead like the authorities had reported last time. Instead he showed up in San Diego yesterday and began to enslave the population with his telepathic control powers. He shows up every once in a while and tries to make entire cities his puppet slaves, I'm not sure why he does it. All I know is that it scares me to no end; the idea of someone invading your mind, seeing your thoughts, controlling what you do. I give an involuntary shudder. Telepaths are perhaps the scariest superbeings on earth. There are no hero telepaths; it seems like a power only villains have access to. I wish Ted was here right now. The story was commenting on how the Extraordinaries, along with the FBI's Division of Supernormal Affairs, had stopped El Esclavador but that it had been a very close thing. The story continues about how there would have to be counseling for the population after the incident. Most of Portland's papers are pro-superbeing so they are running some commentary about how San Diego had a number of legal strictures on superbeing activity and even an ordinance banning more than three Extraordinaries being in the city limits, which almost caused them to fail. Not uncommon in some cities, especially those that lack superheroes. I don't even want to think about how those poor people felt after El Esclavador took them over.

I really wish Ted was home. Reading about the horror stories people told after the attack makes me want him here even more. Getting up I wash out my wine glass and walk to our bedroom. The house, this really nice house in a nice neighborhood that we had bought together, just feels empty without him. It feels too big for one collie. I can smell Ted's scent everywhere. He lives here, but I just don't see him as often as I would like. There is a message on the answering machine. Clicking the button I listen to the sole message.

"Rodriguez, wherever the hell you are, get your tail back here! You can not skip out early whenever you want!" shouts the voice on the machine. It's Ted's boss. Damn it, is he missing work? What was going on? I thought he was more responsible than this. I just leave the message alone and flop onto our cold bed. Where are you, Ted?

The combination of wine, driving, and a long day has a soporific effect on me. I can already feel myself falling asleep on the bed. It isn't late enough for sleep. I'd like to stay up, but worry gnaws at my stomach as I drift off a bit.

Although I can be a sound sleeper, I wasn't really asleep yet. I was just dozing, so when I hear a fairly loud click nearby my eyes snap open. I sit right up and Ted is standing there. I can see his big ears and slender muzzle, his coat of tan brown fur barely visible in the dark of the room. I quickly flick on a desk lamp and with a hint more of accusation in my voice than I feel say, "Where were you?"

"Evening, Jay," Ted tries to say pleasantly. His shirt isn't tucked in and he looks a bit disheveled, tired, and his fur is mussed. What has he been doing to himself?

I get up off the bed and standing with my arms crossed over my chest, I glare at him. "Answer the question, Ted. Where were you?"

"Look, I'm sorry I was late to the dinner. I didn't mean to run late," he says evasively. "Things came up. I ended up doing some clean up."

"Yeah, well all our friends missed you and I ended up being there alone." I glance at the clock. I've only been home a half an hour. Odd, Ted would have had to have taken the bus because we only have one car, but they don't drop off anywhere near now. I shrug it off. There is probably an excuse and I don't want to bother with it right now; there are more important things going on, "This isn't even the first time either. You've skipped out on me and everyone else a lot recently."

Ted sighs, "I know, Jay. I'm sorry there has just been a lot going on in my life; important things."

"More important than me?" I retort testily. He's being evasive and it irks me. I can't help but think how everyone was looking at me at the coffee house, and the drive home which would have been a lot shorter if I had stayed in my old apartment, and reading that paper, and the events in Vancouver. It all just piles on. Not to mention the months, if not years of lying to me. It's not that he hasn't had good reasons in the past but this is getting ridiculous.

"Of course not!" Ted exclaims in surprise looking at me with those brown eyes, his ears folding back as his tail slumps, and says, "You know that you're the most important thing in my life Jay."

"Well you certainly don't act like it," I growl. "You've been leaving me high and dry for weeks now. What happened tonight really hurts."

"Oh, Oreo, I'm sorry," Ted says honestly, using his pet name for me. I believe him too, and I know he is sorry. That doesn't mean he won't do it again.

I'm just miffed at him now, he can't keep doing this and I want to be clear about it. Searching my mind I think about what I read earlier and say, "Oh, just like you'd be sorry if some supervillain attacked the city?"

"What?" Ted looks genuinely concerned about that. "Jay, sweetie have you heard something? What are you talking about?"

"I was listening to the radio tonight. I heard about this huge brawl in Vancouver," I say and Ted seems to visibly relax. "I mean Portland has its own superhero. What if some brawl happens here? What if El Esclavador had attacked here instead of San Diego? Where would you have been? I'd want to be with the man I love, not left alone to fend for myself."

Ted seems shocked by my comment. I mean really shocked, as if I had slapped him in the face. Good, maybe he'll actually think about what he is doing next time. Maybe he'll consider what it means. He stammers out, "Oreo, of course I'd want to be with you."

"So where were you tonight then?" I growl at him pointedly.

Ted licks his nose before saying, "I just got stuck at work, the boss kept me late."

"Ted, damn it, stop lying to me," I growl, my black and white collie tail fluffing out. "This has been going on for weeks and you keep lying to me. Damn it, I'm sick of this! What the hell is wrong? Why are you never around? Are you cheating on me?

Ted's big coyote ears hung low on his head as he looks at me. I hear a slight whimper. He looks genuinely hurt at the idea. "How could you say that, Jay?"

"Well what else am I supposed to think? Tonight you missed a meal with our friends we've been planning to go to for weeks. Last week you were three hours late to our anniversary. You missed our last meal with my parents, which was the fourth time in a row. You come home late five nights in the past week and you've been bruised more than a few times. Not to mention all the other stuff over the years. You give me these cock and bull stories like I'm some sort of idiot. What are you, some sort of kinky pervert who likes to get beat up in bars? I thought we could talk about things. I thought you wanted honesty," I was yelling now. I was furious, but damn it after all the crap we had gone through together including, of all things, getting kidnapped by a supervillain, I thought I deserved better than a late night at work excuse when his office had called asking where he was. My thick black and white fur is fluffed out in annoyance and anger. My thin border collie muzzle spitting out, "I thought you loved me."

"I do!" Ted shouts now his eyes glistening, "Look, can't we just go back to..."

"To what, Mr. I'll-always-protect-you? To me blithely trying to ignore this crap?" I slam my white furry fist into the table in our bedroom causing the lamp to shake. I was being unfair using that sweet line he had told me. When he had held me tight and I felt him gripping me in bed that first night together, when I had felt so totally safe.

Part of me just wanted to grab Ted and hug him. Tell him I was sorry, and yes, he could keep lying to me. Ted is crying now, and those tears sting me for yelling at him. I wanted to say I'd be okay with the lies as long as we were together, even if that in itself was a lie. But I was in rant mode and at this point it was going to be said. "Not a chance in hell, Ted. I LOVE you. I can't imagine living my life without you. But I need to know if you feel the same. We need to trust each other. Or are you just playing with me? Do you love me or am I just a toy? An experiment with being gay like your brother always said."

"I'm not about that! It's just..." Ted trails off and his shoulders slump as he leans against the wall. He looks so defeated. So goddamn smacked around. Bringing his brother into this was truly a low blow and something I regretted the moment I said it. Ted's family was a sore topic between the two of us and his brother's behavior wasn't exactly inspiring. Finally, Ted looks me straight in the eye and says in a low whisper, "Okay, maybe I should tell you. Maybe I should be honest. Just remember you pushed for this." Ted pauses, gulping, "You know how you always wondered about that dresser I built? The one I brought with me that never seems to have enough room?"

I blink. The dresser? What did that silly piece of furniture have to do with anything? That was just my little joke when we had moved in. I mean I kept that crappy scratched up writing desk. Couples that move in together always have knick knacks and oddities they kept for little good reason. I turn and look at the dresser, the brown mahogany pseudo-Moorish design that Ted liked to play with once in a while in furniture. It looks ominous in this light, as if by being tied up with all those secrets it had gained some new facet. Yet it was the same dresser I had always seen, the one I had complained about, the one Ted had even before I met him.

I wonder aloud, "What about it?" My heart beats faster, scared, as Ted slinks over to it, his normally bushy coyote tail hanging low. I can smell the fear rolling off him. What was in there? Weird magazines? Gambling slips? Bodies?

Ted grimaces as he hits a latch I had never noticed before, disguised by a decorative panel on the right side of the thing. He had always been good at wood working, and I hear something slide inside the thing. He opens a drawer and what was inside makes my eyes bulge. A brightly colored blue costume, slinky smooth spandex over body armor, lay there alongside a mask, boots, and a very large utility belt. A bright yellow four pointed star was emblazoned on the chest. It was a very familiar costume.

I still remember when I was falling off of the PacWest Center Building, when those armed robbers tried to loot a city fundraiser party. I remember being caught by firm muscled arms, and being held close to that bright yellow star and feeling myself being lifted into the air. That was the premier of a new superhero, Portland's superhero. Then there was the time with those two vixen supervillains, named Cinnamon and Spice I think, at the marina on the riverfront. Not to mention a host of other times I had seen that blue and yellow suit, and the hero of Portland, flying through the air. I look at Ted, a strange thought worming into my mind. Something I had never considered, no matter how many times I had been saved or watched people being rescued in person or on television. I say my next words in a whisper, my eyes wide, a breeze rustling the fall leaves in the night as I look at him, almost not believing it as I whisper, "Star," I gulp before vocalizing it fully, "Star Coyote?"

Ted nods his head slowly and then, as if to give further proof, Ted lifts his legs up and suddenly he is floating just off the ground, rising a few inches into the air. He hangs there in mid air looking down at me. A slight grin on his snout, a bit of worry there too. Finally he sinks to the floor his feet meeting the carpet with little noise. The beige carpet sinking under his loafers, and I realized that those were a costume too. This was his work outfit, but it was also his secret identity. My boyfriend had a secret identity! I knew I was staring at this point but I can't help myself as I look at my tan and russet furred boyfriend as he stands there before me. Ted still looked the same; nice thick, short fur that I enjoyed running my claws through at night. Same goofy big ears, same toned body. I guess this explained why he worked out so much even when I told him he didn't have to for me. Hell I had started working out to keep up with him. The cute muzzle that just grabbed my attention with its shiny black nose, which kissed me good morning and good night. Only now I could picture that mask on his face and that confident smile as he bantered with some criminal and saved the day.

"So, um, that is my secret," says Ted with a slight chuckle, obviously trying to break the tension.

I plop onto the bed staring at Ted. When you thought about it, the entire thing did make a weird amount of sense. The late nights, the

tardiness, the unexpected disappearances, and the odd regularity with which I had been saved by a super hero, all of it was explained. "That is one hell of a secret Ted," I mutter.

"Yeah," Ted rubs the back of his left ear. It was a nervous tick of his whenever he wasn't sure what else to say.

I wasn't sure either, really, and began to verbalize my thoughts. Things just spilling out of my mouth, something I do when I'm nervous and confused. "Okay, so let me see if I got this right. You are Ted Rodriguez, meteorologist with the National Oceanic and Atmospheric Administration. But you're also the hero of Portland, Oregon Star Coyote. An internationally recognized super hero, who, by himself, took down Doctor Schmetterling before he destroyed Denmark, and stopped the Iron Ravers when they assaulted Kansas City, as well as being the foil to a host of rogues throughout Oregon and Washington. Oh and you're a member of the Extraordinaries, the world's premier super hero team."

"Um, yeah," Ted stood there blushing, "pretty much, though really the Schmetterling thing wasn't that big a deal"

"The entire country of Denmark would disagree," I say with a grin. This is surreal and strange, I know my coyote can be humble but he saved an entire country; shouldn't he be more proud? This is Ted we're talking about, my Ted. I mean I suppose it does make sense. Someone has to be behind the mask after all. I just never thought of Ted being that coyote. I really did think I was used to our world of heroes, unlike my parents, but the idea of Ted being a superhero, the superhero of Portland, Star Coyote, well it knocks me for a loop.

Still looking at his face, his worried face, I can't help but smile at him and say, "Oh and let me see, you are also the Ted Rodriguez who has been dating me for five years next month, and who recently moved in with me. The guy who my parents rather like and call a good influence. Who I find adorably sexy even when he is being a big nerd about Joni Mitchell and Star Trek. Who, might I add, asked me out on a date after spilling a raspberry slushy all over me at the mall. A month before Star Coyote appeared on the scene."

"That too," says Ted with a grin finally breaking across his muzzle as his shoulders slump with relief, "best use of a slushy I ever found."

"And a great way to ruin a dry clean only shirt. Well the fact that you are a super hero is certainly a big secret. So when were you going to tell me?" I ask, tension lessening as the sheer surreal nature of the moment sinks in. Ted was a superhero. A tights wearing jaunty upholder of truth and justice, who had saved more lives than I could count, and my own life a couple times. Who had probably flown into space and fought robot marauders for all I knew.

"Um," Ted scratches his ear again and shuffles his feet.

"You weren't, were you," I say folding my arms and staring at him in disbelief. "You were going to try and keep it a big secret."

"Yeah." Ted's ears flick back a bit in shame as he looks down at the carpet in embarrassment.

"Ted, we've have been living in the same house for almost eight months and dating for nearly five years. Did you honestly think I wouldn't ask? Or that you could hide this?" I quirked an eyebrow at him as I said that. I'm not feeling as angry as I was only a little while ago; more a feeling of that familiar sense of mirth whenever Ted did something without thinking out the full ramifications. Like when he bought that fish tank and filled it up with water outside the house. The idea that he could hide something like this just seems like something only Ted would think of.

"Well, you know, I just figured I could handle it. I mean you believed my excuses before."

"You mean your lies. Sure I believed some of them at first, before I learned your tells," I say as Ted flinches a bit at the word lies. "And you've been a lot less careful lately, Snuffles."

"Tells?" asks Ted. He moves closer to the bed and looking at me slightly confused, not even rising to the bait of that pet name I gave him back when he had that cold. It had become a pet name I enjoyed using for any occasion.

"You always lick your nose before you give me a bald-faced lie," I say with another chuckle. "Not to mention that you wag your tail a little bit too fast sometimes"

"Really?" Ted's finger is fiddling a shirt button, another nervous tick of his. "But if you knew that, why didn't you call me on it before?"

"You don't tell someone you broke their codes unless you have to," I say half jokingly. But when Ted whimpers slightly, I decide I should be more serious. "Okay. I honestly, Ted, it's because, well, after what happened with your parents I just didn't want to press you. I figured you had your reasons."

"So why be angry now?" Ted asks looking at me intently, his ears quirked to the sides in confusion. Bringing up Ted's parents and how I pushed him to come out was always a difficult point between the two of us. It was a rocky time for him and, me as well. The fact that he didn't react to my mentioning it tells me how big a deal this revelation is to him. I pat the bed motioning for him to sit down. He sits down on the edge of the bed looking me in the eyes now. "I mean if you were okay with all of that before, why be angry now?"

I take Ted's paw into mine and squeeze it. Smiling at him and that confused innocent look on his face, "Because we moved in together, Ted. We took a big step in our relationship. I thought we had moved to a new level, that you were finally comfortable enough with who you were to be honest with me. I mean that was what, my sixth time asking you to do it? You've been out of the closet for a while now too. I figured we could start having some true honesty. Instead your lies just got more bald-faced and numerous. It made me angry and a little disappointed. I guess my reasons for why you were lying to me were wrong, but it hurt that you didn't trust me."

Ted looks down at our intertwined paws and puts his other paw on top of them. "I'm sorry, Jay. I didn't mean to disappoint you. I am comfortable with you. Hell, I'm happy to be with you. I just wasn't sure I should tell you."

I smile at the coyote and put my free paw on top of his, reassuring each other. I take a deep breath and continue, "So was this the reason you didn't want to move in with me those other times I asked?"

Ted nods solemnly. "Yeah. I was worried about you finding out."

"But you moved in with me now?" I question leaning closer to Ted's muzzle with a smile. "And I think your fears were justified."

"I was greedy. I wanted to see if I could do this. I wanted to be with you," Ted nuzzles my muzzle. I feel his whiskers brush against my snout his breath on my cheek as we draw closer on the bed. "Even if it was a risk. I wanted to try."

"We would have avoided a lot of arguments if you had been a bit more honest and told me about this sooner," I say at last, my arms around his torso now. Feeling his furry chest under his shirt, "But I'm glad you were greedy. It lets me have you all to myself finally."

Ted chuckles and wags his tail happily. I feel my own tail wagging now as we hold each other. The feeling of holding him and being near him deflating the remaining tension of the argument. Ted says happily, "I'm just glad you're okay with all of this."

I nuzzle Ted and consider that for a moment. Was I really okay with this? I had just said how important honesty was and, honestly, I did not think the word 'okay' conveyed my feelings. The shock was wearing off. That an attractive superhero who has saved my life, was my hot boyfriend was slowly entering my mind. As it did, I was already considering the ramifications. So with a bit of trepidation I say, "Okay is a pretty general term, Ted. I mean this is a lot to take in. This is weird and new territory for me. It's a little scary to consider it all. How many people have boyfriends who affect global politics? I mean how many times have you been nearly killed by some wannabe supervillain? How often have you risked your life? I've watched you on TV fight some whack job du jour with a laser and overblown ego never knowing it was YOU!"

Ted withdrew, breaking our cuddle with a sigh, and flops onto the bed fully, his legs hanging over the edge as he leans away from me. "I was worried you would say that. I know this isn't what you wanted—that I'm wrecking your dreams by being this way."

"What on earth are you talking about?" I wuff, flopping down on the bed next to him. "All I said was that it was weird, not that you were wrecking anything. I really don't know how I feel about this. Except that it is different. You've been a hero for years. You're used to this stuff. Give me some time to adjust. To think about all those times you've had to zip away and do something heroic without me knowing. Was that why you never told me? You thought I'd hate you for being a hero?"

I kiss his wet black nose and my snuffly coyote grins and wags his tail. He always did like that. We lay there together for a while just looking at each other. Finally Ted speaks up, sighing, and looking uncomfortable again. "Yeah, a bit. I mean you've always gone on about how you want a normal life. How we're just normal people like everyone else. How we'd get a little place to ourselves and maybe raise a puppy. Have a quiet happy life. The thing is, Oreo, I can't give you that. I'm not sure I could ever have a quiet life. I'm a freak, Jay."

"You are not a freak, Ted." I growl a bit at the idea of my sweet coyote thinking he was a freak. He should never think of himself like that and bringing up his pet name for me annoyed me in relation to that. "You're not a freak for being gay and you're certainly no freak for being a superhero. I mean hell, you save lives. You've saved mine more than once. You're different, but hell, so what? It isn't anything to be ashamed about. You stop supervillains and save the world!"

"That is just it, Jay. I am a freak. I can lift pick up trucks without breaking a sweat. I've punched out giant robots and fought psychic madmen. Hell, Jay, I can freaking fly!"

"Well okay, yeah, that is different. Like I said this will take some adjustment. I mean I'll need time to get used to it. Just because you wear tights doesn't mean you will not come home to me at the end of the day."

I gently pat his arms and get closer to Ted with a smile. "Keep in mind this is a lot to take in. I mean I just thought you were doing something you had to lie about out of embarrassment. Not saving the city. This won't stop us from being together."

"But what if I can't come home at the end of the day?" asks Ted nuzzling under my muzzle worriedly. "What if I can't be here to grow old with you?"

I consider that, licking his nose, worry gnawing in my stomach as I think of Star Coyote falling in battle. Other heroes had died before. Everyone remembered Marvelous Malamute, Swift Wolf, and The Stranger, the three Extraodinaries who had died for what they did. There were parades and statues and speeches given when that stuff happened. Marvelous Malamute had protected Vancouver, did Ted, well Star Coyote, ever feel weird about going there? Did it remind him of her sacrifice?

For the first time in my life I start to consider what it must have been like for the loved ones who had known their secrets. That would have been lonely and sad. Hell, they probably had to lie to anyone who didn't know the secret about what happened. I push those thoughts out of my mind as best I can. Now was not the time to think about that. Looking into Ted's normally jovial face I can tell he had been thinking about it far too much. "Snuffles, we don't know what will happen at the end of the day. The important thing is that we try to do the right thing and have a good life together. I know you, Ted, you try damn hard to be there for me. I try hard to be there for you. After that, it is all up to chance and the good fortune that supervillains like those two vixens don't get a good shot at you."

"Supercriminals," Ted says, his voice filled with that same tone of pedagogy when he corrected me about what a particular cloud formation was called.

"Excuse me?" I ask quirking my head a little, confused.

"Cinnamon and Spice, the two vixens," Ted looks at me very seriously. "They're not supervillains, they're supercriminals."

"What is the difference?" I was confused, this seemed like a silly distinction to bring up right now, but Ted seemed so serious about it.

"Supervillains are people like El Esclavador and Power Puma, folks who use their powers to try and take over the world or frighten people for their cause. They're terrorists and monsters," Ted says firmly. "Supercriminals are people who just break the law with their powers. Sometimes they do it for fun. Or because they can. Sometimes they have a reason. Sure they're bad guys and they do bad things like larceny and bank theft, but they usually don't kill people. I can understand them. They have a code."

I look at Ted and shake my head. "They're still using their powers to commit crime, so they're more petty, so what?"

"I don't know," Ted shrugs after pausing for a moment. "It's just that they don't go after innocent people. They don't threaten bystanders. They almost seem to respect me. It is a nice change of pace from say that monster Power Puma who will happily hurt innocent bystanders to get his way."

"Sounds to me that you find them compelling." I look at him. "That they are a little bit like you, so you can empathize with them."

And I realize looking at him why Ted could understand the super-criminals. He could empathize with them, because a part of him was tempted to do what they did. He didn't do it though. He was a hero, he protected people, but he could understand the temptation. That was why he needed to make the differences so clear. Heck, for all I knew he considered them a sort of friend, the way he talked about them.

He looks at me and blushes before saying, "You always have to explain everything." Ted smiles weakly and grabs me, his arms wrapping around me as we lay in bed. The tight hug feels nice as I return the favor, our heads going into those familiar positions we had become accustomed to after countless embraces. Our necks craned just right as if we had been made for each other.

Then Ted whispers something else as we hug, words that sound like a lead lump that had been resting in his stomach for a long while, "But what about you? It's dangerous enough being my boyfriend. Now you know my secret too, and that puts you in even greater danger. Being related to a hero is dangerous enough, but if they knew or suspected that you might know other secrets... Last year Omni's husband was killed. Metalyena hasn't had a steady relationship in years. Blitzkrieg lost custody of his daughter thanks to his superheroing. Jay, I'm putting you in danger if anyone found out about you."

"Yeah you are," I interrupt him nodding. "I mean, hell, of course you are. You fight mentally unstable people with death rays. I wish you would have talked to me about it before now so we could work this out together, before you started eating yourself up inside with worry. I mean we are partners. Maybe then you wouldn't worry so much. Ted, I'm here for you. I don't want to be one more worry in your life. You know that. There isn't anything we can really do about the crazies. We just have to try and be careful. But other heroes have families right?"

Ted nods, "A few do."

"Well then, see," I say simply. "Look, I know this will take some work but I'm in for it."

"But it can be so hard, Jay. And you're going to have to lie to your parents. And I'm going to be fighting supervillains and they've told me it isn't easy for the civvies to watch that on TV."

"Well, yeah, I'm not saying it won't be out of the ordinary."

"That goes back to my main point. I can't give you a normal life," says Ted nuzzling my neck, "and I am so sorry for that."

"Hey," I touch Ted's muzzle and look him in the eyes again, those warm brown eyes of his that were always so comforting after a long day, now shining from tears and worries, and I realize something. Something I had never really thought about before now. It had always seemed I had that normal life with Ted. That wasn't true though; the truth was what I say to my snuffly coyote. "Ted, dreams change. I know I said I wanted a normal life but that changed a long time ago. What I want is a life where I wake up in the morning to a smooch from you and to warm cups of coffee on cold rainy days. Cuddling on the couch while we watch westerns and mystery shows, sharing little inside jokes. Your amazing jell-o salad. In short, what I really want is a life with you. That is my dream and I think it has been that way for a long time."

"Oreo, what about everything we talked about? Adopting and the quiet life and … well everything," asks Ted, a hint of a real smile at the corners of his face now.

"Screw the house with the picket fence and the quiet life and the 2.5 puppies," I say flippantly. "My boyfriend can lift a truck and fly."

Ted laughs for the first time tonight. One of those good strong laughs that always starts me giggling. We break our embrace and lay back on the bed just laughing at the sheer absurdity of the moment, our tails wagging. We finally calm down and grinn at each other.

"Jay, you have no idea how relieved I am right now," Ted smiles.

"You're relieved? I thought you were some sex fiend and I was going to have to do something really crazy," I say with my own smile. "Instead, I find out my sexy boyfriend can actually pull off tights."

"That is true. But geeze, thinking back to some of the stories I've heard. Camo has some really crazy ones." Ted is giggling now.

"I get the feeling you Extraordinaries are all relationship challenged," I wag. "I mean seriously maybe you shouldn't listen to those stories."

"I could see that argument. Well, except Solarcoon," says Ted with some thought. "You should see his wife and four kids. I don't know how he pulls it off."

"Isn't he the leader of the Extraordinaries?" I quirk my head a bit. "I had no idea he was married. I had his action figure when I was a teen. How does he pull all that off?"

"Well, the founding members like to say we don't have a leader but Solarcoon is really. I have no idea how, but somehow he does it. He's pretty amazing."

"He is the first superhero," I chuckle. Ted has a reverent look on his face. "I can see how you'd think that."

"He's also a really good dad, though," Ted says with a wag of his tail. "I've met his family. They're good people. You should see how he treats his kids. Besides, his wife makes a really good turkey."

Ted has always had a soft spot for Norman Rockwell-esque families and good homes and that statement about the turkey puts gears twirling in my mind. "Wait, Ted, is that where you disappear to every month? You're little trip to be alone. Are you visiting Solarcoon's family?"

Ted blushes profusely at that and nods, "Yeah, it's a standing invitation to have a Sunday dinner with them."

Now that sounds familiar. My family never did meals, except holidays where Grandpa would cook. Mom was not a fantastic cook and Dad was more of a grill until charred kind of person. Ted's family though, they did big weekly meals for years. I remember the one meal I had with them very clearly, but I am not going to bring that up now.

"Does he know about me?" I ask simply, knowing it is a loaded question. Ted just looks away for a moment. Same old Ted, trying to balance secrets and lead a double life. I feel him tense up a bit as I look at him. He licks his nose but before he can say anything I just say, "Yeah I figured you wouldn't say anything. I guess the others don't know either."

"It is a little hard to tell them," Ted says looking at me languidly.

I take a deep breath and sigh. This feels like a tangled knot that will have to be slowly taken apart. All I can say is, "I know."

"They're some of the best heroes in the world and they're my friends. It is hard to even think about telling them this stuff. These people have saved the world, Jay. I've been with them in war zones, into space and fighting over cities," he says with some excitement.

"And now you are a member on the same team with them," I say with a grin and a wag of my tail. For now, it is time to move on and, really, it is amazing to think of him on that team. "Must have been an amazing day to get your membership"

"Yeah, it was," says Ted with a look of pride on his face, "I'm sorry you couldn't be there for it."

"Me too," I nuzzle him, "but hey, I'm going to be there for your other milestones. Maybe I'll make a scrap book when you personally save the planet from an alien invasion."

With our bodies lying next to each other on the bed, we grin at each other again and I kiss Ted's nose. He laughs and returns the favor happily. It has been a long day by this point. Probably longer for Ted; he had been to Vancouver and back again after putting a day in at work. It is getting late though and I feel myself drifting off while feeling his body heat radiating from him so comforting.

Finally, with a yawn, I say, "Mmm… it's getting late, Snuffles. Let's get ready for bed."

Ted wuffs and smiles, "We already are in bed, Oreo."

"You know what I mean," I chuckle and grab his sides reaching under his shirt and tickling his waist and tummy. He's ticklish right there and it is so easy to make him jump and laugh.

Ted bounces off the bed giggling, "Cheater."

We go about our nightly rituals easily enough. By now we are used to the usual things: making sure things are locked up, lights are off, cleaning up and so on. We brush our teeth at different times because we always get under foot of each other. Finally, we were back at our bed in our boxer shorts. I smile at Ted as I survey his wagging tail as he leaned over getting something out of his bag. "What are you looking for there, Snuffles?"

"This" says Ted lifting up a large silvery pager.

"A pager? What, does NOAA have weather emergencies?" I slip into bed and grin.

"Nah, this is my communicator with the Extraordinaries. Since I joined I have to keep it on hand for emergencies. It is also good for when I need to call for help. The city is patched into it as well, just in case they need me," explains Ted as he put it on his bed side table next to his glass of water. I had the alarm clock on my table since Ted had a tendency to hit the snooze too often.

"You know I never thought of you spandex wearers needing those things. Guess it's a bit silly that I haven't. Surprised it hasn't gone off before," I look at it. Looking a little closer it was it did have a lot more buttons than a normal pager. But at just a cursory glance it looked normal. "I bet it's loud."

"Excruciating. It hasn't gone off for me very often at night. Maybe three times since I got it. The team tries to organize the schedules so we all get decent amounts of sleep and off time. Solarcoon kind of demanded it. Something about how everyone needs off time. Especially the people who can shoot energy rays out of their paws." Ted is looking at me shyly as he continues, "I've been keeping it in my bag since we moved in together, but since you now know my secret I thought maybe I could keep it here."

I look at the pager then the dresser and then at Ted. Looks like our lives were already starting to integrate with his secret world. It felt nice actually; the idea of that silvery pager there and the trust of having it in the open. "Sounds smart to me, Ted."

Climbing under the sheets Ted panted and kisses my cheek happily. I smile and feel his arms reaching around me. Rolling into his outstretched paws and arms, feeling his tight embrace once more, I nuzzle against him as I wrap my arms around him and returne the embrace. As he holds me a thought occurred to me.

"So wait, if you're Star Coyote, how come you haven't broken any of my bones?" I ask looking at Ted.

"Huh? Oreo, I'd never hurt you like that," says Ted surprised.

"Well I didn't mean intentionally. You're super strong after all. No offense, sweetie, but how have you so far avoided snapping something inside of me when we hug? And you're not exactly a languid lover. Should I be looking into taking vitamins for extra bone strength here?"

Ted laughs and rolls back from our hug just chuckling and giggling now. I give him an exacerbated look. I was just trying to be safe after all. Finally he stops laughing and sits up against the headboard, "Sorry, Jay. I guess I can understand why you'd think that. The media just says I have super strength. That does not mean I actually do. I never corrected them because, well, it is a good way to confuse the villains and criminals. Most people don't know what my actual powers are."

"So what are your actual powers then?" I ask curiously.

Ted's paw rubs and pats my shoulder. I slide into the crook of his arm, nuzzling his chest, as he thinks for second and then continues, "Gravity manipulation. I can warp the relative gravity around my body and things I touch. You know, make things weightless or heavier by altering their personal gravity. I use that to mimic super strength and other tricks. So, for example, I can make a car near weightless then throw it. Once it leaves my paws its weight returns but by then relativistic momentum has occurred and you can guess the rest. My super punches and stuff just comes from me increasing my gravity field. The end result just looks like super strength."

"Huh. No wonder you work out then. You need to be in good shape to take advantage of your powers and it's a good back up for other times when you don't want to use them." I say, "Though I do enjoy the end result."

"Yep, I do enjoy that too," he nuzzles my ears "and the fact that you join in now. As for my flight and the super speed, well I think it has something to do with my powers but I haven't figured out how really."

"So some of this is a mystery to you too?" I ask looking up.

"Yeah. Not like this came with an instruction manual. I'm just winging it and trying my best. A lot of it is sheer instinct if that makes any sense. Heck, I wish it did come with a manual. I keep wondering why I can't project my field out and create telekinetic lifts or punches. That would be so useful."

"I bet." I imagine the effects. "That would make cleaning house a snap."

"It's not like it is hard to use my powers most times. I don't even need to think about it really, it just happens. Sort of like waving an arm. You don't need to know how all the muscles work to do it." Then blushing, he adds, "Oh man, when I first got my powers I'd sometimes wake up levitating over my bed. I was so worried I'd end up doing that when we moved in together."

"That kind of sounds fun," I smile. "When I was a puppy and wanted to be an astronaut I dreamed about being weightless."

"You wanted to be an astronaut?" asks Ted, surprised. "You never told me that."

"For years and years. I guess that is my big secret. I mean it is embarrassing. I had model space ships and posters all over my room. I memorized the crews of different ships and even their experiments. I went to space camp. I even studied and memorized star charts and moon maps." I was blushing deeply. "It just never happened for me. My science grades weren't there, among other things. I guess I just gave up on it. Besides I'm a pretty good city planner. I like designing cities and working on infrastructure."

Ted nuzzles my ears and grins, "I think it is adorable, sweetie."

I squeeze against Ted and rub his chest, "Thanks, Snuffles."

As we lay in bed I had an odd feeling that was hard to explain, like I was getting lighter. The bed sheets under me seem to stop rubbing my fur and my tail felt a bit more free. Then I noticed the ceiling was getting a lot closer. I look to my side where the furniture looked weird and then down at our bed. The bed that was very much a few feet below me. The bed I was assuredly not laying on. Our blanket was around us but that was it. We were floating. I turn and look at Ted who is smiling mischievously, his arm squeezing me close.

"Anything you touch?" I ask with a happy smile.

"Yep," says Ted, "now you get to know."

"Yeah, I do," I grin and kiss his nose. "And, hey, we got a bed below us in case you let go."

Ted gives me a mock hurt and then says, "Never going to happen, Oreo."

"Because you'll always protect me?" I ask, cuddling closer and nuzzling his furry chest happily.

"Yep," says Ted with a wag of his tail.

"Why do I always believe you when you say that?"

"Because it is true, Star Collie."

"Star Collie? Because I'm your boyfriend, Star Coyote?" I ask with a grin as we hovere in midair. Oh my God, we were floating in mid air! I try to contain a gleeful giggle as I stretch out enjoying the odd weightless feeling.

"That and the astronaut thing."

"Works for me, Star Snuffles."

"That better not become a nickname for me," said Ted as he rolls against me. We spin in mid air as I adjust against him, our bodies spooning. "With my luck, Force Vixen would hear it."

"That would be a problem?" I ask.

"She enjoys embarrassing nicknames," says Ted simply.

We chuckle and I press against my super boyfriend. His arms wrap around me as we drift off to sleep together floating above the bed. Hovering together against my lover's body, the oddity of being cushioned by air as we float fills me with a childlike sense of glee. Still feeling Ted against me as he presses into my back, the feeling of his breathing getting deeper and slower as he drifts off into sleep is reassuring. No matter how odd the night had become, how weirdly wonderful it was to sleep weightless, and how much I had learned, it was in the end similar to the thousands of other nights we had gone to sleep together and the thousands of nights in the future we'd spend together. My boyfriend's gentle breath against my ears, our fur rubbing together and me feeling content and safe in his arms as I close my eyes and go to sleep.

Chapter 2
Day in the Life

I'm standing on the ledge of a building in my yellow and blue costume, mask on my face as I look out across the Atlanta skyline. I can hear the police sirens wailing in the distance, and hopefully they're evacuating the area by now. Acrid smoke causes my nose to twitch, and I watch as a car is thrown into a convenience store, destroying the store front and hurling glass everywhere. A ball of fire strikes another building, causing a huge explosion inside, and smoke billows from the upper windows in huge black clouds.

Atlanta is in serious danger right now, and I want to leap to the rescue right away. I want to try and stop this from spinning further out of control than it has, but I can not reveal myself yet. We've been preparing for today, there's a plan and I have to follow it. I just have to hope beyond hope that no civilians were in those buildings.

"Give me an ETA," I say out loud, knowing the communicator in my furry ear would pick up my voice. The technology chirps a response and my ear gives an involuntary twitch from the sound.

"It will be 10 minutes and 37 seconds before full deployment can begin, Star Coyote," the deep bass voice of Stratagem says. "But I estimate only 5 minutes until your target appears. Be on the look out."

"Copy that," I whisper. And I watch as a mink on the ground, wearing a far too revealing costume in bright shades of red, is strutting through the chaos, obviously in her element.

She's yelling something now. "Come on out everyone. We have a real educational event right here. This is a historical reenactment of Sherman's march to the sea!" A ball of flame starts to grow in her paw as she says this. She tosses it jauntily between her paws like a normal person would play with a tennis ball. Confident and smooth motions, every pass making it grow larger and brighter.

Her code name is Therma, and I've read the files on her. She used to be a wall flower society girl, until she married a real piece of work. Her husband became the supervillain called Dr. Xerxes, and he used her as one of his early test subjects for his twisted experiments. Some people would say she was one of the lucky ones. Most of Dr. Xerxes' mad techniques end up killing his 'test subjects' in horrible ways. Some say he is obsessed with super powers. I've seen his handiwork first hand and I say he's just obsessed with causing pain.

When Therma ended up with pyrokinetic powers from those experiments, she lashed out at the world. It didn't help that the powers, or getting them, left her unhinged and violent. I watch as she lifts the ball of super hot flame above her head, aiming for the police barricade ahead. A few cops there are running for cover, others are taking aim, but it won't do much good. I'll have to act very soon.

Just before the now basketball sized ball of flame leaves her paw, a bolt of bright blue light hits her in the back. The flame is extinguished instantly as her body is surrounded in a thick block of ice.

"Sorry, Therma, but I think the history lesson is canceled today," a strong, confident voice shouts back. A moment later a ramp of ice hits the ground, trailing off of a building to my right. I grin to myself, watching as my teammate, a husky with a weight lifter's build, slides down the ramp with amazing grace. When his boots meet the pavement he marches towards the figures causing all this chaos. The big husky wags his curled tailed with utter confidence, the icy blue colors of his costume contrasting with the dark grays and whites of his fur.

"Glacier!" shouts a feral looking hyena woman who comes stalking out of the smoke. She has far too many piercings in her face, and is wearing a studded leather jacket smeared with stains. The origin of those stains is something I don't want to think about.

"In the fur, Killa Thrilla," Glacier says with an almost mocking, jaunty salute. All around them the fires are going out, extinguishing themselves seemingly all at once. I know that Glacier is pulling the heat out of the flames. I also know he's worried but he's not conveying it as he marches towards our foes. He's giving us all time to martial our forces.

Despite the warm day I can feel a gust of cool air as the area changes in temperature. He barely needs to concentrate to extinguish the fires. With supervillains, however, you can't let your attention waver that much; especially not with the Terrifying Trio. Glacier smirks at the hyena seeming completely unconcerned by her presence, something we know infuriates her. He holds his paws out wide as he says, "Seriously, did you guys not expect a response when you started tearing apart Atlanta's suburbs?"

"I expect to wear that snout as a jock strap, you fucker," Killa Thrilla yells, and I believe her too. Killa Thrilla was deadly as a normal gang banger back in LA. She was well known even back then, with a long kill sheet to her name. After she discovered her telekinetic potential she got even worse. She enjoys humiliating and killing men, and there are police officers in LA who still don't speak her name. I barely register the flick of her wrist, and in a fraction of a second, knives are lancing out at a frightening speed towards Glacier's body. They're aimed at just the right spots to cause maximum pain and they would definitely be fatal if they reached him.

However, in between Killa Thrilla and Glacier, a glowing magenta energy wall appears, either catching the knives or causing them to bounce harmlessly off of it. That draws everyone's attention as a feminine voice comments, "Now, now, Glacier, they spent all their creativity and thought to make that allusion to Sherman's march. I bet it really strained them. We can't expect them to do something reasonable after that."

"Force Vixen," the hyena growls with malice as a red-furred vixen floats into view above the fight on a disc of magenta energy. Force Vixen has personally taken Killa Thrilla out more than anyone else since they both operate out of LA, and she always done it in such away that she embarrasses the proud hyena. She is at the top of Killa Thrilla's list of personal foes, and the LA Times has even called them archenemies. Force Vixen is dressed in a pink mask and very short pink mini skirt, along with long black boots and a large black leather belt. She's also wearing a smirking half smile that just irritates everyone who faces her, but she never seems to care. Force Vixen being here will make Killa Thrilla ignore everyone else and forget all about team tactics, which is exactly what we need right now. Everyone knows Thrilla despises her at this point and will go for her throat first despite there being other foes around.

"Learning to state the obvious, Manila?" asks Force Vixen with a flick of her bushy tail. "Good for you. Next we'll work on declaratives such as 'I surrender.'"

Blades fling into the air faster than I can see. Force Vixen barely reacts as they bounce harmlessly off of magenta discs that appear and disappear with a thought. Glacier is running to intercept the fight.

"This is who the mighty Extraordinaries send? A snowball hurling weakling and a little girl," howls a deep, threatening voice with a twang of a French accent. I'm on now. That's the cue I've been waiting for. Etenoir has finally shown himself. I can see my target lumbering through the clearing smoke. I aim myself at the hulking figure as I leap off the ledge of the building, my heart pounding as the massive mountain goat comes into view. He is huge, easily eight feet tall and grotesquely muscled in ways no one should be. He has massive curled horns and thick, shaggy, black, woolly, fur. The goat's every step cracks the pavement as he begins to charge towards my teammates.

I lessen gravity around myself to ease my trajectory. I don't need to think about it too much as I zoom forward, manipulating gravity like that has become instinctual for me. I can't believe I am hurling myself at Etenoir. I'm moving too fast for him to react. I suspect the first time he even sees me is just before my fists connect with his chin. By then I've already dramatically increased my gravity field, making myself as heavy as I can. The relative weight and velocity of my blow is enough to send him reeling backwards a couple feet as I pull back from the strike and drop to the ground. A blow like that would have flattened most people, but I don't have much time to enjoy the fact that I actually punched Etenoir. I've already switched from heavy gravity to normal, then to light weight in a second, and even then it is almost takes too long. A meaty fist the size of a manhole cover smashes into the place I was just a second ago, punching a deep hole into the pavement. Water splashes out from a broken water main, but I'm already in the air well above that spot, twisting around in midair for another run.

"Star Coyote! They send you to fight ME!?" I can actually feel the indignation in the howl of rage. I'm honestly as shocked as he is. I dodge another massive fist. Etenoir is easily one of the strongest beings on earth. He's also near invulnerable to all types of harm. He's taken missiles to the chest with little trouble. He tears tanks apart for his own amusement. He's out of my league.

Normally the team could handle this, but this time the only being on earth that could reasonably defeat Etenoir without putting themselves in real danger isn't available. Lady Leopard, the strongest being on earth, is off planet doing a mission for the European Space Agency. We sent a call for her to come back when Etenoir broke out of his prison in Zurich but there is every chance Lady Leopard has not heard it yet. Without her, it's going to take the entire team to take him out.

That's why I'm here, dodging punches that can level buildings. I'm trying to lead him away from the others; flitting around him, irritating him, separating the group so we can whittle them down. Etenoir just isn't taking the bait. He may be strong and psychotic but he isn't stupid. Rumors say he served with distinction in the French Special Forces and fought in Algeria before the experiment that made him into the monster he is today. The French government will neither confirm nor deny those rumors. He does have that accent though and he can speak perfect French. He's also fluent in English, Spanish, Farsi and German. I swoop around him as quickly as I can, landing a couple heavy gravity punches. They don't faze him of course. That first blow was sheer luck and surprise as much as anything else.

Glacier might be super strong and durable compared to most people but he doesn't stand a chance against the ram. They're different weight classes. Glacier can lift Volkswagens, Etenoir has lifted tanks. Force Vixen's fields and constructs have proven less than effective when taking him on. She's a founding member of the Extraordinaries and highly experienced, but she can't fight this guy either. Etenoir is in a weight class beyond pretty much everyone outside of, maybe, Titan Tomcat, Metalyena, and Lady Leopard, and only the last has done it without ending up in the hospital. Metalyena and Titan Tomcat can't fly though, which means I am the only one who can get here quickly that even resembles a heavy hitter. Right now the rest of the team is suiting up, scrambling to get here in time. Meanwhile I am trying hard not to panic. I'm buying time and trying to keep the property damage low until the real power houses get here so we can hit him as a group. No one wants a repeat of Argentina.

The giant ram appeared there a few years ago, before I joined the team. The President of Argentina at the time had refused the Extraordinaries access into the country. He wanted to assert himself and was worried about America attempting a coup on him using the super folks as a cover. He felt the team was made up of puppets to the American government. In the end Uruguay and Brazil called a police action and pleaded with the Extraordinaries to intervene alongside their armies, but it was really too late. The Argentinan army was decimated, the capitol was in flames, and the President was impeached less than two weeks after the conflict ended. The death toll was never fully tabulated. Titan Tomcat, Toronto's superhero and a recent addition to the team at the time, was in intensive care for a month.

When Etenoir escaped this time, Blitzkrieg, Berlin's superhero, ran to the prison and was there in under thirty seconds to confirm his escape from the latest cage. Etenoir never sticks around those prisons long and somehow he always eludes capture until he makes his reveal in some rampage. Even with a super fast wolf zipping around Switzerland looking for him, Etenoir escaped. He made his appearance now, a week later, with his cohorts that the media has dubbed the Terrifying Trio. That makes three supervillains who like to cause as much property destruction as possible for less than understandable reasons. Hell there can't be any profit in this, it's just senseless violence.

A back draft of heat smacks into me. Damn, Therma is out of her ice prison. That didn't take too long. I can't turn to see what is going on of course. Etenoir is running at me now and I need to keep dodging him. Etenoir has a lot of advantages over me but he isn't as fast or as maneuverable. I'm using that to my advantage, just as I have learned in training. I don't have invulnerability. If he hits me with even one blow, I'll be a pancake. I have to hope things are continuing according to plan for everyone else. Namely, isolate and cauterize the Trio until the rest of the team arrives and we can contain them fully. Together the Terrifying Trio is a massive threat. That's why Glacier froze Therma first, despite the fact that she could counter his freezing power, because Therma is the team player. The other two, while smart and effective, tend to be loners and that is how they fight. The biggest advantage we have over them right now is team coordination. Therma could tell the others what to do or give them backup, so she had to go down first. That's why we brought Glacier here early. Hopefully by now Killa Thrilla is neutralized, and it's just Therma. Glacier and Force Vixen can handle her. I hope. THOOOM goes a fist into the ground. That was far too close to my face. The big goat is getting irritated.

I twirl around yet another blow from the huge goat and smack into a joint with as much force as I can muster pushing hard, straining my powers and body. I'm not holding back but Etenoir just chuckles a deep malicious laugh. I fling myself back before an over sized mitt grabs my head.

Then I hear an ear piercing shriek. Something beyond loud, it seems to dig into my skull. A wave of air pushes past me as I hear metal tearing and things breaking. I look over to see some raccoon girl in a brilliant acid green shirt, black jeans, and over sized sunglasses decorated with odd buttons and necklaces. She's cackling, and the pavement in front of her is cracked. Windows all around her are broken, and a couple cars that weren't already hit in the fight have been flipped over and scattered. I don't see Glacier or Force Vixen anywhere.

Crap, it looks like the Terrifying Trio has gone into the Quartet business. We're outnumbered and very likely outgunned and I've been so busy in trying to distract Etenoir that I haven't paid attention to my communicator or what has been going on in the rest of the fight. I know I've seen that face before, but I can't remember where. I'm worried now. I don't know this one, her powers or her style, and I'm not sure the others can handle this alone. But if I leave Etenoir mid fight then who knows what will happen. I don't even know where back up is or when it will get here.

The uppercut from the goat's huge fist nearly connects. I let my attention wander too much. I was lucky to have pulled back in time. Etenoir chuckles, a deep menacing sound, as he says in quiet voice, "Ah, it seems the cavalry has arrived."

I fly overhead, just out of reach, wondering what I should do. This obviously was a plan of theirs to keep us off our game. Score a dead hero or three perhaps? Okay then, this fight needs to end quickly. Where are the others? Shouldn't Blitzkrieg be here by now at least? Then I see it—holy cheese and crackers, I see it!

All those self defense classes and training exercises Solarcoon has put me through just paid off. I had to learn basic hand to hand and martial arts after joining the Extraordinaries, and it is surprising how much that helps out in the crime fighting business even when you have super powers. You tend to forget how useful that kind of knowledge is when you can fly and lift boulders. Etenoir has forgotten it too, because his stance is way off. He has been swinging at me so much his huge legs are in a terrible support position. He's a good fighter but he's over confident about his abilities and I see an opportunity.

I swoop in behind him as quickly as I can. I know he'll follow my movements, screwing his stance up even worse, twisting his body to take a swing at me. At this point, if he were a normal opponent, a simple kick or punch would send him sprawling, making him land prone, an easy defeat. Etenoir is not normal. Even with my gravity turned up as far as I can go to mimic super strength, I wouldn't budge him. That's not the point anymore. I reach out and touch the back of his knee with my paw, lessening gravity over as much of his leg as I can. The idea is simple enough: remove his balance. Now the big goat is near weightless on one side, and his own strength makes Etenoir slip, his feet taken out from under him as he flips up into the air sprawling out and bellowing in surprise. Once his feet leave the ground, I make his whole body weigh next to nothing, enough for me to push him up further, and as he flips up into the air, I quickly let go.

As he flies into the air and back down again, I'm zooming into the sky. I hear him hit the pavement loudly. I don't look. I need to press this advantage as much as I can. My ears pop as I fly into the air, zooming ever upwards, my tail swishing about in the wind. I feel myself straining to fly as high and as fast as I can. I feel my nose drying out and the air is lessening. It's getting hard to breathe now. I reach a height I feel comfortable with and twist about until my legs are pointing down. I've made myself as light as a feather to zoom up here. The communicator chirps, Stratagem is questioning what I am doing, but I don't answer. Instead I take a deep breath and will my personal gravity field to increase as much as I can. Normally I like to make the transition smoothly, normalize myself before switching gears. I feel strained if I try to move too quickly. Right now, I need to do this maneuver with all haste, not comfortably. It feels like time is standing still, and then I'm dropping. I'm dropping very quickly. I feel my nose bleeding slightly, the wind whistling past my ears. My tail feels like its going to be pulled out and I grit my teeth, straining myself, pushing my power, forcing myself to become even heavier and drop ever faster.

I close my eyes hoping I've aimed right—hoping Etenoir hasn't moved too much or been quicker than I expected—hoping my powers will cushion me enough that I won't break apart. My feet connect with something very hard, slamming into it with an audible, cracking boom as the pressure changes around me. I open my eyes quickly. YES! I've landed right onto Etenoir's solar plexus. He's dazed now. I think I just winded him! My heart is pounding now, working on pure adrenaline. My muscles and bones straining, I run up his chest to that huge snout, keeping my increased gravity turned all the way up to hold him down. I lash out hard, smacking him in the muzzle with my seemingly far too small fists. Once, twice, three times I hit him hard in the face. I risk a fourth blow and then leap backwards, breathing hard and slamming my feet back into where I first landed. I hope this worked, I don't know if I can dodge a strike from the goat now. My head feels musty and sluggish and my body strained.

No blows come. Etenoir is breathing but it seems labored. I glance about. It seems eerily silent right now. I hit him so hard the ground has indented around his body. He isn't moving. I look up. His eyes are closed and he seems unresponsive. I count the seconds mind whirling with thoughts as I watch. At thirty seconds of standing on his huge chest, my weight turned all the way up, I know what I've done.

I've punched out Etenoir. He is out for real. Holy crap! I punched out ETENOIR!

Then things seem to get a lot louder. Sound seems to rush back onto me. My communicator is chirping like crazy. Blitzkrieg is reporting from Newfoundland. He's heard the news and is turning back. Metalyena, Camo, and Titan Tomcat are standing down. Stratagem is standing us down from the high alert and sounding an all clear to all concerned agencies. I hear Solarcoon's warm and gruff voice over the communicator, "Excellent work, Star Coyote, a truly superb use of your skills."

That sends a thrill up my spine from my tail to my snout. I feel like I should be doing a little victory dance. All I can do is grin goofily at the thought. One of my favorite heroes, a man I idolized even before I got my powers, the leader of the team, just praised my work.

I hear the calls of reporters now. How do they always get past those barricades? Cameras are flashing. I'm hearing cheers from other places. I look around trying to find Glacier and Force Vixen, worried if they are okay or if they need help.

They don't. They have the other three well in hand. Thrilla Killa is frozen in a block of ice looking shocked. Therma has been contained in a magenta energy force field bubble and the other girl looks like she's been knocked out. Glacier waves at me to come over. I grin and wag my tail which causes me to finally start listening to my body. My legs feel like rubber, as if I just ran a couple miles full tilt. My muscles feel strained and ache; I'll be feeling this for a few days. The cameras are watching me right now. I know I can't appear weak or that this wasn't part of the plan as opposed to the Hail Mary pass it really was. I let my gravity return to normal and step off of Etenoir, giving him a jaunty salute and walk over to the others, trying hard not to let my knees wobble.

Glacier is grinning from ear to ear. We joined the team at the same time, trained together for hours, and I've worked with him more than anyone else. We're essentially best friends in the tights business and outside of it as well for the most part. I know how Paul thinks. He's proud of me in a way few other people would be. He knows where I

have been. I think he's trying to hold back from giving me a hug and cheering like some of the crowd. He can't help but blurt out, "Star, that was amazing! Holy hell, dude!"

Force Vixen is more reserved right now. I'm not sure how hard she is concentrating to hold in Therma, but it doesn't look like much. Therma seems truly shocked and isn't putting up a fight in that bubble. Force Vixen smiles at me, and it is one of those genuine smiles of congratulations. I don't think I've ever seen something like that on her face before. It really makes her look beautiful. "Good work, Star Coyote." Wow, she even used my full hero name. Normally it's some nickname from the tough as nails, pretty in pink vixen, and some correction about what I did wrong.

"So who is the new girl? I think I've seen her before but I'm not sure where," I ask looking at the knocked out raccoon.

"Oh this is Raver. She's had run-ins with Solarcoon mainly. I'm not sure why she is here. Something for a DA to ask," says Glacier, holding Raver's limp body up. "She's pretty green though. She should have hit us with her sonic wail instead of showing off beforehand. Glass jaw too, which is ironic."

"Well let us just be thankful she didn't get the chance. And that isn't ironic, it is just unfortunate for her," said Force Vixen with a grunt. "Good reaction this time, slushball, but you should have been watching my back and seen her coming. I was busy containing Therma."

"Hey now, I was doing my job and I thought there were only three," Glacier responds defensively.

"Exactly, you thought there were only three. Never assume anything like that," Force Vixen comments with utter confidence. "Star Coyote did his job and even anticipated beyond the requirements of moment, ending up with a fairly impressive takedown and the Extraordinaries not having to come out in full force. You were too rigid on the plan"

"Well, the plan worked," says Glacier.

"Because Star was willing to anticipate beyond the plan," says Force with a smirk.

I'm trying hard to not grin from ear to ear, I am blushing and I can't help that. I hear sirens as the police approach with back up and containment systems. Maybe this time Etenoir can be held. I doubt it, but it is a nice thought. Police officers, and it looks like military personnel, approach the three of us. By now the Governor of Georgia has to have called the National Guard and a couple of other organizations to discuss containment.

"Well, everyone, game faces," says Force Vixen with a slight flourish of her tail. "Make the reports, try to avoid talking to the media and no boasting. Make it clear we appreciated the hard work of the police getting people clear."

We nod at that, she is the senior leader on this one and her instructions make sense. Both of us are grinning though. We pulled off a fight with the Terrifying Trio plus one with only one senior member present.

The chief of the Atlanta PD, Anderson Pinjay, meets with us. The cameras are flashing as the older wolverine speaks to us in a thick drawl, "The mayor wishes to extend his heart felt thanks at the speedy intervention of the Extraordinaries. I'll admit I'm not sure I like you mask wearing vigilantes dealing with normal crime but I'm glad you were here today."

"Just doing our job officer," says Glacier with a Colgate smile and then more seriously, "Do we know what the damages are yet?"

"More casualties than anyone would like but it would have been worse if you weren't here so quickly," Pinjay says with a somber nod. "I lost some good patrol men when they started this. Would have been worse if you hadn't frozen the tart in red," he says gesturing at Therma, though he's looking a bit reprovingly at Force Vixen.

"She'll be getting a nice asbestos padded cell soon enough," Force Vixen says with a swishing flourish, her very short skirt made obvious with a twist of her hips. She does feel the need to needle him a bit at this point. She does that to a lot of people.

"Yes, well," the Chief seems a bit uncomfortable with all the cameras rolling; he doesn't want to share his real feelings about all this. He turns to me, "Star Coyote, that was amazing work. The mayor of Atlanta wants to make sure you know that if you ever want to leave Portland you'd be welcome here."

I'm shocked at that. Atlanta has always kept up a very aggressive zero supers policy. Pinjay himself has been one of the strongest anti-supers voices in the city, if not the country. I grin and say easily, "Sorry, officer. I'm a Portland coyote all the way. Maybe Glacier will want to move from San Antonio."

Before we continue talking, all of us putting off the inevitable clean up work, my utility belt rings. Or more accurately my cell phone rings. Shoot I thought I had it on vibrate. I blush as everyone stares at me.

"Is that your cell, Star?" asks Glacier surprised. "I've never heard it go off before."

"Uh, yeah, sorry about that." I'm a little embarrassed, giving a nervous laugh as I reach my paw down to my pocket.

"Is it important?" asks Force simply.

"Well, just some personal stuff," I say hoping that it won't go further than that.

"You have personal stuff?" exclaims Glacier in surprise. "Wait, you've never talked about personal stuff."

Force Vixen gives an exacerbated sigh, "Go. Handle it. We'll deal with clean up."

You don't have to tell me twice. Vixen has never let me out of clean up duty. I'm in the air in a second. Yeah I'll be feeling this battle for a few days; whatever lets me fly is complaining from the strain. I just float up to the clouds then come back down near the battle on an undamaged roof top. Better to be nearby just in case. I take my phone out without looking at the number. I know who is calling me; this cell phone number is known by only one person.

"Hello," I say.

"Hey there," says a very familiar voice. I grin and can't help but wag. I can just picture Jay with his cell phone calling me, "Hope I'm not pulling you away."

"Not from anything important," I say happily. We had talked in the days after I told him my secret and we agreed not to use our names or nicknames over the cell phone as an extra measure of protection for the two of us. Too many people out there have weird technology or super hearing. We could go without the phone but it is really nice getting a call from my collie after a battle.

"Impressive things on TV. That was some fight in Atlanta," he says simply. I can imagine him leaning against that bench outside his office building as he is talking, wearing that button up shirt his furry chest plumps out slightly, poking through the top button, his tail lazily moving back and forth.

"Were you worried?" I ask. I know he won't answer with complete honesty there, but I want to ask.

"You had it handled. You should watch your left side though. He nearly got you a couple times."

"Yeah, I know, but let me tell you this is one outcome I wouldn't trade for anything," I say, still grinning ear to ear.

"I'm proud of you," Jay says over the phone and I know despite his worries that he really is right now. And that, more than anything, makes me smile and float slightly above the roof. The fact that he is proud of what I've done today makes it seem even more impressive. "You did a great job. I know you were scared about this happening."

He's right, I had been. The team had been on high alert for a week since the escape, and everyone was on edge. I had told Jay why after a day or two of me jumping and snapping at him. It scared both of us that I might have to fight Etenoir. We both had looked at that beeper every night in fear. I had finally just put it in my sock drawer so I could ignore it. "Yeah I was."

"Me, too," he says, "but you did something incredible today, and the fear didn't stop you and that is why I am so proud."

"So what are you doing now?" I ask changing the topic even though I am now floating off the rooftop slightly. The great part about being honest with Jay is that right now it is like we're new lovers again, exploring each other in different ways, seeing new parts of each other. We've both been a bit more affectionate too. We've been calling each other more and just chatting, giving each other more attention.

"When I saw the special news report I took a coffee break. Everyone did really. I'm just outside the building now," he says.

"Having a good day?" I ask just wanting to keep talking now.

"I've had better. I got a lot of extra work on my desk today, some new proposal stuff. You know the drill."

"Yeah, my boss is going to be angry for me getting back so late."

"I'll bet," he says with a throaty chuckle. "Is it just me or is Force Vixen's skirt getting shorter and shorter?"

"Maybe her skirt is getting shorter," I say sticking out my tongue a bit. "Why, you jealous? Worried she'll tempt me away from you?"

"Nah. We both know you're a neck man," he says and we both laugh. He then adds, "Hey, see if you can make it an early night tonight, I want to celebrate with you."

I grin from ear to ear, "Well, let me check with my people but I bet I can swing it."

"I better get going back to work," he says. "Oh, and remember we need eggs, so pick some up on your way home."

"Of course," I say happily. I'll probably also get some more coffee too, we were low this morning.

He pauses for a moment and then adds with a slight tremble in his voice, "I love you."

"I love you too," I say as we hang up the phones. Yep, he really was worried. I tuck my phone back into my utility belt making sure to set it to vibrate this time and sigh, wishing I was home right now. Well, better go help with clean up. I turn around and there standing on the roof are Force and Glacier. Force Vixen has a self satisfied smirk on her muzzle and Glacier is grinning at me in undisguised glee.

"Well what do you know, Star Coyote, has a giiiiirrrrlfriend," says Glacier with a wide teasing grin.

"A girlfriend threatened by my skirt no less," says Force Vixen with a flirtatious smile. "Well at least your paramour has taste, Star Puppy."

I am blushing full force now as I look at them, "Um, how much of that did you hear?"

"Pretty much all of it," said Glacier walking up to me and wrapping an arm around my shoulder and holding me close in a friendly hug. "Atlanta PD has got most of this and the UN's special Etenoir peace keeping force is here to help contain the big goat, so the Chief kindly asked us to scoot. Especially since the hero of the hour had already left photo opportunity range."

"Ah." I say nodding. "You guys know you did a great job too, right? I mean I only did one thing. You took out three dangerous super villains."

"False modesty will get you nowhere," says Force Vixen, "especially in trying to change the topic"

"Yeah! I mean seriously Dude why didn't you tell me you were seeing someone? I tell you all about my dates. Hell, do you know how many double dates we could have done? Is she not a coyote? I mean you know we're not speciesist here," says Glacier quickly, and I think he's actually a little hurt.

It is true, he does tell me all about that stuff, we talk a lot. Sometimes we go out for drinks together or hang out between missions. It is nice having a friend who knows where you are coming from, and hell, I'd call Glacier my best friend after Jay, and I know he feels the same way. But how do I explain to him that it is a 'he' not a 'she' that has my heart? I mean I don't want to risk our friendship. He's a Texan for goodness sake.

Jay tried to hide it, but I know he was really miffed that I wasn't out of the closet on the team. He thinks it a step back for me personally, since it took forever for me to come out to my parents. But after what happened when I told them, why would I ever want to risk my friendships on the team that way? Besides, how would people feel if I was an out loud and proud hero? Wouldn't some people have real problems with that? What if the city of Portland kicked me out? What if they kicked me off the Extraordinaries?

I can hear that voice of Jay's in my head lecturing me that if people are going to freak out about a very small part of my personality then they aren't really friends and they're not worth my time. I've wanted to be an Extraordinary ever since I got my powers. These are people I idolize, and this doesn't feel like a small part of who I am. I've got a boyfriend I live with. I wish Jay could understand what a big deal this is to me.

"Glacier, leave him alone. Just because he doesn't talk about his one night stands is no reason to pry into the privacy of whatever chippie he is with this week even if she's a porcupine or something," Force Vixen says testily as she taps a booted foot and calls the bunker.

"Um ... border collie," I say hoping the extra information will be enough for now.

"Oh, a herder hmm. Yeah those can be fun, especially in the sack! Very commanding and in charge if you like that," says Glacier with a little of that old fraternity dog shining right through. I can not help but blush further.

"Mmmm. So does she know your secret? That phone call was oddly timed," asks Force Vixen.

"Yeah. I, uh, told my secret a month ago," I say. Oh good gravy, I'm playing the pronoun puzzler game again. It's been a long time since I've done that. Maybe I should just be more honest.

"A MONTH!!!" shouts Glacier, "And she's sticking around? Geeze, Ted, why were you keeping that under your hat? I've never told anyone I date that stuff. How did that go?"

"Glacier! Code names!" growls Force Vixen looking about worriedly.

"Lot of yelling about honesty, some massive reassuring and a couple days of really awkward conversations," I say now with total honesty.

"Dude, you are going to tell me everything now," says Glacier with a wag of his fluffy tail, "seriously."

"Okay, gossip girls, hush," says Vixen touching her ear and nodding. She's getting a communiqué from our base. "Stratagem wants us back at base for debriefing and medical checks. No arguments."

"We'll just continue there," says Glacier with a grin, looking at me with undisguised glee.

"Fine and dandy," says Vixen offhandedly, obviously not caring enough at this point. "Now get ready for the teleport."

"Oh hell, not the teleporter again," says Glacier irritably.

"I could just fly there," I say. I hate that device, I really do.

"Do you think so?" Force Vixen with mock interest, "Want to carry us there as well?"

"Well … not sure I can do that right now," I say scratching my ears. "Think you can make it there?" asks Vixen. And I know that she knows I pushed myself. How she always knows I have yet to figure out. "No," I admit.

"Right then, got all that, Stratagem? Okay then, begin the sequence now," she says and I see her disappear in a flash of golden yellow. My communicator chirps that I am next. I try to brace myself.

* * *

I hate the teleporter, I really do. I feel the energy around me pulling me in a direction that might be left or right or maybe neither, if that makes sense. Next it feels like I'm being pushed through a key hole. Not necessarily painful just tight and uncomfortable. Finally after that feeling passes I feel myself materialize on the pad; upside down this time, surprisingly not one of the worst ways to appear on this thing. However my upside down position causes me to smack my head against the floor and flop over. I hate this thing; I swear it just wants to embarrass me. I scramble up to get out of the way so that Glacier can move through next.

Back when the Extraordinaries were founded and the Bunker Base was created, The Stranger handled getting people to base. The jackal's power allowed him to manipulate space and time, letting him teleport people to and from the Bunker with ease. It was seen as a secure way of maintaining the location's secrecy and it was convenient. Stranger's temporal manipulation bubbles were also quite snazzy in later years. The best part was that he was amazingly precise about it, and could move large groups as long as he was touching them. He even helped hollow out the caverns that would become the bunker. As a founding member with Solarcoon, Force Vixen, Swift Wolf, Stratagem, and Lady Leopard the team had gotten used to his services.

After he fell in that fight with Doctor Schmeterrling, Stratagem had put tremendous effort into creating a device that could mimic the convenience of Stranger's powers. All you had to do was look around the huge room the teleporter was in to know he hadn't gotten there yet. Easily the size of an octagonal ballroom, the floor of the room was covered in odd circuitry patterns that looked sort of like I-Ching symbols leading to the central point the teleporter drops you on. The device can only teleport one person at a time, tends to have odd side effects, and can be pretty imprecise. That and it was uncomfortable. From the stories I heard, Stranger's teleporting was quicker and didn't leave a sensation, outside of an odd ticklishness once in a while when he was tipsy from the annual holiday party. And it never left you needing to brush your fur afterward.

Across the room, Force Vixen is adjusting her costume. Her mask is askew and her skirt looks wrinkled. She is brushing down her fur with a folding brush because her cranberry red fur is sticking out at odd angles right now. I heard one time the teleporter didn't materialize her costume. That might have been Camo blowing smoke under my tail, though. He and Vixen have a rocky relationship.

"How bad is it this time?" I ask. We both know I'm talking about the static charge that causes your fur to stick out. No one ever knows if the static will affect them on any one trip. It is more embarrassing than anything else. Most times I just look like I have a bad case of bed head.

"You've had worse," she says glancing at me. "Your head fur looks a little off but that's it."

I've taken to carrying one of those folding brushes in my utility belt as well, so I take it out and try to comb my fur down slightly as I hear that hum of Glacier's arrival. I glance over to see how bad it is for him, and it is intensely hard to not fall to the floor laughing.

Glacier's usually thick, soft coat is sticking up with a full static charge, making his entire body appear to be a bulked out giant fluff ball. His costume looks far too small on his now puffed out body, which does not help me to stifle the giggles.

"Not that bad this time," Glacier says with a wag of his tail. Seeing that poof wagging his tail is too much for both of us, and Force Vixen and I both start laughing. I nearly fall to the floor chortling. Glacier is oblivious at first, but he looks down at himself and sees his fur sticking out and says with resigned exacerbation, "Of all the days to forget to bring a brush."

Vixen and I both hand him ours and he starts to struggle with controlling his fur as we leave the teleportation chamber. The Bunker is a pretty expansive underground complex. A couple labs, holding cells, trophy rooms, even a few apartments to handle housing situations. We're headed to the central meeting room. That is where the main computer used for monitor duty is located along with a couple other key systems.

Entering the main meeting room, I glance at that huge table we use for actual meetings. Most times it is empty or has one or two heroes sitting at it working on something for one reason or another. I still can't believe I get a seat at that table. Or that my own logo is on one of the chairs.

Stratagem is at the main computer control center running operations and watching out for situations the Extraordinaries might be needed in. The stocky badger is probably also using that computer to run some investigations of his own, and some computer game of the day. He has never been clear what his powers really are outside of his brilliant mind. Personally I think it is multitasking. Though he is an amazing detective, outside of what I heard about Omni, he can pull together clues like no one else. We're lucky he was on monitor duty today. He can't take it all the time. He has his own life to live in Boston and his own work, projects, and criminals to handle. Not to mention his civilian identity's life and job, though I don't know what he does or how he finds time to do it. He plays things really close to the chest. I wave at him with a grin as he turns around and gets out of his chair to look down at the table from the raised platform.

Stratagem is a pretty impressive badger in a lot of ways. He works out hard and it shows on his body. He doesn't have that weightlifter huge muscle guy look of Glacier. He's got more of a stocky firm look that seems to compliment his badger body frame nicely. He's in great shape for a superbrain. He certainly looks like he's got super stamina or strength in that silvery gray body suit costume he wears. It is a bit looser than tights but does reveal his musculature enough to be imposing. Most times he has a utility harness and belt on along with a black trench coat that conceals a frankly terrifying array of gizmos and gadgets. Over his eyes is a pair of large gleaming goggles. He let me try an extra pair on once. They look simple and a bit old fashioned but in actuality they're highly miniaturized super computers that he created to give him a constant data feed. I still have no idea how he processes it all.

Stratagem is looking at a watch and comments, "That was the third fastest take down of Etenoir without Lady Leopard on hand by 0.39 seconds."

"Well I think the large part of the credit for that should be given to Star Coyote," says a deep baritone voice. I turn, not realizing others were in the room. I had missed the two heroes standing to the side when we walked in. One is a large hyena with dark brown and tan fur and black spots, Metalyena. He's wearing a white tank top, loose brown cargo shorts, big workman's boots, and a red bandana mask to hide his face. His hair is tied back in a pony tail which just seems to highlight that relaxed slacker look the powerful hyena has always had. No one doubts his dedication now, but when he first premiered there was some talk of him being too lazy to be a hero. Metalyena gives me a warm smile and walks over. Shaking my paw, he asks, "So how did it feel punching out that jerk?"

I grin and take his much larger paw in mine shaking back. Metalyena has actually defeated Etenoir in combat. It wasn't easy but I know he can relate. I smile up at him as he gives me that firm jovial hand shake and I answer, "I still can't believe it worked."

"It was an interesting way of using your abilities, Star Coyote," says Stratagem as he absentmindedly tapped on a key board, "very much based in the idea of keeping an opponent off balance." He mumbles to himself for a moment, "Hmm, there we go. I just shut down that Cartel that had been bringing in that high grade cocaine into El Paso." I grin a bit. Stratagem often verbalized his computer events. I think he records it for some reason. I used to be more impressed, but he does them so often, not to mention he's always working on four things at once.

"It was awesome to watch," says Glacier giving me another one armed hug. He continued with a broad wag of his fluffy tail, "Metal, you would not have believed it. I was shocked when I saw our Ted here slam that ram. I think Etenoir was shocked too."

"We saw it on the screen," Metal says, chuckling with one of those brotherly laughs he always gives. He's always been an easy guy to work with, laid back and willing to go with the flow, very even tempered. I think it comes from having a big family. It is surprising that his powers then revolve around implacability. When he turns into living metal, Metalyena becomes impossible to hurt and super strong. It's some sort of alloy of powerful tensile metals that even Stratagem can't identify fully. Not that it stopped the badger from using the hyena as a basis for some of the stronger metals in the base and in his own equipment. Heck, even outside of his metal form he's got the build of a powerful athlete and can take a lot more than most people. That is why his costume is so relaxed. Unlike most of us he literally changes his body and doesn't worry about much when it comes to his personal safety. Other people are a bigger concern for him and when he works with the team he has a tendency to dive in front of attacks taking them before it hits anyone else. That has caused problems when we have intricate plans, but it is hard to convince an invulnerable hero not to take one for the team. He continues, "I had already metalified myself and I was about to get into the teleporter when I saw it happen"

"This one dragged me away from an important meeting. So let's see if next time we can speed it up with the interesting use of powers," says

Camo, lurking in the corner of the room. Camo is a jaguar in a black full body jumpsuit. The only thing breaking up the uniformity of the tight black suit is a line over his torso leading to a stylized letter C on his shoulder. Camo's mask is actually a pair of large golden sunglasses that wouldn't have looked out of place in the 1980's. He's been voted most stylish hero four years running by some fashion magazine. I never pay attention to those things, which I suppose makes me a bad gay man, but it was something he gleefully reported to Glacier and I on our first day.

"If you are both here you could have joined us instead of watching the TV," Force Vixen responds to Camo with a slightly raised eyebrow.

"Hey, it isn't my fault the teleporter had to have a system reboot after I got here," says Camo, flicking his tail in irritation.

"And yet you want the fight sped up, Mister Sight-Unseen," says Vixen with an arched eyebrow. "Though I do wonder what a guy who can only create illusions would actually do against a behemoth like Etenoir."

"Hey, Metal and I have taken him down before," growls Camo his pride a little hurt. Camo's powers are subtle and he uses them well, but it does seem incongruous that such a powerfully built leopard's abilities reside in being so subtle. He can turn invisible and create illusions. He learned ventriloquism to increase the effectiveness of his powers. There are some in NYC who feel they need a more powerful hero and say so openly in the Post and Times. Never mind Camo's dedication or the drop in crime since he started patrolling the city, it remains a sore point for him when people mock his abilities or effectiveness. Something Force Vixen knows all to well. Like I said, they get on each others nerves.

"As I recall that fight, it was Metalyena handling the situation. And he ended up with a broken arm and actual cuts in his supposedly invulnerable skin," says Force Vixen, her words almost dripping with acid.

Metalyena sits back in his meeting hall chair and props his legs up on the table while giving Glacier and I one of those looks. He's seen this one before. Camo and Metalyena got their powers at the same time while roommates at Princeton. They both played football there and knew each other extremely well, so they premiered together and fought crime in New Jersey. Now Metalyena works out of Chicago and Camo handles New York City.

There were all sorts of rumors about how intimate the two were back then; heck Jay looked disappointed when he heard they weren't a gay couple. I know a couple guys who have Camo's posters up on their walls. He does a couple every few months and the proceeds he would receive go to a string of charities of his choice, mainly scholarships and

New York youth programs. For team publicity, and to fight against shoddy knock offs that flood the markets, Camo has convinced team members at various times to do photo shoots for assorted merchandise under the same system as his own. The profits always go to charities but it gets a lot of press and as I understand it, they sell really well. The company Fredrickson Publishing has the copyrights and lawyers to defend the team's image. Jay had one of Metalyena flexing when I first met him. Then after I saved his life twice that poster disappeared and I found a Star Coyote one I had done when Camo convinced the team to get them as a set, the only time he has been able to get Solarcoon to pose for it. I hear the Force Vixen ones outsold Camo's, much to his chagrin.

Jay had blushed a lot about having a poster of me. I felt flattered. He had gotten rid of that poster before we moved in together saying that with all the times Star Coyote had saved him he didn't want me to get the wrong idea. Jay and I had a nice long chuckle about that one after the fact; though he did convince me to strike a similar pose for him that night.

Stratagem clears his throat to break up the standoff, "If I may. The teleporter failure was my fault. I strained the coils getting Glacier there in time to contain Therma, and it couldn't handle much after that." Camo gives Force Vixen another dirty look but they stop their verbal barbs for now. Stratagem continues, "Now then, Lady Leopard hasn't reported back but I will send her an all clear signal so she knows not to rush. I have been in contact with the UN and the Attorney General's office and they are already preparing Etenoir to travel to a new secure prison on Midway Island. I believe it will have a 62.7% chance of containing him. Metalyena, they requested either you or Star Coyote to supervise the transport."

"They requested TED!" shouts Glacier still extremely happy for me. "Wooo!! Way to go buddy!"

"Really?" I say surprised, flabbergasted actually. Normally the UN only wants experienced heroes who have been on the team for a long while to handle that sort of thing. I only joined the team three years ago, so being asked to help supervise is nothing short of amazing.

"Well you did impress a lot of people," Metalyena grins, "but since you took him down, why don't I handle the transport? I'll call my worksite and tell them I won't be in for a few hours."

"They need two and a half hours for preparation," says Stratagem, "so you have some time to head back to Chicago using the transporter. They're confident they can keep him out with the number Star did on him and that drug cocktail they have for him."

"I'll get out there now. Best not to wait," says Metalyena as he stands up, "Good work again, Ted."

I grin and wag my tail happily. I almost start to float again. All I can say is, "Thanks, Kyle."

Stratagem continues talking, drawing my attention back to him as Camo and the hyena prepare to leave. "Now then, I need you three in the medical bay for a full health check. We need to make sure there is no real damage."

"Oh, come on. Therma didn't lay a hand on us and Killa was out in minutes," Glacier grouses. He hates medical check ups.

"Rules are rules, Glacier," says Stratagem while folding his arms, making it clear there won't be a discussion. "I also need full reports from each of you, then you can go."

Glacier grumbles a bit but I nod. It does make sense, and Stratagem probably wants to figure out how we can speed up a take down next time. His genius for tactics is after all how he developed his moniker. Then I realize something. Maybe now is a good time, with Stratagem right here, to bring up an issue.

"Oh, uh, Stratagem can you also pencil in time for a personal meeting with me," I ask as Camo and Metalyena begin to head towards the door once more.

"Of course, Star Coyote. May I ask what it is about? You know monitor duty is when Vixen signs off on it," says Stratagem trying to guess what I want.

"Trust me, you don't want that," from Camo.

"No, it isn't about that. I, um, well," I shuffle my paws, feeling everyone looking at me now. Maybe this wasn't a good idea. I blush slightly and blurt it out, "I wanted to talk to you about getting Alpha Level Security for someone."

Everyone is staring at me now. Camo and Metalyena have stopped dead in their tracks. The team has several levels of prodedures and tools for the protection and safety of Extraordinaries' families and loved ones. Alpha level, the highest level, is for when we need to have the entire team ready to defend our families. It implies a lot of trust in the team and that the people under guard are extremely important to the member. I should know. I once spent a week's rotation guarding Solarcoon's wife and kids when Baron Xanadu attacked Omni's husband and we didn't know if he had other identities or had told anyone else what he knew.

Alpha level security is for the most important people and it means a lot of extra bells and whistles and a lot of risks because of how much the person being protected finds out.

"I see," says Stratagem slowly. "Ted, you are aware that Alpha security is only for extremely close relationships correct? These are certain by laws that are followed with it because of the intense security it implies, the danger, and the level of trust afforded to team members. An Alpha class has a high chance of learning more than one secret identity. It is also a large commitment of resources for all of us. There are only 12 Alpha class security people. Four are children."

"I know. I read the rules," I say. I sat down with Jay and we talked about it. A lot. We read the rules together too. I thought about asking for just Gamma level, maybe Beta. Why raise attention and issues, why risk the team finding out, but at the end of the day Jay is just too important to me. I have to at least ask about it, even though it is uncomfortable for me to do so.

"Then you know it means the person needs to know your identity in full," says Stratagem.

"They do," I say.

"That the person has to have a very clean record. No criminal records, they can't even have tangential contact with a super villain," continues Stratagem.

"Beyond reproach," I say evenly now.

"It means me entering their name into the central computer. That every Extraordinary will know about parts of your personal life should an emergency come up," says Stratagem. He's referencing Titan Tomcat's hesitancy to put the name of his wife in and Stratagem's own silence on the matter. A part of me wonders if he already knows about Jay, and is giving me an out.

I take a deep breath, "I know."

"That you need to have been in a long term committed relationship for at least three years," says Stratagem.

"We've been together five years," I say. "And we moved in together eight months ago."

"Five YEARS!" shouts Glacier. I turn and look at him. He looks very hurt at that admission. Actually everyone is staring now. Camo has taken off his sunglasses. Metalyena's face looks shocked, his powerful square snout hanging open slightly. Even Force Vixen seems a little taken back. Glacier continues, "Ted, you've know this girl since before you joined the team?"

"Um … a month before I even put on a costume," I say and I really wonder if now is the right time to correct him on the gender, but he just looks so shocked.

"I can not believe this," says Glacier at last.

"I'll say. Talk about playing it close to your chest," says Camo. "I had no idea you were even dating."

"Obviously that was the point," says Glacier acidly. "Did you not trust us, Star? I mean you've met Metalyena's brother. You've met Vixen's fiance. Hell, you've met my father and he doesn't even know I'm a super hero!"

"It wasn't that," I protest. "Look I just compartmentalize my life a lot."

"Hell, now that I think about it I've never met your parents," continues Glacier angrily. I flinch at that. A part of me wants to growl back at Glacier. Rise to the bait and tell them about how my parents called me a pervert and kicked me out. About my brother's condescending attitude and how he tried to blackmail me when he found out about Alex, my first boyfriend. I want to make him eat his words.

"Like that is a big deal," Vixen says stepping between us before I say anything. "Some people don't get into personal details like that, Glacier, and some families aren't that close. I see no reason he should have introduced you to his parents."

"It is a surprise though, Emma," says Metalyena. He then looks at the fuming husky, "Look, Glacier, it was his choice. He's taking a big leap to now ask for Alpha level. We should all calm down and just accept that this is how it is."

"Accept it!" Glacier shouts his eyes glowing. I think he is actually having trouble containing his powers, "Five YEARS! Five of them! Hell, you didn't even tell this chick you were costumed until a month ago. Obviously it isn't that close!"

Metal glares at Glacier. We all know about how the hyena had once told someone very close to him, and how that person rejected him. Called him a freak and broke off all communication completely. Glacier obviously regrets saying that now as the hyena growls at him, "Paul. Go to the showers. Cool off. Make your report later." Glacier stares for a few moments then turns and leaves. Things feel really tense now and I know it is my fault.

"Yeah, I better get back to work," says Camo finally, walking quickly through the door and out into the hallway.

"We better handle this now," says Stratagem.

"It can wait until after the check up and reports," I say, feeling like I need a breather right now. "I really do not want to cause everyone a lot of stress about this."

"Team bylaws are clear. Alpha class requests take immediate priority over everything outside of Code Indigo threats," says Stratagem. "Frankly, this is a lot of work for me personally and I need to get on it right away. Is this girl aware of the background check I'll be running?"

"Yes," I say. That background check is legendary and I had warned Jay about it when we first started reading up on security levels.

"Good. I'll assume an awareness of the in person meeting I will need to run, as well. Now come with me. I take it secrecy is important so we'll run this in my lab. Metal, please head back to Chicago. I'll give you an alert when the UN needs you."

I follow Stratagem through another door and into his laboratory. The room is expansive. He keeps a lot of captured dangerous supervillain technology in here for further study, along with a number of personal projects he doesn't think will be safe in his laboratory at MIT. The badger once mentioned he has one hidden there, but I don't know if he actually works there in his civilian identity. He's sort of a cipher in a lot of ways towards the team. He sits down at his workshop table and points at a stool across from him, which I sit down on.

"Now then, first of all is this person in my data banks?" he asks as he taps at his computer.

"Yep," I say, "Epsilon level."

Stratagem sighs and says, "Of course. Epsilon is the lowest level, in which I barely have any work." He clicks a button and a large screen turns at my side so I can watch the work Stratagem is doing. A folder opens up. A host of pictures fly by. People important to me: friends, family and coworkers, about thirty of them in all. I see Jay's smiling face, his parents, his sister, Abby my office buddy, Frank from down the hall, my boss, his boss, my parents, neighbors and other people. The badger glances at me as he works and says, "I can understand a wish for discretion, Star Coyote, but you realize even a Beta class level could be entered by you, and doing so wouldn't have been known to the rest of the team except in very extreme circumstances. I would have done at best a cursory background check if the computer found something. Alpha class means I need to do a lot of this research by hand and cannot be delegated to my computer intelligence programs."

"Yeah, I guess so. I just wasn't sure about going to that level," I say after some thought. "I want the safety and security."

"Well, I would complain but honestly I'd be a hypocrite," Stratagem says offering me a rare smile from his usually very business like snout. "I tend not to talk about my mother or sister and I put them in Gamma. You're being braver than me. So what is the name of this mystery lady?"

I barely register that Stratagem has just told me the big secret of who he considers most important. My mind is on the fact of what I have to say. I take a deep breath and tell the truth, "His name is Jay Carson"

Stratagem stops tapping at his computer for a second. The lack of movement is different from his usual pace and while it only lasts a second at most it feels like the air is sucked out of the room. I start to tense up. Then Stratagem starts to quickly type with his fingers, a flurry of movement on screen and from him. I watch on the screen, and I see Jay's image come to the foreground. Suddenly, documents are streaming in front of me. I see his licenses, his passport, his medical records, recent credit card purchases, and a host of other things as Stratagem starts to work. I see the status under his name go from Epsilon to red letters in capitols "ALPHA PENDING". I sit quietly for a few minutes as Stratagem works in silence.

Finally he looks up at me. I saw a file whiz past on the screen. It looked like my father was there arguing with Jay. The computer is obviously thinking and needs a break from Stratagem's speed. He leans forward and says, "I think I am beginning to see why you have been keeping this relationship under your mask."

"Yeah," I say scratching my ear, unsure what the heck I should be saying here. Should I tell him about how we met? How I really wasn't looking for a boyfriend after that break up with Alex? About how we had the same taste in movies and books? When I knew I liked guys? I hate the fact that there is no protocol for this stuff.

He clicks some more buttons for a moment and reads text moving far too quickly for me to discern, "I can also see you've been with this man for some time. Very much in an exclusive relationship as well, from nearly the start, a wise move as that does cut down on certain risks. He likes pistachio ice cream. Well, no accounting for taste. I see you bought a home together. Looks like a nice bit of property, though the bank's mortgage rate seems far too high for this area and your credit histories."

"Yeah," I blush. I keep forgetting that somehow Stratagem can put this stuff together. I've heard him lecture Glacier about safe sex before so I know he isn't talking about my being gay when he mentions risks.

He taps at his screen a few more moments before saying, "I can understand the concern, Star. Worrying about him, perhaps concern about how the public would react, and so on." He leans forward now and looks at me. I can see his eyes behind those goggles now as he stares at me, "But please understand this fact. Even before today you've proven yourself to be a hero of quality and skill. You have worked hard and the team has benefited from your membership. You have saved lives. You are an Extraordinary. You deserve respect for what you have done. Everyone who knows of you will never doubt that, who you date does not and should not matter."

I stare now. This is the most personal Stratagem has ever gotten with me and his sincerity is disarming. I feel relieved and my tail quirks up as I say, "Thank you, Stratagem."

"I'm just being honest. Jay looks to be a smart man from these files. I am sure he has said something to the same effect." Then seemingly back to business he continues, "Now then, I'll need a little time here while I work out this preliminary material. Why don't you hit the med lab and clean up, maybe start work on your report."

"Yeah, of course," I say getting up and heading to the door.

"Oh, and, Ted," Stratagem calls and I turn to look at him, "I won't tell anyone before you are ready. Please keep in mind however, that my findings will be publicly accessible by the team, and something could come up—it would help if people knew. You've started a ball rolling and you will most likely have to tell everyone sooner rather than later. Alpha security is no place for secrets."

I smile and nod and walk out. I stop off in the medical laboratory. Stratagem's computers run the basic diagnostics and Force Vixen is there to help operate them. It is what I expected, some strained muscles and obvious stress but nothing serious. There is no way to really test my powers, or where they come from and how they connect to me physically yet, but I practice them out a little bit and I know that while I stretched whatever gives me these abilities it hasn't been broken, it just feels like a stiff muscle. Vixen doesn't talk about the events in the meeting room or the fight with Etenoir. We do have a pleasant chat though about a few things. She brings up the recent tennis game that we both watched last night, our thoughts and opinions about who was going to win the tournament and who needed to work on their backhand. It feels good to just not think about this crazy morning right now. Get into the normal everyday stuff. The computers give us a clean bill of health. That was expected in the end.

"You know, Star, I think I need to clean up a bit," says Force Vixen after we leave the medlab. "I suspect you do as well. Why don't you hit the showers and we'll make a full report after that."

I nod and we split off to the locker rooms. I'm halfway there when I realize she was pointing me into the locker room that Glacier is most assuredly occupying right now. I am not sure what else to do, so I continue on and enter the locker room door.

The team's locker room has the usual look: tile floors, benches, showers, lockers, and irritating florescent lights. We just have our insignias on the different lockers, more space, and larger than normal lockers. I keep an extra set of clothes and a spare costume in mine along with toiletries. I hear a shower running, probably Glacier. He loves long hot showers, he told me once that it was one of the first warm things he could do once he got control of his powers. I worry that I have really screwed things up between us.

I open up my locker and look inside, taking stock and making a mental list of what else I might need in there. Getting low on clean socks. I always keep a few extra pairs because I hate wet and dirty socks over my pawfeet. Yes, even in costume, when the boots are connected to my leggings, they can still get wet and gross. As I think about it, I admit this costume is a little dirty itself. Actually, it is rank and has rubble and some rips from the fight. Maybe switching into my clean one would be a good idea.

I have my torso essentially out of my suit when I hear the shower turn off. My right ear quirks in that direction of the showers as I hear the blow dryer turn on and hum away. I pause in taking off my costume. I have time to just put it back on and leave quietly. Why the heck am I thinking this way? I beat Etenoir today! I've faced down a lot worse than this, but Glacier is my friend. Hell, one of my best friends in or out of costume, and I really did hurt him by not telling him about Jay. Maybe I am just scared of dealing with that, of dealing with all of it after everything that happened, and the fact that maybe I have to tell him scares me.

I hear clawed toes clicking on the tiles and I turn as he rounds the corner. Glacier has stripped out of his costume, even his mask. The only thing he is wearing right now is a towel. His strong furry chest is exposed and my eyes shift that way a little bit. When I first joined the Extraordinaries it had surprised me to learn that certain parts of the bunker were mask optional. The locker rooms for instance fit this bill perfectly. So I pretty much learned what all of these legendary people looked like sans mask, except Stratagem. It is an issue of trust and very much a way to relax. The bunker is one of the few places we can be open about our powers, identities and just unwind. It took me a month to finally take mine off. It felt really good to do it finally. A barrier that was worth removing

He isn't wearing a mask so I can see those piercing blue eyes of his, a very light blue that can be very charming when he smiles. He isn't smiling right now. Our lockers are across from each other. I turn back to my locker and continue to strip out of my costume. Pausing to take my mask off, I slip that into the locker. I hear a locker door slam. Turning I see Glacier resting his head against the door.

"I hate being a liar," he says turning to look at me.

"What?" I ask, wondering what he is talking about.

"I hate having to lie. I lie to my coworkers, my dad, my civilian friends, and everyone else. Hell, I lie to the cops too. It sucks. I know why I am doing it. It is to protect people because I do all this hero work. Doesn't change the fact that I am lying to people I trust," Glacier says, walking over and sitting on the bench near my locker.

I finish slipping out of my suit and sit down on the bench as well, wearing only my boxers. I think for a moment and say, "Sometimes you have to lie. It is part of what we do."

"My mom always told me not to lie. When she died she told me to always be true to myself," says Paul looking down at the ground. "Every time I lie it feels like I'm not living up to her request."

"A bit maudlin there, Paul," I say, turning to him and wondering if he's joking. He looks pretty serious. I put my paw on his shoulder. He doesn't shrug it off, so I continue. "I think your mom would understand. I mean you're protecting your dad and everyone else. You know the secret identity thing protects us as well."

"I wonder if I would have lied to her if she had lived to when I got my powers," he says sighing. He looks me in the eye now saying, "I thought when I joined the Extraordinaries that I wouldn't have to lie. That at least here I could be honest about things. I figured every one else was being honest with me too. I mean zero masks and using our real names? Heck going out for drinks or pizza. Ted, you've even slept over at my apartment."

I break eye contact with him and look at the floor, "I just don't see what is so great about honesty. Being honest means you get hurt or you hurt others. It isn't like I have been lying either. I just don't tell you everything. I want to keep my costume and my daily life separate."

"Lie of omission. Hell dude, you've been seeing someone the whole time I've known you and I never knew. I want to know that stuff. I told you all about my relationships; you could have joined in telling me all about this. Truth is always better than a lie, Ted," he says simply.

I glare at him for that one, his Boy Scout demeanor is really wearing on me at this second. "Yeah, right, because people you trust won't slap you in the muzzle and turn their back on you when you tell the truth right?"

"Well, yeah!" The husky sounds a little offended at that, I think, and then he seems to realize how sincere I am and his face softens. "What? Do you think I would do that? Do you really think if you told me the truth I'd hurt you? Isn't it supposed to be bros before hos?"

I have to laugh at that feeling a little less tense. Paul smiles too and I know that was a joke from the former frat dog. "A little crass there Paul. You might want to make sure Force Vixen or Lady Leopard don't hear you say that."

"Hah, yeah, I know." He leans back on the bench. "I guess it is just a surprise to me that you trust someone more than me and I didn't even know they existed."

"Not like I talk about the amazing Glacier and his dating habits over dinner you know," I say with a grin.

"I just want to be your buddy, man. I thought I was," he says a little sadly.

"You are." I nod and smile at the big husky and then say more seriously, "This just isn't an easy place for me to talk about. This part of my life is something that has never been easy for me to talk about."

"How so?" asks Paul, quirking his head and looking at me. "What, did you have some bad break ups? Look if some ladies screw with you, well that sucks but no reason to clam up on things."

I think about giving him a neutral answer something easy and noncommittal, another lie of omission. Another part of me rebels against the idea. Here is one of my best friends talking about being honest and how much he hates lying. Here we are down to our skivvies pretty much laying everything bare. Of course that highlights a problem, as I've always been worried the locker room would get uncomfortable if they knew. But looking at him I know that if I don't tell the husky now it just means more lies than I think any friendship can stand.

"Who says I'm dating a lady?" I ask leaning forward on the bench trying to sound neutral, but my legs are shaking. My breath quickens and my chest tightens as I think about leaning against the fence in the backyard, flashing back to when I once told someone else very close to me the truth.

"Huh?" Paul seems confused by that.

I turn and look at him and I try to open up more. I have to tell the truth now that I'm on the path to telling it. "I mean, who says I am dating a woman? You're kind of assuming that aren't you? What if I'm not?"

"But you asked for Alpha level and you said it's been like five years and I heard you say I love you. I don't..." I can see the gears turning in his head then his eyes widen and he sits back staring at me. I hear his breath getting a little quicker. He finally says, "Wait. Ted, are you saying that you don't have a girlfriend. That, uh, you well... um..."

"I'm saying I have a boyfriend, Paul. I'm saying I am gay." It should feel like a relief but instead I just feel tense. I'm waiting for the reaction. I can just feel it, the room is far too quiet and it's getting hard to breathe. I'm watching Paul and I see his paw gripping his towel a little too tightly. He's trying to process this. I think he might be thinking about all the times I've seen him naked too. I know this reaction pretty well, a roommate in college moved out after I came out to him.

"So this collie is a dude?" Paul finally says. "I, uh, guess you do like being taken charge of in the sack."

Wait was that supposed to be a joke? Glacier grins at me and I realize it is a joke as I grin back giggling a bit, "Assuming that one again."

"I don't wanna know!" he says in mock anguish, shaking his paw at me. "Keep my virgin ears clear of that!"

I laugh and giggle at that one. "Oh, sure you say that now after telling me all those stories about those girls getting freaky, but if I just happen to return the favor you get all concerned about virgin ears. You know my ears are a lot bigger than yours."

"Hey, that was more for your edification," Paul says with a wag of his tail, "besides, I'm not sure I want to know if you're the woman with this guy. I have a hard enough time with my masculinity knowing Lady Leopard could punch a small moon out of orbit."

"Yeah, well... girls are grodey," I grin, "besides, we take turns."

"Now I'll know that forever!" he grips his ears and actually falls off the bench in a fit of giggles.

I laugh too and wag my tail happily smacking it against the bench. Wait, are we actually having one of those weirdly friendly coming outs?

My husky buddy is still giggling on the floor rolling about a bit. Finally we both stop laughing and he looks up at me and I look down at him for a bit.

He says something first, "So wait. You're serious? You've got a boyfriend and everything?"

"Yeah, his name is Jay." I nod looking down at Paul as he slowly picks himself off the floor.

"And you've been together for five years?" he continues standing over me now.

I grin looking up at the big husky, "Yes, five very interesting and fun years."

He looks at me now and sighs a bit, "I'm not sure what I should be saying here, Ted. I mean, I don't think I've ever ... well, had a gay friend before. I mean I guess I have, for nearly three years, but you know what I mean."

"Yeah, I do." I've heard that before but Paul seems pretty sincere about it.

"I mean, maybe someone I knew was gay but they never told me," the husky says, clearly thinking about it now.

"I don't know about that, Paul, but if it helps you can ask me questions. I'll try and be honest."

"Have you been checkin' me out?" he asks without any thought and then seeming to think about it he adds, "And should I even be asking that?"

"Probably not, but hey, you asked," I smile at that and stand up in my boxers and reach into my locker grabbing my spare costume wagging my tail as I answer. "Well, Paul, let's think; you're an incredibly fit guy who walks around with his shirt off on a regular basis. I'm not exactly blind. Of course I've looked."

Paul tenses up, gripping his towel and gulps, "Well, uh, yeah, um, you know I like boobs right?"

I laugh at that one, "I'm in an exclusive relationship, Paul. Jay and I are not into playing around. Just because I see the eye candy doesn't mean I really want it. You're cute but I already have a great guy in my life who is more my type and very sexy. Why is it everyone always assumes that because I'm gay I want to jump them?"

"Pride?" suggests Paul with a smirk. "I dunno, Ted, maybe guys like to hear that people find them attractive or something."

"That makes some sense. Still, what is the right answer to that?" I ask scratching my ear after I pull my costume on and start to clip it together.

"No idea. I'm not even sure why I asked," says Paul, nodding his head a bit as he goes over to his own locker and starts to pull his costume out.

"I understand if this makes you uncomfortable, Paul. I'm not sure what I can do to change that fact and I am sorry. I guess you can see why I didn't want to tell you," I say with a slight smile looking at him and then grabbing my mask out of the locker before shutting the door.

"That is total baloney and you know it, Ted," he says looking at me after putting his own mask on.

"What do you mean?" I say surprised as how forceful that was and how earnest it sounded.

"Ted, maybe you were thinking about that, but I bet you were always worried about me rejecting you. Right?" says Paul with a warm friendly smile, obviously putting everything together. "The thing is that while, yeah, this is something I am not used to, you're still the same old Ted I've known for years and the same Ted who has saved my life and went three sheets to the wind with me when Tina broke up with me."

I'm surprised by that and can only respond, "Are you telepathic?"

"Nah, I'm no mind freak. Trust me if I was I bet I'd have to wear black and cultivate an evil laugh. I just know you," he says simply with a grin. "You're my buddy, Ted. I asked for honesty and you gave it."

"You know for a frat dog boy scout you are no meat head," I respond with a happy grin, my tail wagging rapidly behind me.

"Eh, I try," he says with a confident smile. "It helps that they did this entire sensitivity training thing at my job. Being a high school teacher you have to be ready to run into this sort of stuff."

"Sensitivity training in Texas?" I joke with pleasure as we turn and start to walk out of the locker-room. "What is the world coming to?"

As we leave Paul turns to me and says, "So wait, I'm not your type?"

I chuckle at that one, "Nah, sorry, Paul."

"I'm just going to be curious now," he says.

"Well maybe we should fix that," I say with a wag of my tail feeling a lot more confident as we walk down the hall.

"How?" the big snow dog asks.

"Dinner. You, Jay, and I go out to a nice place," I say nodding my head, "and you get to meet him and see for yourself."

"That would be nice," said Glacier with a wag of his curly tail. "I get to meet this guy and I get reciprocation for all those other times I dragged you to meet somebody."

"Yeah," I say with a genuine smile, glad for the first time in a long time that I have come out to a close friend. We walk into the meeting room where Force Vixen is already filling out her report and get to work. Vixen gives me a conspirator's smile seeing the both of us walking in wagging our tails.

* * *

Making reports is easy enough, if a bit tedious. I'm done within half an hour. Stratagem tells me that if he has any questions for the clearance he'll call. He's a found a nest of power Puma supporters who were planning some sort of terrorist action in Des Moines, I know he's juggling Alpha clearance as well, so he's a bit distracted. Force Vixen has already teleported back to Los Angeles. Glacier is staying later as he still needs to undergo the medical check up and he always puts off those reports and procrastinates. I briefly consider just flying back to Portland but I still feel a bit stiff and I don't want to stretch myself too much so I risk the teleporter.

It isn't too bad this time. I'm dropped off right side up and only a block from where I wanted to be and I have all my clothes on. I make it back to my office complex easily enough and slip over to my drop site. I found this alleyway years ago. It is secluded enough for me to change out of my uniform and into my civilian clothes. Tie, button up shirt with pocket protector, slacks and belt on, along with my penny loafers and a quick brush of my fur, and I'm Ted Rodriguez, meteorologist with NOAA. I stow my costume inside the hidden latch of my briefcase, a trick Camo taught me. Before that I had been putting it in a duffle bag and that got me odd looks at work. I could walk through the front door but despite the amount of time I've been gone I want to see if I can slip inside with minimal fuss. The front doors have security guards and cameras so that might be trouble. I float up to the roof and open the access door. It is supposed to be locked but the lock has been broken for years and no one is in a rush to repair it after all it is on the ninth floor. Who could reach it? Well, besides me.

I use the roof access to walk down the stairs a few floors. I'm on the third floor and turning the corner into my office when I hear a rough, smoky voice growl my name. "Rodriguez."

I turn and look at the face of my boss. Doctor Davidson might be a foot shorter than me, plump from years of desk work as well, but the chipmunk is still intimidating. He's looking me square in the eyes right now his grizzled gray muzzle somewhere between a sneer and a snarl. I try to put on a pleasant nonchalant grin for him, "Dr. Davidson, is something wrong?"

"How long is your lunch break, Rodriguez?" Davidson growls. I'm still surprised a chipmunk can growl, but I swear that is what it sounds like.

"An hour, sir," I respond wondering if that was the excuse I gave when my communicator went off and I flew to Atlanta. I can't remember as it seems like ages ago now. Shoot, I need to be careful here. I'm still on thin ice after skipping last weeks meeting to deal with that sinking ship in Seattle. It is not good if I can't even remember my excuse.

"An hour. Just sixty minutes. Not an hour and a half?" Davidson says leaning in closer nearly bumping against my muzzle. "Don't pull this with me, Rodriguez. You might be a damn good meteorologist, but if you keep this up I will take action."

"Yes, sir. Sorry, sir. I lost track of time," I say quickly. An hour and half? I can't look surprised, but I know Davidson is too smart to have missed that I was gone much longer than that. So someone is probably covering for me.

Davidson glares at me, "Get a better watch. I do not need my office turning into four hour work days and you can NOT keep skipping things."

With that growled delivery, he stalks away back to his own office. I turn and open the door to my office and walk inside, putting my briefcase down by the door. Abby is at her desk, the older chocolate Labrador glances up and waves at me as I sit down at my desk and start to arrange my projects into a semblance of order.

"Well, well, look who finally showed up," she says with a wry smile. "Finally feel like sharing your presence with us?"

"Well, you know sometimes I just have to walk among you mere mortals," I joke, "by the way thanks for the cover."

"I have no idea what you're talking about," she says as she looks over a model of a storm system on her computer. "Incidentally, it seems the Fairweather Island project found its' way to your desk."

I glance down and try to suppress a moan. Not the Fairweathers again. Well, that is obviously the pay off. I know Abby covered for me with Doctor Davidson. I was gone for three hours at least so she couldn't cover all that time, but she did save my tail again, and now I have to cover some of her work load. Abby is a decent woman and I like working with her. We've built an understanding over the years. She doesn't ask where I go and gives me cover at the office, and I do extra work for her and let her get the credit. It seems to work for us. She is a smart woman and she does good work by herself, but she'd be an idiot to turn down a lessened workload. I put the islands into my queue and begin to work, tapping away and filling out paper work. Abby is humming to herself and I suspect she is rather happy to be rid of this albatross. The Fairweathers are the headache of the entire department. Those islands just don't seem to obey the basic rules of weather patterns. They're one of those anomalies that make everyone scratch their heads.

For the rest of the day, different people stop by and give their thoughts on the fight. It is hard to remain neutral on this stuff. There is also a lot of talk of Portland Pride. Dylan even has a t-shirt on that has some coyote, probably some model off a bus, in a poor facsimile of my mask and logo and the city skyscape with the words "Portland's Own" under it. A lot of the team members hate these knock offs but I love those things. The knockoffs make my identity a lot easier to keep because they confuse people about what I actually look like. I don't really care about the identity theft anymore.

I have to work late to get everything on my desk done. I call Jay to tell him that. He is far from surprised. Fortunately for me I work pretty quickly and, other than the Fairweather project, most of my load isn't too bad. I'm done maybe an hour later than I would be on a normal day where there aren't behemoths trouncing down the suburbs of Atlanta. I can understand why Metalyena hasn't been dating that much. Most heroes do have to keep longer hours just to keep a balance between things. Lady Leopard is lucky she owns her own business.

I go up to the roof, making sure no one is following me, and change into my costume. I strap my briefcase to my back after filling it with my clothes. It is getting darker out earlier, so I am pretty sure no one will see it. The night is warm and there is a nice breeze. A perfect night to fly outside and I don't want to bother with the bus. I'm in the air in a moment and taking a lazy slow glide home. I can smell the scents of Portland as I fly over the city. I really do love this town. I dip lower once or twice flying between buildings. When I do that I hear actual cheering. One guy on a balcony, obviously a little drunk shouts, "Way to go man!!!" Others wave or point at me smiling. I could get used to this adulation. Portland has always been a welcoming place for me, but tonight it is especially jovial. People are going out of their way to congratulate me. One building is hanging a homemade banner celebrating me. I'm blushing intensely as I fly by it.

I'm near the Fifth Precinct so I fly over there and hide my briefcase on the roof. The Fifth has been my adopted police precinct since I started being a hero. The captain there, Belinda Remirez, was and has been the most accepting of my super hero career in the city and has helped me with processing as well as tips and equipment in the name of helping the city out. Most of the beat cops know me pretty well by now. They're a good bunch. I wave to O'Bannon and Sanchez as they leave the front door. The mayor made the Fifth into the official home of the super crime prevention division maybe two years ago. The cops were more used to it because I kept dropping off costumed morons so most of them got promoted to that division, getting a slightly bigger salary in the process, as well as equipment improvements.

I head to Captain Belinda Ramirez's desk. Belinda has been at the Fifth since before I started. She's worked dispatch, crime, vice, you name it and she has her ear to the ground more than anyone I know. I often hit her desk for any tips or opinions on where I should patrol and she has become a good friend of mine. It works nicely and she coordinates with the officers, EMTs, and fire department for me. She has the frequency to contact my communicator programmed into her phone

"Hey there, Belinda," I grin and lean over her desk and look at the coyote as she puts down the phone. She is a gray furred coyote with a thick mane of black hair which she wears in a braided pony tail. A lot of women do that, it's been a really popular look ever since Lady Leopard, and her ever present ponytail, showed up.

She flicks an ear and gives me a smile and says, "Well, well, hail the conquering hero."

I roll my eyes and wag my tail a bit. Laughing, I say, "Oh, hush."

"Pretty nice stunt in Atlanta today, Star Coyote," she says as she looks at me from her desk chair. "You know, I've been fielding reporters' calls all day because of you. They want to interview folks here at the Fifth."

"You knew the risks when you started talking to me," I flippantly flick my tail. "So anything on your desk you want a hero to help with?"

"What? Today?" she says in mock surprise. "Not content to rest on your laurels are you? Some would say taking down a super villain that gets his own prison would be enough for one man."

"I guess I'm just better than most men," I say as my shoulder gives a slight twinge and I shift my feet slightly. Belinda gives me one of those soft motherly looks I know she gives her son, Hector, when he pushes himself in little league. Well I have been very honest today, might as well go for the gold, "Okay, I do want to take the night off, but I wouldn't be a superhero if I didn't ask if I could help."

"Fair enough," says Belinda with a smile. I know she wants to tell me something so I wait for it as she shuffles a few papers about and then continues, "Well, let's see, the east side Dingos and the Banditos were about to start a little turf fight but, oh, what is this? They called it off and a few of them turned in their weapons or themselves."

"Guess they gave peace a chance," I say with a wag wondering what that has to do with anything.

"A tiger tried to steal a couple million in diamonds but confessed to the crime and returned the loot, along with blowing the whistle on his fellow conspirators," says Belinda, looking up at me with an arched eyebrow.

"Odd," I say nodding my head, "his conscience strike?"

"Vice had three drug dealers walk in and surrender their goods," continues Belinda with an ever wider smile.

I quirk an eyebrow in surprise at that one. Vice and I often work together against the illegal drug traffic in Portland. Having a superhero does help out in a lot of fights. Most of the dealers are very territorial and tough these days, thanks to our combined efforts.

"Oh, here is a favorite," says Belinda looking on another page then at me with a wide grin. "Cinnamon and Spice admitted to a plot to rob the city treasury and hold the mayor for ransom and said they wouldn't be doing that."

"Are you kidding me?!?" I shout in surprise. My snout feels like it should get lock jaw. Cinnamon and Spice are a duo of vixens that have been a constant burr in my side. The two of them love nothing more than causing trouble and escaping with large sums of money. I've taken them out more than once. The only thing worse than their complex schemes, is the tendency of those schemes to embarrass me and everyone else in authority. They're pretty much my archenemies, in a weird way, because of all the supercriminals and villains I have faced they have given me the most respect. I have to ask it. "Why did they admit to that?"

"Well, it all seemed to happen after a certain coyote took down a giant French monster," says Belinda tapping some papers on her desk. "Though I suppose it could all be a coincidence if you ignore the comments like 'just make sure that coyote doesn't get me' and 'I am not taking on that super freak' to name a few. Cinnamon had some very charming things to say I might add before she and her sister escaped custody once again. We actually caught them after they confessed to their plot."

"Really?" I am genuinely surprised. I wasn't expecting that. "They actually surrendered because of me beating Etenoir?"

"Here is one more," continues Belinda with a smile, not answering my question. "Eye witnesses say they saw Rigger zooming out of the city about three minutes after you took Etenoir down."

"How do they know it was Rigger?" I ask. Rigger is a fairly subtle criminal and most people don't know him on sight until he does something in that Victorian era costume of his. He's an older otter and rumor says he's one of the first superbeings. No one is exactly sure who he was before putting on the mask and committing crimes.

"How many otters do you know who have rocket shoes made from Red Devil vacuum cleaners and twine?" she says pulling out a photo that shows just that. Rigger has been up and down the west coast for the past year. Actually, he's taken on every member of the Extraordinaries at one time or another. I still remember that popcan gatling launcher he made from a pair of magnets, some yarn, and a recycling bin. Fortunately, as criminals go he's more of a 'rob the bank' type. So he's not dangerous unless you enjoy carrying around large sums of cash. He's also nonlethal as a fighter, and I think every hero appreciates that.

"Not many," I say with a smile.

"Point is this, Star. Go home. Enjoy the night off. You've officially made every cop's day easy, no one is going to pull anything big. You've either won their respect or fear today. So live it up a bit," says Belinda, "and good job by the way."

I don't argue with her. I just smile and walk out of the precinct amid some cops clapping me on the shoulder, giving me thumbs up and promises to pay for drinks sometime.

I'm in the air again and flying out to the suburbs, briefcase in hand, going home finally with a feeling like I've done both my jobs well. It is rare that I feel that way. I land in a park a few blocks from home and change clothes in a restroom in the park. I walk the rest of the way. This park is a perfect place for me to land and change out of costume. It is also close to where the bus stops, which is a great cover for why Jay has a car but I don't despite both of us commuting to work. I do stop off at a corner grocery and grab half a dozen eggs, remembering at the last moment.

I'm soon at the front door of our little ranch home. I smile and wag my tail thinking about that. Our little ranch house. It needs a bit of work, but we're going to commit to it. Jay and I picked it out together. It has everything we want in a home. A nice backyard, big bay windows, a larger kitchen than either of us has ever had since we went to college, and a very nice bedroom. I unlock the door with my key and step inside.

Jay is at the door waiting for me wagging his tail. I drop my briefcase by the door and the grocery bag with the eggs and smile at him. He slides in close and gives me a hug saying, "Welcome home, Ted."

We both still enjoy saying that. I hug him back happily, "Sorry I'm late. I had a long day."

"It happens," Jay says evenly holding my paw and leading me to the kitchen/dining room. I can't help but think about Paul's little comment about herding as he leads me and I start to giggle slightly. Jay looks at me and quirks his ears, "Something up?"

"Nothing, just something a friend said," I respond with a grin. We sit down to dinner, a really nice meal. Jay really knocked himself out preparing it and he timed it perfectly thanks to a police scanner he picked up. My clever collie figured out that if he listens in on them and has a map near by he can figure out when I am coming home. The chops are delicious, as is the rest of the food. Jay tells me about his day first. Busy but not bad, I nod appropriately and grin at the stories about his office. He mentions the mayor came by his office and I have to ask.

"Hey, Abby mentioned something about a statue," I state with amusement, "any truth to those rumors?"

"A statue? To Willa Cather perhaps?" he says with a chuckle and grin.

"Well, someone told her that maybe there would be a statue devoted to me," I say perhaps a little too hopefully.

"A statue to Ted Rodriguez?" asks Jay, being coy. "Whatever for?"

"To Star Coyote you big tease," I grouse in mock annoyance.

Jay just wags his tail, "Oh, I see. Him. Or is that you? The pronouns there always confuse me. I'm sorry to say that is a no. Trust me, I'd be the first person to hear about something like that, it would have to cross my desk. But I heard the rumor too, it came from an aid in the PR department."

"Ah. Well good. I won't need to get my costume pressed," I say, a little disappointed. But it is true I won't need to have my costume cleaned. "So you were saying about that guy, Carmichael?"

"Just some prattle. Nothing as important as your day," says Jay easily and happily leaning forward and looking at me.

"Don't say that!" I retort quickly, "I enjoy hearing about your day."

"Well, you have to admit my stories lack the charm of these," Jay replies as he pulls out newspapers from behind his chair. Most look like late and afternoon editions. He unfolds one and reads, "Such as this from the Portland Tribune 'Pernicious Parisian Pounded by Portland Powerhouse' or from the Oregonean 'Star Coyote Outshines Etenoir' and of course the Herald has stated simply 'Star Coyote Saves Atlanta.' I'd have to say it puts my day in stark perspective."

"How many of those newspapers did you get?" I ask incredulously glancing behind his chair.

"Only six, well seven if you count this one I got at the deli near work. That was mainly for the coupons. I think I'll make that scrap book I was talking about," Jay says puckishly. "Literally saving the day does tend to contrast with a day doing paperwork and working on a new residential zone."

"People have to live somewhere, Oreo," I say as I take a pesto laden bite of chicken, "besides I did a lot of paperwork today too. I need to hear about your day, it helps me make sense of the craziness of my own. I mean between punching a super villain out and regular office stuff, I had a weird day."

"Fair enough," Jay nods, "But I am curious about your day. What happened with you?"

"Well, after the fight in Atlanta I went back to the base with Glacier and Vixen. We made reports and so on. After that back to work where I got chewed out for taking a long lunch break," I relate quickly. "Not much else to tell."

"Except that Cinnamon and Spice surrendered to the cops," says Jay with a big smile. "Bet you're glad to not have to deal with those tarts."

"They didn't surrender so much as admit their plan and then escape custody," I correct him before continuing, "I really think you have a jealous streak about those superwomen I know. It isn't like I'm interested by any of them. I like my women with a Y chromosome," I say with a mischievous grin. "After all, shouldn't you be more worried about Glacier and I?"

Jay dismisses that with a wave of his paw, "Not really. After all I am only having a little fun with you. Besides, those two women are just creepy with how they like to tease you. As for Glacier he doesn't know you're gay."

"He does now," I say taking a big bite of pasta and gleefully chewing it slowly, enjoying the taste and texture as well as the flabbergasted surprise on my boyfriend's muzzle.

Finally Jay asks, though it sounds more like a demand, "You told him? You told Glacier today?"

I nod and wag my tail a bit to show it is okay. Jay grins as well as he see me do that. I swallow; reach over to feel Jay's paw and respond, "Yep. I also applied for Alpha Security for you, Jay."

"Wow. You have been a busy mutt today," Jay says with a warm smile. "Coming out of the closet, beating up Etenoir, inspiring a city, and getting paper work done at the office. See why I said you put my life into stark contrast?"

"Well I'm not totally out with the team," I say. Then I tell him everything that happened at base except for the real names of my team mates. I'm not comfortable with that yet. Jay laughs at the right times and agrees that Glacier might be one of the better coming outs I've had.

"There is one other thing," I say as Jay gives me another chop. He always remembers to cook extra for me.

"Oh? What?" Jay asks evenly as he sips his wine.

"I set up a dinner date with Glacier," I say with a contrite grin and, seeing Jay's confusion I continue, "I mean between the three of us."

Jay is silent for a while as he mulls this and then with a content sigh says, "Sounds like you've got a really good friend there."

"He's a boy scout," I say flicking an ear in amusement. "You're still my best friend."

"I think that was so saccharine I'll get tooth decay, dear," Jay rejoinders, causing me to snort.

We both laugh at that and continue eating dinner. We talk about where we'll eat with Glacier and when, along with other things. Jay thinks it is best that we wait until after he gets security clearance. I wanted to do it sooner, so I wouldn't be as worried. I have to relent in the end. After all, Paul can't wear a mask to dinner. Jay will know his identity and it really is best if he gets Alpha clearance before hand. I'll contact the snow dog in the next few days. Jay smiles happily. I can tell he is excited at the idea of meeting another hero.

After dinner and the clean up of the kitchen that follows, we curl up on our couch together. Jay rests in the crook of my arm as I lean back in the seat and sigh happily. The meal is already having a soporific effect on me. This is our favorite position for watching TV or listening to the radio. Jay's tail lazily wags back and forth with contentment as he nuzzles against my chest, once in a while nuzzling my neck.

I had been rushing everywhere today just sitting down and relaxing on the couch with Jay feels wonderful. I didn't even realize how tense I had been feeling with all that zooming about from one thing to another. I yawned a bit starting to relax finally. Jay nuzzled my shoulder the wrong way and I hissed in pain as a flare of tense muscle hit me. Still felt a little over stretched and sore there.

"Something the matter?" he asks looking up at me worriedly.

"Oh, nothing much," I reply rubbing my shoulder and smiling at him. "Just a little strain from the fight today."

"I thought you said you were okay," he says with a worried look on his face.

"I am it's just a stretched muscle or two. Nothing I haven't had before," I say sitting up a bit and pausing the audio book that's playing so I don't miss anything.

"Oh, I see." Jay twists out of the crook of my arm and I feel him push me a bit onto the couch until I have my back to him. I feel his paws start working into my neck and back, squeezing my body. It feels nice as he gives me this attention and I mumble happily as he turns the audio back on so I can hear my story. His paws feel wonderful as he gives me his undivided attention and I wag my bushy tail panting happily.

We stay like that for a while with Jay just lavishing me with attention. This feels wonderful even though he isn't the greatest masseur in the world. The fact that he is giving me attention like this feels great. It just makes me feel nice and enfolded the man who loves me; I turn my head smiling at Jay.

"So when do you want to switch," I ask moaning slightly in comfort, loving this attention, and a part of me just wants to return the favor.

"You've had the harder day," as he kneads a knot in my back making me squirm.

"You had a long day too." I wiggle my fingers while enjoying the feeling of my collie on my back.

"Not like yours." I can feel him tensing up at that. I smell a whiff of worry and concern. We're both canines, we can pick up that kind of scent easily. I've learned his moods and their scents.

"Is there something you want to talk about?" I turn my full attention to him now.

"No," says Jay sitting back, "No not really."

"I thought you wanted honesty, Jay," I reply

"Now don't start that," Jay says with some exacerbation.

"So talk to me."

"We were having a good night," he says slowly.

"We'll continue to have a good night. I know I have had a great night," I reply with total truth. I have to wonder if he is going to ask me the question. I've heard about the question before from other heroes when they talk about their family. I'm not sure how I will answer.

"It's just," Jay pauses and thinks for a moment then continues, "Snuffles, I could have lost you today. I know I didn't and I know there are risks with you being a super hero. But I had all these plans today. I got the food days ago. I found this great audio book for you and I was so excited. Then I see the TV and you're fighting a guy who has put heroes in the hospital and who has killed I don't know how many folks. It scared me and a part of me was angry at you for letting this happen on this special day even though you didn't know."

I can only nod as Jay says this. He looks guilty about admitting this. Is he worried that he is wrecking things?

He presses onwards, "It was amazing you took him down, and I was really happy, Ted. I still am so proud of you. But it scared me that I'd lose you today. And I keep thinking what if you have to fight on an anniversary or a holiday? What happens if you're needed Thanksgiving and I lose you then? I know it is silly, Ted. I mean you're an amazing guy and you can do stuff I can't even conceive of really, but you're not invulnerable. I mean part of this is all about being lucky, you're lucky they shoot at your chest and that star because you have Kevlar and you're lucky in these fights. It became clear how much luck you depend on when you took Etenoir on in a fight."

"Yeah, I know, sweetie. I know," I say. It is true it doesn't matter how careful I am, what I am doing carries risks and those risks are huge. I look at Jay and he looks scared and worried. I twist and turn and hold him tight in a hug.

"I just don't know what to do, Snuffles," Jay says as he hugs me tight.

I look him in the eye and see that worry and I realize I have to ask the question, because he can't bring himself to. "Jay, when I started being a hero it was my choice. I mean it was all about me. Now we're together and we're close, closer than I've ever been with someone. What I do effects you. Do you want me to stop?"

Jay looks at me for a long time looking me over a paw reaching up and feeling one of my ears. He's mulling this over. I wish I had telepathy. Then he answers, "No."

"That was definite," I say with a grin.

"Do you really think I haven't thought about asking?" Jay asks incredulously. "I thought about it your first night on patrol after you told me. I've considered it before a couple times, like that bank robbery last week, and every time I come back to the same conclusion—I can't ask you to do that."

"Why?" I'm genuinely curious as to his answer.

Jay licks my nose and thinks for a moment deliberating his words and then says, "You chose to be a hero before we even met. I know that because you had the costume all worked out and had practiced your powers well before your premier and I think you would have let something slip if you got your powers after we met. You continued to be a hero as we dated. You lied about it for a lot of reasons but you did continue with it. And there were more than a few times you tried to break it off with me because being a hero and having a normal life are obviously difficult. Thinking back, there were times you tried to quit being Star Coyote as well. At the end of the day you tried to make a compromise. Be a superhero and still have me. Right?"

I stare at Jay for a long time surprised. He's not only thought this one out, he's directly on the money, "Uh yeah."

"I thought so," says Jay with a satisfied grin. It is the same one he gives when he solves the murder on TV shows in the first ten minutes, which is pretty much always. He continues, "Ted, the way I see it being a superhero is something you don't just want to do because it is fun or you like the danger. I think you're doing it because you feel you have to do it. I'm not sure it is my right to ask you to stop. I think you have to feel you can stop."

I think about that for a long time, my mind whirling over what he said. "I think you're right, Jay. I never thought about it like that. I mean, before I got my powers I didn't want to be a super hero. I didn't plan on it. But when it happened, when I got these abilities, I just couldn't stand by. Every time I heard about a car jacking, a bank robbery, a rape, or a murder I wondered if I could have stopped it. I wondered if maybe I could have helped. Then there were the super villains and I found myself thinking that if I used my powers I could have stopped them. I mean I have these powers, how can I just stand back and not use them?"

"I don't know, Ted," Jay says resting against me, "I don't have powers. I've never thought about it."

"It took me a year of seeing headlines and watching the TV until I decided to do it too," I say.

"Do you like it?" Jay asks nuzzling my neck.

"Yes," I say simply. "I do like it. I like being able to fly and lift cars. I like my superhero friends and I like knowing the secrets that come with being a superhero. I like being able to do something almost no one else can do. But I really like the feeling of saving someone, of protecting people, of changing things for the better. I like knowing I saved the day."

"So you feel responsible because of your powers. You like doing it. I can't stop you from feeling this way. I certainly don't want to stop seeing you. I mean I thought about that, after all the risks are huge. But at the end of the day I want to take those risks. You're worth it to me," Jay says smiling at me. "I mean every time I think about the risks and I get worried I think about days and nights like this too. You save my day, Ted."

"Now who is being saccharine," I laugh even as I feel all warm and content at the thought.

"Well it is true. I don't have many other options then where we are. I'm going to stick this out. It is just that today was an off day for that," Jay leans against me as he sighs.

"I can see why. It doesn't mean today was bad though. You got things done. So did I. You also gave me an amazing gift and a great welcome home on a great day," I grin, "and this was a great day. I took down Etenoir, stopped a car jacking, and I came out to a friend and for once it went really well. Something you helped make happen. Glacier accepting me for who I am is something I wouldn't have without you. You saved my day."

"We're both being really overdone today you know," Jay says.

"Doesn't mean we're not saying the truth." I yawn. "Been a long day. How about we turn in?"

"I'm up for that," Jay says with another smile after a yawn of his own.

We kiss, our muzzles meeting and I know we've crossed something important. Our kiss lasts for a long while as we cuddle close on the couch. I grin at Jay after our lips break, our bodies close together. I look at my wonderful boyfriend; he makes it all worth it. I smile and lessen gravity, floating us above the couch. I push us slowly to levitate over the floor for a moment, gently lowering us until our legs touch the floor, still hugging.

"Show off," Jay says happily as we walk back to our room.

CHAPTER 3
CLEARANCE

It has been a long two weeks since Ted applied for alpha level clearance for me. I kept waking up in the middle of the night worried I wouldn't pass the background check. Thinking back to past boyfriends and wondering if any had put on masks and tried to take over a small country. Thinking of Tyler that way would put me in a fit of giggles, but there were guys in my past who where doing who knew what these days. This of course led me to think back to every bad thing I had ever done. Every speeding ticket and mistake I ever made haunted my dreams, along with the less savory parts of my past. I mean this is the world's only team of superheroes. The vanguards of decency and justice who lead as much by example as anything else and I was seeking to be a part of their world. That is more than a little daunting. There are things I am not proud of in the slightest in my life, stuff from before I met Ted. Ted told me not to worry but I couldn't help it. Getting this was important. Ted needed to feel I was safe and this would help me become part of his life. I knew he was probably right that I shouldn't worry; still, in the dead of night, what else can you do?

Then early last night, I got a call on my cell and a deep voice asked me when a good time for me to discuss clearance was. I agreed to the next morning, I called in sick for this, the voice gave a very exact time down to the millisecond for my teleportation to base. My analog watch wasn't that exact, but I agreed to it. Hopefully the teleportation device wasn't based on some sort of temporal field or something equally crazy.

Ted couldn't wait with me; he had wanted to of course, but an early morning call from the police for some assistance put a stop to that. I was left bleary eyed and alone to ponder what was coming next as he rushed out before even the sun had risen, saying something about a street gang fight. These early calls always seem to leave me tossing in bed, considering the cooling of the sheets and fighting my urge to sleep in, as well as my worry for Ted as he zoomed to assist Portland.

I see he had left the TV on when I go out to the kitchen for breakfast. I glance over at CNN. Nothing local. They were talking about how Nth Knight had just attacked Munich, Germany. I've been paying more attention to superhero fights since Ted revealed he was Star Coyote. How could I not? I watch the TV and the attack as I drink a cup of strong coffee. Nth Night is a St. Bernard who wields a sword and wears a breastplate that seems to allow him to fly. Sometimes he has clockwork automatons fighting with him, brass and steel ones with gears that seem almost as anachronistic as Nth Knight. European heroes deal with him more than anyone else as he shows up there on a regular basis. He's probably insane, since nobody can figure out what his motives are or even what he is trying to do at times. He steals petty cash and other things, but other times he attacks government buildings or parks. Nth Knight has also done some mercenary work too. He seemed to come out of nowhere, so no one is sure where he truly came from and he doesn't seem to have an identity like most villains do. He wouldn't be a truly credible threat except that for some reason his sword can actually hurt Lady Leopard. Ted told me that Stratagem carries around some sort of staff made from special alloys that can counter it, but everyone on the team gets worried when he shows up. He's erratic in his motives and actions and that always worries them.

Blitzkrieg is on the scene in moments. The burly brown wolf is Germany's hero and so he gets to be the first responder. Technically, he's Berlin's hero but when you can run across the globe it makes your area of operation much broader. Ted told me a while back that the reason heroes operate out of cities is personal convenience. The cities are often their homes, the places where they have friends and family, and where they want to set up protection. The accepted tradition, thanks to the founders of the Extraordianries, is pretty much to work within that city and if possible expand outwards. So while Glacier can only really defend

San Antonio, Star Coyote can defend much of the Pacific Northwest due to his ability to fly. As such, Blitzkrieg tends to protect Germany as a whole, along with the parts of Eastern Europe that will let him. He makes pretty short work of the St. Bernard, who looks surprised anyone showed up to stop him. Did the anachronism really think attacking a government office wasn't going to draw attention?

The newscasters seem to think the story was essentially over except for commentary, so they switch to some other news. El Gato Cibernetico, Mexico City's resident hero and cyborg, had launched a defense of his city against the beaver supercriminal Interrutorre. Interrutorre is a Canadian hacker genius who likes to rob major computer systems and engage in acts of technological terrorism for the right price. I only know about him because he once tried to hold Portland for ransom. You can guess which superhero coyote stopped him. You almost have to feel sorry for Interrutorre, but if you're using super science and are stupid enough to take on a technological superhero, you deserve a beating. Besides, who wears black form fitting suits with twinkle lights when they're that overweight? By the time the very short fight was over it was time for me to leave. I stepped outside into our backyard and waited. It felt weird just standing in the middle of the backyard in the early morning, dew still on the grass, hearing some of the neighbors getting up, the daily lives of people around me just starting while I moved towards a very strange and possibly life changing event. Surreal hardly covers the feelings of worry and anticipation that swirled in my stomach.

Fortunately, I didn't have to wait for long in the backyard. Ted tried to warn me about the teleporter. He would have preferred to fly me to the Extraordinaries' base personally but apparently the rules were clear: this had to be a private meeting without my boyfriend present. They also didn't want to risk the location and the teleporter was a good way of keeping that information secure.

After the odd and uncomfortable sensation of being pulled in every direction and yet not, and the feeling of every follicle of fur standing on end, I could see why Ted disliked the thing. I close my eyes, trying not to think about those feelings; it was just too disconcerting. I think I now get why Ted keeps a gigantic bottle of Maalox in our medicine cabinet. When the sensations evaporate I feel my feet on hard ground, not the compliant grass of the backyard. I open my eyes and look around the huge room with its odd octagonal shape and strange flooring. It was also cooler temperature without the sun shining on me. My fur feels odd; I look down to see my thick long collie fur sticking up at weird angles.

Taking out the comb Ted gave me, I brush at my fur concentrating on getting it into better shape and step away from the center of the room. Finally, I glance up from my arms when I hear a door open.

A well muscled stocky badger stood in the doorway. He looks broad shouldered and fit. More muscle development than Ted, but it is hard to tell for sure because his costume obscures his body slightly. I can't get much sense of him beyond the feeling of a very fit badger. His costume is some sort of gray cloth that was not the same sort of spandex bright colors that Star Coyote wore, and I can see a harness as well covered with pockets and items, thick cloth pants held up with a large utility belt, the entire outfit half covered by the long black trench coat he's wearing. Over his eyes a pair of large aviator goggles. In one hand he was carrying a long bronze colored staff with a stylized letter Q on it, which seems very out of place.

Despite the staff I know who he is: Stratagem. One of the least well understood heroes on the Extraordinaries team, and yet one of the first superheroes and a founder. There are few photographs of the Bostonian hero beyond the official poster. He avoids being photographed, even when taking on supervillains. He's not a grandstander like Ted can be and he will not do interviews. He claims, as I understand it, that he has no time. No one is really sure of his powers, but they have to have something to do with super science. He has strange sonic weapons, tensile capture nets, his odd ability to be at the right place at the right time, and everyone knows of his most famous battle when he took Atomic Lion down with some sort of containment foam. I think Ted knows more but I am pretty sure it is not my place to ask. I learned most of that from some web surfing while I waited for the call.

"Jay Carson, I presume," he says evenly as I walk towards him.

I nod my head, "I guess you're Stratagem and this is the base?"

"Correct on who I am, though this may not be the base. After all this is an interview to clear up details. I haven't given you full clearance yet," he says very matter-of-factly. "I apologize for being late in my retrieval."

I look at my watch confused. The time seems to have matched up well for me, "Late?"

"I was off by 37 seconds," he explains simply. I quirk an eyebrow at that. The guy had a teleporter, it wasn't like I was waiting for a train, but he continues talking, "The problem was that there was an emergency in Boston this morning. Ms. Q decided to attack an armored car convoy filled with discontinued bills. I had to step in to stop her."

I glance at the staff in his hand, "So you won."

"Invariably," says the badger now with a slight smile. "Ms. Q had been planning this for a while but she left herself open. The Boston police and I were ready for her strike."

"You saw it coming?" I ask as we walk out of the teleportation chamber.

"Ms. Q is many things. A mad genius fennec whose Q rods can do astounding, even physics defying things such as creating bolts of energy, or allow her to fly, or a number of other things. She is also a spoiled woman who hates to get her hands dirty. She always hires a selection of lackeys who she dresses in matching tailor made uniforms to do her bidding before a crime. Usually she dresses them to match an outfit of hers that she wears for the actual heist. It tends to leave a money trail, and this one I picked up on a week ago," Stratagem explains, I think with some satisfaction but it is hard to be sure. "I had hoped to find her hideout before today but she was clever enough to hide it after the last time we combated each other. Fortunately I was able to figure out when she would attack and plan my day accordingly"

"Thanks for fitting me into your schedule then," I say with a wag of my tail, wondering if he was joking. I look at that rod he is carrying and I have to ask, "So isn't that police evidence?"

Stratagem glances at me and then at the rod, "Yes, perhaps, however the DA's office has learned from bitter experience not to have any of her Q rods in the same building as Ms. Q, and I have an agreement with the city of Boston and MIT to share any data I find from my investigations of these devices."

"What about evidence contamination," I ask now curious about the entire thing. I remember that investigation in my own office years ago over graft and the problems tainted evidence caused.

"It was brought up before, but by now most officials trust my findings. Besides, they have more than enough to handle Ms. Q this time around. Meanwhile, I wish to continue my investigations of her devices and keeping this in an evidence locker would impede my research," he explained as we walked down the corridors,

"I thought you were one of the smartest men in the world," I say as we stop at a large door that looks like it has a lot of extra security on it. Stratagem takes the time to type in a series of codes on a key pad and have his paw scanned.

"Some have said that," the badger responds as the door opens and I see a room filled with weird ray guns, cannons, swords, robots and other things. "I don't see it that way. For one thing, I believe myself to be sane and many of these so called brilliant minds like 'Doctor' Schmetterling and Ms. Q are clearly unstable. However their inventions escape my understanding in how they do what they can do. Perhaps their madness allows them to make intuitive leaps I can not see. Perhaps they have powers which pervert the natural order of things. Fortunately, I do not work alone. MIT and a host of other schools and governments have scientists that pour over the records we have and other artifacts. Perhaps one day we can turn some of these 'mad science' inventions to better purposes. I do not work alone and I stand on the shoulders of thousands of brilliant men and women. I have support and perhaps that does make me look more intelligent but it wouldn't be that way without all the minds working with me. I just have a skill for utilizing their findings and seeing patterns where others do not." It sounds like something he's said many time before, and perhaps he has. Everyone must ask him what I did.

"Well," I continue, hoping not to sound too new at all this, "Can't anyone use those mad science inventions though? I mean, I remember that some of these mad scientists give their men laser pistols and stuff like that. Like that Baron Xanadu guy when he attacked Washington, DC a few years ago." Strategem enters the room and puts the staff on a table. I remain outside. I'm pretty sure I wouldn't be allowed in a room filled with contraband super science.

"Oh yes, other people can use them but we haven't found a way to reproduce the science that creates them or how they work," Strategem explains as he leaves the room. I hear numerous locks going into place as the door closes behind him. The goggles still obscure his eyes, and they gleam in the light, giving him a slightly menacing look as he continues, "As a scientist I dislike that. The very heart of science is reproducible results that anyone can with the right tools recreate and use to their betterment. Not some cackling madwoman with a penchant for fois gras. But we are not here to discuss that, we're here to discuss your clearance. Please follow me."

We walk down the corridors taking a couple of turns in silence. The place is confusing and I'm not sure I could find my way around here without someone leading me. I guess that is part of the point. Finally, we come to a door and step inside. It is a bit shocking to see this room. It looks like your average office room: carpet, nice wood desk, two chairs, a table, and a book case filled with books make the room look far different from the futuristic corridors we walked through to get here. Strategem sits down behind the desk. I sit in the other chair facing him.

"I'll start by saying this," Stratagem says leaning forward on the desk, "you need a new PIN."

I wasn't expecting that, "What?"

"You're father's birthday is far too easy to guess. Try a series of nonlinear prime numbers, that works very nicely," Stratagem says as he takes out a stack of papers from the desk and shuffles them into order.

"You looked into my bank accounts?" I say a bit angry as well as surprised.

"I'm sure Ted warned you about my thoroughness. People have complained that it is invasive, and perhaps it is, but I needed to know these things. I have also looked inside your safe deposit box, just so we're clear," he says without a hint of apology as he holds up the first piece of paper.

I feel angry and a bit betrayed at the idea of someone digging into my accounts and box like that. I mean I knew this was going to be a thorough investigation, but still, he could have put it better. What? Did he look inside my underwear drawer as well? I look at him and he's got a good face for hidings these things. He's impossible to read. I'm not sure if I want to know where else he has looked. I do know this: it is done and I did essentially ask for this. I take a deep breath and try to calm down, "Alright. I'll consider that."

"Good. Now then let's take a look at a few things. During my investigation I came upon a few points I wish to have clarified," he says with a slight smile.

"Fine with me," I say. "Honestly, it will be good to have this over."

"You have a relatively clean record," says Stratagem looking over his papers. "Besides a few minor glitches such as using a fake ID when you were in high school and a speeding ticket you paid off quickly I can't find much."

"Well, I try?" I say evenly unsure of how else to respond. How the heck did he find out about that fake ID? I had been a stupid kid to try it but no one had caught me with it. A lot of people do stupid things as kids. Fake IDs are pretty innocuous over all but it is weird that he found out about that.

The badger sets the first piece of paper to one side, face down. "However, there are a number of questionable acquaintances of yours I'd like to discuss," says Stratagem. I stare at the heap of paper. Shoot, here come the old boyfriends, this was going to be a long day. "To start with, let's discuss Simon McConnel," he says calmly.

That throws me for a loop. I can honestly say I was surprised as I ask, "Simon? My brother-in-law?"

"Yes, married to Tessa Carson four years ago, one child, Billy, age four." Stratagem says looking at me. "How would you define your relationship with your sister and her husband?"

"Nonexistent," I say evenly, trying to not let resentment seep into my voice. The badger motions for me to continue. I have to sigh before saying, "Theresa never really took well to my coming out. When she left for college she stopped talking to me. After she met Simon it got worse. The guy is pretty homophobic, he doesn't like having me around, and he hates it when Ted is near by. He has issues with interspecies dating and he considers coyotes too separate from dogs. He pretty much told me to never go near my nephew."

I leave out the 'jokes' that jackass has told me and some of the more colorful language I could use for him. In my opinion Tessa married a real slime ball of a collie.

"Yes, that seems to confirm my findings," says Stratagem. "I was curious why you and Ted went to your parents on Thanksgiving and your parents went to your sister's for Christmas."

"It is the way we divided up the calendar so we don't see each other," I explain. Oh what the hell, the guy knows freakish amounts of details about me. I might as well tell him something personal. "My parents are pretty accepting of who I am and they love Ted. I know they'd love for all of us to get along. I think it really hurts my Dad to see Theresa and me so estranged. I've never even met my nephew—but you probably know that."

Stratagem grunts and nods and then looks at me with a look of what might be empathy as he continues, "I only ask about this because Simon McConnel has some very questionable associations and backgrounds. For instance he has had low-level connections to a number of criminal organizations in Seattle, Washington, not to mention his support for Power Puma."

"He supports that freak?" I nearly shout in surprise. I can't believe it. Power Puma is often pointed to as the first true supervillain. Yet, it makes a kind of sense. Power Puma is a neo-nazi who believes his powers come from his refined genetic stock. He's deeply speciesist and committed a lot of terrible crimes before the superheroes began to appear and deal with him. Everyone in the GLBT community remembers his attack on the Castro district of San Francisco. He's attacked other groups as well, like those species he considers lesser beings. Hell, he still makes people shudder in fear. I know more than a few people who won't go near mountain lions because of him. Not to mention his cadres of followers, supporters, and how good he is at organizing super criminals and villains into helping him. He's a consummate manipulator who can lift cars. He's just sinister.

"He gave to his legal defense fund and is on a mailing list for some of his more troubling propaganda. I'm unsure how much he supports the man beyond that," explains Stratagem. "He also seems to have done some courier work when he was younger, for an organized crime syndicate known as Pour Liberte et L'Amour."

"Yeah, my sister chose a real winner there," I say with an eye roll.

"Well, he is now involved in what I believe are legitimate business ventures. Still, I wished to check how knowledgeable you were about these things," Stratagem says in what I think is supposed to be reassuring manner as he turns the paper over. "I must admit if you were closer to the man I'd be very hesitant to give you Alpha clearance. He has questionable links and would be a security risk."

"Oh, that would be fun. Simon causing me to lose this," I say offhandedly as Stratagem put that piece of paper aside. I think Ted would smack him around if that were the case and I know my coyote can do just that, even if Simon is a bit more developed muscle wise.

"Now then. What is your relationship with Aaron Lewis," Stratagem continues.

"Aaron?" I ask in surprise. I have to shake my head and think about my answer before responding, "I haven't thought about Aaron in a long time. We grew up together. For a lot of years we were best friends. We did everything together from baseball to tire swings and when we got older our friendship got older too. After we went to college, we sort of drifted apart. I saw him at my high school reunion. We traded numbers but I really didn't talk to him afterwards. We used to be a lot closer but I let things drift. So did he. Not really a good excuse for letting a friendship end, but there you go. Why?"

Stratagem nods and checks something on his paper before sliding it away. "Hmmm. Yes, I figured that was the case. In my investigations I found out that his accounting firm has deep connections to Doctor Xerxes, Veneno, Doctor Schmeterling, Madame Dye, Raja Raksha, Baron Xandu, and a couple other high level threats. They launder money through their books and set up a number of accounts that help these villains fund their goals. I've been trying to find this one for a couple years and without this background check into you I would have still have been scratching my head. Thank you."

I blink at that. I never thought of those guys needing anything as banal as money. It isn't like they knock over banks. Those are all high rollers. Kids in European countries are taught to run for shelters thanks to Dr. Schmetterling. Veneo has barely been stopped from taking over Brazil once or twice, and even once tried for all of South America and nearly got away with it. They're the kind of super villains people build bomb shelters against. I think about Aaron and I finally have to say, "Aaron can't knowingly be involved in that."

"Oh, he is," says Stratagem simply, setting the paper aside. "Your loyalty is commendable but I can assure you of this fact. Now then, one more question."

I'm still in a bit of shock as I sit in my chair considering all of this. One of my childhood friends, mixed up with the kind of people who terrorize entire countries. I look at the heap of papers, and I'm almost frightened to ask him what the next question is but I do so anyway.

"Can you sign these please?" the badger says handing me a pen, and turning the thick pile of papers towards me.

I blink and start looking them over. It looks like really dense legalese. Even I have trouble parsing some of it and working in city planning I'm used to dense documents. There are post-it notes marking where I need to sign. I finally glance up at the badger, "What are these?"

"Nondisclosure forms, a couple injunctions, protection slips, permission slips, accountability forms. The usual legal paper work for Alpha clearance," Stratagem says.

It takes probably less than a minute for me to realize what Stratagem just said. I can feel my eyes widen as I ask in disbelief, "What? You mean I'm in?"

"Of course," says Stratagem with a smile now as he looks at me. "You passed my screening easily enough and despite these few glitches," he waves at the three pieces of paper he's set aside, "you are very clean."

"Some glitches," I say, still thinking about Aaron and all the men who I'd had relationships with in the past, "I'm surprised some of my past, um, interests didn't raise some questions."

"What makes you think none of that came up?" Stratagem asks evenly holding up another, very thick looking folder. "Such activities might have come up but I had no questions about them."

"Um… so… did any of my old flames come up?" I ask, now curious.

"Well I'd hate to violate their privacy," the badger says, and I think he is joking. It is hard to tell. I also am pretty sure I don't want to poke this any further.

I start reading the forms and signing them, asking a few questions whenever I am confused. I've learned to always read these things as best I can. It is all pretty impressive and complex, covering I don't know how many bases. "Who wrote this thing?" I finally ask as I sign the tenth page.

"The Extraordinaries have a legal firm on retainer. We had them work out these documents for national and international law. It took a lot of work but it is worth it for general security. They're designed to be legally binding in just about every nation except Iran, North Korea, Zimbabwe and Poland. I'd have you sign some of these NDAs anyway, even if you didn't pass my clearance standards considering you've seen Star Coyote without his mask on."

"Among other things," I say with a slight giggle. Stratagem blushes slightly. I might have pushed a button there. Still I am excited, I passed the background check. I'm getting Alpha clearance! I think it is okay for me to joke a little bit and this guy knows a lot about me. I sign the rest of the documents after reading them carefully. After I finish signing the last one I pass them back to Stratagem, who straightens the signed papers and puts them in a folder.

"These will be kept in a specially sealed folder at certain key sites. Your name will not come out of these file unless the situation is warranted, and that would be only in the most extreme circumstance. No government can compel your identity from us thanks to an agreement with the UN Security Council. But I want to warn you, the other team members do have access to the basic information, and some of them will find out who you are," he explains, standing up with the paperwork in hand. "Now, please follow me."

I gather myself up and follow the badger down the hall silently. I'm lost in my own thoughts as we pass a number of larger doors. I don't really notice them right now. I'm still mulling those documents I signed and the fact I have passed and what that means. My life just got an added complication for one thing, but Ted and I are now a lot closer legally in some ways. However, when we enter a pair of very large doors I am snapped out of my thoughts.

I stare agape at the large room. A huge computer with a massive view screen fills one wall, and a large circular table with chairs marked with the sigils of each Extraordinary member fills the rest. I can see Ted's chair with his four point star symbol. The room has other screens and computer stations around the edges and is impressively huge. A catwalk above us creates a second floor. It gives me a feeling of tremendous

security and scope. Televisions are on in different places broadcasting different news organizations in a number of languages, all muted right now.

"Welcome to the central meeting room," Stratagem says walking forward past the table, the lenses on his goggles glowing from the screens' lights.

"I've heard about this place before. Time magazine had an article on it, I think, a couple years ago. I thought only Extraordinaries could see it. Hell, you didn't even let the Attorney General see it when he took a tour," I say looking about in surprise at the huge room. Now I knew I was in the Bunker. Seeing this place, a spot few if any people get the chance to see, it is just amazing.

"That article wasn't perfectly accurate. We made sure to plant some incorrect information so as to fool our enemies," says Stratagem. "That aside, after today you are an Extraordinary."

"What?" I ask confused, "Last I checked I didn't have superpowers."

"Alpha clearance makes you a member of the team; honorary at least. According to our bylaws and rules you are a full member in good standing. The team comes to your defense and helps you. The Extraordinaries watch out for you. It is one of the major reasons we formed the team, mutual defense as much as coordination to defeat enemies we could not hope to deal with alone. Now that you are a member, you will also have this," says Stratagem opening a key pad locked drawer under the large computer and pulling out an oddly shiny circular beeper. It looks very familiar to me.

"That," I pause staring at the technology in his paw as he proffers the item towards me. "That is the same communicator as Ted's."

"Well not exactly the same," Stratagem says opening a latch and showing five colored lights that are turned off. "This is the civilian model Mark 2, I designed it myself. There are only six others like it in the world. Each one is handmade personally by me. Here take it, this one is yours."

I take it in my paw. It feels heavy and it gleams slightly. It looks like a normal pager except for being circular and the extra buttons. I look up at Stratagem, "So what makes this one a civilian model?"

"Oh, a few minor additions. It still functions as a communicator. You can still use it to call the Bunker, or any member with their own version. It uses a special frequency that only the Extraordinaries have access to," he says as I look the communicator over. "You can use it as a digital key to the base as well as call any version of law enforcement and emergency responder you can think of. Just like the others. I originally did not have them do that but I had too many complaints. Stranger's wife, she was his girlfriend at the time, kept needing to call for help on it."

"Okay, wow, that is a lot of responsibility," I say seeing on the small screen a call screen of numbers. Ted's is at the top. I could call any hero on here. Heck, it looks like I have a direct number to the National Guard.

"Unlike the superhero versions, these also carry a tracking device of my own creation on an oscillating frequency only I have access too. That way we can find you in an emergency. I try not to watch them at all times, but I do make periodic checks once in a while or when requested. I doubt Ted will need to know where you are at all times. It also has a locator beacon that will get you to your panic room," Stratagem continues.

"Panic room?" I ask in surprise, "I always thought those things were jokes. I doubt they work."

"Perhaps in most cases they are, but I, along with other members, feel there needed to be an alternative to waiting in an unsecured location for a superhero to come rushing to your aid, another option in case we are busy dealing with a crisis. For threats like Power Puma, Dr. Xerxes, and Raja Raksha there is often little time to spare in defense. Hence the panic rooms of my design. You'll have one in your office, your home, and your parent's house," Stratagem explains matter-of-factly.

"Won't my parents notice that? I mean I thought you guys wanted to keep the secret identity thing. If they're going to find out, I'd like to tell them," I say with some hope that I could avoid lying to my parents.

"I've had a look at their home's blue prints and schedules along with yours. Trust me, I can install the panic room there easily without them having to find out."

"Oh," was all I could say. Ted and I had talked about telling them and decided not to, but it wasn't like I liked the idea. Sure, kids lie to their parents, but I had tried to tell them the truth since becoming an adult.

"The rooms are useful," Stratagem continues. "I realize it seems a bit much but let me assure you with some of the threats we face it is best if those untrained or unready to deal with super criminals to get out of the way and into a safe location. Such as a reinforced bunker designed to take frontal assaults from laser canons and not be scratched."

"I see," I say, a little worry creeping back up my spine. What was I getting into here? A part of me selfishly wondered if there was still time to back out, to forget all of this. But how could I do that and still have Ted, I rationalize.

"Now then, the most important feature on your communicator is the warning codes," says Stratagem pointing to the five inactive lights. "Those are each color coded to deal with certain situation and help direct you. The color is defined by my computer systems or any member of the Extraordinaries can tell your communicator what color to blink."

"Cute," I say looking at them. Going from left to right: green, blue, yellow, red and what looked like black.

"Green is an all clear signal," Stratagem starts. "That will tell you everything is okay and not to worry. We put that in to help calm certain member's worries. Force Vixen's fiancé in particular, since she never calls to let him know she's alright. We usually give it off after a fight has concluded or when an emergency has been resolved, but before clean up efforts begin."

"Got it," I nod looking at the green one. "Pity. Blue is my favorite."

"Blue is for general alerts," Stratagem says, pointing at it, "For when local law enforcement needs aid, or we're busy dealing with a crime or low level emergency. Its main use is so no one interrupts or calls while we're dealing with something important."

"I'll keep that in mind," I say trying to hold back a chuckle from when I had tried to call Star Coyote when he was on a stake out. That was before I knew, but it apparently had ruined a week of work for my super boyfriend.

"Now when it glows yellow, you need to pay attention," Stratagem says and I can hear in his voice a bit of greater concern. "That means either a serious crime is occurring near you, a dangerous supervillain is loose in your general area, or the Extraordinaries have been called together to deal with a serious threat. I highly recommend in such a situation you get to a radio, TV, or Internet connection and find out what is going on."

"Well, that makes sense."

"Ideally you should proceed to cover or a secure location as well. I'd like it if you headed to the panic room but no one ever follows my advice there."

"Nice guilt trip," I say with a bit of a laugh.

"Just consider the idea that when it glows yellow you should head to safety and away from trouble. Unlike, say, Metalyena's brother. Technically, if it is blinking yellow you should find cover and not even look to find out what is going on. That is a subcode for greater concern but I think I'm the only one who bothers with that," Stratagem grouses. He's obviously put some work into this.

"And then red is what?" I ask looking at the communicator.

"Code Red is our highest level threat that has been used to date," Stratagem says with deadly seriousness. "It means you should seek shelter immediately. A serious risk has been detected in your area, an Etenoir or Raja Raksha level threat. The situation is highly dangerous and you have to be on guard. More than likely a team member will be with you shortly to check on you, defend you, or evacuate you. I highly recommend getting to your panic room at that point. It is also the signal we use when a fellow team member is in danger and needs help but that won't appear on your communicator unless you are in the general area. I would still get to a panic room in that situation."

"How often do they happen?" I ask looking at the currently dark red light. It looks ominous and the idea of it flashing when Ted is in mortal danger is scary.

"It happens maybe once a year at most. It used to be more common but as the team has coordinated better we've learned to deal with problems more efficiently," Stratagem explains and then his face seems to darken as he continues, "Now then, this is very important. If the red light starts blinking then that is very serious."

"Why? What does it mean?" I ask.

"It means that a supervillain or enemy of the Extraordinaries has discovered either a secret identity or a name or names of our civilian allies and family, and perhaps even their locations," Stratagem says. "When that happens, protocol goes out the window. More than likely a secret identity has been breached and there is the risk other secrets have been learned as well."

Stratagem looks deadly serious as he says this. I'm worried too and maybe even scared, as I say, "What should I do when it happens?"

"I'm unsure," the badger says guardedly. "I'd suggest the panic room but they may not be safe anymore. Play it by ear and be on guard. More than likely Extraordinaries will be rushing to every Alpha member's location. I wish I could give you better advice," Stratagem says and then his shoulders slump a bit, "But it has only happened once, and sadly to a Beta class security member"

I don't need him to tell me when the 'once' was. I can guess what happened and I know it did not go well. "Alright. Well I'll try and be careful and follow your suggestions. What about this last one?"

"Code Indigo," Stratagem says, "I'm not even sure why I keep it on there. We've thankfully never had one."

"What is it?" I ask, "What is Code Indigo?"

"Code Indigo is declared when I and two founding members agree that a situation is beyond the Extraordinaries' abilities to deal with. A situation or extreme danger where the odds against survival look to be impossibly high," Stratagem says. "We've never had one."

"What happens when a Code Indigo is declared?" I ask more curious than anything else. The idea that the Extraordinaries can't handle something seems ludicrous to me. They have Solarcoon, Force Vixen, Lady Leopard, Metalyena, Titan Tomcat, and Star Coyote on their team. Those are all heavy hitters. Good gravy, they've saved continents from disaster. Alone, each of the members, even Camo and Glacier, the supposedly weak members, have taken down dangerous foes far greater than their abilities would lead you to believe. Together, well for a normal person like myself, I can't conceive of anything stronger than the team. Even the worst supervillains have been taken down by them.

"That is when the warning lights flash in more than a few offices and military HQs around the world," Stratagem says. "For instance, Agent Jon Crick of the FBI's Supernormal Affairs Division will get an automatic call as will the Prime Minister of England, the German Chancellor, and a host of others alerting them to the situation. Then the computer will begin contacting every superhero outside of the Extraordinaries and asking for their assistance."

"All of them? I thought most of those guys didn't make the cut because of lack of power or something," I say a bit bewildered.

Stratagem gives a grunt of irritation before saying, "The media likes to make that claim. There are more than a few pundits who like to spout that nonsense as well and point out how many members are from the United States of America. It is true there are a lot of heroes in the USA, but it is folly to assume we have all the power players. There are plenty of powerful beings who choose not to join us. For instance India's superhero The Guru is nearly an equal to Lady Leopard, if not stronger. We asked him to join but he turned down membership feeling his first duty was to India and shepherding its people spiritually."

"I find the idea that he's equal to Lady Leopard a little hard to swallow," I say with a lot of skepticism. I've seen Guru once or twice in the papers and on the net in my search for information on super beings. He doesn't leave the Indian subcontinent much and there isn't much information on his activities beyond his first major one, which was cleansing the Ganges River somehow. He's an extremely well built tiger who goes around in a vest and pants and does not seem frightened by bullets or much else. Not a big newsmaker stateside. I do remember when the UN pleaded with him to leave Kashmir during a recent dust up of hostilities but that is it. Lady Leopard on the other hand, heck she's picked up ocean liners out of the water and rescued oil tankers. She's beaten giant robots and smacked meteors out of the air with her fists.

"Oh believe me, he is. Personally I am glad to not have him here. I find it a little hard to believe his claims that he is empowered by the Hindu Pantheon of Gods to shepherd the people of India to enlightenment. Still, he is frighteningly powerful and in the case of a Code Indigo I'd be happy to have his help. In such a situation I believe the world would be in danger, and he would come to our aid." Stratagem says sagely and I almost believe him. Still a part of me can't imagine anyone stronger than Lady Leopard or better trained than Solarcoon, or able to out do the other members.

"Who else gets the call?" I'm curious to know who would be left out at this point.

"Well," he says, pausing to think for a moment. "We'd probably call in Shaleighleigh in Dublin. She is a bit new still but she has promise and abilities we might need, though we are considering asking her for team membership if she continues to perform well. Bollywood Bard from Mumbai, though he grandstands. Sfumato from Rome despite the interpersonal issues with Force Vixen, Kilimanjaro in Nairobi, he's very new but seems highly capable. Wavefront in Wellington would be helpful, she has a lot of power but she isn't a team player and she refused membership when we asked. Barrier from Sydney, who we rejected because of his lazy attitude. Alias, if anyone can find him or her," Stratagem seems irritated at that one. I don't think even he knows how to contact Alias, but then who does? No one even knows what the Baltimore superhero's species is. He continues, "Getsumi from Osaka who declined joining the team a few years ago citing the language barrier, Omni will be asked though I doubt she'll leave retirement or Richmond, Mandala Aicha from Hyderabad, India, is new but she shows promise, and El Gato Cibernetico in Mexico if the Mexican Government will let him."

"I saw him on TV taking out Interrutorre a few days ago. He seemed pretty effective," I add helpfully. That techno wizard beaver is known for high tech crimes. I suppose it makes sense for a cyborg feline to defeat him but he they don't often clash. Interrutorre is more of a Canadian foe of Titan Tomcat's and Ted's. I do have to ask. "Why would the Mexican Government have a problem with him helping the Extraordinaries?"

"Ask them why they declined our offer for membership. El Gato Cibernetico is the only successful state sponsored superhero and the only successful artificially created super hero to date. Everyone else's powers seem to come from accident or birth, but his were on purpose. Let me be very clear. That is highly remarkable, and the US, Chinese, and Russians Governments, among others, would love to study him to find out why. All their attempts have failed. The Mexican government uses him carefully, points to him as a major source of pride, and the Mexican people love him. They see him as a major asset and would like to protect him." Stratagem explains.

I decide to change the subject. "Huh. Seems like it would be a lot of power to handle this hypothetical threat, but it sounds like it would be amazing to see. Hope you never have to use it."

"So do I," Stratagem says with a nod of his head. "We only plan to ask during an Indigo threat and hopefully one of those will never come. Personally I am against the idea of adding to the roster to combat a threat. None of those heroes have worked with the team. I was voted down on that matter. This was more Lady Leopard's idea. I also keep records and contacts for some of the more morally ambiguous villains."

"To catch them?" I ask.

"No. To add to the team if need be, which is another Code Indigo prerogative. People like Rigger, Cinnamon and Spice, Thrum, or Slipstream. The super powered people who sometimes do heroic things despite being criminals," Stratagem explains tapping on the computer showing pictures of all of them.

They're not as famous as the real villains. Well, except Rigger but he seems to have been around for years. The only ones I know very well are Cinnamon and Spice, and that's because they often commit crimes in Portland and hit on my boyfriend.

"Wait! They've done heroic things?" I ask surprised at that. I just never thought of supervillains or supercriminals doing good deeds before.

"Well yes, they have," Stratagem says carefully. "Rigger once helped me shut down a drug ring in Boston. He was immeasurably helpful and he does hate drug traffickers. Each of those so called villains has their causes. They have helped us before. Thrum was, excuse the pun, instrumental in helping stop Doctor Xerxes once. Cinnamon and Spice often tithe their ill gotten gains, once laundered, to foster care parents and orphanages. They commit crimes to do what they feel is right. Though Rigger, I admit, commits most of his crimes for fun, even he seems to want to help people if presented an opportunity. I have seen him go out of his way at times to protect people who catch his interest, especially other aspiring supercriminals. I suspect he has trained most of the ones on this list over the years and tempered their more dangerous impulses."

"So what is the problem?" I ask as I put my new communicator in my pocket.

"Nothing on paper, but I dislike the idea of letting people like them near our base or giving them some of our secrets. Our success comes as much from surprise as our abilities and training. Letting any of them in would be an association I wouldn't trust," Stratagem says. "There are a couple heroes I'd like to background check too."

"You haven't?" I chuckle at that a bit grinning and wagging my tail. "Should I be surprised? After all the work you did on checking me."

"Solarcoon and the other founders requested I never do a background check on heroes as intensive as I do on civilian members. They've been concerned with actions of a person after gaining super abilities and the privacy of members, and they claim that they do not want to know about the darker pasts of some individuals. So I have not done the same thorough research I like with our super powered team members or with other unassociated heroes," Stratagem says. I think he is actually chaffing at not being able to research people like that. "Except for Alias, who remains an enigma."

"Sounds like you have a hard time trusting people," I observe with a raised eyebrow. It does at that. He really seems to dislike the fact that he doesn't know these things.

"Perhaps, though I think it has more to do with the fact that I like to know what is going on," Stratagem explains with a slight smile. "I like to know situations before I get into them. Plan them out appropriately. I always have enjoyed knowing things, and unlike the others I lack true invulnerability and the powers others possess. For threats like a super strong Neo-Nazi it is best to be prepared."

"Yeah. I do admit I wish Ted was a bit more careful and thought things out more," I say with a nod.

"Yes, he is a brilliant young man, but he has a hard time conceptualizing long term situations sometimes," Stratagem nods. "Just be glad I got him to let me interweave Kevlar armor into his costume. My polymer weave is very strong and has probably helped a bit."

"I can not believe he went out there without Kevlar at one time," I say more resigned than irritated. That is too much like Ted.

"You know that he is a very capable hero. He has done a lot of good and protected a lot of people. I'm very happy he is on the team," Stratagem says, "Though his powers remain a bit of a mystery to me."

"They're a mystery to me as well. I think I'll have a couple more chances to seem them in action as time goes by. I never expected to interact with super heroes, Stratagem," I grin and wag, "but I think it will be interesting."

"I suspect so. But please call me Samuel," Stratagem says as he reaches up and takes off his goggles revealing his strong square jawed badger face. His eyes, a remarkable golden yellow with a hint of brown, look at me unhindered and draw me in. I can't help but stare in surprise. A super hero I barely know, one of the major heroes, a founder of the Extraordinaries and a man who has worked as a hero for much of my life, just revealed his secret identity to me. He continues, "More accurately, Professor Samuel Bernadette of MIT's arithmetic department."

I stare at him for a second as he proffers a paw and then I take it and shake his gloved hand, "Pleasure. Jay Carson."

He grins and then puts his goggles back on as he turns back to his computer, "Welcome to the team, Jay."

I didn't spend the rest of the day in the Bunker. Stratagem had monitor duty and then had to get back to his city. I didn't want to stick around. After all, Ted still hasn't talked to the rest of the team about me and I didn't want them wondering who the collie in their base was. So I got teleported back home, may I never have to use that awful thing again. I ended up at my front door instead of the back. Fortunately I had locked up and carried my keys with me. I spent the rest of the day cleaning up the house. Handling the minor chores around the house gave me time to consider all the events of the day. I walked around wondering where Professor Samuel planned on putting this panic room. What would happen next? How had the other family members reacted to getting clearance? Could I really handle all of this? All this information, all the strangeness, all the oddities, can I really deal with this?

Ted came home fairly early, thankfully stopping me from mulling it over too much. He brought flowers too, which was a nice touch. I greeted him at the door happily.

"Hey, sweetie," my big coyote said as he walked inside. "Have a good day?"

I close the door not saying anything. I want to draw this out a little bit as I walk into the living room. Ted follows behind me and I could feel his worry seeping off of him.

"Oh no," Ted began, a hint of his sudden fear in his scent. "Look, Oreo, I'll reapply, I'll talk to Stratagem, I'm sure we can get you Alpha clearance."

I grin at him and take out my communicator showing it to him including the little E insignia on the bottom. Ted looks at it for perhaps a second and then leaps into my arms, enfolding me in a hug.

"YOU GOT IT?!?!" He shouts gleefully hugging me tight, "Oh my god, Jay, this is fantastic! You got clearance!"

"I certainly did," I laugh and nuzzle Ted happily, feeling him bark and wagging his tail furiously. I also feel a sensation that is starting to become very familiar, "Now, Snuffles, I know you're excited but perhaps levitating the two of us in front of our picture window for the neighbors to see is bad idea?"

"What? I'm not," began Ted but he looks down and sure enough both of us were dangling in mid air a few feet off the ground, "Whoops! Sorry, dear!"

We gently touch down on the floor. We don't break our hug though as I snuggle against Ted happily. I'm just happy he's so excited. "It's okay, Star Snuffles."

"Ack! Don't start that now!" Ted giggles and smiles at me. "Any problems?"

"Well, I learned we're getting a panic room, an old friend apparently works for super villains, oh, and my brother-in-law is a slime ball, so nothing new there," I say with a smile. "I did get a futuristic beeper though."

"Wow, Theresa's husband is slime. There is a surprise," Ted jokes and licks my nose happily smiling at me. "Oreo, you have no idea how happy this makes me."

"Oh, I think you can show me," I say with a sly smile. "By the way I saw your chair, very nice spot, and Samuel is a really nice guy. Maybe we should take him out to dinner after Paul."

Ted blinks for a moment and then says, "Who is Samuel?"

I quirk my head at that a bit confused, after all how could he not know a team mate's name, "You know, badger, wears a trench coat, goggles for a mask, has oddly golden eyes?"

"What?" Jay says in surprise pulling back and looking me in the eye, "Are you... Are you saying you saw Stratagem's face? That his name is Samuel?"

"What, didn't you know that?" I ask in surprise. Then I think about it a moment. Stratagem only tells people things if he can plan out the results. He trusted me with very personal information because he felt he could, but he's never done a real search on Ted before.

"No," Ted says in surprise. "He never told me his name, heck he never takes off his goggles. The guy is a cipher to everyone but the founders."

"Oh," I nod along, thinking about it. That does make an odd amount of sense.

"So his name is Samuel. Wow, okay, so what his last name? Did he tell you what he does? I always assumed it was a MIT or Harvard or something but I never was sure. What is he like without the goggles?" Ted asks quickly looking excited, "I mean there is the betting pool on base about all this stuff. Maybe I can win it."

I take a deep breath and sigh, "Sweetie, I think I've said too much."

Ted looks surprised at that and says, "Oreo, come on. You know I was joking about the betting pool."

"No, Ted, it isn't that," I look around avoiding his eyes. After all this talk of honesty it's hard to think about keeping secrets from him but I know in this case I have to. "Look, Stratagem trusted me with some very personal information. Obviously he was comfortable doing so, and I don't know if I can betray the trust he's shown me."

"Even for me?" Ted asks crestfallen, his ears lowering.

I kiss his nose and smile, "Ted, we've always shared things, but this isn't my secret to tell. It's his. I can't go around telling it, even if you are adorable and the man I love."

"I know," he says. "It is just a surprise that you get to know a secret I don't."

"Part of the world we live in it seems, dear Snuffles," I say breaking our hug and holding his hand. "Now come on. It is time for dinner. You can talk about your day and I'll tell you everything I can about getting clearance and being a member of a superhero team."

Ted draws up beside me and smiles, "I'm happy to have you part of it."

"Good," I say and I feel it to the tip of my tail as I wag and hold my super powered boyfriend's paw confidently, "Because I don't intend to leave anytime soon."

CHAPTER 4
DINNER DATE

I sit back in my chair and take another slow sip of my red wine. It is one of my favorite wines and I'm trying to savor it, make it last the night. The waiter, a white rodent, is giving me a look of annoyance. That is understandable, I have been here over twenty minutes and besides the bottle of wine, I haven't gotten anything to eat, and I'm taking up a table for four. I lean back in my chair and wait for Ted to show up. Unfortunately for the waiter I am ready to wait a good while longer.

After all, keeping to a firm schedule when you date a superhero is nothing short of crazy as I have unintentionally learned over the years. Since revealing his identity Ted has only gotten worse, as he now feels he can get away with not having to make up excuses for his lateness. There is always something to distract and draw a certain gravity manipulating coyote, and after seeing three police cars drive by with their sirens on, I could just tell I'd have to wait a while longer. I used to think Ted had a problem with being on time. Knowing the truth gives some perspective. He does have trouble with being on time and it is only exacerbated with his duties and need to help people.

I chuckle a bit thinking about that for a moment and sip a little more wine. There was a time I'd have gotten more than a little irritated by Ted being late. Now though, I'm taking it all in stride. Maybe I should get some bread to go with the wine. I haven't finished my first glass, but it would be a bad idea for me to be tipsy tonight.

Ted and I chose this restaurant because it is one of our favorites. Cozy atmosphere, great food, good wine list, it's a nice neutral place. Better for meeting new friends and others than, say, meeting at a club. We've come here a lot of times and it is always good. I'll admit tonight I'm a little more on edge. I want to make a good impression. Tonight I meet Ted's friend and teammate, Glacier, and I want this to go right. Ted and Glacier have worked together for a couple years, and from what Ted has told me they're very close. Not that it takes a genius to see that. A couple passes over the internet and you get the gossip about them. None of it is even close to reality, and while one blog was going on about how they were a couple, it was obviously an anti-supers blog trying to find dirt.

I'm still trying to figure out where I fit into this aspect of Ted "Star Coyote" Rodriguez's life, celebrity superhero gossip aside. I do know I've been more defensive of the supers since learning his secret, but at the same time the people behind those masks are a big question mark. I really don't know anything about the team outside of their amazing acts and general gossip. I might know Stratagem's name, but somehow I don't think the badger is someone you can just call up and chat with. Considering how the media accounts of Star Coyote's powers are completely wrong, it leaves me with a lot of questions about them.

I feel the odd weight in my pocket and my white furry paw drifts down to touch it. The oddly circular beeper still feels weird and heavy. I got it two days ago and the thought of it being there still surprises me. I've been trying hard not to take it out and fiddle with it too often, especially in public. I don't want to draw attention to my Extraordinary communicator after all. It is a sign of how far I've come and, perhaps, how I fit into all of this and right now it is a bit reassuring.

My ears perk up and I look over to the door as it opens, and Ted comes into the restaurant in a very nice dinner jacket and tie. Beside him is a thickly muscled husky with a dark gray fur and a surprisingly bright white muzzle and chest markings. Sadly for both of them and their obvious attempts at dressing up, it has all been for naught. Their fur is mussed and disheveled; they must have used that teleporter to get here. The waiter from before is really giving them a look. Oh yes, he's getting a nice tip, I think as I roll my eyes. I wave at them and Ted sees me and gives me a big smile as he comes walking over to the table. The husky, who I assume is the famous Glacier, follows him.

The husky has a very pleasant tone to his fur that looks very soft and gives him an air of cuddliness. I can't help but notice how in shape the guy is. He obviously works out, he has that weight lifter look with really firm musculature. He is also stuffed inside a very tight looking suit that is in serious need of alteration. It really shows off his shape though and that curled tail lazily wagging behind him, along with a pleasant grin on his muzzle, gives him a very pleasant brotherly look. He has a sweet muzzle and alert eyes. Even for a husky this guy looks good.

Ted slides up to the table as I stand up, smiling and wagging my tail in what I hope is a non-threatening manner. Ted is smiling too, and for once he looks genuinely excited over this kind of meeting as he puts a paw on my shoulder.

"Paul Valdimos, this is Jay Carson," Ted says with a happy smile as he looks at the husky and turning to me he says, "Jay, this is Paul."

I stick out my paw and shake Paul's hand. He has a really nice grip, not too hard but firm.

"It's great to finally meet you," I say as we shake.

"Same here," Paul says breaking the handshake. We're all smiling at each other but we've hit an awkward pause in the conversation here. I'm not sure how to continue and neither are Ted and Paul. How are you supposed to start a conversation like this? The pause is small though, as I finally think of something to say.

"Well let's sit and look over the menu. The waiter is peeved enough at me already," I say and the three of us sit down. I sit between them with Ted to my right and Glacier, I mean Paul, to my left. The chair across from me is empty. We open up the menus and look through them, even though I've already decided what I want.

Paul is the first to say something after a minute or two of looking at the menu, "So what is good here?"

"A lot of things," Ted says with a grin. "I've heard the rib roast is to die for."

"Heard?" Paul glances up at that and looks at Ted, "I thought you said you've been here before."

"We have," I give him a grin of amusement, "But mister originality here always orders the same thing."

"Oh, I do not," Ted grouses, his tail held high in amusement.

"I certainly don't remember you ordering anything else here. Heck, I got this wine because it will go well with it," I say easily enough.

"What is it he always orders?" Paul asks. His voice has a slight Texas twang, and I suppose that makes sense, after all he does come from San Antonio. He has a look of puppy-like curiosity as he leans forward. It is very endearing. "C'mon, tell me. I've never been to a nice restaurant with this guy. We've mainly done pizza."

"Oh, please. I order all sorts of things," Ted says. "And we've done more than pizza and beer, Slushbreath."

"Okay, there was that time we got Mexican, but we were in Tijuana on a case looking for Los Hermanos, so that doesn't count. I mean he's a circus performing coyote who teleports and turns into sand. It was all business, and getting pizza in Mexico would just be wrong," Paul says as if he was talking about a spreadsheet, rather than being a superhero. Then he looks directly at me and asks, "So what does he always get?"

"Osso Buco, yams, and cauliflower with extra onions," I say with a grin. "I used to think it was just a stereotype that coyotes love that stuff. Then I met this guy."

"The lamb shank is fantastic here. That is why I get it and I don't always ask for that. Besides I was thinking of getting the …," Ted pauses as he looks over the menu for a few moments obviously trying to find something and then says, "The bouillabaisse!"

"You hate white fish, love," I say with a grin and a wink at the husky. We both chuckle at that.

"I'll say he does. I remember when we had to fight the Disrupters in Quebec and Rigger used that fish hose he created out of some rubber waders, a staple gun, and bike pump. You spazzed out completely when it hit you. Never mind that it didn't hurt," Paul says with a grin and I have to laugh at the mental image.

"Oh, I remember that. You smelled like fish for a week," I say remembering the very lame excuse of falling into a fish stand while on a survey a few years ago. The Disrupters didn't last long as a supervillain group. They broke up quicker than a lame garage band after a few beat downs from Titan Tomcat. I only heard about them because of all my internet research. They were mainly adventure seeking supercriminals. Canada seemed to be the only place they operated from. The Extraordinaries as a whole took them on maybe twice. I continue with a grin, "I've never seen a guy take so many showers."

"I did not," Ted sits back in his chair in mock agitation. I know he really isn't bothered as he asks, "What is this? Rail on Ted night?"

"Well it's good to know Paul and I have that in common," I say with another grin. "Seriously, Ted, get the shank. You love it. Personally Paul, I'd recommend the steak with the onion marmalade. I've had it before and it is quite delicious."

"Sounds good to me," Paul says with a wag. We order our meals, I get the rib roast, and then it's back to sitting and looking at each other. This kind of introduction is always difficult. Ted has known both of us for years and we've known Ted, but we've never really met each other or known anything about each other. Where does one start with introductions like that?

Finally I ask the obvious question, "So I saw some police cars zoom by. Anything to do with you two?"

Ted leans back and chuckles, glancing from side to side make sure no one is close enough to hear. Paul gives a big smile at me and nods his head.

"Oh you better believe it did," Paul says at last with a grin as he points as his tousled fur. "Ted flew me here. We didn't use the teleporter. I'd like to add how sad it is that flying at Mach 3 doesn't mess my fur up as much as teleporting."

"So what happened?" I ask leaning forward. "I've used that thing twice and it is embarrassing what it can do."

"Well, as we're flying into town, Ted here gets a beep on his communicator, just code blue, local police asking for assistance. The usual deal, some silent alarm goes off in a strip mall jewelry store and they're asking for general action. So we thought 'it's probably nothing. It will only take a minute and we're early.' I mean it has to be just some punks or idiots trying to rob a strip mall right? They just have the bad luck of getting two superheroes" Paul says with another grin while absent-mindedly trying to smooth some of his head fur down.

"I've heard that before," I say with a sidelong glance at Ted who holds up his paws in mock surrender

Paul continues, giving Ted a sidelong glance, "Next thing we know, someone hurls a tree at us as we land. Who do we see walking out of that jewelry store with at most a thousand in profits but Whirlwinder."

"Wait, The Whirlwinder?" I ask looking at them both. "That wolf with the welder's mask and really awful fashion sense? Always wears a big flowing cape and bright orange costume with green markings? The guy who once stole a blimp to rob a museum in New York? That Whirlwinder?"

"Way to play into stereotypes, Jay," Ted says with a grin, commenting on the fact that I brought up fashion sense, "But, yeah, that's him."

"It took you two that long to take him down?" I ask incredulously looking at my watch. Even online the Whirlwinder is considered a joke.

Paul chuckles at that, "Well he caught us off guard. I mean what super powered person bothers to rob a jewelry store after it is closed?

The receipts are locked in a safe, the profits are often taken off site, and the high end stuff is always locked away. Unless you're a super brain like Rigger or can tear open a vault, it's a huge waste of time."

"Better words to describe Whirlwinder have never been spoken," Ted says acidly.

"Not a fan then?" I ask Ted

"The guy can control the wind, create tornados out of thin air when it should technically be impossible," Ted says and then takes a deep sip of his wine. Our appetizer arrives; we got a tomato tart for the three of us. I think we look a little odd clamming up when the waiter comes by but we didn't have anything else to talk about. When he leaves Ted continues, "It just offends my professional sensibilities as a meteorologist. I mean theoretically, with his Winder Gloves, he can control air currents. I bet with some tinkering, that sort of thing could really make a difference. He could control the weather with some training. Think what you could do with that power for farmers, hell for the general public, when storms hit. What does he do instead? Knock over liquor stores and Zip-marts."

"Yeah, well, he was ready for the two of us," Paul says idly as Ted takes a bite of his tart. "Or so he said. The guy is a huge windbag, excuse the pun, besides being a lousy dresser. After chucking a tree at us with a mini tornado he proceeds to yammer on and on about how he's got this one all planned out. How he'll be the one to win this day this time. He sends up a couple wind bolts from his gloves at Ted, who flies up in the air; total distraction of course. I don't think it even registered with Whirlwinder that I was there. The rube kept trying to catch Ted in a mini cyclone but Ted flies around them easily and even dissipated some of them."

"Old trick." Ted comments dismissively. "He never realized that I know enough about wind and tornados to counter them. A little super flight in the right direction and they get flummoxed. The problem is making sure nothing gets hurled at bystanders or that property damage is kept low. He isn't very precise. Unlike, say, Rigger, Cinnamon and Spice, or Lux. Those guys actually go out of their way to avoid hitting the bystanders."

"Yep, well anyway I get close enough for a precision shot with my freeze vision and freeze his gloves. After that Ted gives him a smack in the snout and he goes down for the count. We break his gloves for good measure, but he's probably got more," Paul says and then finally takes a bite of the tart. "Hey, this is good!"

"Don't be so surprised," I laugh at the husky's look of pleasure. "This is a good place to eat. So Whirlwinder goes down. Why did it take you so long to get here?"

"Well we needed to gather up all his loot, bad idea to let that sort of stuff just lay scattered on the ground, and wait for the cops to secure the scene, which took forever because of the property damage, and then we got out of there. After that we needed to change out of uniform," explains Paul

"Not to mention attempt to control our fur, Whirlwinder does do a number on coifs," Ted says. "All that blowing wind makes it feel like being in a wind tunnel even if you're just nearby."

"Well, seems like a good reason for being late to me," I say looking at the two of them. I figure I need to keep things moving so I ask, "So, Paul, what do you do?"

"Me?" asks Paul and then he seems to realize what I am asking. "Oh I'm a high school teacher. Geometry, but I also do some PE and I'm the coach for the wrestling team."

"Really?" I say surprised looking him over as he starts to blush. "Sorry, it is just I expected you to say something like construction worker or body builder with a body like yours."

That makes Paul blush a bit more, "Well, ya know, a guy has to eat. Besides it would be a bit unfair for me to do that stuff with my super strength."

"Sorry, it just surprised me," I say with another grin. "Must be hard to balance that with being a superhero."

"It can be, but I have a pretty good cover of being a volunteer fireman for Extraordinary cases, and you'd be surprised how many criminals and super criminals act outside of school hours. Besides, I can really help some of those kids by being a superhero even when not in my mask. If you can keep your ear to the ground, you get all the gang news in plenty of time for a switch to tights," Paul explains.

"So it's one more way of being a hero?" Ted asks in surprise. I guess he didn't know either, or at least not about that aspect. "I mean, I consider my work stuff to be a break from the tight wearing duties."

"Nah," Paul says those bright blue eyes shining a bit. "It's just a dividend. I like being a teacher. It works for me."

"Did you always want to be teacher?" I ask conversationally.

"No, I, uh," he pauses there he looks like he's thinking how to respond until he just sighs and says, "Someone else convinced me it was the right way to go."

Obviously this is not a good line of discussion, so I try to shift the topic a bit, "Yeah, I didn't think about civil service until after college when I went to a career fair. It worked nicely for me and it fits my lifestyle."

"I was always a nut about weather," Ted says with a wide grin. I think he missed that pregnant pause. "So the idea of getting into it as a career really worked for me. Of course, had I known it would lead to me getting super powers I might have not pursued it."

"Wait… how did your study of meteorology lead to you getting super powers?" Paul asks, glancing at me.

I have to admit I am curious too, "Don't look at me, he's never told me his origin."

"Playing close to the chest again, Ted?" Paul asks with a playful grin.

"You realize with that lead in, you have to tell us," I say playing off of Paul easily for this.

We stop as our food arrives and I smile happily. Ted is positively gleeful as he smells the rich aromas of his food. He is a man who appreciates food and I admit I like seeing him enjoy it. Paul takes a bite of his steak and a smile breaks out on his muzzle.

"Well this beats my plan of a large pizza," he says with a grin.

"Told you," says Ted happily.

"So you were saying about your powers," I prod as I cut my meat.

"Oh, right," Ted blushes a bit. "Well, it was summer and I was just finishing off my doctorate degree. I decided to do an extra credit assignment to bump my GPA up just a bit. It was a camping trip where I took measurements and gauges for a month by myself in the wilds of northern Maine. Four weeks of doing NOAA data collection about a hundred miles from civilization. It turned out to be just the right thing for my resume for me to get hired right out of school."

"Was this before or after Alex," I ask looking at Ted.

"Alex?" Paul says looking between the two of us, "Who's Alex?"

"Old flame," says Ted with a dirty look at me, "and during, thank you, Mister Nosey."

"Oh," Paul nods, "I guess you would have other people in the past too. I just never thought about it."

Ted gives me a sidelong look and I just smile and take a bite of potato as he continues, "Anyway, it was lonely work, out by myself in the middle of nowhere, but it was also refreshing. It made for a really nice break from my parents, from school, from everything. Being out in the woods with just my charts, my thoughts, and some Zane Grey novels was well worth it, or so I believed. I took to sitting outside and just looking at the stars. Anyway, one night, about midway through my trip, I'm looking up at the sky when I see a shooting star, or what I thought was one, zooming across the sky. Only it's very, very, low and when it passed over my camp site, it lit the entire ground up like it was day. I was shocked to be seeing it and even feel the meteor impact. Well, being a scientist and being paid to be out there observing, I noted the time and direction, grabbed my note book, and rushed off to find out where it landed. I didn't know much about comets or meteors, but I did a lot more research afterwards, let me tell you. Right then, though, I was just curious. So I hiked over to it. It was easy to find because it lit the forest up. When I get to it, it didn't look like a meteorite or anything I saw in movies, or anything else I've seen since. There was no crater, heck the trees weren't even knocked over. What I found was some sort of glowing white-gold colored orb hanging in mid air. I'm not sure how to describe it except it just looked like energy."

"Freaky," I say just imagining the sight. "Let me guess, you poked it with a stick?"

"Oh, c'mon. Ted wouldn't do that," Paul says looking over at my coyote.

Ted blushes a great deal at the hulking husky's glance and then mumbling says, "No. I poked it with my hand."

"You're kidding," I say incredulously, "Ted, that was really dangerous!"

"Well yeah, I know but I wasn't thinking and it wasn't hot. It had a weird, um, comforting feeling. Anyway so I poked it with my paw and there is a flash of light as the orb seems to disappear into my hand. Next second I'm standing in empty, pitch black woods with nothing there except for the stars overhead. It was really weird but I just wrote it off, thinking I had had a few too many that night."

"Oh ho. I think I see why you poked it with your paw now," Paul comments with a chuckle and pokes Ted in the ribs with a big finger.

Ted just rolls his eyes at that. "I didn't think anything weird or strange had come from it. I just went to bed and forgot about it. That was until I woke up the next morning floating about three feet above my bed."

I have to laugh at that. I can just picture Ted's face as he woke up levitating. He probably panicked too and I could see him flailing about over his bed. Very unlike how I woke up my first time levitating, nuzzled up against Ted's reassuring embrace.

"After I figured out how to fall again, I then proceeded to break my favorite coffee mug just by picking it up. I started to realize that what happened the night before wasn't some dream," Ted explains to the both of us with a motion of his paw as I take another bite of my ribs. "I spent the rest of the month training and figuring out how to control my powers well enough to enter town. I broke a lot of things those first few days from increased gravity and I had to learn to make sure I slept inside so I wouldn't float off a couple miles." Ted grins at me, pointing a finger at my smiling muzzle, "And yes, that happened. Flying took even longer to learn."

"Ugh. I hear you," Paul nods along. "It took me a month to learn to control my abilities and it's still hard sometimes."

"Yes. Ted still accidentally floats or breaks things when he's not thinking," I say adding into the conversation. I can't help but think of the new glassware we bought when we moved in together, which has been decimated by Ted's lack of forethought at times.

"He had it easy," Paul says. "Try being a living heat sink. I literally drain heat into my body to create cold. Moisture condenses and freezes around me. I had a snow storm develop inside my apartment in that first month when I was learning to control it."

"A snow storm in an apartment?" I ask surprised, thinking about how awful it would be to suddenly find a snow storm in my home.

"It was terrible. I take a nap thinking I've got my freezing under control after concentrating for hours to hold it back. Then I wake up to find myself in swirling snow," Paul says resting his head on one paw. "This was after accidentally freezing all my food and breaking the pipes in the building. I'm still surprised no one called the cops on me considering all the damage I did to that place."

"That would be disheartening. Still you've got your ice powers under control now," I say helpfully.

"For the most part, yeah, but that first month with them was hell. I felt comfortably warm the whole time but everything that touched me froze solid. I couldn't go near anyone. I had to learn to eaten frozen food and most of my diet became icicles. For a while there I had to wear gloves if I shook anyone's paw." Paul looks at the two of us, "Heh, I've never told anyone about this stuff."

"I remember you mentioned your power made you enjoy hot showers," Ted says. "Why, though, if you always feel warm?"

"Because taking a hot shower and not having the water turned to ice around me even as I relaxed a bit meant I finally had my abilities under control. It took me a while to finally get up the courage to touch people afterwards but it was worth it. I still remember how great it felt to take that first shower, though. I had accomplished something really huge. It meant I could be a normal person again," Paul explains. "And that meant a lot to me. It meant Doctor Xerxes didn't win."

"Doctor Xerxes, what does he have to do with it?" I remember how Ted had talked about the insane man and his obsession with super powers a couple weeks ago. He's not a nice guy. His experiments, sometimes on the willing, sometimes on the not, never end well.

"He's the guy who gave me powers," Paul sighs.

"Wait. He succeeded?" Ted says shocked. "I didn't know this. Why didn't you tell me that?"

"Succeeded?" I ask.

"Xerxes has always, as far as I know, been looking for the cause of super abilities. The source, so he can create an artificial army of super soldiers among other things," Ted says. "At least that is what he's always said."

"Don't believe that sadist," Paul says angrily with a vicious look on his face as the water in his water glass turns into an ice cube. A chill floats over me, like a cold front passing overhead. "The guy may claim what he does is for science, but he just enjoys experimenting on people."

"I'm sorry," I say reaching a paw over and touching Paul's paw reassuringly. My hand feels numb instantly as I touch his, but it seems to calm Paul down as he gets that look off is face and I feel the temperature start to creep up again. I can only guess at what happened and how Paul got his powers and I suddenly feel very bad for even talking about this. While Ted and I treat his powers as a gift, as something wonderful to have around and use, I guess for the big husky they're a reminder of bad times.

"No, I'm sorry," Paul says with a sigh. "We're out trying to have a good dinner and I'm bringing up this sour stuff. Its just learning to use them was hard and the price was steep."

"Would you give them up?" I ask curiously.

"Not now," Paul says with a shake of his head, "they're part of who I am."

"Yeah, same here," Ted nods. "I do want to know what that thing was that gave me my powers but so far there hasn't been anything else besides my abilities so I'm not questioning it."

I'm about to say something when I see a big wolf out of the corner of my eye come through the front door., "Ted, 9 o'clock."

Ted looks over as well and his ears fold back in bemusement. "No way. Anything we can do?"

"Not that I know of," I say as he catches sight of us. "We did offer up our time after all."

"What are you two talking about?" Paul asks, about to turn around when the wolf arrives at our table and greets Ted by wrapping his huge muscled furry arms around the coyote and hugging him tightly.

"Hi, girls," the big wolf says very happily. Gary Manhower, one of our biggest friends in Portland. He slips over into the empty chair and looks at the three of us with a huge grin. Gary is a big wolf with a very square jaw, he's big in every way actually. He's the very epitome of the gym rat, working out every day. He's got light grey fur that seems almost white over most of his body except his muzzle and throat which are colored with a rich reddish brown which tints the inside of his ears as well. Ted and I both know that red brown fur trails all the way down to his thighs. He's wearing a tank top and jeans today, and I'm sort of impressed he's dressed this much. Gary has always liked showing off the body he works so hard for. He's also pretty much the biggest poof I've ever met. He's one lisp and a limp wrist away from being a toxic stereotype. He looks at the two of us with his big tail wagging. Ted is giving him a bemused look, I'm trying to contain my exacerbation, and then he turns and sees Paul who seems more surprised than anything and says, "Well, hello there," in the most lewd, near lisp possible.

"Uh. Hi," Paul says unsure what else to say. It might be the lavender tank top.

"Oh, I love a chatty fellow," Gary says with a big grin. "I'm Gary, and where have these two Marys been hiding you?"

"In Texas, Gary," I say with a raised eyebrow, hoping he'll walk away at this point. I love Gary. He's a good friend but now is not the best time for his particular brand of behavior. "So any reason you hunted us down?"

"Because we know that you had to have done that to have found us here," Ted adds simply . "Paul, this is Gary Manhower. He's been our friend for years. We used to go clubbing together."

"Before you two decided to settle down fully with each other." Gary gives a theatrical eye roll at that. "Not that it was a shock to the gang or me. Still, being together doesn't mean you're in a suburban convent."

"Oh, we still go out," I say defensively.

"Yes, once a leap year," Gary rejoinders easily with a wide grin. "Maybe."

"Har har, we would have been out last week if someone didn't call us in tears," I say right back at the big wolf. It's a verbal jab that Gary is used to.

"Jay, be nice," Ted says. "So what's up? Still need to talk about Silas?"

"Nah, I'm fine really. If he wants to go to Vancouver to pursue his career let him go," Gary says and I note a hint to his voice of it cracking. Silas and Gary had been a lot tighter than most of Gary's pick ups. Last week he was in tears over it and I find it hard to believe that Gary, Mr. Overly-Romantic, got over it this quick.

"So you're here for what reason?" Ted asks.

"I don't know if you heard the news but HE is in town," Gary says with a gleam in his eye his tail wagging rapidly a broad smile breaking out on his face.

It suddenly occurs to me exactly what he is talking about, but Ted doesn't register what he means until far too late, "Who? Who's in town?" After saying that, he seems to realize what is going to happen, but it is too late now, there's no stopping it.

"The hottest hero ever! Glacier!" Gary says, throwing his paws into the air with glee and relish, and he's so obviously pleased to break the news that he doesn't notice Paul nearly choke on his bite of food.

"Oh? Is he?" I ask wishing I had telepathy as I pat Paul's back heavily. They need to try and act nonchalant here. I could see the use of it at this moment, despite the morally questionable nature.

"He was spotted over by that strip mall on Walsh with Star Coyote, taking on that super dud Whirlwinder. I can't believe that hot husky is in town," waxes Gary with an obvious sigh and smile. "I even got to see him in person! I was there to see him defeat Whirlwinder."

"Wasn't, um, Star Coyote involved," Paul asks innocently blushing slightly.

"Pssh, please. That boy tries, but it was all Glacier. And let me tell you, Jay, our little debate with Brandon is over," Gary says with a waggle of his eyebrows and I almost shut my eyes hoping he wont say what I know is coming. "Because let me tell you, that you are so right, that husky does have one mighty fine butt. Especially with the way that tail curls. I took pictures with my camera. Want to see?" he says excitedly, pulling out his digital camera.

Well gee, I haven't wanted the ground to swallow me up since junior high. I suppose I was due. All I can do is say, "No thanks," while avoiding Paul's gaze.

"Aww, okay but I think I'll keep them around," Gary says with a big smile and I really hope he won't say something lewd. He doesn't normally but I know how much of a fan he is of Glacier.

"What was this all about, Jay?" Ted asks looking at me with a quirked eyebrow. He's enjoying this. Despite how Paul is blushing and my embarrassment he's enjoying it. I can just tell.

"It was a stupid conversation Brandon started three years ago," I start to explain.

"Well maybe a little longer than that," Gary commented rubbing his chin with a big paw as he smiles wistfully. "Ted, I think you've heard the tail end of it a few times. I swear, Mr. Big Husky, I don't know how you stand it! This one is always late to everything! I've given up on why Jay is so accepting of it. Anyway, Brandon started us on what heroes are hottest or who we'd do. Right after movie stars of course, it's just a fun thing to talk about."

"And, uh, what do you all say?" asked Paul a little worriedly.

"It varies just like with movie stars," Gary says waggling his eyebrows. "Jay here has had the same answer for years, Star Coyote. I still say it's because the guy saved him. I'm a fan of Glacier though. I mean have you seen that guy's shoulders? Not to mention fashion sense with that robin's egg blue uniform, compliments his body and fur very nicely. Jay sticks by his guns but he's been on my side when it comes to Glacier more than, say, Metalyena."

"Oh really!?!," says Ted with a very wide grin. "And he's said that for a few years?"

"Yeah," Gary nods looking at the three of us a bit perplexed.

"That is actually pretty sweet," Paul says.

"So anyway. Find anyone interesting these past few days?" I ask trying to change the subject to Gary's dating habits and hoping we can get off of this particular topic.

"Oh, I think so," Gary says leaning over and playfully squeezing Paul's bicep. The husky grins in bemusement at that one. He has no idea how to react to that. He seems like a guy who is used to showing off his body so the attention from Gary is a bit unexpected.

"Um, Gary, I hate to tell you this but Paul is straight," Ted says with a worried look.

"Oh my stars and garters!" Gary leans back from Paul quickly. "I'm so sorry. You just look too cute to be straight."

"Um, no problem?" Paul says trying to sip his wine and blushing at that, avoiding eye contact. Typical straight guy there. Ted and I share a look at that and nearly burst out laughing. The entire thing does have a surreal quality that makes it funny and I am glad to see my coyote feels the same way. Paul seems to have relaxed as well so hopefully this won't cause a long term problem.

"No, that is a problem," Gary says dropping his flame act a bit now. "Here I am yakking about a hot superhero and groping you. Hell, I was even downplaying Star Coyote and everyone knows I'm just as proud to have him as a hero here in Portland as anyone else. I mean he defeated Etenoir. I am so sorry." Gary looks really worried that he's offended Paul, and I know it's not an act.

Paul stumbles a bit but gives the wolf a slight smile, "Its, um, okay I guess. Hey, at least I get how some of those girls in college felt."

"Well as long as it is a learning experience," Ted says with an amused grin, resting his head on his paw and looking at the two big muscled canines.

Paul laughs at that and it is a nice deep throaty laugh and infectious. We're all chuckling soon as his big bright blue eyes twinkle, "Yeah I suppose it is. Next time though, let's not make it a lesson with visual aids."

"It was really nice seeing those heroes though. It must be amazing being them," Gary says wistfully. "I love seeing them do what they do. I remember what it was like before they came on the scene."

"I think we all do," I nod along remembering the news reports when I was a little kid. Those were dark times before Solarcoon appeared, and dangerous too. "I'm glad they're out there. They take so many risks for us."

"But what they can do is so amazing. I wish I could do some of that stuff. You know I used to be a hockey player and figure skater for years. I'd love to have the power to make ice," Gary says.

"It is not all its cracked up to be, I bet," says Paul offhandedly with an eye roll as he sips his half thawed drink.

"I don't know. Looks amazing to me," Gary says with sheer gleeful exuberance. "But hey, just like checking that cutie Glacier out, a guy can dream. I bet you can relate. Don't most of you straight guys look at Force Vixen or something?"

"Unattainable," Paul says dismissively with a smile. "I like my women a little more down to earth."

"Fair enough," Ted says with a chuckle. "Though that doesn't explain Gillian."

"Hush you," Paul says with a chuckle, giving Ted a happy look I've seen from plenty of ex-lovers and friends. I know I've given Gary that look myself.

The four of us chat happily for a while, and by now our food is done, but we're not ready to leave just yet. Gary orders some coffee for the table to make up for horning in. Gary's a good guy when you get to know him, but I can tell he might be a bit smitten with Paul. I've seen that look on his face before, and when the two of them are discussing something he seems to light up, Ted glances at me and shakes his head at the wolf, and I can tell he's thinking the same thing. Hopefully that won't blow up in our face. At least it seems like Paul's having a good time and were all laughing and talking about little things.

As we sip our coffee, Ted brings up something. "So what I've always wondered is why are there always more supercriminals than superheroes. I mean the first superbeings recorded were guys like Rigger and Power Puma. Solarcoon, our first superhero, didn't show up for at least two years after Power Puma, and Rigger was active well before that."

"Yeah that bugs me too," says Paul folding his arms a bit a slight look of irritation on his snout.

"Really? Seems fairly obvious to me," I say sipping my coffee.

"So why then, Mister Smarty?" Paul asks jovially.

"Well, let me put it this way: I don't know too many people that if they got super powers who wouldn't misuse them a bit. If not misuse them a lot. Most of the so called supercriminals are just people who use their powers to take what they want or do what they feel like. I can understand that. A feeling of not being constrained by the law and doing it because they can seems to be the main motivation for them. The excuse is that they're crazy but really it's more because they can," I philosophize for a moment tapping the underside of my muzzle, "and supervillains are just people with very strong beliefs. A lot of them are terrorists and nut jobs but they have beliefs and want to accomplish goals. I could see a person gifted with powers going about that kind of act."

"Part of what makes the Extraordinaries heroes is the fact that they do so much for us. They decided to use their powers for everyone, to protect our laws rather than break them," Gary adds nodding his head. We've never talked about this but he seems to agree with me. He has more reverence in his tone than I would, but then he's always been a fan of superheroes. He once confided in me that one of his first crushes when he was a teenager was Solarcoon. "It isn't their powers that make them super, it is their actions. They're heroes and unlike some people they really seem to mean it. I mean, I still remember where I was when Solarcoon stepped up to save Phoenix and declared that he would do everything he could to protect and serve the law."

"Right," I say with a wag of my tail. I had been in school at the time and our teacher had gotten a TV and showed us the incident. She somehow guessed it would be a life changing event. I think about it for a moment, all that power and responsibility that Ted holds and I add, "I don't know if I could do what they do. I don't know if I could be strong enough for it. I don't even know if I wouldn't be tempted to act like some of the criminals and get a little revenge or do something terrible if I had powers."

I feel a leg brush against my leg and I look at Ted our eyes meeting as we glance at each other and he smiles at me. That happy smile full of hope and joy as he says sincerely, "I know you'd do the right thing, Jay."

I smile at the big goober and blush slightly. Paul and Gary are looking at us and I know Gary is missing the subtext but I think Paul gets it.

"It's a theory," Paul says easily enough, finally breaking the silence as he looks between the two of us.

Gary excuses himself after we pay the bill. He says something about seeing Brandon and Mattie. He's just excusing himself after breaking into our meal like that. I'm positive he has something else he wanted to talk to us about, something beyond spotting his personal hero Glacier. That was just Gary trying to be polite and not bring up something personal in front of a stranger. The irony that he was sitting next to the heroic husky isn't lost on me. We part ways, and the wolf heads home while Paul, Ted and I continue to talk as we wander around the downtown area for a little while.

"So when can you two come to San Antonio?" Paul asks finally as the night winds down.

"Heh, you want us to?" I ask with a wag as Ted smiles very broadly and happily.

"Sure. You're a really nice guy, Jay, and Ted is my best friend," Paul says with a smile. "I wouldn't mind hanging out with you guys here again, but why not try some of Mission City?"

"Well I think seeing San Antonio would be neat. A nice change of pace from the Rose City," I say trying to contain my glee. Paul actually might like me. Good, he seems like a really nice guy too. I can see why he and Ted are friends.

"Hah, yeah, San Antonio is a great place. One of the many reasons I am a hero there. That and it's just fun," Paul says. "So, Ted, think you can fly me home? I really don't want to use the teleporter."

"Oh sure, Paul," Ted says, "As long as you don't mind me holding you tight."

"I'll survive. Now that I know what your type is at least," Paul says with a conspiratorial grin.

Ted just laughs at that. I have no idea what they're talking about. I give it a pass and we look for a place for them to get into costume. While we're doing that Paul hands me his cell number and I do the same for him. Our communicators can call each other but those are for official business. Ted and Paul switch into their costumes at a public restroom. I won't comment on that too much except to say we're cleaning that costume when he gets home, and the two of them are soon flying away as Glacier and Star Coyote. I head back to my car, grinning happily. It's been a good night.

Driving home I smile to myself. All things considered it's been a good introduction to Glacier. He's a great guy and we had a fun time. I feel like I'm becoming more a part of Ted's superhero life and that is worth something to me. There is also the fact that Paul seems to be a really nice guy, an ally in all of this craziness, and that is immeasurable in its value. It shouldn't be a surprise though; he is a hero, just like Ted.

CHAPTER 5
THE INTERVIEW

I brush my black and white fur for what feels like the millionth time. I try hard to look good most days: brushed fur, shirts that are not wrinkled, clean pants, and so on. Today though I am in my good suit and I spent extra time grooming everything. Today is special, I'm representing my offices and the city of Portland and I need to make a good impression. I look over some documents as I wait. I'm going to try and not sign them for now; I will need to look over them carefully before I send them out and I'm a bit too nervous right now to be 100% trustworthy.

"Ah, welcome," I say standing up when Elizabeth Clay enters the room. She closes the door behind her with a smile on her long, thin muzzle. The famous Philadelphia reporter looks just like her byline photo. She has black fur that seems to have a slight gray sheen like polished igneous rock, with long pointed ears accentuating her height. She's thin and lithe, the very epitome of her jackal heritage. Her brown eyes remind me of mahogany and that slender muzzle gives her a very crafty appearance. She's wearing a silver bracelet and a white blouse along with a skirt that matches her tan jacket. It gives her a comfortably professional look.

I have to wonder, as I look her over, if perhaps she uses her looks to disarm those she is interviewing. Does she wear the same thing when she interviews the President? When she was investigating Erbe Corporation for its illegal business dealings that bilked billions from stock holders? When she ended that slum lord's business? When she shut down that hospital that was involved in a black market organ program?

"Mr. Carson?" she asks lightly with a smile as I proffer my paw.

"Please call me Jay, Ms. Clay," I say with a smile of my own indicating the chair on the other side of my desk. We shake paws easily. Okay time to put on my poker face. I've interviewed with the press before. I need to avoid showing too much emotion and I need to be very careful with my answers. This might seem to be an innocuous interview but you can never be sure, especially when the interview is being conducted by Elizabeth Clay, one of the best journalists in the country.

She single handedly put the Philadelphia Enquirer back on the map. She interviewed Doctor Schmeterling once, has been in a battle of words with Power Puma, and brought dictators to their knees with her stories. Heads of state have taken questions from her as have CEO's, politicos, and anyone else she can get to. For a woman in her thirties she has a frightening resume. I should know, I've read many of her stories. I'm a huge fan actually, even her Philadelphia-centric articles are engaging and interesting.

"Only if you'll call me Lizz," she says disarmingly with a slight tilt of her head and a smile. She sits down giving off a relaxed confident air.

"I have to say I'm a bit surprised at your request for an interview," I say with another smile. "I didn't think there would be that much interest in Portland's city planning for the city of Philadelphia."

"Well every city needs its infrastructure and long term development plans. This is part of a larger story comparing urban planning across major American Cities. I'm starting with Portland but I'll be going to other cities," she says pad and pen in hand. "People need to know how these things can work so they can give informed input. You've been on a number of projects yourself. Water treatment and reclamation, city parks, and a massive new residential complex for low income families that you took point on—all things Philadelphia has been grappling with. Maybe an outside perspective will help."

"I'm only too happy to try," I nod along as I nudge my paper work with my paw, making sure it is all there, reassuring myself more than anything. She knows my resume very well. I wonder how much investigating she has done on me. I shouldn't be too worried, Stratagem did look into my records and didn't find anything and I know he covered his tracks and played cover up for me.

"I'm sure you will," she says with another smile and a glint in her eye. "However, I am sorry to say that is not the real reason I am here. I have some other questions to ask you."

"Oh?" I say as pleasantly as possible, wondering what she is going to ask and fearing the worst. "What do you want to know about?"

"Star Coyote," she says simply.

I don't take a deep breath. I don't move my tail or flick my ears, I even try to make sure my eyes don't widen as I say in what I hope sounds like an easy tone, "Well I'm afraid he doesn't work in our offices. The mayor's office does have a press agent that will take questions for him or set up an interview. Do you want her number?" I slide my hand over to a drawer.

"Oh that won't be necessary, I spoke to Polly Paulson an hour ago," she says.

My paw stops and I try to give another pleasant smile. Damn it, there goes my easy out. "Oh, well, I'm not sure how I can help you there then."

"Oh, but I think you can," Elizabeth Clay says with another smile, the quirk of her lips giving me an odd feeling of being caught between a rock and a hard-place. "After all, you were the first person Star Coyote ever saved."

I chuckle at that. I really hope this is what the interview is about, "Oh, of course, but by now he's saved thousands of lives in this city alone. You might recall a month or two ago he defeated Etenoir."

"Yes, but he seems to have saved you a number of other times. An anomalous number of times really," she says. "In fact, I'd say you were very lucky to have him around. How many people can say they've been held hostage by a supervillain after all?"

"Well honestly I'm very accident prone, and I've just had some bad luck getting into situations. Besides Thrum might be a squirrel who can control sound with his inventions but he isn't really dangerous. He just likes to rob places," I say trying to brush her off. Damn it. I'm not ready for this. I don't have a cover story for this, because it's true. I have been saved a dozen times by Ted's alter ego. Ted and I have tried to think one up but neither of us thought of anything plausible. Okay, I have to calm down. She hasn't said anything that isn't public knowledge. I've been interviewed before about being saved by Star Coyote. She might be more famous, but she's like every other reporter.

"Hmm, yes I suppose you could say that. Though perhaps Star Coyote played a little too rough with the Thrum that time," she says with a certain dismissive tone, pulling something out of her briefcase. "Care to comment on this picture that made its way onto the wire?" She hands me a photo with a smile.

I look at the picture, and it shows Star Coyote in full costume flying through the air. I'm cradled in his arms. I try to keep an impassive face, "Looks like Star Coyote saving a collie."

"It was taken two weeks ago yet no calls or emergency reports were filed involving a collie."

"Not everyone reports these things. Something I'm sure you're very used to as a reporter," I say giving her another smile, and trying very hard to not panic. Damn it, that was from a surprise date Ted took me on. We had flown off to have dinner in Seattle; a picnic on the space needle's roof. It was our first date using his powers to go somewhere crazy. I didn't think anyone had seen us. He was just showing off.

"Very true," Lizz says. "On the other hand I do find it very interesting. Especially where it was taken, when you consider what the police have to say on the matter of Star Coyote."

"The police?" I ask, a bit confused by the sudden shift.

"Yes, did you know the police keep transcript records of their communication? They're fairly extensive but a little digging and you find an interesting trend. They'll tend to note when they see Star Coyote. Never anything dramatic, but they do bring up how they've seen him flying over one neighborhood or another. Over the past year he's been seen an unusual number of times flying around one neighborhood. The same neighborhood this was taken in."

"Oh?" I say trying to be as noncommittal as possible, "Well, what neighborhood is he flying into?"

"That is just it," she says with a grin. "He never flies directly into that neighborhood or out of it. He's always seen around it. Why would a superhero try so hard to not been seen in a nice middle class section of the city?"

"I have no idea," I say placidly while cursing silently. I can see where this is going and I can't think of any way of distracting her.

"Well you do live in the neighborhood, Jay," Elizabeth says. "I thought perhaps you could offer an idea."

"We don't have much of a crime problem there," I say with a slight smile. "So why would we need a superhero dropping by?" Ted has always been careful about not flying directly home. How could we have missed how suspicious that looks?

"So then why is he seen almost every night flying in that direction or away from that area?" the jackal asks while tapping her notepad with a pen. "I think I should also point out something else. Demographics: there are only seven coyotes that live in that general area according to census data and city government records."

"That seems like an odd bit of demography. Perhaps my offices should look into it and try to find a way to ensure the coyotes of Portland feel welcome in that area," I say trying to round it back to city planning. How did Ted and I never notice that? Hell, his very moniker gives off a huge honking clue. There aren't a very large number of coyotes in the city after all, unlike say Albuquerque or Fresno. Of course there's only going to be a few in our part of the city.

Elizabeth Clay does not seem perturbed by this as she continues, "Four of them are women. Of the men one is a teenager in foster care, another is a retired dock worker who used his pension to buy a very nice home with his wife, and the third is a Ted Rodriguez who happens to live with you."

"I make no secret of my lifestyle or my boyfriend," I say gesturing to a photo of Ted and I on my desk. Maybe some faux indignation will throw her off of me and give me a moment to get my thoughts together. "Do you have a problem with a gay dog working for the city of Portland and dating outside his species?"

"Hardly," she says with a quirked eyebrow. "You know what is also odd? Star Coyote's superhero career has had a number of weather moments in it. For instance when fighting Whirlwinder a few weeks ago he used his ability to fly at superspeed in a clockwise fashion to undo a tornado while Glacier disarmed him. He's famously used a storm pattern to defeat the Iron Ravers outside of Kansas City. In a couple interviews he's even talked about the weather in very informed terms. This is despite the fact that his powers seem to have nothing to do with the weather or seem unaffected by the weather."

"Maybe he just hides that fact well," I say as I wrack my mind for an answer to throw her off. "If his powers were affected by the weather he'd want to keep that quiet wouldn't he?"

"Yes, that is possible," she says her tone giving me the impression that she finds it highly unlikely. "I find it interesting that your boyfriend Ted is a meteorologist with NOAA."

"Are you implying something, Ms. Clay?" I ask carefully. I know I'm walking right into it now, but I just can't see a way to avoid her asking the question. I can't let on how close she is to the truth; I have to play dumb even if it means setting her up.

The famous reporter gives me a smirking smile as she looks at me. I think I now know how some of those officials and others have felt when she's caught them. This is not a woman who messes around, "I thought I was very clear, Mr. Carson. I'm saying that you are dating Star Coyote."

I try to keep my face impassive but it feels near impossible under her gaze. My tail quivers slightly and I try to keep placid and cool as she continues to look at me, those brown eyes piercing me almost as if she is reaching into my mind.

"I am saying that you are dating one Ted Rodriguez," Lizz continues, "who is also the masked crime fighter and superhero Star Coyote. The same Star Coyote who only a few months ago defeated Etenoir. That Ted Rodriguez is a member of the Extraordinaries." She's pressing the point now, trying to make me crack. "You've been dating him for years and you know his identity in full," she says calmly. All the while, she's talking as if she was discussing the economics or city planning. As if this was standard fare for her interviews.

"That is the craziest thing I ever heard," I say in what I hope is a dismissive tone. My heart is pounding though, and I feel weak in the knees. This is not good. Ted's secret identity has been blown wide open. I caused the outing of my boyfriend's secret identity just by sitting in my office.

Elizabeth Clay then does something I did not expect. She starts to give a very warm laugh, "Oh, you do play the game well."

I am honestly confused at that, "Pardon?"

The jackal continues to smile as she leans back in her chair, getting comfortable, the air of professionalism dropping away. "Usually by this point I have a person gasping in fear or at least shaking a bit. Diane Lee was hyperventilating right about now."

"I'm sorry I don't follow," I say, and in the back of my mind I have to wonder: Who is Diane Lee?

"Yes, perhaps not," she says reaching into her purse. "Perhaps this is more of an 'I'll show you mine if you show me yours' moment."

She pulls a pager out of her purse; a very familiar pager, silvery colored, a lot of extra buttons on it. I reach my right paw under my desk towards my pocket and feel the reassuring lump there. It can't be like mine. She flips a latch and shows a string of five colored lights, all off right now. Green, blue, yellow, red and what I now know is indigo. What did Stratagem say? There were only six others like mine in the world. A reporter has one. How did she get one? I reach my paw into my pocket. This isn't about Ted and I anymore, this is a security breach. I try and give a noncommittal answer, "Show me a beeper?"

"Oh I wouldn't do that," she says with another smile at me this one a bit more comforting despite the situation.

"Do what?" I ask my fingers fumbling over the controls.

"I wouldn't call Samuel about this," she says. "Your communicator should only be used for emergencies after all. I think he'd hate to be bothered about a visit from little old me."

That stops me once again. I know for a fact very few people have Stratagem's real name. Not even Ted knew that. Only founding members and the Alpha class people he trusts know his full name. I have to ask, "How do you know that name?"

"He told it to me when he gave me my own communicator," she says pleasantly. "And finally I have some confirmation. You have a good poker face, Jay."

I slump back in my chair surprised, my eyes widening. That throws me for a loop. I take out my own communicator and stare at it and then look at hers again. I open the latch and look at the unblinking lights and she sees mine as well now.

"He gave you one?" I ask in disbelief.

"He gives everyone with Alpha level security a communicator. But then you obviously know that," she says with another smile.

"Alpha level security ... but that would mean..." my voice trails off as my mind races at the thought. It means she knows someone on the team. Not only that but she is intimately connected to that hero and the hero has told her everything. Then it hits me like a punch to the gut. Oh god, I even know which hero trusted her. Fortunatly, Elizabeth continues talking, covering my momentary distraction.

"It means that I know a lot of things which I don't report on and that I have access to the Extraordinaries," she says with a smile.

I can't help but smile as the tension floods out of me, my muzzle breaking into a wide grin. I knew intellectually there were other people out there, people like me, and in my situation. But I never thought I would meet one. Let alone learn that one of them was a famous reporter who would ambush me in my office.

"I'll give you this, Jay. It was hard to find you," Lizz says.

"What, after all those clues you laid out?" I say with some surprise. "You made it sound like I should go underground or something."

"Hardly," she says with a little pride, "First of all, Stratagem does an excellent job covering up tracks as he works. I have to give the man credit; he knows how to hide these things. I've gotten lucky most times finding the other Alphas. Though in your case you have one of the best covers for a romantic connection I've ever seen."

"I do?" I ask, leaning forward. "How so?"

"Well to be honest it's because you are a man," Lizz says matter-of-factly. "You would be surprised how many people wouldn't make the connection. Most people I think assume Ted, if I can use his real name, is straight."

"And here I always thought he had a pretty unmistakable flamey twinge," I say with a chuckle, "but then I've always had pretty decent gaydar."

Lizz gives a snorting laugh at that, "Yes, perhaps so, but internet rumor and general opinions put Glacier or Metalyena as more likely to be gay than Star Coyote. If you discount the obviously fictional accounts and the 'everyone is gay' argument, then Ted has a very deep cover."

"Glacier? HIM?" I'm surprised. "I admit I don't go surfing the internet for that kind of thing, but people can't actually think that. I mean c'mon that guy is almost painfully straight."

"He does wear a light blue and form fitting costume," the jackal says with a smirk. "Are you telling me you never thought about it?"

Actually I'd be lying if I said no; Brandon and Gary's long running talk about sexy superheroes comes to mind. There are a lot of guys I know with posters of Metalyena, Camo, or Glacier, or sometimes all three. I always assumed it was because they were all pretty jacked, whereas Star Coyote might be very fit but he's more lithe; like my body type, trim but not over muscled. "Valid point. Still, after meeting the guy it is hard to think of him as anything but straight."

"You've actually met him?" Elizabeth asks with an intrigued grin.

"Well, aren't you active. I've only seen him at the annual holiday party. To be fair, I have attended only one party since he joined and I've never had a chance to talk with him."

"Well Ted and Glacier are friends," I say unsure if I should use his actual name here. It is hard to tell who knows what. I'm also a little surprised that there is a holiday party. Ted never mentioned it though I suppose I can guess why he wouldn't have brought it up.

"Ah, yes, the infamous friendship of those two," she says with a grin. "If I was in the gossip columns like Madeline Lee I would make plenty of hay out of it."

"I'm sure you would," I say with a smirk, "but you're a serious journalist."

"That I am," she says in a satisfied tone. "Still, those columnists do have their ears to the ground; they can pick things up I miss. Even the morally bankrupt ones like Madeline. Part of your great cover is the fact that most people don't even suspect Ted's alter ego is gay. It gives you more wiggle room than the rest of us. I don't think anyone could find a connection easily."

"Thanks, I guess." I say with some bemusement. It isn't like I chose any of this consciously.

"I'll add of course that part of the trouble in finding you was that we didn't know who had asked for clearance. Technically that is supposed to be top secret. Stratagem hates for team members to gossip about it; especially with their civilian friends and family. Unfortunately for him, while he may tell the heroes to keep mum, things do slip out. Holly got the first clue when her husband had to skip out on a parent teacher conference and take monitor duty because Stratagem was busy investigating. He was vague but Holly is hardly a fool. She figured it was something pretty big and called the rest of us." The jackal grinned, "At that point it becomes a sort of game as we try to put it together from the clues the heroes drop. We've been down this road before after all, and we figured someone was getting Alpha clearance. Who exactly was less well known." Elizabeth explains recounting the events, "Brian got the next big clue when his brother told him about a fight Glacier had with Star Coyote. He was more worried about team dynamics but it matched our time frame. Diane got a confirmation out of her boss, and then the race was on to see who among us would figure out the mystery."

"Wait. All of us?" I ask questioningly

"Ah and here was come to the main reason I am here," Elizabeth says. "You see, while the superheroes in our families group together out of a shared interest, well so do we."

"What?" I ask confused.

"All of the people who know the secret identities and are in on the Extraordinaries: We talk to each other. Send e-mails, call each other up, write letters, and have meetings," Lizz recounts with a vaguely wistful smile on her snout. "Shoot the breeze; complain about how our super spouses skip out on chores. The usual thing."

I think about that for a moment and it comes to mind what that could be called, "Sounds like a support group to me."

Lizz gets a sad smile on her face for a moment and then says, "I suppose it is. It helps that we're all friends."

"It also sounds really nice," I say at last, looking between our two communicators. People who have been doing this for years and know what this is like. I try not to let Ted know about my concerns or worries, but holding it in and not talking about it has been difficult. I can' tell any of my friends about this. I can't tell my parents. How do you explain worries about your boyfriend getting killed by a supervillain? Or explain the surreal nature of watching him fight on TV when no one else knows who is behind the mask.

"It can be. Actually we're having our bi-monthly meeting next week," Lizz grins. "We like to get together, share some food, have a few drinks, and compare notes. See each other face to face. Normally we're separated by borders and oceans but it is our way of getting around that," she says, and then more conspiratorially, "of course it annoys the bejeezus out of Lady Leopard and Solarcoon, but that is icing on the cake if you ask me."

I have to laugh at that. She says their names with such familiarity and talks about doing something so mundane. Not mean spirited, just an interaction, "So this isn't Extraordinary sanctioned?"

"Not in the slightest. This is Super Family sanctioned though," she says with a self satisfied grin.

"Corny name," I reply as my ear twitches slightly in amusement.

"You try to think of one better," the jackal says breezily. "They don't like it because they think it's a security risk. We're just getting together with friends."

"So why haven't they stopped it?" I have to ask. "I mean Stratagem alone would be able to do that."

"Most of the team knows that it isn't a good idea to try. A few arguments and a bit of deception," she says with another conspiratorial smile, "and we've made it work."

I nod and say, "Hmm. I suppose that makes sense, though I'm not sure how I feel about lying to Ted."

"Well to be fair, he did do it to you for quite a while right?" Lizz asks.

"He had his reasons," I try to respond, though she does have a point there and honestly this does sound like something I would like to try. "I suppose you speak from experience. They really don't have a problem with it?"

"I'll admit Stratagem used to have a real problem with it. He tried to shut us down when I started arranging them, but eventually he stopped," she says, nodding her head with a thin smile. "I figure either the other founders convinced him to put his energy where it was really needed or he decided it was all right. So are you in?"

I don't even have to think for a second. "Definitely."

"Excellent. I had $20.00 riding on this one," she says.

"Huh?" I grunt surprised at that. And, for what feels like the thousandth time, I ask, "What do you mean?"

"Oh nothing, you'll see," she says with another smirk as she scribbles something down on a piece of note paper and hands it to me. "So we're meeting at this address at 6:00PM Eastern Standard in Queens, New York City."

"What?" I say surprised, looking at the address. "Um, well, that is pretty far."

"Well we can't all meet in Portland, some of us do live in Oxford, Toronto, and Chicago," she explains.

"Oh," is all I can say a bit chagrined. I hadn't thought about that at all. "That might be a problem for me."

Elizabeth quirks an eyebrow with what looks like genuine confusion, "How? Your boyfriend flies. Most of the rest of us are taking planes and trains. And in one case the teleporter."

"Wait. You're suggesting I ask Ted to fly me to the meeting?" I ask in surprise. I hadn't thought about using his powers to get me places before. I mean for our date in Seattle sure, but that was together, and he planned it that way.

"Well of course. Stuart has his wife fly him all over the planet for conferences. It saves him, as well as the University, a ton of money. Holly uses her husband's powers as well to get around at times," she says as if it's the most ordinary thought in the world. Then with a little more understanding she says, "I've been there before, Jay. We all have. Give yourself permission to ask Ted for this kind of thing. It is a perk you should try to enjoy and if he has a problem with it and you're in a good relationship he'll tell you. Let me assure you there is nothing sacrosanct about his powers. You can use them too. Fudge the truth to get to NYC if you have a problem with that, too. I've done it before"

I consider that for a bit. I bet she has too. She does have a point though, it wouldn't hurt to ask. I don't want to lie to Ted to get to the meeting, but I still want to go. Then I think of something more important than that, "Oh. There is another problem. Ted isn't out to the rest of the team."

Lizz seems truly surprised by that, "He's not? Isn't he aware that your name is already out there on the records? They don't let the other Alphas see them, but anyone on the team could just go and look."

"Oh sure he is, but he's just not open about it. I think he's hoping it won't come up," I say with a roll of my eyes. "Honestly, Ted has had some drama, to put it lightly, when it comes to being out. I'll admit I'm a lot more comfortable with being gay than he is."

"I think I see what you mean," she says leaning back in her chair. As she thinks about it, she passes a pencil between her fingers. It looks like a nervous tick of hers and I doubt she does it during her regular interviews. This seems more relaxed and personable right now. Then her muzzle breaks into a very wide grin, "Oh ho! This will be good."

"Uh, why?" I've only just met her and I can tell she's planning something.

"For once, we civilian team members know something most of the heroes don't know. For once we have a secret over them," Lizz says with obvious relish. "Oh, this will be fun indeed. Trust me, Jay. No one will blow Ted out of the closet. We've all wanted a secret for years."

"I'm not sure I want to help exacerbate relationships," I say laughing a bit; the idea of a group of civilian family members wanting a secret over their superpowered spouses seems so hilariously silly.

"Unless his dating a guy is somehow dangerous or threatens the team I can assure you no one will be that worried about it or try to tell. This is more for fun," she says. "Oh yes, a great deal of fun. Leave it to me to handle this."

"Got it," I smile. Perhaps I'm trusting her too much, but damn it feels nice to talk to a normal person who knows where I am coming from, even if she is famous. I continue to smile at her, "Well, you can count me in."

"Good," she says, opening up her note pad. "Now onto some actual questions."

I smirk a bit, "Didn't you already ask a few?"

"Those were unofficial," she says. "I'm also here for this city planning story, so now I am interviewing you about your job, unless of course you want the story to be your paramour. I do after all need to satisfy my editors about this trip out here."

I laugh and smile putting my communicator away. "No, I think city planning sounds about my speed."

We talk for another solid hour about my job, the city's growth plans, our layout, the modernization efforts for infrastructure and spending. A lot of ground covered. She's good, too. She did her homework and goes right for the meaty questions, not wasting my time with easy questions you could look up in a basic text book or on the internet.

Finally she is done and gets up from her chair. I ask, "So want to grab some lunch?"

She smiles at me sweetly, "Sorry, Mr. Carson, but we need to maintain the cover story. I can't be too buddy-buddy here. I'll see you in Queens."

She leaves the office and I sit back resting my shoes on my desk in relaxation. Good interview. I might have given her a bit more on city planning than I had intended but it feels good to be so honest with someone. I'm sorry to see her go, but I'm looking forward to this meeting. Now I just need to figure out a way to tell Ted or get there myself.

I get home at a reasonable hour tonight. Besides the interview I had a pretty light load today. I suspect my boss was trying to make things easy. People are curious as to what was said in my office and I'm still worried about it a bit as I want Portland to come off well. Elizabeth Clay does not strike me as a woman who pulls her punches.

Still, I get home and I can't help but smile. Ted is home before me. It is very odd so see that. He might be planning on a late night patrol. He tries to keep off a strict schedule. That way people don't plan around that and cause trouble when he can't react quickly. Keeping a varied schedule keeps them off their guard.

I'm all too happy by the greeting I get at the door. He's in a good mood and I think that will help me when I tell him what happened today. That and I do enjoy being greeted with a kiss at the door from my hunky boyfriend.

"Hello, there," I say as our lips break and we smile at each other. "Have a good day?"

"Oh, yes!" Ted exclaims with glee. "The Fairweather project is done and I don't think I'll have to see it for a while. I had a good lunch, caught some gang bangers well before they did anything truly bad, and stopped a drunk driver. I also stopped a mugging, but hey, those are getting easy to stop. I feel excellent!"

"Good to hear," I say drawing him in close for a hug and nuzzling his neck for a moment. His tail is wagging rapidly and he makes a happy sound in my ear. He might not be thinking about patrol tonight right now.

We break our embrace eventually. I loosen my tie with pleasure. Ted has already removed his and thrown it over a chair. Neither of us really enjoys those things. My thick chest ruff tends to bunch under them and Ted just hates the constriction.

Neither of us really feel like going overboard for dinner, so we start digging out some leftovers and putting together a salad to go with them. As I toss the salad Ted asks, "So how was the interview?"

I take a deep breath at that and consider my answer before finally saying, "Very interesting."

"So what Portland paper was it for this time? What were they asking?" Ted asks as he pops some dinner rolls into the oven, obviously not hearing my answer.

"Didn't I tell you who was interviewing me?" I ask in surprise. I thought I had told him.

"You might have but the past few days have been crazy," Ted says. Then a little more chagrined, "Sorry, Oreo, I wasn't really paying attention. I mean it was just one more interview, right?"

I'd be miffed at him not paying attention but he is right; the past month has been crazy for him. Big projects at work, two intercontinental flights on Extraordinary business, and a couple late nights with the police. This has probably been a breather for him today. I also don't usually talk too much about interviews. Still, this is pretty important and I might as well get it out of the way. I clear my throat and say, "Actually, it was an interview with the Philadelphia Enquirer."

I hear Ted drop the plates he was holding. I turn and see one of them has broken on the ground. He tries to laugh it off, "Oops, clumsy me."

"Are you really going to try that line, Ted," I ask quirking an eye brow. "It was Elizabeth Clay, just to confirm what I know is going through your head."

"Oh," is all Ted can say as he stands up. I get the broom and dust pan and we clean up the shattered plate. As I take down some clean plates and put them on the table he finally says, "Oreo, please believe me. I would have told you if I had realized what was happening. I'm so sorry."

I get some wine out and pour a glass offering one to Ted. He shakes his head turning it down. Yep, patrol night. I pour him some cider as I say, "I know that. I get the feeling that while I might technically be an Extraordinary I'm not trusted with everything; especially with identities of the other civilians.

"Yeah. Stratagem and Solarcoon are pretty strict about this stuff," Ted says. "I'm glad you're okay with that. I've heard the stories about her ambushes."

"It was pretty impressive actually. We're going to have to change our routine a bit and be a little more careful," I say as I take the leftover chicken out of the oven.

"Well she probably covered our tracks for us a little," Ted agrees as we sit down at the table, "but yeah, always good to be more careful."

We're both silent for a bit as we chew our food. Ted looks a little less excited about the day. I think the news of my little interview and some guilt over not telling me might be deflating things.

Finally I have to ask, "So how would you feel about flying me to New York City next week."

Ted looks up brightly, "Oh, hey, that might be fun! I haven't spent much time in New York. I bet we could get there in under an hour, too."

What do you know? He is okay with me asking for these things. "Yeah, that would be fun. But I was thinking for a drop off for a meeting. Still we could plan to just spend some time in the Big Apple."

Then Ted's face get serious as he is obviously realizing what is going on. His ears fold back slightly, "Wait a second—meeting—New York City—Elizabeth Clay. This isn't a meeting of the other civvies is it?"

"Sorry, Snuffles. It is," I answer truthfully.

Ted sighs, "I'm not sure I want you to go to that."

"Why?" I ask more to keep the conversation going than out of curiosity.

"It's just that Solarcoon and some of the others really don't like those meet-ups. They're big security risk. All our families in one spot is a huge target," Ted says.

"That might be true, Ted, but unless some enemy already knows a number of identities they wouldn't know we're all connected to you guys. It might even be safer as the group would know to react quickly in calling for support," I say taking a bite of food.

"You assume," Ted adds as he gives me a look. He does have a good point and that was a lame excuse. It would be somewhat dangerous to gather like this. I want to try it though. I want him to understand that.

"Maybe I am," I say as I put my fork down and look at Ted. "But maybe it would be a good thing anyway."

"And maybe it would let too many secrets out," Ted says and an undercurrent of anger in his voice.

I know where this is going but right now I don't care. "And maybe you shouldn't be afraid of some of your secrets being known."

Ted slams his glass down onto the table, "This is not about that and you know it."

"Right, of course not. Just like how you telling your parents you were going out with 'Marcy' for the first two years we were dating did not have anything to do with me," I say back angrily.

It was a low blow. Ted has never been proud of that one. He growls at me, "Not the point, Jay, and you know it."

"Well, what else can it be?" I ask glowering at Ted.

"It isn't safe and it means the other Extraordinaries will get mad at me for breaking the rules," Ted says through clenched teeth as he looks at me. "Just like I said."

"If they really wanted to stop it they would have already," I say confidently. "These are some of the most powerful people on earth. Lady Leopard alone can do the impossible. She's on the side of the meet up too. Her husband is coming all the way from the UK."

"Only because it stopped the arguments between them," he said plaintively. "No one on the team likes these things. I don't want to add to it. Why do you want this so much?"

I don't answer his question. I don't want to voice my reasons. I only respond, "They'll be quiet about it." I look at him. I know he's scared about being outed but I realize a lot more of this is a wish to not to have the rest of the team angry at him. The team is filled with people who are his friends and who he deeply respects. I can understand that, but a childish part of me still wants to go to the meeting to push this thing.

"You've never even met them and you think they won't blab? That they won't mention how I helped you get there? Or anything else? Besides the fact that one of them visited you, what do you know about them?"

"The other Extraordinaries trust them like you trust me," I reply. "That trust is the reason I wouldn't lie about this. If the others feel the same way, then I think they'll keep our secrets."

Ted stands up shaking his head, "I can't believe this."

"What is so hard to believe?" I ask looking up at Ted. "After meeting Glacier I know the team has some good people on it."

"You don't know them and you don't know how it is with these meetings. You can't understand," Ted retorts.

I stand up now too, knocking my chair back slightly as I glare at him. "Don't pull this, Ted."

"Pull what?" Ted growls.

"Don't pull the 'I'm-a-super-hero-and-you'll-never-understand-what-that-means' junk. It is true I'll never be able to lift heavy objects or freeze things with my eyes or create force fields from thin air or run to Taipei in under half an hour, but that isn't what this is about. Seems to me I know exactly what this is: a group of people wanting to gather together and their loved ones have a problem with it. And you have a problem with it because you're afraid how your teammates will react," I say, glowering at him.

Ted turns and starts to leave the kitchen, "I'm not hungry."

Now, as a collie I suppose it's genetic that I don't like it when things don't go my way, or people leave my presence without permission. I suppose it also means I don't back down from things easily, or so the stereotypes claim. Really that is just an excuse. I can be pretty thick headed and I know it. Case in point: I know that following my coyote and continuing this discussion is a bad idea, but I find myself following him into the living room saying, "No, Ted, you don't get to do this. You don't get to pick and choose where I am in your life. We're boyfriends ,you have to let me into your whole life."

"I have!" Ted shouts rounding on me, growling as his ears lay back against his head. "I have damn it. Do you think this is easy? Do you think I liked lying to you? That I like putting you in danger when I put on the mask? That I like the idea that you knowing my secrets puts you in even greater danger? You don't get to pull your sanctimonious crap with me, Jay. Not here! Not over this!"

"Well someone should, because you've got your head so far up your ass I'm surprised you don't need a flashlight," I growl back, tail fluffing out as I glare at Ted. My nostrils are flaring and Ted's fangs are bared at me.

"Fuck you," Ted says. "You don't know anything, Jay. You don't know what it is like seeing someone's loved ones murdered because they're related to a hero. You don't know what it is like facing down some mad man who doesn't care about victims, or laws, or anything beyond their grandiose but petty plans. You really don't know shit about this."

"And you don't know what it is like knowing you might not come back to me," I say angrily.

"What?" Ted growls looking confused, "What does that have to do with anything?"

"Do you think I'm an idiot, Ted? Do you really?" I ask angrily. "Elizabeth Clay is from Philadelphia. She is a reporter who has never left that city. She knows who you all are. It doesn't take a genius to put it all together, Ted."

Ted looks at me with his ears back, and I can see the anger fading from him as he starts to realize what I'm saying. I didn't want to bring this up. I didn't want to talk about this again. I've been trying so damn hard to get some peace over this; to find a way to come to grips with it all. A way to not weigh Ted down with my issues, because I know my empathetic coyote would feel guilty about it, but I'm letting it out now.

"Elizabeth Clay was married to The Stranger, wasn't she," I say. It isn't a question. I know it is true, it has to be. Ted nods now, looking a little dumbfounded that I figured it out. I don't know why he is. This isn't exactly a mystery. Stranger had been a jackel and Philadelphia's hero for years, and after meeting Lizz it was easy to figure out. I continue, "She was married to one of the founders of the Extraordinaries, the jackal who sacrificed his life to save the world. I saw it on TV, Ted. We all did. Schmetterling had hijacked all the world's transmissions to focus on him and his spatial distortion device. We all saw him lose control of the damn thing. We saw it as it started to distort reality. We all heard that it would have destroyed everything as it unwound space and time. We saw, I saw, The Stranger leap into the center of the vortex. I watched him die on live TV, just like you did." I'm panting now, the tension escaping me as I speak. Later on, it was explained by Stratagem to the UN General Assembly, that The Stranger figured out that his powers could be used to stabilize and shut the distortion down. That his teleportation abilities worked on the same principals, and he could close it from the inside. It worked, but the whole world watched him die to save everyone. I take a deep breathe and finish, "We all saw it, hell we saw the parades, and the President dedicating the statue in Philadelphia."

"Yeah," Ted nods, a bit stunned by my outburst. I doubt he's talked about this much with the team. It happened a long time before he joined, and I don't think they would enjoy talking about it.

"That means Elizabeth Clay watched her husband die; saw him die on TV with everyone watching. Saw him sacrifice himself for the entire world," I say. Then more quietly, "The same way I might see you some day."

"Oreo," Ted begins to walk towards me. I stop him, holding up my paws

"Let me finish, Ted. Look, I know you. You're a hero because of what you do, not just because of your powers. I know you well enough to know that if the same situation occurred, and you could stop it, you would. You would save the world. I know that, Ted. It makes me proud to know you that way and incredibly happy that you want to be with me.

But it means you'd have to leave me; that I wouldn't have you any more. That I could never tell a soul about why you were gone and I was alone. I know it sounds greedy, Snuffles, but that is the truth. "

"If you want me to stop…" Ted begins.

"We talked about that, Ted," I interrupt, "I don't want you to stop and I don't think you could stop."

"Then what can I do?" he asks looking at me. "I want you to be happy, Jay. I don't want you feeling this way."

"I am happy, Ted," I smile at him. "Really I am. Just because it could happen, doesn't mean it will. Elizabeth Clay reminded me of all of this. She lived through it."

"Yeah, she did," Ted nods. "I hear she was a wreck for a while."

"It explains her sabbatical from the paper," I say. "I guess her husband didn't leave her; that was just the cover story."

"Stratagem and Force Vixen tried to make up a better one, but after Madeline Lee printed that rumor in her gossip column, nobody would believe anything else," Ted said sadly and a worried look crosses his face. "I guess that could happen to me, too."

"It might not," I say with a grin, "neither of us are famous reporters."

"True," he nods, "but what does that have to do with meeting the other civvies, Jay?"

"It has everything to do with it," I say looking into his warm eyes. "Ted, think about it. She has been through the unimaginable. Who would you talk to? Who else did she have to talk to but the others? These are all people who are essentially in the same position as me. They know what it is like to be with a hero. They know the risks. They know the challenges. Best of all, they can talk about it. I would never be able to talk to people in the office, or Gary, Brandon, Charles, Lilly, or Mattie. Under no circumstances could I ever talk to my parents about anything like this. I'm not even talking about you sacrificing your life. I'm talking about the general stuff, like hearing about you on the radio taking down some criminal and saving lives. These people know what it is like."

"I guess they do," Ted says as he nods.

"I mean I thought I was going to have to be quiet for the rest of my life. Never risk talking about it with other people, except other heroes and you. No offense, Ted, but that isn't the same," I say with a slight smirk on my muzzle. "But when Elizabeth revealed who she was, I realized I didn't have to be alone with this. There are others like me. You know how that feels?"

"Yeah I do," Ted is nodding along now. "I guess I didn't think of it that way."

"It happens," I say with a smile, the argument feeling like it is now miles behind us. Ted wraps me in his arms and we hug tightly. I think Ted is still worried and we're both a bit jumpy from the fight, but it still feels good to hug him. "So then, New York City next week?" Ted asks, breaking our hug.

"If you're okay with it," I say after looking into his eyes for a little bit. I want him to have an out, and if he says it isn't okay I'll let it drop, no matter how hard that will be.

"Only if you tell me everything afterwards," Ted says licking my nose with a smile on his face.

"Back to dinner?" I ask. Before Ted can answer, his communicator beeps.

Ted looks at it for a moment and then chuckles, "Afraid not love. Looks like the police need me."

"Go," I say with a roll of my eyes as Ted rushes off to get his costume on. I go to the kitchen and make him a chicken sandwich. He's in his uniform in a moment and I hand him his sandwich and kiss him before he zooms out the back door.

Chapter 6
The Super Family

I've never actually been to New York City. In fact most of my life has been spent on the West Coast. At best, I've been on some road trips into Nevada and a trip to Wisconsin to visit a great aunt. I did a trip to Chicago, a graduation present from my parents when I finished college. I've been to parts of Canada more often than other parts of the United States. I've been told I need to get out and see Boston, New York City, and the other big cities, butI've never had the chance.

I somehow doubt anyone who told me to do that pictured me flying out gripping my boyfriend's neck tightly while he cradled me against his chest, zooming far into the sky at amazing speeds. Star Coyote is still not sure how the mechanics of his super speed flying work. I'm pretty sure it would make a physicist's head explode. Whatever the case, it is pretty interesting flying out across the continent in his arms. Planes feel safer but we're quicker. And I have to admit, pressing against my guy's muscled chest is rather nice. I think he grips me a little tighter than necessary for the same reason. It is chilly though. The meeting is set up for a Friday so we both took a day off work. Ted's boss is a lot less helpful than mine on this one. Ted has been zipping around so much that he has to sneak out of work at times and his boss is no idiot. Still, Ted got a major project done along with some smaller ones and has turned his work in on time, or early, and worked ahead, so he didn't say no. He just groused at the idea.

So we got to tour the city together, spending the day in New York, and behaving like actual tourists with Ted's costume stowed in a backpack. There is a lot to see and only having a day feels like way too little time. Now I wish I had looked into a hotel, but we did the major tourist spots. We saw the Empire State Building, the natural history museum, Central Park, and a few other things. It was far too little time to see things for real. I count us as lucky that we didn't see any crimes taking place. That was mainly so Ted wouldn't feel the need to intervene. It was nice to just spend the day together.

All too soon, it is time for me to head off to the meeting. Ted's plan is to fly back to Portland and do some patrolling there. Then he will come to a prearranged meeting spot. Elizabeth Clay had sent me an e-mail with the locations of twenty buildings in Queens with rooftop access that people off the street can get to. I'm not sure if she put the information together or someone else in the group did it. I don't know anyone else yet and I didn't want to ask for names or details over the phone.

I take the subway over and get off a stop away and walk the rest of the distance. I get the feeling we all want to try and keep exact locations to a minimum. Rounding the corner I see Lizz Clay on her cell phone. I wave to her and she smiles waving back. As I walk up she seems to be finishing her conversation.

"Don't worry, it will be done by the end of next week," she says into the phone and nods her head, rolling her eyes slightly. "Trust me this one is in the bag, Lou."

She snaps her cell phone shut muttering something about editors and then smiles at me. I wag my tail slightly and offer my paw, "Well, I made it."

"So I see. Everyone is just getting here, there are a few stragglers as always. Come on, we're a block away from the restaurant," the jackal grins as she leads me forward.

"Excellent. I would hate to be late after all," I say with another grin as we start walking. We only move a few feet before we hear someone shout.

"Hey! Lizz over here!" We turn and see a fox and a hyena walking towards us. As they get closer I get a better look at them. The hyena is a broad shouldered guy in a t-shirt and jeans. He's pretty big and well muscled with a round muzzle. His fur is a deep dark brown that almost seems to obscure the black spots on his face and his hands have a deep mahogany gloved effect. His t-shirt is a light gray with four red stars emblazoned over his chest, the Chicago flag I suddenly realize as a bit of trivia floats forwards in my brain. He looks odd in the t-shirt, as if he should be wearing a uniform that fits his striding gait, if that makes any sense. The large boots he is wearing seem to fit him the most.

The fox, the one shouting, smiles at Elizabeth as they catch up, "Good to see you again. It's been far too long."

He's wearing a really nice suit: black jacket, bright white shirt, understated belt buckle, silk tie, wing tip shoes. It all screams class and confidence. He seems extremely professional in it and his trim fit body just accentuates it. Most foxes look thin in my experience but he seems to have a more solid look. Not wispy or feminine, just very fit. His slender grinning muzzle reminds me of someone. His slightly large ears are tipped in white instead of black or red. That is what finally throws the switch in my head.

I should know that face anywhere: Adam Fairchild, one of Los Angeles' most famous district attorneys. We used to get briefs up in Portland about what he did. Fairchild is considered one of the best lawyers in the country. He was one of the first DA's to truly prosecute super criminals for their crimes. He led the charge for special judicial reforms in his state. His most famous case was the one against Power Puma that shut down his political organization throughout the west coast. He did a pro-bono case afterwards getting millions from Power Puma's estate for his victims.

Everyone was surprised when he retired from his DA job a few years ago. It was so unexpected. After all, there were rumors that he'd run for governor. Despite his young age and the stigma against lawyers he was respected, well liked and had built a career as a defender of the public interest. I hear he now works for a civil rights law firm closely tied to the Southern Poverty Law Center.

"Adam, good to see you're looking so well," Lizz says with a smile. "Still keeping fit, I see. The personal gym is working out for you."

"Well Emma would kill me if I started putting on weight now," he says patting his stomach. I'm standing off to the side, so I don't even think he noticed me as he continues, "After all, she does work out herself, so why shouldn't I? She does lead a more active lifestyle than me, to be fair, but that's all the more reason for me to try a little harder."

The hyena coughs into his paw theatrically, I think to garner attention, and Lizz turns to him, "Sgt. Wilson, I see you're doing well."

"Lizz," he grunts, "Nice seein' you too. Let's talk at the restaurant though. I hate catching up where anyone can listen in."

He gives me a sidelong glance and I get the feeling he's talking about me, and that he wants me to move along. Elizabeth just smiles though and says, "Of course, Brian, but as everyone here is in the family I don't see too much trouble talking here."

"In the family?" Adam quirks an eyebrow and looks at me. I think he's finally noticed me. His eyes widen with recognition, "Lizz, did you do some investigating?"

The hyena, Brian, is also looking at me now and has a toothy smile, "I think she did, Adam."

"Jay Carson," I say offering my paw to the big hyena. His hand seems to dwarf mine as we shake.

"Brian Wilson," he says gripping my hand very tightly

"Adam Fairchild," the fox says offering me his paw and I take it my hand feeling a little sore after the hyena's grip. I can't believe I'm shaking Adam Fairchild's paw. I also can't believe that Adam Fairchild knows Force Vixen. It's the only thing that makes sense if he is here. Los Angeles is where Force Vixen works out of, and I know Adam Fairchild used to work closely with the heroine on cases as the DA. He was also her biggest critic when she messed up and made mistakes. Is she the reason he abandoned his political ambitions and left the DA's office?

"Well, now that we're all introduced," Lizz says with the air of a woman who wants to move to more important matters, "Yes, I have done a little investigation. None of you ever put the time into it to get it right. So I did, again."

"Oh, I'd have found out eventually," Adam says with a grin.

"No you wouldn't," Lizz rejoinders easily as we start walking again towards the restaurant.

"So, did she not mention I was coming?" I ask looking at the fox as we start to walk to the restaurant.

"It's standard procedure for Lizz. She loves a good surprise," Adam says with a chuckle. "I'm still not sure how she does it, finding all of us. You know she found everyone in our little group, though Holly was the one who organized us to actually meet up and created the phone tree."

"Footwork," she says with a smile. "And you boys are paying for my drinks tonight."

"He's the Alpha?" Brian says with undisguised shock. "I thought this was some Beta security person you found and wanted to invite. Like Michelle."

"No, I'm an Alpha," I say with a look at the hyena, "and what happened to getting off the street to talk about these things?"

"Sorry, just surprised," Brian says while looking at me. "I do try to keep a lid on this stuff, but I was expecting someone else for the position is all."

"Michelle was a unique case and you know it," Lizz says easily. "And trust me, Jay here is a perfect addition to the group."

"I'm surprised that she didn't tell anyone," I give a look at Lizz. "She does that all the time," Brian says with a groan. "Little Miss I-Have-A-Secret, who only tells when she is sure to make a splash."

"We're used to it by now," Adam says as he opens the door to Three Mugs Tavern. I had looked it up online. It has really good hamburgers and fries according to online chatter. As Lizz and Brian enter he continues, "Don't take me wrong, she just loves getting a reaction."

"I suppose so," I say entering the restaurant. The Three Mugs Tavern is one of those faux taverns meant to evoke the myth of the warm old drinking houses of yore. It does a decent job, and there's even a big bay window so you can see people walking by on the street. Business seems to be doing well; there are a lot of people here. A hand shoots up at a table in the back and waves us over.

A large table back against the wall has two other people sitting at it. The one vigorously waving us over is a very effeminate lioness. She has a very petite muzzle and a winsome frame. Thick auburn hair on her head tied back in a braided pony tail. She's wearing a bright blue sweater and very tight jeans.

Beside her is a raccoon woman with bobbed hair. The woman just seems to scream wholesome sweetness. She has a warm smile on her plump round face and her mask just accentuates her rounded features. Just looking at her makes me think of mom and apple pie. She is the first one to speak when we come over, "Well now, it appears everyone is getting here on time for once."

She says it with a very amused tone and Adam chuckles, saying, "Not for lack of trying, Holly. Hello, Diane."

"Addy," the lioness says happily, "Brian, Lizz."

"Who is left?" Brian asks sitting down in his chair which creaks slightly as he sits. Lizz sits down as well and the positioning of everyone leaves three seats open. Two on the end that are away from everyone and the other seat is corralled between Adam and the raccoon named Holly. I think I'm supposed to sit there. Periphery seating might be a bad idea for the new guy. Hopefully I'm not making a faux pas.

"Stuart is a little late, but he called ahead," Diane says. "After all, he is coming the furthest."

"I'd feel bad about that but Jane can get him here easier than anyone else," Adam says.

"Oh, and Michelle said she is coming," Diane says, "But she's stuck taking the train so who knows when she'll arrive."

"Ugh. Well, they're lucky. I had to use that irritating machine to get here," Brian says resting his head on his paw. He doesn't have to actually say which machine, I can guess.

"Yeah, I've been warned about that thing," I say taking out a folding brush. That causes a round of laughter from the table.

"And with that we know for sure you're one of us," Adam says with a smirk. "It removed my tie one time. I'm still not sure where it ended up. Brian and I met up in the bunker. We got the fish eye from the big shiny metal one."

"So the others will know soon enough," Holly says easily, taking a sip from her glass. At that moment the waiter comes over and takes our drink orders.

As the beaver leaves, Lizz grins at Holly and Diane, "Well now. Does everyone want to pay for my meal or just give me the cash now?"

"Ah, so he is the new Alpha," Holly says easily, nodding at me. "I assumed you'd find out before anyone else."

"Jay Carson," I say with a smile shaking Diane's paw which shoots out quickly and takes mine before she turns back to the bright blue drink she is sipping. Holly gives me a matronly smile and takes mine as well. She has a very warm, soft paw.

"Holly Jefferson," she says, "Actually since you're new why don't we do the more formal introductions."

"Ugh, those," Brian rolls his eyes. "Do we have to? They're dangerous."

"Oh they are not," Lizz says, and the jackal gives a dismissive wave of her paw.

"Reveals a lot of secrets is all I'm saying," Brian cautions, and the big hyena's face is serious. "There is a reason certain people don't like these meet ups."

"Tough," the lioness says, "He'll learn this stuff eventually. At the very least he'll get an earful of gossip from me and Michelle before the night is through."

"Why don't you start, Holly," Lizz says ending that line of conversation as she nods at Holly. "We'll go around the table and then Jay can tell us a little about himself."

"Sounds fair," I say with a happy smile and a wag of my tail to conceal my nervousness.

"I'm Holly Jefferson," the raccoon says. "I'm a grade school teacher in Phoenix, Arizona; where my husband, Bill Jefferson, is a state patrolman. I have four lovely children; Jenny my daughter is the oldest, followed by the triplets Mark, Luke and JJ."

She takes out a wallet and shows me pictures of three identical raccoon boys, a tween raccoon girl with her hair growing long and oddly blond, and finally a very large, muscled raccoon man. There is no mistaking who he is. I'm looking at the civilian face of the first super hero, Solarcoon. That shock of blond hair on his head gives it away if nothing else. He's resting against a pickup truck with Holly leaning against him. They are both smiling very happily.

"I'm Diane Lee," the lioness says pulling me away from the picture. "I live here in New York City. I'm a personal assistant to Wallace Fredrickson. Currently single. We work at Fredrickson Publishing Company's fashion magazine Blush."

"What happened to Zach?" Adam interrupts.

"He had issues with the amount of time I spent on my job," Diane says sipping from her flamboyant drink, "too much devotion to the boss."

"He wasn't worth your time anyway," Brian says offhandedly.

"You're tons better than he'll ever get," Lizz says. "And if you want, I bet I can run an expose on him easily."

"He wouldn't have kept the secret anyway," Diane says dismissing what everyone is saying. "The boss depends on me. Besides, plenty more guys out there. Not to mention I doubt you could dig up that much dirt, Lizz."

Wallace Fredrickson, well, there is only one hero that could be, Camo. His personal assistant knows the truth huh? Odd, but not surprising I guess. He must need her to know so she can keep everything organized. Still, for a guy who turns invisible, it's interesting that his assistant knows at all.

"I guess that explains why Fredirickson has the poster and calendar deal with the team," I say perking up my ears and grinning.

"Oh yes, that turned out to be a real boon. Wally had no idea it would sell so well. That, on top of some of his other deals, got him that nice office and I got a very nice desk out of it," Diane says with relish, "and everyone said he was going to be the unsuccessful son."

"Oh, so it is Wally again," from Adam with has a teasing lilt and a waggle of his ears.

"I have no idea what you mean," Diane says coyly.

"I'm sure," Lizz smiles. "I do admit, that calendar and poster deal was a great idea. It really sells well. I guess people like licensed images of their heroes."

"That and it really did a nice job breaking up all those counterfeit and fake deals," Diane says. "Wally always did hate those things. Far too shoddy and expensive."

"Sorry I'm late!" calls a voice and I turn to see a dark grey striped tabby cat walk up to the table and place her trench coat on a hook nearby. She is rather small looking, but she seems proportional even though I'm pretty sure that she'd only come up to my shoulders if we stood next to each other, discounting her ears of course.

"Its fine, Michelle," Holly says congenially. Everyone smiles as she sits down next to Diane. Holly continues, "How was the trip?"

"I swear those trains couldn't run slower if they tried. I sometimes wish Alan would just break down and let me use the teleporter. I swear the man can grow twenty stories into the air but he can't solve public transit," the tabby grouses as she sits down, then turning to looking up at the table she spots me. "Oh, hello there! I, um, didn't see you. And by teleporter I mean, uh, hmm." She freezes, unsure what to say.

"I doubt you need to worry, Michelle," says a man with a robust English accent. A snow leopard in a tweed jacket pulls out the last chair and smiles at all of us sitting down. His fur is close cropped and he has a pair of spectacles on his nose. His grey and white fur has a nice sheen to it and his thick fluffy tail waves back and forth slowly. There is only one word to fit the way he looks, professorial, "I doubt anyone who was not part of our little group would be sitting this close or be having such a tight conversation."

"Michelle, Stuart, this is Jay," Lizz says with a sly grin, "and you both owe me dinner."

"Oh!" Michelle's eyes widen, "Should I leave the table?"

"I'm sure you've heard enough from all the members of our august group to no longer warrant that," Stuart says. "And a pleasure meeting you, Jay."

"Introduction time," says Diane with a smile, "and it is your turn, Michy."

"Well that's a fine how do you do." She smiles at me. "I'm Michelle Green, and my husband Alan Green and I live in Toronto. I run a florist shop there and my husband helps. Technically I'm Beta class security, but Lizz found me and convinced me to join up for these little meetings."

I find it somehow hard to believe that Titan Tomcat helps run a flower shop. I guess you never can tell. Alan Green has to be him though, Titan is the only hero in Canada after Marvelous Malamute fell. He's also a tabby cat so it would fit that he's married to Michelle.

"You know I have a hard time seeing the big guy arranging flowers," I say with a grin. "Didn't he punch out those, um, bikers?" Hopefully the others will know that is a code word for the Iron Ravers.

"Well those 'bikers' weren't expecting him," Brian says with amusement, "and the 'roid freak didn't see his smack down coming either." Obviously Brian means Etenoir there, and I smile with shared pride at what Ted accomplished that day.

"It is also unfair to say he's a florist. Actually he's an accountant," Adam comments as he sips his beer.

"He just works out of Michelle's shop and handles her books," Lizz explains.

"I like my description better," says Michelle, who clearly takes a bit of pleasure from teasing her husband on the matter.

"Well I'm just as amazed he's an accountant. He certainly doesn't look it," I say nodding my head, trying to imagine Titan Tomcat doing something like that. The guy can control his density and size at a whim. The most iconic image of him was the time he towered over Toronto in his red and white costume to stop the robotic attack dolls sent by Dr. Schmetterling. That was before he joined the Extraordinaries. This is a guy who has taken on Mishmash, the Iron Ravers, and Etenoir, and he is an accountant working out of a florist shop.

"The charm of a good secret identity," Lizz says with amusement. "No one ever expects the frumpy little accountant to be the guy who has swatted down airplanes and defeated Frost Giants in Norway. It gave me a real run when I was looking for Michelle."

"They gave him a parade for that you know," Michelle says. "I loved Bergen. What a lovely city and a lovely country."

Brian leans over and whispers conspiratorially, "I had the same reaction when Lizz brought her to the meetings."

"If I may," the studious snow leopard coughs and we all turn to look at him. "My name is Stuart Everheart. I'm a Classics Professor at Oxford University. I live in Oxford with my wife Jane, who runs a book store in town."

"I went to Oxford for a conference a few years ago," I say with a smile. "I really enjoyed it. A great old city and the schools are amazing to explore. I spent a little time in the Somerville Library. Although, I do have to be critical of the maze-like roads."

"Ah yes, an extensive collection," Stuart muses ignoring the comment about the streets of Oxford. "What conference were you there for?"

"It was an urban planning and development conference a few years ago. All about planning the cities of the future," I comment. The waiter comes by at that moment and we make our orders. Most of us are getting hamburgers, though Michelle is apparently getting a chicken sandwich. Holly briefly considers the fish sandwich but is convinced by Adam to get the cheeseburger.

It isn't a surprise to me that Lady Leopard runs a book store. It seems to fit her personality. Despite the fact that she is the most powerful being on earth, she always seems understated, cool and polite. I had always assumed she lived in London, too, since she's often in that city dealing with the criminal element, but given her powers she could live anywhere in England.

"Why don't I continue," Brian says as the waiter leaves, tactfully skipping over Lizz. That seems natural, I don't think she wants to speak and everyone knows she already introduced herself to me. There's no need to bring up The Stranger. "I'd like to know a bit more about this conference," Stuart says with a smile that would be overly toothy if not for the avuncular purr underneath.

"It sounds interesting," says Adam to my side. "I take it that you work for city government?"

"Okay you guys hold it," Lizz says with a grin on her slender muzzle. "As much as I enjoy a good cross examination, I also like building suspense. Why don't we wait until everyone has gone to find out about him."

"Spoil sport," Diane says with a flick of her tail, but the lioness is smiling as she says it.

"Go for it, Brian," says Adam with a chuckle and a waggle of his ears. "We might as well keep to the unofficial rules and embrace Lizz's amusement."

"Okay then," Brian says with an eye roll. "Anyway, I'm Sgt. Brian Wilson. I'm a cop from Chicago and I work in the Hyde Park area. My brother is the reason I get to come to these things."

"I was wondering about telling family members," I say with a nod. So at very least Metalyena told his brother. Shame Ted and I don't have siblings who would understand.

"It was more I discovered it. Kyle hasn't been great with keeping secrets from me or my sister," Brian says taking a sip of beer. Our food arrives and everyone remains quiet. Oh yeah, we're keeping a low profile I think to myself. We're the biggest group in here and we clam up every time the wait staff comes anywhere near us.

"You know I never heard this story," Holly says as she munches on a fry.

"Well," Brian looks down at his food, "You know how it is." The big hyena doesn't say more, but I can tell the table isn't going to let him drop it.

"I can say I'm curious now," Adam says leaning over toward Brian. "Now be nice and share."

"Yes, after all I did relate the story of how Jane told me," Stuart says as he takes sip of his beer. The snow leopard grimaces and says, "Honestly, Diane, you have to find a place with better beer."

"Oh please, Stuart, stop being a snob about your alcohol," Diane says leaning back in her chair, "besides the mixed drinks here are great."

"No drink should be that color of blue," Stuart says definitively looking at Diane's drink, "or, for that matter, color coordinated with one's clothes."

"Back to Brian's story," Adam says, his fluffy fox tail flicking about. I'm curious at this point as well so I nod in agreement.

Brian chuckles and rolls his eyes, "There isn't that much to tell. Kyle had just graduated from college. He got some pretty good marks, but instead of going on with his plans to be an architect, he announced to our mom and everyone that he got a job as a construction worker. Mom freaked out, of course."

"Why would she do that, it isn't a bad job," Holly says.

"No, but it was if you knew Kyle from before the accident. The guy's pretty smart, whatever he looks like, and he wanted to be an architect for years. He'd spent his life wanting it, and suddenly his plans change. All that hard work he did; all those applications, the late nights, the studying and working for scholarships, and now he wants to be a construction worker? It was just weird to everyone who knew him," Brian says. Now, it doesn't surprise me that Metalyena is in construction work, and it wouldn't have surprised me if Brian had been too. The hyena is pretty ripped and I know Metalyena, Kyle I guess, really is too. There are the posters out there showing him flexing after all. My friend Brandon has a truly frightening collection of them. Gary sometimes comments how he wishes he could be that size and Gary is no small fry.

"We all figured it was some sort of weird phase. Like how he kept missing parties and anniversaries," Brian continues, a big smile breaking out across his muzzle.

Everyone starts chuckling at that. Lizz is chortling and leaning back in her chair. Adam hunches over the table snickering. Stuart cracks a wide smile, chuckling in a dry British way, and Diane nearly falls out of her chair laughing. Even Holly giggles. I have to admit I'm a little tickled as well. It happened to me too after all.

"Oh don't get me started on missing events," Diane says. "I don't care what any of you have. Try to balance out a meeting schedule and calendar around super nutjobs sometime. Meetings canceled for bank robberies, dates mussed by actions on another continent. I swear Dr. Schmetterling lives to throw my schedules into a kerfuffle. Not to mention the ass kissing I need to do over the phone. If I have to comfort one more starlet or writer with a bruised ego I'll scream." The lioness sighs and sips her drink.

"Mmm. Try getting someone to do yard work," Holly says with a throaty warm chuckle. It reminds me of my Grandmother when she baked cookies. The plump raccoon continues in a deep tone, mimicking her husband, "Oh no, I can't help with the weeding today. I have to run off and stop a couple car thieves. No, can't help with the plumbing, off to Los Alamos again." She sighs wistfully. "I get more post-it notes from the man than actual help or conversation. Not to mention all the parent teacher conferences missed. The kids are helpful now at least, but that year when the triplets were born—never again. Why last week we had some time set aside to do planting in the garden and he had to rush off to stop some attack by little Ms. Haltertop."

"Oh yeah," I chime in as Michelle snorts in her drink from the nickname Holly just gave the supervillain terrorist Veneo. "I remember that. Someone was supposed to go with me to meet up with my parents for a day to help them out with shopping. I end up coming alone and trying to figure out a way to not mention that a certain someone is in Sao Paulo."

Holly pats my shoulder, "Oh we've all had that. I just give the excuse that work called. That is hard when we visit his family in Zuni or my own in New Hampshire, but it has a surprising success rate."

"We all have our stories on that front, that's for sure," Lizz adds and then with a sad smile continues, "You would think a man who could teleport would be able to get somewhere on time, but Nick never did. It can surprise you how much you miss it when it stops. I'll look at a full trash can some days or a pile of dishes, and think back to some random call from the police."

Everyone looks at Lizz for a moment and the table gets quiet. Lizz with a half hearted smile adds, "Oh like I can't contribute." The jackal shifts a bit uncomfortably and the table looks away from her.

Holly leans over and begins to whisper, "Nick was, well,"

I wave my hand, "I figured that part out."

The table remains quiet for a little while longer until Adam clears his throat, "It's just that this is the first time you've said his name in a long while."

Brian rests his paw on Lizz's for a moment and everyone remains quiet before he decides to continue, "I didn't know all that at the time you see. Then I find out he's working a second job as a mechanic to help pay off his loans. That cheeses me off. He worked so hard, got amazing grades, put in all that effort, and can't handle the loan payments except to have a second job. Worse, neither job he has is in any way backed up by the degree he worked his tail off for."

Lizz just nods, "I see where this is going. Nick was the same way when he put the mask on."

"Right," Brian grimaces. "Well anyway I get to his apartment and knock. No one comes to the door so I go in and wait for him. He gave me a key after all, and what do you know? He sneaks in through his own window. I didn't know it was him of course, and I'm a cop. All I saw was a mask climbing through a window. I pulled my gun and badge, he moves towards me without identifying, and I sort of, well, I shoot. Of course the second he hears a bang, the guy turns into pure metal, so I find out about his secret."

"By shooting him?" I say quirking an eyebrow.

"Hey, it works," Brian chuckles a rich bass sound as he eats some fries. "After we got over the mutual shock I got the details."

Adam grins, "Oh that is a fun one. I still like how Emma told me."

"Well proposing to a young woman and having her say no because she can create force fields is a surprise," Stuart says quirking an eyebrow.

"I still say that was very romantic," Diane says with a grin, "besides, she said yes in the end."

"Fifth time is the charm I suppose," says Stuart with some amusement.

Adam flicks his tail jocularly as he says, "It's what I've always said."

"Charming really," says Michelle. "But I don't understand the connection between his hobby, and him not becoming an architect."

"I bet it was the same reason Nick had," says Lizz. "Nick didn't become an EMT because that was what he wanted to do; he became one because of the flexible hours. Not to mention an erratic schedule he could use as an excuse for missing things. He was going to school to become a doctor before he developed his abilities."

"Wait," Adam says in surprise putting down his burger as his eyes widen. "Nick was going to go to medical school?"

"That was the plan," Lizz says off handedly. "He finished pre-med but decided medical school was too much when trying to be a caped crime fighter. He wanted to help people, so he dropped his MCAT scores and forgot about it. He wouldn't even consider being a nurse, which would have been a better job than an EMT. Maybe if he had lived he would have done it."

Brian is nodding sagely as he squeezes her paw for a moment longer. Diane seems to be watching his large paw as well but my attention is drawn back to his face as he continues, "Kyle is the same way. He really wanted to be an architect but he can't do that and still run all over town at any time catching bullets and stopping supervillain plots. He's always pushing himself, pushing his abilities and body so that he can do more. I think it is because he blames himself when someone gets hurt and he knows he could have stopped it with his abilities"

"It's crazy," Diane chimes in. "I mean Wally is able to hold down his job just fine, but he does the same thing. I think that is why he has so many one night stands."

"Wally had a lot of help from his father securing his position," Stuart adds as he considers his meal carefully.

"He's earned it by now," Diane says and she looks a bit offended at the idea that Wally didn't work for his job. "Besides he gives up a lot, too and I have to cover for him when some moron with an axe to grind and way too much power decides to cause trouble."

"I can see it, too," says Adam looking down at his plate. "Emma does the same thing. She's a brilliant legal assistant. She could be an amazing lawyer; hell her LSAT score was great. 177. Better than mine!"

"But?" asked Holly.

"But she can't see how she can balance her other duties with working in the courts. Judges don't like excuses much and law school devours your time. So she helps me but she keeps deferring the actual arguments to me so that she can do her pink thing."

I don't say anything. A part of me wonders about Ted. He's always wanted to be a meteorologist. He's trying to pursue his job and interests but it is a huge strain at times. The hours he puts in and the trouble he has with his boss is practically legendary. He's lucky his office mates are so understanding and helpful. But he still does a lot and pushes himself to balance these things. It would be easier if he didn't have to though. What has he given up for his mask duties? Heck, I know we had our own troubles thanks to this. Then there is Paul. I remember from dinner how he talked about being a teacher. I can't help but feel he's doing that for other reasons. As if he's sacrificing himself for this.

"Anyway, I suppose I should talk now," says Adam. "I'm Adam Fairchild and I'm a lawyer in Los Angeles. My live in fiancé and I, as you can guess, have found a way to make things work. You can guess other details about Emma."

"So when are you going to make an honest woman out of dear Emma?" asks Holly with a jolly smile, trying to break the morose mood at the table.

"Any year I'm sure," chuckles Adam, "as soon as she gives up miniskirts."

"And I suppose hot pink," Diane says. "Honestly, how a red fox can pull that off I'll never know."

"Yet she does," adds Michelle with a nod.

"I wasn't aware this was fashion hour," Lizz says with a slight quirk to her eyebrow.

"Oh, let them have their fun," Adam says. "I know Emma enjoys it when people react to her dress. I don't mind one bit."

"That is surprising to me. I've heard people say such, well, unreasonable things about her," Holly says.

"Well, of course I don't like it when people call her a tart or a slut," Adam adds looking at Holly defensively, and then adds, "But there is damn little I can really do about it. After all, we all have our covers. No, it's fine Emma that dresses the way she does. She dresses to make an impression and she truly does not care whether it is positive or negative."

"Better reaction than I would have if my sister was running around like that," Brian says.

"Yes, well there is a rather large difference between sisters and fiancés," Adam counters. "Besides, the look has a certain classic feel for me."

"I would agree," Lizz states. "I actually like the look she pulls off. It gives her a real sense of femininity that I like. She does draw attention at least."

"Oh, I enjoy it too," Adam says with a waggle of his eye brows. "I always have. She's a pip though, I'll say that. She loves using that look to push people's buttons."

"So enough about fashion, lets get onto the juicy parts," says Diane with relish as she turns and looks at me.

"Oh yes indeedy," grins Michelle as everyone looks at me expectantly.

I gulp. No really, I've never gulped before talking, but now all eyes are on me. These people are married to, in love with, or family of some of the most impressive people on earth. I am too, but still; I'm sitting next to Solarcoon's wife. I've also got one heck of a secret compared to these guys.

Well no way to put this off, so I start with, "Hi, I'm Jay Carson."

"Hi, Jay!" The table shouts, nearly bowling me over with the combined noise. I didn't' expect that, and they all start giggling and laughing at the way I jump.

"Sorry, Jay," Lizz comments from the end of the table. "That is our little welcoming joke."

Smiling I sit up and continue, "I'm Jay Carson and I'm from Portland, Oregon."

"Really," says Holly with a smile. "Well that is interesting."

"Shoot I had real money on Sheleighlie," says Michelle.

"She isn't even a member of the team," Stuart observes, "I was expecting a friend of Glacier's."

"Sorry I'm a Star fan all the way," I smile. "I'm a city planner in Portland where I've lived most of my adult life. My family comes from Oregon. And obviously I know a certain Coyote."

"Heh, another coworker friend," Michelle grins, "new point for our side."

"Um," I pause at that, then I can't help but blush a bit. "Actually I live there with my boyfriend, Ted. Who has saved my life more than once."

Okay, there I said it. I just dropped the secret, and I'm sure they get the subtext. Brian's eyes have widened. Stuart has looked up from his meal and quirked an eyebrow. Adam looks a bit surprised too. Diane nearly does a spit take. Lizz just watches their reactions, grinning like mad.

Holly is the first to say something, "Oh! Well that is different."

Everyone else is staring now, so I take a deep breath and continue, "We've been together five years. We just recently got a home together . Though, he had, well, concerns about my safety."

"Nice to know some things are universal," says Adam leaning back and taking a drink.

"Yes, that is true," says Stuart at the end of the table. "Jane always has the same concern. I do believe when you become immune to bullets that you reset your standards when it comes to other people's safety. I honestly think I am one head cold away from quarantine."

"It isn't like we're totally helpless," says Diane with smile. "You know I once smacked Whirlwinder upside the head with my keyboard?"

"It isn't exactly hard to get the drop on him," says Brian wryly. "I mean I once clubbed Wrecker of the Iron Ravers."

"Which caused you to end up in the hospital for a week, don't forget that part," Holly comments while looking over at Lizz and smiling. "Lizz has some great stories from her investigations. The number of times you've been in danger and gotten yourself out of it amazes me."

"I've just been lucky," Lizz says with a smile on her slender muzzle.

"I've been there. Luck can play a lot in it. I see their point though, it isn't like we're in a good position to defend ourselves. Even with my self defense classes I'm nowhere near qualified to take on someone competent like Lux." Adam looks at me and he asks, "How long did he make you wait before moving in?"

"Three years," I say with a chuckle. "After about two years I knew I wanted to take things a further. He eventually broke down and we finally got our place together."

"You'll have to tell me what you said in detail sometime," says Adam with a roll of his eyes. "It would be nice to have a clue in how to get a certain Vixen to finally set a date."

"Well to be fair he told me his identity only a few months ago. That was interesting," I say with a chuckle and a wag.

Stuart laughs as well as Michelle, "Oh my, yes. I remember when Jane told me the big secret. We had a rather large row that day."

"Same here, Stuart," I say with a smile. "Well, more me yelling at him but I get the feeling you know the deal."

"Indeed I do," from Stuart with a grin on his muzzle, "Though perhaps yelling isn't the right word. It is when Jane gets very quiet that you know there is trouble brewing."

"Alan was just annoyed I was going through his laundry and found his costume," Michelle says. "I used to wonder why he insisted on doing it. Looking back it was so obvious that he was a, well, member of the team."

"I just walked in on Wally while he was taking his costume off," Diane says with a laugh. "He couldn't deny it at that point. After that I've been locking his office so people can't barge in on him."

"Wait a second..." Brian chimes in, as if suddenly remembering something, "How come everyone here had a bet on me being Kyle's lover but no one is paying up for this secret?"

"Well I never thought Portland's buddy was into guys," says Diane.

"Ditto," says Michelle. "Though I guess you never can tell."

"Can I just say I'm shocked at all of you?" I say with a chuckle. "Ted is not exactly the best at hiding this."

"I had no idea about you either," Diane shrugs. The lioness swishes her tail as she says, "And you would think I would know considering how many gay guys I work with."

"Might have to get your gaydar checked," Adam says with a grin. "Though yeah, I had no idea either. Good surprise, Lizz."

Elizabeth Clay bows her head with a mischievous grin, "I do try to please."

"What is it with all the heroes keeping their identities like that," Holly says as she turns back to her meal, and everybody begins to eat now that introductions are over.

"What do you mean?" I ask.

"Well I can see not telling extended family, but Bill and I talked long before he put his mask on. We talked about the risks he was taking and when he got his powers he told me all about them," Holly explains. "All our children know as well, even though it is a risk to his identity, we wanted to be honest with them."

Lizz grimaces slightly, "Simon and Penny don't need to know right now. They're far too young. It isn't about honesty with them."

"Simon and Penny?" I ask Adam under my breath.

"Lizz's children," Adam says in a whisper. "This is a perennial disagreement between the two."

It suddenly dawns on me. I've heard of Simon and Penny before. I read about Lizz's children in her articles. She mentions them every once in a while, but now I know they're the children of Nick "The Stranger" Clay as well. I just hadn't made the connection.

"I'm still surprised you can get the block bands on them," says Holly evenly.

"I've figured out ways," says Lizz.

"Block bands?" I ask conversationally.

"Something Samuel cooked up. It blocks out 'abilities," says Brian using Stratagem's real name.

I nearly do a spit take at that. Sputtering I say, "Block out? Really? Haven't they been trying that for years in prisons for super criminals?"

"Well it only works with a holistic understanding of the abilities and talents of the person involved." Stuart says in his professorial tone. "Each one has to be specially made for the wearer, and they work better on children. Teenagers and adults can resist them and eventually overcome their effects. Further, there are certain risks to the wearer. It is just safer than the alternative."

"Which would be what?" I ask quirking an eyebrow at that. What could be considered worse than unknown risks to children?

"Super powered toddlers," Lizz says with a sly grin.

My eyes widen at that possibility, "That could actually happen?"

"Oh, it has happened," says Holly with a smile. "All of my kids have their father's abilities. Their first exposure to sunlight seemed to jog it."

"Mine developed them a little later, but I suppose the ability to alter spatial relativity would be a bit more complicated," says Lizz.

Adam explains, "Samuel theorizes that abilities are a dominate gene. That they are always passed down and manifest eventually. He thinks it only happens if the parent's powers have already manifested before conception. Blitzkrieg's daughter hasn't shown any powers but she was born before he got hit. Though he hasn't really tested his theory."

"Hence the creation of block bands for the super tykes," says Brian. "And the hope that no one like Doctor Xerxes ever finds out about the kids."

"What happens eventually to them?" I ask in surprise. "I mean these bands don't take away their powers forever so what is the plan?"

"Only a parent has the ability to take the bands off," explains Lizz, "and we'll make the choice of when they can use their abilities responsibly. It is true that eventually the bands will become less effective as they get older, but by then maybe we can get them to use their skills responsibly."

"And I thought my parents were rough cause they wouldn't let me drive a car when I was a teen," I say taking a bite of my burger.

"We let the kids use their abilities in a controlled environment with their father on hand. So they know what they're doing," says Holly, demurely eating her food.

"I guess this just strikes me as a huge surprise," I say at last, "Ted never told me."

"Well to be fair, would this really come up?" asks Adam.

I think about that for a moment and nod as I chew. This does explain why Ted always shies away from talk about artificial insemination. I just assumed he liked adoption better, "That is fair I suppose."

"What I'm surprised by is that no one on the team has let slip about Star," says Michelle.

"Well…" I pause and then say, "They don't know."

"They don't," Adam blinks thinking for a moment. "They don't know?"

"Ted is very in the closet at times," I explain. "He hasn't really told the team outside of Paul and, um, Samuel."

"Wow, I had no idea," says Michelle. "Wait who is Paul?"

"Any reason for being so secretive?" asks Stuart easily and then to Michelle, "I would assume Paul is a certain ice cube."

"He's had some, um, rough spots in the past," I say trying to be diplomatic. "I personally think it would be better for him to just tell everyone. I mean they aren't bad people. The team won't care."

"I wouldn't be too sure 'bout that," says Holly, her face thoughtful. "People can surprise you about these things."

"What's that? The matron of honesty isn't sure someone should be honest," says Lizz, mockingly quirking an ear at Holly.

"All I am saying is that people don't always know what to do when they know these things," says Holly evenly. "I don't know how Bill would feel about knowing this. He's very old fashioned in some ways. I'll admit I'm a bit shocked as well. Ted is a wonderful man, and if this makes him happy then it isn't my place to judge. Bill works in a much more conservative job though. He might be uncomfortable with this revelation."

"It can be a very personal issue," says Stuart diplomatically.

"People just need to get over it. It isn't like, um, Ted hasn't done a lot of good, so who cares?" says Diane boisterously.

"That may not matter to some folks," says Brian. "There are people on the force who are open about being gay. They sometimes get flack from the other cops, and some churches have written letters of complaint. I mean what if people knew and Ted couldn't intervene because people were fighting him off?"

Adam nods at that. "Remember when Force Vixen first appeared and some people called her a lesbian? It did cause a lot of trouble when she was trying to save some people. There was one case when she tried to help rescue people from a fire where some zealots actually formed a human chain to stop her."

"That was years ago," says Diane waving her paw dismissively.

"Whatever the case," interrupts Lizz, "I'm sure we can all keep this secret."

A very wide grin breaks out on Adam's face. It looks conniving and a little sinister. "Wait a moment, are you saying we finally have a secret to keep from all of them?"

Similar smiles break out on Brian, Diane, Michelle and even Stuart's muzzles as they eye each other gleefully.

"Well it seems, Lizz, you've really brought us a good new member," says Stuart. "This will be amusing."

"I thought you boys would enjoy this," Lizz says with a quirked ear and a grin. "After all, how often do we get an opportunity like this?"

"I'm not sure I'm comfortable keeping things from Bill," says Holly worriedly. "We don't often keep secrets."

"I used to wonder where Bill got his steel rod-like moral rectitude, and then I met you," comments Lizz with a slight twist of sarcasm. "As for keeping it a secret I don't see how this will come up. I mean unless he asks you point blank, I say don't even mention it."

"I'm still not comfortable with it," says Holly, and her motherly face creases with worry.

I turn and look at Holly and try to give her a comforting mile as I rest my paw on hers reassuringly. "Holly, I swear I'm trying very hard to make Ted comfortable with all this and get him to come out. I'm not happy with him not telling anyone and I want him to be honest. Can you just wait a little while until he's comfortable?"

"I suppose. Ted has done a lot for my family. He is a sweet boy and I enjoy having him over at our place. I just dislike the possible lies," Holly sighs. Everyone else is looking conspiratorial, though I do have to agree with Holly. I'm not really sure I'm comfortable asking them to lie for me. They're all amused at this for now. I think it is a bit of pay back, and I can understand that wish. I'm just relieved that I didn't lie to Ted about their keeping his secret.

After that, we talk and eat for a long while, just enjoying each other's company. All of them are really nice, and they make me feel like a real part of the family. We spend a while talking and chatting, comparing notes on our families and each other and eventually it came back to identity revelation.

"I can't believe you had to yell at Ted to get him to reveal his identity," says Brian as the meal winds down.

"I still can't believe you shot your brother," I say with a smirk.

"Total accident!" Brian exclaims. "Besides he's invulnerable. He wasn't hurt by it."

"Still, it is a funny little story," begins Adam. Before he can finish, the glass picture window at the front of the bar explodes into the room with a loud bang. Without even thinking, I'm pushing Holly down under the table and shielding her. Screams fill the air and I smell smoke.

"Come and face me if you dare traitor!" shouts a voice full of rage. I look up from the ground, trying to see what is going on. Diane is shielding Michelle against the wall, the bigger lioness covering the slim tabby. Stuart is holding the waiter down to the floor, the beaver's drink tray spilled across the floor from when the leopard pounced him. Brian and Adam are standing at the head of the table, looking towards the front of the bar. Adam has taken a stance I know is from self defense and Brian's paws are clenched into fists. Lizz is glaring that way too, her body tense as she moves in front of another table, as if she is going to use her body to shield them from something. Looking towards the front I can see why.

Power Puma, the super strong and far too perfect looking mountain lion, is standing only a few feet away from us. He's got his trademark red, black and white costume on, and a belt full of weapons. Crap, did one of the world's first supervillains, as well as one of the toughest, just find us? He looks a lot tougher in person. Bigger, too, then I expected from seeing him on TV. A shiver of fear runs down my spine seeing him.

I can almost feel the group's collective tension and concern at the sight of him. Everyone knows Power Puma's beliefs and his behavior. He appeared out of nowhere right at the beginning, claiming he was proof of the mastery of the feline race. He believes fervently in separation of the species and the natural rulership of felines over all others. He took a lot of that from his neo-Nazi parents as I understand it.

At least he doesn't have any followers with him. The problem with Power Puma is there are plenty who agree with him and who saw his powers as proof of his agenda. He built a large following of people on every continent that would let him spout his garbage. He's incited riots. He's vicious and he cunning and very dangerous.

When Solarcoon appeared for the first time and smacked Power Puma around it was one of the greatest moments ever televised. I still remember the parties. People were proud, especially since Puma has such a low opinion of mustelids and raccoons. It was a tremendous insult that a raccoon had beaten him in every way.

The guy is a dangerous monster. I stare at his bulging muscular form and reach into my pocket to get my communicator. Holly's paw stops me and she shakes her head. She mouths the words, "Not yet."

"You won't be escaping today, Puma," says a voice from outside. As I look to the shattered exterior of the building, a hero stands there in a black and silver jumpsuit with a stylized C on the shoulder wearing his golden sunglasses: Camo.

"Watch me, race traitor," growls the puma nastily, almost spitting. I've seen looks like that before. Frankie, a previous boyfriend, was a house cat who always looked that way when cornered either metaphorically or physically. He hated being put in a submissive place.

Camo steps into the room confidently, and all around the bar people are cowering away behind tables or chairs. The jaguar seems to exude confidence and skill, and the patrons are staring at him. Some even look less afraid. It is as if Camo has Power Puma right where he wants him. He seems to glare at the cougar as he says, "Did you really think you'd get away with your attack on that youth center?"

"It was disgusting," growls Puma, flexing his hands, and I can see one drifting to his belt where a very large gun is holstered. He doesn't look all smooth and confident like he tries to appear when making some statement on TV. He looks riled and angry, and oddly unsteady on his feet.

"Yes, kids playing basketball is a terrible thing," smirks Camo. "Just give up before you embarrass yourself again, Puma."

"Never!" howls Power Puma as his hands twitch. I've never seen anyone move so quickly, the gun is in his paw and he's firing. No one could dodge that!

Loud reports fill the room as he fires point blank shots directly at Camo. The jaguar can't possibly escape them. He'll be killed! He's not invulnerable! I look over at Diane worriedly, but instead of looking horrified she's smiling.

Instead of falling to the ground bleeding, Camo just smirks at Power Puma. The bullets haven't touched him.

"HOW!" growls the puma, tail lashing in fury as he keeps firing.

"Damn, you're thick," says Camo but his lips don't move. In fact the voice seems to have come from our direction.

Suddenly Camo disappears and reappears at Puma's side. A fist lances out, smacking into Power Puma's far too symmetrical face, causing him to stumble backward and drop his gun as sparks fly from the gloves on Camo's paws.

Camo smirks and flicks his tail, "You always fall for the same trick, Puma. You'd think after the fifth time you wouldn't, but darn if you don't keep proving me wrong."

Camo disappears in a shimmer and suddenly three Camos are surrounding the puma, "Remember? I make illusions and turn invisible, you dunce."

Power Puma struggles to his feet growling, shards of glass from broken bottles and steins spilling off of him his skin unmarred. "Simpering trickery you fool. Fight me like a man!"

"Let me think," and suddenly another fist pops out of nowhere and sends Puma reeling with a loud crackle. "No. Considering one of the NYPD got you with that tranquilizer dart and I'm wearing these taser brass knuckles Stratagem made we're actually in a fair fight."

Power Puma regains his balance growling and reaches to his side, then stops in surprise. "What?"

"Looking for these?" asks another Camo, showing another gun and a hand grenade before he disappears again. I can hear his voice flitting about the bar as he says, "Yeah, I'm really stupid enough to not to disarm you and remove that junk from your utility belt. I mean, who would think of taking the trinkets of destruction off the crazy lion when there are civilians about?"

A powerful kick into Power Puma's gut causing the lion to crumple back onto the ground winded and we all see Camo reappear again finishing off a round house kick. "Oh right. I would have thought of it. A ten year old would have thought of it. Moron," Camo sneers.

Power Puma tries to stand, growling, "How are you doing this?"

"Like I said you were hit with a special drug cocktail the NYPD cooked up just for you. The diamond tipped darts were hell to make but those drugs are messing with your usual skill at taking a beating. Add in my taser brass knuckles and an odd amount of pleasure smacking that smirk off your muzzle," says Camo from nowhere again. Suddenly Puma's paws are forced behind his back, and we hear an audible click as Camo reappears behind the lion and using the leverage of his postion he slams Power Puma to the ground grinding a knee into the mountain lion's back. "But I'm getting sick of out gunning you in a battle of wits, Pitiful Puma. Here's a clue, if our multi-cultural, multi-species city offends you, then don't come back to New York City. We're getting sick of your ugly mug and we're ready for you now."

Some of the patrons and the bartenders cheer at that and there is clapping. Puma growls and thrashes but his strength doesn't mean anything at this point. Camo's got him in a classic hold that stops him from getting any leverage to use his amazing strength. Camo grins, "Now as the cops will soon be telling you: You have the right to remain silent, and here is a clue, twit. I'd take that one seriously because I think the NYPD and I are getting sick of your nonsensical tirades. Here is a thought maybe you can understand. Just stay down and enjoy the friendly prison lifestyle."

Power Puma squirms helplessly. Camo motions at the door and a couple cops rush in and snap stronger restrains onto the lion and then heft him up. They all look very big and tough, and while I know that Power Puma is super strong, they seem to have him well in hand.

"Thanks, Camo," a large wolf policeman growls. "We didn't know how to handle this one."

Camo grins, "I'm glad to help take him down officer. That is what I'm here to help with. Eh, the guy's a twit and dangerous, but don't worry. With his little gang in custody and Officer Willoughby's little shot he's more than pacified for now. Let's try to keep him locked up this time?"

"We'll do our best," a tiger growls as they starts to force the puma out onto the street. "We got a special paddy wagon just for him this time."

Camo turns and grins at the bar, "Sorry for the inconvenience folks. Feel free to sue Power Puma's estate."

Camo salutes the bartender and slides out of the building confidently. A moment later he takes a grappling hook out of his belt and fires it into the air. He's soon swinging into the sky as people begin talking excitedly now that the danger is passed.

"And with that I do believe our meeting is over," says Stuart jauntily as we get up and dust ourselves off.

"Very gentlemanly tackle there, Jay," Holly says with a smile.

"I wasn't thinking," I say truthfully. "Sorry if that hurt."

"No, no," Holly smiles happily and pats my arm. "It was very sweet. I can see that Ted has found a gentleman."

Everyone chuckles and we pay our bill. It is odd but while everyone else still seems in shock or amazed our little group is taking it in stride. I guess we've all gotten used to this, even me. We all leave a nice tip for the wait staff. They've had a hard day. Then we're out on the street. Everyone gives me their phone numbers and other forms of contact. I get the feeling this dinner was as much an interview of me as anything else. Adam shakes my paw saying, "If you ever need to talk about something feel free to call. I am after all in your time zone."

The entire group nods at that and I happily trade my number back with the same words. We go our different ways, splitting up and trying not to travel in a group. I wander off alone. It is dark now but I don't care, I feel like I'm almost floating with glee. I soon get to the rendezvous point where Ted and I agreed to meet. Standing on the roof I smile. New York is a great city, and despite the way it ended, today has been really good.

As I take in the night breeze, I feel a tap on my shoulder. Turning, I see Ted in his blue and yellow costume, his mask on as he smiles at me, floating just above me. I smile back as he lands on the ground and I feel his arms enfold me. I lean up and our lips meet in a kiss as I feel him against me.

"Hi there," I say when our kiss breaks.

"Have a good time?" he asks with a wag of his tail as I look into his masked face and grin.

"Yeah," I say enthusiastically. "It was great. Thank you so much."

"No problem, Jay," he says nuzzling my ears as I pant happily. "You know that."

"It was a shock when Power Puma showed up though," I say with a grin as Ted's eyes widen and he steps back.

He nearly shouts, "WHO showed up?"

"Don't worry," I say with a wave of my paw. "He didn't know we were there. I doubt he would have suspected a thing. Camo beat him up."

"Why didn't my communicator go off? I would have rushed there to help out." Ted is looking down at his communicator device.

"Camo had it handled and we couldn't call everyone in, it would have been suspicious," I explain.

"That is a huge risk, Jay. Don't assume things like that again, just call. We'll cook up a reason," Ted says hugging me closer, worried now. "I don't want you taking stupid risks."

"Very sweet," says a voice causing us to break our embrace as we turn around looking about. The roof looks empty.

I glance about but Ted just glowers saying, "Nice one, Camo. Come out. What are you doing here?"

Camo suddenly appears on the roof only a few feet from us, his arms folded. He looks almost as angry as Power Puma did as he says, "Well, let's see. I saw a group of people who have been told not to gather in one spot, gathering in one spot. I saw a good friend of mine with them. I also saw a new face in the group. All while I'm battling a psycho who has taken hostages in the past, and who made sure I couldn't call for back up with his damn EMP gun. Where shall I start?"

"Um," Ted gulps a bit and grins, "With how much you, uh, just saw?"

"Well, after following the collie here," Camo points at me, "everything."

"Oh," Ted's ears lower in worry as I look between the two.

"Okay, so no big deal," I say at last. "Let's not worry here. Power Puma didn't see anything, so we're okay."

"Okay?" Camo's tail bushes out in anger. "OKAY?!? Are you kidding me? First of all, Star Coyote here just violated a bunch of bylaws and rules by helping you get here and not telling anyone about this damn meeting."

Ted blushes at that. "C'mon, Camo, you know the others don't tell either," he says, a bit of pleading in his voice.

"Yeah, well, that's what you think! Maybe we do tell each other and make protective plans, ever think of that? Maybe those of us with family in them put extra security around these meetings. Maybe we like to know who everyone is so that we can properly defend them," growls Camo. Then looking at me he says, "I won't even get into the stupidity of not using your communicator to call for help when a super villain shows up."

"It happened very quickly," I begin to argue, looking at the furious jaguar

"That is no excuse," Camo says stomping closer. "Will that be an excuse if Xanadu shows up at your door? It happened so fast?"

"Camo, Xanadu is in a wheel chair," begins Ted earnestly. "Remember? Omni put him there."

"Oh and then," Camo continues ignoring Ted's argument completely as he looks at him, "Then I trail back here to watch a hero kiss his boyfriend while his mask is on. Never mind how many damn shutterbugs might be about. Or the fact that said boyfriend was just with a group of Alpha class friends and family. Finally, that brings me to the little matter of one of the team's heroes being queerer than a three dollar bill!"

"Now hold on I don't see how that is any of your business," I say angrily moving towards Camo and getting into his face a bit. "What he does on his own time is no one's business."

Camo glares at me. "Nice sentiment, kid," the man who is my own age snarls, "but I live in the real world and let me tell you if this came out there will be a lot of trouble and people making a big deal."

"Camo, I've been discreet, I don't think this will…" begins Star Coyote.

"You mean like you were just now?" Camo says glaring between the two of us. "Between your arrogant stupidity and your lying to me and everyone else on the team I should file you for probation. Hell! Forget that, I should get you kicked off the team!"

Ted's eyes widen as he whines worriedly, "Camo, that isn't fair I…"

Camo interrupts him before he can say more, "No, it isn't fair. It isn't fair that you put a lot of lives at risk today, including your boyfriend's. It isn't fair that you put the team at risk for not telling us about this. It is especially not fair that you put us over a barrel if something happens and you get found out. Do you know how many countries won't let us in if they learn about this? Iran and Russia aside, there are a lot of people out there who won't like you for 'just being you,' Star. I've seen it first hand."

"It isn't like I chose this," begins Ted worriedly and I have to step in at that.

"If they have a problem then that is their problem. If they don't want help from someone because of who they love then they're idiots," I say angrily. "And if you have a problem then the same goes for you. We are not doing anything wrong by being together. We made mistakes tonight. Fine. I can accept that, but Star is not wrong for being who he is or who he sleeps with."

"He is for not telling us honestly," says Camo. "Our team demands honesty so we can function properly."

"Honesty? You're one to talk. You just admitted you're keeping these meeting secret from some members of the team when you make your 'protective plans'. And what does it matter if Star is gay?" I ask gruffly staring into those sunglasses, now very irritated. "It isn't like you would have kept him off the team if you had known. Or is it?"

"It makes things more complicated than they need to be," Camo says irritably. "If you can't see that you're a fool. We need to work out a contingency in case this gets revealed. We need to be preparing for the fallout and figure out a way to cover the team's collective ass. Never mind all the other dumb risks both of you took."

"Fine," I say angrily. "But don't threaten him with dismissal for being gay, you jerk."

Camo glowers at me for a few moments and then looks at Ted, "We'll talk about this later. You're damn lucky no one got hurt." He then turns and leaps off the roof. I hear his grappling hook go off and he swoops away into the night. Or so I assume. The guy does turn invisible after all.

Ted picks me up without saying a word and kicks off the ground. We're high into the air in mere moments. It is cold up here. I can hear Ted snuffling and feel him shivering but I know it isn't from the temperature.

He doesn't talk to me. Not one word, even when we get back home. Ted locks himself in the bathroom and I can hear the shower turn on. I put my new phone numbers into my bed side table and sit on the bed and wait. Ted takes a very long shower. Afterwards he comes out, and still he doesn't say anything to me. He looked worried and scared and unsure. I want to hug him but I know he doesn't want that right now. He had the same look when his brother found out about us. Right before, and then after, he came out of the closet to his parents. We can't talk right now. I know, though, that this time he's not just disappointed in himself. He's disappointed in me too. I should have called him.

We just turn off the lights. He doesn't say a word as we sleep on opposite sides of the bed for the first time in a long time. I had been getting used to floating above the bed as we cuddled into the night. It has been a long day. It feels like it is going to be a long night as well.

Chapter 7
Confrontation

"Why Minneapolis again?" Metalyena asks as we stand on the roof of a building as night falls. He looks a bit strange in his costume because he hasn't turned into his metallic form. When he does that he is much heavier. After that incident in the wharfs of Seattle a few months ago when shoddy construction caused him to fall through the roof and spoil a sneak-up-on-the-nefarious-criminal-mastermind-plan, we made a team rule that he can't activate his metal form on rooftops unless it is an emergency. "I mean it is a bit chilly up here tonight," he shifts his feet.

"Chilly in Minneapolis?" Glacier says with a grin, and his voice crackles with static as it comes through the radio built into his helmet. The husky isn't wearing his normal costume tonight, but a full body suit that even covers his tail. The helmet is connected to the suit, and it doesn't even have a faceplate. Glacier's normal costume is pretty revealing since temperatures and wind chill don't concern him, which is why he's stuck in the environmental suit tonight. That outfit would be stifling even in this chilly weather, but not to him. So he just chuckles at the rest of us as we shiver, adding, "What a shock."

Night has fallen on the Midwest, and the twin cities of Minneapolis and St. Paul are lighting up. I grin, perhaps a little too much. There are times I really enjoy these jaunts across the globe as part of the superhero biz. Even with all the stress and worry lately this feels worth it. The lights are coming on all over the city, towers becoming bright and lights from below us become ribbons of light as people go about their normal lives. This is just cool, no pun intended, even if it is in North America. I've never been to Minneapolis before and it looks like a nice city. I never thought I would be here, even visiting to fight crime.

Force Vixen pulls me back to reality as she speaks up, "All right. I'll recap once more, but everyone please try to pay attention during briefings next time. The major banks figured out years ago that their armored cars make tempting targets for super criminals, so they've been trying to be more careful about shipments of money. They've been a lot more secretive about routes and placements. The World Bank has been leading the effort with the creation of an international advisory committee which helps to coordinate different organizations, helping them to combine resources. Tonight an armored car division will be traveling down this street here in Minneapolis. Its carrying securities, cash, computer codes to important banking institutions—you name it this thing might have it. It is heading to St. Paul for special holding and disbursement. Stratagem estimates the value at well over fifteen billion US dollars. Of course the US Government has been mum about exact numbers."

"Stratagem believes this is a team effort strike," Camo says as he plays lookout. "He's positive that a group of supercriminals are going to try and take this themselves. Someone got some top secret information and they're making a move. Stratagem, of course, saw it coming before anyone else. He's positive this is a nascent group forming, probably the first real test for their leadership and teamwork skills, and that works for us. We have the experience. They won't be as coordinated as we will be. These convoys are well guarded and we think they're going to plan on that but they won't expect an intervention from the Extraordinaries. After all, the twin cities don't have a superhero."

"Well, we'll make an impression and remind them not to start any funny business in supposedly 'safe' cities," says Force Vixen looking over all of us with a sly smile. "Stratagem convinced the Minnesota government to let us act here as extra security. They don't want us driving the trucks but they gave us the route. He's positive this is the spot where this cabal will make its move."

"So we'll be here if they try anything," I say waggling my eyebrows at Metalyena who can't help but smile. I remember my first team up on nights like this. I was giddy and smiling the entire time too, and it was just great a thrill being with people with powers who were trying to help. We stopped the bad guys, and as I recall shut down a pretty big cartel. I look over the assembled group. Force Vixen is in the lead right now as the only founder present, with Metalyena, Camo, Glacier, and me. We should have had Blitzkrieg or Stratagem here as well, but the plan changed a few hours ago.

My communicator chirps, and I can hear the fight occurring in Asia right now. Doctor Schmetterling decided today of all days was a good day to build a giant attack robot to rampage through Kazakhstan, so we split the team in two. We needed to be here to guard the convoy and stop a team of supervillains. If we let them have any success as a team it would give them impetus to work together and train, which would be bad for us, but we couldn't leave that robot rampaging around. Fortunately Solarcoon, Lady Leopard, Blitzkrieg, Titan Tomcat and Stratagem are on the situation. I'm pretty sure with those five handling the problem we can be here. Everyone is a little distracted. Having every Extraordinary active on one night is pretty rare and we've been running around a lot recently.

"Now then," Vixen says looking between all of us, "since we've now played catch up, here is the game plan. Metalyena and Glacier you two are on point. Metalyena, you handle any heavy hitters they brought to take out the amour and defenses of the convoy. Glacier, you know who your target is."

"Makes sense to me," says Metalyena flexing a powerful bicep. Glacier smirks at that as well. He might not be the strongest guy on the team but he can heft a Volkswagen with the best of them, and with the very durable and super strong Metalyena we have more than enough muscle.

"I'll handle defensive lines and get civilians clear," continues Force Vixen. Then looking at me and then at Camo she says, "You two are back up and reserve. Keep the field clear, we're not expecting any major threats but there is obviously a supersmartie or two involved in this. Handle anyone who tries to make a splash and act in support."

"I'd suggest putting Star Coyote on the front lines," Camo says. "I can handle any surprises."

Force Vixen gives Camo a withering glare, "I think my plans stand where they are, thank you very much."

Everyone is staring now and I'm blushing. Camo looks chagrined as well and Force Vixen is fuming at the both of us. She hates when people question her command decisions, so this really isn't a surprise. Camo looks at me, and I try not to look back. We have been having trouble lately. I've been worried sick about what the jaguar would say to the team after he found out about Jay. It has been nearly three weeks since the incident in New York City. Power Puma escaped from jail, killing two guards and an inmate. He apparently hunted down the marksman who shot him, Officer Willoughby, and, well the guy was a raccoon married to an otter. He and his wife didn't make it. Camo has been really upset about that and I think what happened with Jay just makes it worse. I know he hasn't said anything, yet, but it has me on edge now too.

Metalyena and I are still getting along fine and none of the founders have said anything to me either. In the mean time the jaguar and I haven't been working well together. Camo holds a grudge and I'm second guessing my moves around him too much. He's been arguing with me as well and we've both been trying to shift duty rosters to avoid each other. Unfortunately, Force Vixen hasn't been cooperative.

At least it has been better than how things are going with Jay. I'm still upset at him for not using his communicator and for going to the meeting at all. I've been spending a lot of late nights at the office or on patrol, avoiding talking to him and seeing him. He's tried talking to me but we've both been on edge and I've yelled at him a few times. I know he is sorry for what happened and what went wrong, but it is hard to forgive and forget. At the time it made sense, but now too many bad things have come from it. It makes me feel like he manipulated me. It really stinks but all my worry about him, anger at him, and fear about being outed are all tied up together right now. I didn't even tell him I was going to Minneapolis. I had been telling him about any trips before they happened if I knew beforehand. I could call him before the convoy gets here, but I tell myself it is too late to make the call privately.

Force Vixen is obviously done talking and everyone starts getting into position. I look out over the edge of the building, not hearing Glacier approach until he rests a paw on my shoulder.

"Star, what's going on?" he asks plainly worried, and I can just see his concerned eyes through the thick faceplate of his helmet. "You and Camo have been at each other's throats for almost two weeks. I know it can't be what happened with Power Puma. Camo knows what a psycho he is and so do the police. He has really been riding you and that isn't like Camo."

I look up at the big husky and smile. He's being a good friend. I didn't tell him about what happened but he's been trying to find out. I think he's even called Jay. I guess I should say something, "Camo found out about Jay."

Glacier's eyes widen, but before he can say anything, we hear an explosion on the street below. The convoy is here and so is the enemy. We didn't see the set charge under the street, and it blew a manhole cover into the air with a pillar of fire, stopping the convoy cold. At least the explosion didn't kill any of the drivers.

"That's my cue. Is anyone else tired of Stratagem always being right?" says Glacier quickly.

This isn't a busy road, but people were on it just the same and I can hear screams of shock and surprise as people start running in every direction. Then I hear a howl. It is primal, frightening, and loud. A being races towards the front of the convoy. It looks like some sort of amalgamation of hundreds of different species, it has scales and feathers and fur and a twisted snout.

It's Mishmash, the genetic monstrosity. I've seen him on TV and in the team's files. He's some sort of genetic accident. Either a scientist or a victim, I'm not clear on the details, but he's got a chip on his shoulder for being a freak and thinks the world owes him. He has a long record of robbery, mercenary activities for some very dangerous groups, and destruction, all with superheroes stepping in to stop him. It isn't like the cops can do anything to get in his way, he's very powerful. He can absorb the genetic information of anything or anyone he touches, adding them to his body. He's been able to demonstrate super abilities just by touching someone, and that alone makes him frightening and dangerous. Worse, he is dangerously strong and durable.

Unfortunately for Mishmash, we figured out he would be here. Glacier is already racing up the street in his specially made suit. That uncomfortable costume will prevent Mishmash from being able to find even a strand of fur from which to gain Glacier's powers. The monster is distracted as he grabs the front of the armored truck and begins to lift it into the air, metal bending under his fingers. He doesn't see the fist until it connects with his misshapen muzzle.

I can almost hear the smack as Glacier's gloves connect. Mishmash can take a lot of punishment so Glacier isn't holding back. The punch sends the beast flying back from the truck's front end. Mishmash has about the same the same level of strength as Glacier, but Glacier has other abilities at his disposal and we are backing him up.

Glacier growls and takes a defensive stance, his arms akimbo as he stares the beast down. He gives a confident wag before saying, "Sorry, Mishmash, no withdrawals today."

Mishmash just howls in anger and charges back at Glacier. That's odd. Normally Mishmash banters a bit more. I don't think about it long as Mishmash charges again at the muscled husky, and the battle is starting in earnest as a green flame shoots out of an alley and strikes near the armored car.

Atomic Lion strides into battle, the gargantuan feline growling and flexing his oversized body as he advances, his mane licked with green flames as he lumbers towards the convoy. "Damn it, we've got an Extraordinary here. There might be others. Mishmash! Be on guard I'm going to get the loot."

"Awww, now don't be sad, Atomic Lion," says Metalyena, as he runs forward with his fist raised. He's all metal now and should be all business but I guess when you are invulnerable you can spend time making quips. "I'll play with you too." The lion roars and charges at the hyena.

WONG! The metallic sound echoes across the street as Metalyena lands a direct hit with his fist right onto Atomic Lion's jaw, and the lion is sent reeling backwards. He shakes his head, glaring at Metalyena, and when he roars green flames leap up around his body as he shouts Metalyena's name and the two start brawling. Atomic Lion is a dangerous supercriminal. He's super strong and durable and he can shoot out radioactive fire, but that isn't what makes him truly dangerous. When he's angry or using his super strength, he puts out hard radiation and the more he uses his powers the worse it gets. Metalyena's metallic body can take a lot of punishment and when in metal form he's inorganic, so the radiation isn't a problem for him. The rest of us are going to have to keep our distance though and I'll be taking iodine tablets after the fight.

Mishmash is fighting in close quarters and getting really vicious, teeth and claws appearing and disappearing in the seething mass that makes up his body as he tries to tear a hole in Glacier's suit. Glacier's fists are too dangerous for him to really approach though, and whenever the husky lands a blow a thick patch of ice forms on the monster's hide. Mishmash has to be freezing at this point, but he keeps pressing on. I can see Glacier's eyes glowing beneath his faceplate as he prepares a blast of freeze vision even as he struggles hand to hand with Mishmash. Before Glacier can blast the monstrosity, a wave of vibrating sound hits the husky and throws his aim off.

I nearly take off at that, but as Thrum sends out another blast of sound waves towards Glacier a pink energy field stops it and intervenes before Glacier can be truly flanked. Force Vixen doesn't say anything as she swoops in to deal with the situation. The squirrel looks worried now as Force Vixen prepares her energy fields confidently. Thrum is a low level super criminal, a genius of sonic and sound. He's created devices to control sound in a multitude of ways but he doesn't rise to the level the other two are. He doesn't go after civilians and innocent people like the other's do either, but he's competent and he complicates the fight by sending out waves of destructive sound.

Even as she moves in towards Thrum, Force Vixen is setting up defenses around the street. Her magenta force fields intercept the various blasts of atomic fire, shrapnel, and now sound waves from the vicious fights going on down there. She's buying time for the civilians to make a run for it, and the armored car drivers and guards are withdrawing to a safe distance, regrouping just like their training dictates and letting us take the brunt of the fight. A few are helping get the last of the people of Minneapolis off the street , which makes it easier for us. Force Vixen's abilities with her force fields can be incredible but they have limits. Over time she has learned to create multiple fields around her but it takes a lot of concentration and the more there are, the weaker they get.

I feel a tap on my shoulder as Camo says, "Eyes on the game." He points to the roof of another building. I can't quite see what he's pointing at, the shadows are too deep, but a sudden glow on the roof gives me just enough light to make out the silhouettes of three figures there watching the battle. Camo has us hidden of course so I know the villains can't see us. I grab his paw without thinking and launch us into the air. Camo grimaces slightly, I am not sure if it is our holding paws or from having to rapidly change his illusions so they can't see us. Shoot, I should be taking my time here or the jaguar's power won't shield us. We're hovering over the roof in seconds though. It looks like Ms. Q, Lux, and Therma are the other three.

"Blast it all what are all these supersimpletons doing here," says Ms. Q waving about her latest Q rod as she glowers at the fight. How can the fennec fox think she can pull off heels and an evening dress as a costume for these things? The ornate opera glasses she is using to spy on the fight are a nice touch at least.

"Looks like I called it, Q," says Therma tossing a small fire ball between her paws. "I told you this caper was too top heavy with overpowered muscle heads."

"Should have just been us and Thrum," squeaks Lux. Lux is a mouse scientist who discovered a way to manipulate light. Her advanced technology is highly focused on creating light, dimming light, powerful concussive light bolts, and even creating low level illusions. Camo's powers are better for illusions but the mouse can do things he can't. She's very reserved compared to most villains and she's probably why we didn't spot these three before Therma began playing with fire like she always does. Camo is often the one who handles her. She's worked with Thrum a lot lately and the water cooler gossip is that she is dating the squirrel.

Lux being here means she's changed her pattern, but she's been getting more and more mercenary recently. She used to just steal advanced technology to improve her control of light, but now whenever she shows up it is with Thrum and money is more and more of an issue. I hope the rumors aren't true. A duo of super geniuses of light and sound would not be fun. They're both foes of Camo more than anyone else, and he's often commented how valuable their skills would be in Hollywood or entertainment. I think it galls him that they waste their talents by being criminals.

Ms. Q's rod flares with energy and her irritation is obvious as she glares at both of them. "Don't question my brilliant schemes! I might have not accounted for the Extraordinaries, but this will still work. We'll get the money yet! Mishmash is at least doing his job and stopping anyone from gaining an upper paw."

"Imagine what he'd do if he still had his brain," says Therma testily, obviously irritated at working with the flamboyant felonious fennec. Okay, I love alliteration. Jay has been teasing me about how much I use it in my banter, but she's the woman committing crime in an opera dress and six inch heels. She practically demands that kind of thing. Anyway, we hang in the air listening in as Therma continues, "The guy's not much more than instinct at this point. What did you do to him?"

"Wouldn't you like to know," says Ms. Q slyly with a flick of her tail.

"We had better get down there," says Lux beginning to glow, her big white furred mousy ears twitching. "Thrum is out of commission in that ice cube, Atomic Lion is on the ropes, and Mishmash isn't anywhere close to taking Glacier and Force Vixen down."

"Hold," Ms. Q smirks. "We all know the Extraordinaries always keep someone in reserve for these fights. Well this time I had someone in reserve as well."

"Great, someone else we have to split the profits and the action with." Therma grouses. "Who is it this time? It better not be that squealer Thrilla Killa. After the crap in Atlanta I'm not working with her again."

"Hardly," Ms. Q deadpans as she points into the sky.

I glance up, and I feel the boom more than I hear it. I grip Camo's paw tight so he doesn't get separated from me, and watch as Glacier is sent tumbling across the street in the backwash as something flies down the street at super sonic speeds. The big husky crashes into an armored car, leaving a big dent. Ouch that does not look fun. Thrum vibrates out of his now fractured ice prison Glacier created around him, sending shards of hard ice flying everywhere, and Force Vixen has to bubble herself defensively. I see a blurring streak fly into the air laughing as the mayhem as even Metalyena and Atomic Lion are shaken. He stops and hovers above the others, and I can see what looks like a jackrabbit in a very form fitting black and gray costume and an air ace's cap from the 1940's. His long ears flop forward and his toned body gleams in his form fitting streamlined costume as he strikes a pose.

"Slipstream," says Lux with a grin. "How did you get him? I thought he was holed up by the Canadians."

"Oh, like she'll tell," says Therma irritably.

Camo whispers to me, "Alright, listen up, Star Coyote. Slipstream is bad news here. Everybody down there is exposed and you're our only flier besides Force Vixen, and she isn't fast enough to tackle him." The jaguar points at the laughing rabbit and says, "You handle him. I got these three."

"Camo, that violates the team rules and you know it. You can't take on three supervillains at once," I say, shaking my head, "especially not those three."

"Oh now you're concerned about the rules?" Camo growls, his eyes narrowing at me. "Now drop me on the roof. I got these rubes."

Oh, I'd like to drop him alright. I glare back at him, my ears flicking backwards. There are three competent and experienced criminals down there and they're all tough guys to fight. I'm not sure I can just leave him here.

"Do it, Star." Camo growls and I hesitate, second guessing myself again. Camo is an experienced hero, he's fought these villains before, and Slipstream is already coming around for another strafing run. Force Vixen is keeping Thrum occupied while Glacier collects himself, but that leaves the civilians fairly undefended and Mishmash is rallying. If Glacier can't stop him from reaching Force or Metalyena, the tide could turn against us.

I drop Camo, seeing him land on the roof easily and quietly and then disappear fully from my view. I fly up into the air quickly so the three on the roof don't see me and aim for the flying rabbit. Slipstream Jackrabbit is not someone I've taken on before, but I've read Stratagem's reports about him and actually remember them for once. He's taken on Titan Tomcat, El Gato Cibernetico, Glacier, and Force Vixen, I know that. I think the rabbit has purposely avoided me because I can fly so fast. That makes sense, because while he's fast, he's also inexperienced and he doesn't have any powers beyond flight. When he's flying he has increased strength and stamina, but it's really all based upon his ability to fly. I swoop into the air, the wind blowing through my fur as I angle in from his side. He doesn't see me; he's too busy diving in for another supersonic swoop at Glacier and Force Vixen. So when I slam against him he's genuinely dazed. Shaking his head, his ears flopping about, he looks up as I come around to take him down.

"Aw SHOOT!" Slipstream turns and starts to fly around quickly, trying to out maneuver me. He's no idiot at least. He's faster than me obviously; much faster. I push myself, flying after him as he begins to race across the city. To those who cannot fly it is hard to explain what its like to push yourself like this. It is something like running on the track during a long run and forcing yourself to go beyond your normal limits. Slipstream may be faster, but I think I'm just a bit more maneuverable. I don't need to be faster than him. I just need to be fast enough to out think him.

We're both zooming about quickly, swooping around the city, trying to gain an advantage. I can hear windows rattling in buildings as I fly after him. He's making an obvious mistake for a flier by weaving and dodging about. Something I learned from training with Lady Leopard is that maneuvering about isn't going to help you outrun somebody. If he was just flying straight out he'd out pace me easily and be home free, but he's wasting time and energy flitting about. I'm smiling now, reaching out a paw. I might not be sure what to do in my personal life right now, but catching a low life like this guy, that is something I can do easily. I smirk as my paw latches onto his ankle.

"What!?!" shouts Slipstream unimaginatively as he tries to shake me off. Too late though. I've got him and he doesn't realize it. His levitation and flight are a neat trick, but he obviously still obeys the laws of physics to some degree. Laws which I can rewrite, and since we are touching I can force him to obey my rewritten rules. I start to fly back to the battle, pulling him behind me while increasing the gravity field around us. He's struggling kicking about but he isn't anywhere near ready for this.

"What is going on here?!?!" Slipstream shouts as we plummet out of the sky, obviously worried and freaked out by my actions. "What is going on? How are you doing this?"

"I think it is obvious," I grin. "You're going in and I'm taking you down. Literally." We're falling like a stone now, and I can see the rabbit's shock and fear.

I just keep pulling and weighing him down. He's too panicked to aim a good kick at me now that I have both paws on his ankle. Fliers like him, and to be honest me, don't like being forcibly grounded. Flight is like the ultimate freedom in some ways, and losing that is really disconcerting. Soon we're back at the fight, and I make it so we touch back down lightly in the street; Slipstream all the while trying to worm his way free.

The fires are out by now, so Glacier must have had time to them extinguished. Thrum is down for the count, as is Atomic Lion who is struggling in some super strong bonds that Metalyena has used on him courtesy of Stratagem. Glacier has Mishmash in a choke hold now, and the monstrous man looks more blue than usual as the husky subdues him. Before Slipstream can run for it, Force Vixen has a bubble of pink energy around him.

"Hmmph" Force Vixen snorts. "If that is the last of them then? It appears Stratagem overestimated their brain power."

"Oh, goody," says Glacier when Mishmash finally passes out. Though one of his arms shoots out and twitches for a few moments, turning black furred and thinner before he sinks to the ground, his rapid shifting falls still as he goes down. Glacier rubs his shoulder as he glances about the field, taking in the sheer destruction the fight has caused. "How about next time he overestimates their muscle power." The big husky reaches up and peels open the seal of his suit, taking his helmet off. Underneath, Glacier's thin mask covers an exhausted look on his face. "Yeeowch, I hate being the team punching bag."

"Well we can have Metalyena do it next time if you're going to be a wimp," needles Force Vixen with a grin.

"Wait a second," I say looking about. "Where is Camo?"

"I assume on the rooftop where you left him," said Force Vixen. "Why?"

"He was taking on Ms. Q, Therma, and Lux alone!" I shout as I begin to fly upwards into the air.

"And you left him alone?" shouts Force Vixen angrily, a barrier of magenta forming over my head causing me to smack my skull into it painfully.

"Hey!" I shout back. "He ordered me to take down Slipstream." I growl as I angle around the barrier and head for the roof top.

"Just following orders?" Vixen fumes. "Is that the excuse you're going to make? God damn it, Star! Metal, Glacier, follow Star Coyote up there now!"

"No need," says Camo as the jaguar comes stumbling out of an alley way. His costume is ripped and singed from flames, his sunglasses are cracked and askew but overall he looks okay. Dragging behind him are two cuffed super villains. Therma and Lux are knocked out and he has the Q rod in his other paw.

Force Vixen rushes forward as does Metalyena. "Oh hell, Camo, are you alright?" Metalyena asks while worriedly looking over his friend.

"I've had worse," the cat grimaces and staggers forward as I float back to the street. His left leg looks a bit twisted and he's limping badly. "Here, I caught these two."

Force looks over him and seems to relax a bit. Obviously she doesn't think he is too hurt. This is probably why she growls at him, "Yes, you caught them. Where is Ms. Q?"

"She got out of the fight once I grabbed her oh so precious Q staff," Camo says with a smirk. "She got away for now but I'm sure we can catch up with her at this point. She can't run far in high heels."

"So you took a dumb risk and only caught two of them," says Force Vixen irritably, her bushy tail flicking back and forth as she crosses her arms in irritation.

"Hey," Camo growls back at her his ears laying flat on his head, "I made a command decision. Star Coyote followed my orders and did his job. End of story."

"And you could have been killed for it," says Force Vixen under her breath as she glares at Camo. "Taking on three supervillains is moronic if you can avoid it."

"It was handled," Camo says. I glance about trying to look for something else to do right now. I don't want to be in the middle of this. Its odd, but I can't help but notice how the shadows on the street seem to be lengthening.

"Maybe we shouldn't be doing this in public," Metalyena says as a way to get the two of them to stop yelling.

"Stay out of it," they both shout at him and then turn back to glaring at each other. Camo's tail is lashing just like Force Vixen's is and the jaguar has his hackles up.

"What the hell is wrong with you, Camo? You and Star have been at odds for weeks and now you pull a stunt like this?" Force Vixen is growling now. "Are you still trying to prove something, or are you just an idiot?" I glance at Glacier, who worriedly looks between the two of them. Weird, it seems darker around here now. Much darker. Is the moon behind a cloud?

Camo snarls at her. "Hey, don't start with me Miss Pretty-in-Pink. I did my job and I took them down. Star had to take out the flier, because you couldn't have." The jaguar says accusingly, "Not with those three trashing the street."

The street is quiet for a moment as all five of us breathing heavily, Camo and Force Vixen bristling in anger as Glacier, Metalyena and I look on in shock. I can see the angry storm clouds forming on Metalyena's face as he prepares to defend his friend, and even Glacier looks about to wade into the argument.

"Wait." Force Vixen blinks, as if shaking herself out of something. "Metalyena is right. Why are we fighting like this? Unless..." Force Vixen stops her voice trailing off as she glances about around her surveying the scene.

"I can't believe my brother is a faggot," says an all too familiar voice. My eyes widen as I turn about quickly. That sounded like my brother, but he doesn't know about my costumed identity and he can't be in Minnesota, can he? Everyone else seems confused as well. Did they hear him too?

Then Force Vixen starts shouting orders, "Non-superheros get back! Metalyena, Glacier twelve o'clock! Now!" Her tone of voice is suddenly filled with fear and the commands jerk us out of our anger.

I look where Force Vixen is pointing and my eyes widen. I can't believe I was so idiotic! How could I not see a huge cloud of inky blackness creeping down the street? Why did I not see that?

"What is that thing?" shouts Glacier as he runs towards it. Metalyena just grunts and he looks like he knows. Metalyena's hide is still lustrous metal as he pumps his legs, heavy stride hitting the pavement, cracking it from the force of his footfalls and his weight. I take up a defensive stance and got ready to do, well, something. What could I do really though? It's a huge cloud of blackness. I glance over at Force Vixen, who is staring past me wide eyed.

"Damn it, he suckered me," says Force Vixen under her breath, "he played me."

"Who?" I begin to ask but I stop as turn my head to see what she's looking at. Behind us, I catch a glimpse of Camo's face and arm being swallowed by another wall of darkness as he's dragged into the alleyway behind us.

I turn back to where Metalyena and Glacier are to scream a warning, but I'm too late. The shadows rear up near Metalyena as he passes a lengthening patch of shadow. They look like black tentacles as they wrap around the big hyena's body. Metalyena growls and struggles as the thick bands of inky blackness grip and pull against his powerful muscled torso, metal muscles flexing as he struggles with them. Even as he struggles I can see more lancing out and gripping him, pulling him prone to the ground. I want to run to his aid, to drag him out of the mass of darkness surrounding him, but I can't seem to do it.

"Yes, foolish child continue to struggle," says a velvety voice, dripping with condescending amusement; a lilting sound like someone from a Bollywood film. It only added to the menace for some reason as he strides out of the darkness—a large muscular tiger dressed in blood red and purple robes with a wide turban a top his head where a fist sized sapphire rests and a large peacock feather graces his turban. The tiger walks with perfect grace, a smile on his muzzle revealing far too sharp fangs. It's Raja Raksha. I've heard of the Maharaja of Madness but I never thought I'd face him. Didn't he die in that battle with Guru in Mongolia a few years ago?

"Alright, hold it!" shouts Glacier his eyes glowing again as he prepares a bolt of freezing energy. He's running up to Raja Raksha, his powerful frame ready to barrel into the tiger like a semi.

Raja Rakasha just quirks an eyebrow, looking at the charging Glacier, "I don't think I will. Tell me, boy, do you think any of this will change the fact that Kevin is dead?"

Glacier skids to a stop, reeling backwards as he stares at Raja Raksha. He looks like he's been slapped in the muzzle as he gasps, "What?"

"I said," Raja Raksha muzzle breaking into a smirk as he purrs, "Do you truly think any acts of bravado or courage will ever make up for the fact that Kevin died thanks to your cowardice?"

Glacier stumbles backwards, staring horrified at Raja Raksha. Why isn't he attacking? Raja Raksha flicks a paw and a shadow rears up beside the husky and slams into Glacier, sending him flying into the air and smacking painfully into a wall. Glacier looks dazed and confused, I am not sure if it was from the physical force or what Raja said. The shadows around him start to close in on the husky as he sits there, eyes wide in shock.

I stare at the advancing tiger, unable to look away. I feel paralyzed, unable to move. I can see Force Vixen fumbling with something, her normally confident movements uncoordinated. Force Vixen's energy bubble surrounding Slipstream fades as Raja walks closer to us, the magenta energy flickering away to nothing.

My head feels musty and it is hard to think. I hear my communicator chirping excitedly. Force Vixen activated a code red, a call for general assistance before she dropped her communicator. As Raja begins to speak, I feel like the air is being squeezed out of me. "I must say this plan is going very well."

"What plan?" asks Force Vixen as she starts to create a pink force fields around us, trying to cut the team loose from their shadowy bonds. Normally if Force brings a field into existence inside something, she cuts the thing in two, but the shadows just reform when the fields flicker and die away.

Raja Raksha just smiles at her as he coos, "Silly woman, you know you can't cut through those. As for my plan, it is simplicity itself. I found Mishmash wandering in the Gobi desert after he had escaped to that wasteland from his inglorious battle with Getsumi on the island of Kyuushu." The tiger's voice is a deep purr as he says, "It was delightfully easy to rip his mind apart."

Mishmash growls and moans from his position on the ground, rolling over to kneel in front of the advancing tiger. Even with his face constantly shifting, I can tell he's staring with adoration at Raja Raksha as the tiger grins down at him. "Breaking his mind and will with my power was simple, and in doing so I saw an opportunity. A way I could bring you foolish Extraordinaries to heel and for the world to finally recognize my power.

I merely had to have dear Alex Yeltsen, or as you know him Mishmash, attack a major city such as Minneapolis, and watch your team arrive to try and stop him. Then that simpleton Ms. Q improved upon my plan."

With his attention focused on Force Vixen, I try to levitate off the ground and gain some height, clear my head and maybe find something to throw at this guy. My body wobbles as I try to lift off. I get maybe a foot off the ground until Raja stares at me with his piercing yellow eyes. I remember terrible things: Alex breaking my heart. My brother finding out I was gay. The locker-room with Paul just before I told him I was gay. Turning down that job offer from Director Prichard of the National Hurricane Center. I wobble and fall to the ground gasping. What is he doing? The memories drown out my other thoughts.

"Gathering a cadre of criminals here for an attack? Little did she realize that Atomic Lion was in my employ and Mishmash was my thrall. All part of my plan to gather you heroes here," Raja says as he inspects the street. "Getting a few extra powers from these petty villains will be useful too, I'm sure."

"Why?" growls Force Vixen as she holds her paws up trying to direct a force field at the tiger. I don't know whether to protect herself or block his power. It doesn't matter though, the pink energy doesn't even finish forming before it winks out.

"Foolish little girl," the tiger smirks and those three words seem like a slap across Force Vixen's face. "How you ever became a leader on this team I shall never know. It is a shame some of your other members are off in Asia but that worm Schmetterling has a way of being a nuisance at the worst of times. As for why I did this, it was so that I could have Mishmash absorb all your abilities. Did you know he can do that and hold that knowledge for years? Why, I got here because he had once touched The Stranger and absorbed his teleportation skills. He did not even realize it was still inside him before I took him under my gentle tutelage." The tiger's paw reaches out and caresses Mishmash's face, and the way his face shifts under the tiger's touch is disconcerting. "I will destroy all of you and have him absorb your abilities. He will be an unbeatable slave with the powers of the Extraordinaries. Perhaps I'll even let a few of you live enslaved to my will as well. Then the world will cower before Raja Raksha"

That smile on his face tells me one thing: he knows he's won and he's reveling in the moment with malevolent glee. He's just doing this to torture us. The tiger looks about at all of us smirking, "Now, where to start."

His eyes fix upon me and that smile grows wider, predatory, filled with malicious excitement. His voice coos like that of a man inviting someone in for tea but it is filled with a deep viciousness, "Ah, yes. Star Coyote, I don't think we've had the pleasure of meeting before."

I want to move, to back away, to fight, or run, or I don't know what, but his eyes have me transfixed. I can feel tendrils of shadow creeping up over my costumed body, crawling up my wrists and legs gripping me tightly. I can hear my mother and father screaming at me. My brother's mocking laughter. Voices from high school taunt me from the past.

"Leave him alone!" shouts Force Vixen, her voice cracking so it sounds like she's almost pleading. I can see another force field forming between Raja and myself even as I remember Alex's exact words as he broke it off with me.

Raja Raksha turns and growls at her, "Learn your place, girl."

The force field collapses and Force Vixen falls to the ground as shadows start to creep over her pink costume. I think I hear her as the

shadows pick her up and slam her to the ground flat on her back, she is struggling like mad. The tiger menacingly smirks at me as the shadows engulf her completely. "Now then, on to you, little one."

I can feel him getting closer even as I watch him. The presence of the Maharaja of Madness is filling the space around me and clouding my vision, the darkness getting deeper. I can hear voices in the shadow. My parent's angry, shouting voices are getting louder. Alex cursing me. Samantha. Joshua. Camo. I can hear the explosions of a car. The sound of a gun going off, a memory from before I even put on the costume. I can see that poor man dying in front of me because I wasn't brave enough to intercede. Too scared to be a hero then, even though I didn't have powers.

"Simpering little fool," the tiger coos down at me, "do you really think dressing up in a garish costume can make up for all you've done?"

I whimper now as I hear my brother trying to blackmail me. Alex saying he found someone else, someone better than me, someone who would be worth his time. Why am I thinking this? How can I not? I have to try and fight him, but what can I do? He has me trapped as he leers down at me and it is so hard to think.

"You'll never change what you are," the tiger condescends as he talks to me, "no matter what you do, you are a perversion. You are less than nothing. You're an abomination against the natural order."

I'm crying now. I know he's right. I am broken. I'm wrong inside. I know it. I remember thinking it at night as teenager. I could hear my parents saying it over and over again, talking about other gay people they knew, about how wrong they were. All the while, I knew they were talking about me even though they didn't know the truth then.

"You can wish it wasn't so. You can strive against it," the tiger smirks, "but you will fail. Just the way you have failed everyone here today."

Tears are pressing against my mask now. I want the voices to stop. They're yelling and chattering and telling me, reminding me, of everything I already know. All my mistakes, all the things I know are wrong with me.

"You're all alone," the tiger smiles at me and he's so close that his whiskers brush across my face, his voice dripping with sweet honey, and I know he's telling the truth. I am all alone. I've failed so many people. What kind of freak am I? I'm a faggoty little gay coyote. What can I do to help anyone?

"All alone and worthless. A pervert. A freakish little thing. Trying to make up for what you are by playing hero," Raja Raksha says evenly and I know he's right about that too. I put on this foolish costume to hide who I was, but everyone can see it. He continues with a smile, his sharp teeth gleaming as he traces a claw down the front of my costume, tearing the fabric right across the big ridiculous symbol on my chest. "Why, even your own mother hates you."

I want to cry out loudly now, just to make a sound, to howl my sorrow to the world, but it feels stifled in my throat as Raja Raksha leans down close to my thin muzzle, almost nuzzling me as he whispers, "You aren't a hero, you little sissy boy. You're just pretending to be one." I know he's going to kill me now. I can feel it coming, he's going to tear my throat out with those claws and I just want him to end it. The voices, his voice that sounds like mine now. What have I ever done that is worth anything?

Raja leans back, and the shadows holding me force me up to eye level with him as he smirks at me. I try to look away from those eyes. I just want this to stop, the voices telling me the truth, I want to escape to run away like I've always done as he says, "You're all alone in the world. You have nothing. You're worse than nothing." His paw reaches out, and I can just feel the tips of his claws at my throat as he says, "You're an aberration and an incorrect thing. You aren't a hero and you never will be. You are the furthest thing from a hero. You're all alone."

"You couldn't be more wrong, Raja," says a voice. Suddenly a bright blue gloved fist flashes across my vision and connects with Raja's muzzle, slamming into him forcefully and sending him reeling backwards away from me.

A blinding light fills my vision; bright warm and golden yellow. The light flows out from a point beside me, dispelling the shadows around me with ease. I drop to my knees, but I can see the street again. I can see my team mates and the armored cars, and the damaged buildings around us. It feels like a warm summer day. It reminds me of fields I used to play in. The day I truly learned to fly. When I joined the team! It reminds me of that wonderfully sunny day when I met, and I have to gasp as the memories come flooding back into me, the day I met Jay. Jay! How could I forget Jay? His face fills my mind. That sweet nose of his and his comforting voice—the way his arms feel around me. The feeling of Jay's soft fur and the richness of his scent comes rushing back to me, filling me up inside. I remember Jay now and the voices become quieter as I blink back tears and look up at the man beside me.

Right beside me, standing proudly, is a raccoon, his muscled torso made powerful from years of hard work. I've seen him before, but my memory is still hazy from Raja's attack, and I feel giddy like I did the first time I met him.

There's a hard look on his confident muzzle, and he has wide rounded ears and a shock of blond hair crowning his head. He's wearing a pair of rounded, mirror sunglasses over his chocolate brown raccoon mask, and the beaten old jeans on his legs are caked in dust. Bright blue gloves adorn his paws as he balls them into fists, and a large sky blue and yellow jacket accentuates his powerful shoulders as he stands there, the light radiating out from him as if he were a second sun. My mind begins to clear, and I smile weakly. I know there is a sun symbol on the back of his jacket. It was the only symbol that made any sense for the world's first hero.

Raja Raksha glares at the figure as I try to talk, my mouth feeling so dry I can only whisper, my voice cracking. "Solarcoon," I manage to say, relief flowing through me.

He's speaking again, that warm fatherly voice a deep reverberating growl, "Star Coyote is a hero. A man who has done everything he can and will continue to do so. I have seen it and I know that he does it for the best of reasons. He will never be alone. No one with as good a heart as his ever will be."

I feel his large raccoon paw on my shoulder, squeezing it reassuringly. The light begins to fade around me but the shadows have retreated and are gone. Night returns but I can see the moon and the streets lights shining. It's just night, not the otherworldly darkness that filled the street before. The other Extraordinaries are free as well, and staring at Solarcoon. Atomic Lion and Mishmash are standing up and flexing, preparing for another round. The other supercriminals are loose, but they seem shaken and unprepared. Raja's attack probably wasn't any kinder to them than it was to us.

"Screw this. I'm burning you freaks down," says Atomic Lion, green flames wreathing his paws. "I agreed to this to see some Extraordinaries dead and if that froo froo tiger can't deliver, at least I will!"

Solarcoon barely reacts to that except to arch an eyebrow. As he continues to look at Raja Raksha he says, "Lady Leopard, take Atomic Lion. Titan Tomcat you have Mishmash. Blitzkrieg—Thrum and Slipstream are loose. Detain them. Stratagem, help our friends. Raja is mine."

I glance behind me and I see them. The rest of the team is here as I see a flash and the teleporter delivers our last member onto the scene. Lady Leopard is standing there looking stern and powerful, her arms akimbo on her hips her pony tail wafting in the night air, her tail fluffed out the only sign of agitation. Titan Tomcat, the five foot tall gray tabby cat in his bright red and white costume, a red maple leaf emblazoned on his chest. Blitzkrieg, his stout fireplug body tensed for action, power seeming to flow from him with sparks of electricity. Stratagem is in the back, glowering from behind Blitzkrieg, his goggles shining as he looks over the field of battle.

Lady Leopard moves quickly and deliberately, launching herself forward and ramming into Atomic Lion at a frightening speed, slamming him down to the ground. She's immune to his radiation and much stronger than the big lion. He tries to send out a bolt of flame at Metalyena as Metalyena picks himself up from the ground, now flesh and fur, the effects of Raja Raksha having caused him to turn back from his metal form. Lady isn't having that though; she blocks the bolt of flame easily with her body and slams the big lion with a fist that sends him flying up into the air like a doll. She flies after him quickly. I think I hear her say, "Pity. I overestimated that one."

I look over as Mishmash roars and starts running at a prone Glacier, eager for revenge on the husky. Titan Tomcat runs between them and I watch as the small cat squares off against Mishmash, and he looks far too small against the shifting behemoth. Then Titan starts to grow rapidly, the cat's stance widening and growing fluidly as he expands to a much larger size, easily grappling with Mishmash now and pushing him back hard. I don't know who is more surprised when Metalyena slams into Mishmash toppling him over. Titan Tomcat just shakes his head and rushes forward to help, not even questioning it.

Blitzkrieg streaks forward, a blur of color and brown fur as he stops a rallying Thrum with ease and begins to spin around under Slipstream, creating air currents the rabbit has trouble gaining leverage in. A smell of ozone and the sound of crackling electricity trail behind him as the Germanic wolf does his job. Blitzkrieg's superspeed proves more than a match for both criminals as his legs pump and his body becomes a blur of motion as he runs about.

Raja Raksha gives a throaty mocking laugh, "You think this will do anything, Solarcoon? You have merely fallen into my trap along with the rest of your pathetic teammates."

"I'm taking you in, Raja Raksha. I won't let you threaten my team or endanger these innocent people anymore," Solarcoon says, leaving my side and advancing upon the tiger. I believe him—he has such confidence in the pronouncement. Solarcoon might not be the most powerful member of the team but I've seen some truly dangerous people cower when he walks and talks like that.

Raja Raksha just gives a spitting laugh, "Do you think me a fool? It is night time here, Solarfool. Your powers depend upon sunlight. How much of your internal power have you wasted with your little lightshow? You have no power left and you cannot resist me." The tiger raises his arms, shadows swirling around his paws.

My eyes widen as I realize Raja Raksha has to be right. Solarcoon would have had to drain his internal power reserves to create radiance like that. He depends upon solar energy to empower his abilities but his bioluminescence always drains his energy, it is why he doesn't do it very often.

I have to help him! I try to stand, lifting myself from the ground pushing up my legs wobbling, I feel lightheaded, and weak, like I just gave blood and skipped lunch, but I have to help. I feel a paw on my shoulder pushing me down gently. Stratagem's voice whispers in my ear, "No, Star Coyote, you're still weak. Let Solarcoon do this."

"He needs help," I say staring at the shadows creeping up on Solarcoon as he stares resolutely at Raja Raksha.

"He can handle it," Stratagem says evenly as he takes a light out and shines it against my mask as he talks softly. "What I need to know is this. What is the name of your boyfriend?"

My eyes widen in shock as I stare at the badger. "Jay. Jay Carson," I whisper worriedly. How can he bring this up now? In public no less!

"And his parent's names?" he asks evenly betraying no emotion.

"Belinda and Frank Carson," I answer wondering why he would ask me in the middle of a fight.

"Good," Stratagem offers me a rare smile. "If Raja had gotten to you like some of his other victims then you wouldn't be able to remember details like that so readily. Listen, Star Coyote, stay down, sit this one out. I need to check on the others and you've gone through too much."

I can only nod as the badger gets up and rushes to check on Camo. I just sit there watching as Solarcoon advances on Raja, the tendrils of shadow from the tiger's paws snaking out to around the raccoon's raised fists as Raja Raksha growls at him, "You have no powers and no ability to withstand me. This time I shall defeat you, gnat. How a little mortal man like you thought he could resist me is beyond contemplation! I, the lord of nightmares and the king of demons, will not be defeated by a mere man."

Solarcoon flexes his arms and pushes forward, walking towards the tiger without a concern. The shadows trying to hold him back snap apart as he marches towards the tiger, who stumbles back surprised as

189

Solarcoon says, "Lord of nothing. You're a bully, Raja Raksha. Nothing more, nothing less." Solarcoon's fist slams into the tiger's nose, knocking him backwards his nose starting to bleed. "You parasitically feed on people's sadness and pain and their regrets, which you stir up and manipulate without even understanding or truly knowing them. I won't let you bully my friends. With or without my powers I can—I will stop you."

Solarcoon's fist cracks into the tiger once more, who seems genuinely surprised and pained now as Solarcoon advances upon him again. The strong raccoon seems to radiate conviction and righteousness as he takes up a boxer's stance and begins to punch forward, slamming into the tiger's body and making the ornately dressed tiger wince and buckle.

I turn away as I hear a loud crash. Glacier is up and he hurled a small wrecked compact car into Mishmash, slamming him to the ground. He and Metalyena are circling Mishmash, preparing to fight again, drawing his attention away as Titan Tomcat rushes up from behind. The tomcat stretches and lengthens growing larger and larger, his body stretching and growing outward as he towers over the buildings around us, now several stories up. Mishmash finally notices the looming cat, but it is too late as the red and white garbed cat slams a big red booted footpaw directly onto the misshapen monstrosity.

Titan's voice booms over the area, "Struggle all you like, Mishmash. You don't have the leverage to push me off and my rubber soled boot doesn't have any DNA for you to absorb."

A part of me wants to laugh at Mishmash essentially being squished like a bug. Glacier and Metalyena turn their attention on Thrum and Slipstream as Blitzkrieg lets them go, speeding off to grab Lux who was trying to sneak away.

Slipstream raises his paws in the air saying, "Aw, screw this. You guys got me."

I can't believe the battle has turned around so quickly. I turn and watch as Solarcoon pounds Raja Raksha like a heavy weight boxer, his fists easily breaking through the tiger's shadows and smacking into the tiger's flesh. Raja's feeble attempts at fighting back are countered by the better trained and more accurate raccoon. Every blow from Solarcoon reverberates inside me. I can almost feel the tiger weaken from the onslaught. Solar isn't taking pleasure in it; it is almost like he is a force of nature at this point: a force of pure unbridled justice.

Raja Raksha curses and spits glaring at Solarcoon as he stumbles back, his turban askew. "You win this day fool. Your sunny optimism will be the end of you one day though." After saying that, he growls a word while touching his turban, and seems to disappear in a shimmer of bright light. Solarcoon glares and looks around saying one word, "Stratagem."

Stratagem comes forward and inspects the area looking about as his finger's twitch, obviously teasing out information with his glove keyboard. He then says, "It appears that Raja Raksha teleported away."

"He can do that?" asks Lady Leopard as she lands on the ground, dropping the unconscious body of Atomic Lion onto the ground.

"No," says Solarcoon, his ears twitching backward for a moment. "At least not as far as I know."

"He claimed he had Stranger's power through Mishmash," Force Vixen says as she walks forward, obviously disheveled and unsure on her feet.

"No," Stratagem says. "It wasn't that. There are certain signals of Stranger's power being used. I know that. This was obviously an artificial teleport. It has a completely different signature."

"Troubling," says Blitzkrieg his tail twitching as he runs up to them, a thick German accent rolling off of him. "It means he hast gained dangerous technology. Correct? He could, hrrm, use that badly yes?"

Stratagem smirks, "Not really. I've gotten more familiar with the technology over the years. This was an obvious emergency teleport. He might be anywhere but he won't be able to use it again easily and its targeting looks to be off. He probably has not landed where he wanted to go. Now that I know he has such a device I can watch out for purchases of the equipment he's obviously fried using it."

"We'll find him," says Lady Leopard nodding her head and putting a gloved paw on Solarcoon's shoulder. I wonder if she is reassuring our leader or herself. Even Metalyena seems shaken by this.

"We better," Glacier says grinding a fist into his palm. "That arrogant jerk needs a firm pounding."

"I think Solar gave that to him already," Force Vixen says rubbing her head obviously drained.

"Alright, team," Solarcoon interrupts further discussion. "Metalyena stay here with Lady Leopard and report to St. Paul. Give them a full account of what happened and make sure there aren't any other surprises. Blitzkrieg make a run around town. See if you can find Ms. Q. The rest of us are going back to base. We have wounded and we need to assess what happened."

Camo is still unconscious and Lady Leopard cradles him gently in her arms before handing him to Titan Tomcat who has shrunk down to only seven feet. Mishmash is lying on the ground like a doll. Unmoving and blank eyed, he looks like a puppet with his string cut.

Stratagem begins to teleport us out one by one. As the glow of the teleporter enfolds me I can't help but feel shame. I failed the team. The others were strong enough to shake off Raja's effects. They did more than I did. It feels like another long night ahead of me.

CHAPTER 8
MANY MEETINGS

It is several hours before we're all in the Bunker meeting room. We had to take our time with the teleporter coming back, and besides, Blitzkrieg, Lady Leopard, and Metalyena needed some time to finish their tasks. Apparently Metalyena stayed in his metallic form in the mayor's office and put a hole in the floor with one of his feet. This of course has not helped relations with the city of Minneapolis, but Metalyena was staying in metal form to keep himself stable, so it couldn't be helped. Apparently it helps him stave off mental duress as well as physical damage, so we'll try to pass the floor off as collateral damage as well, but we'll see how the Mayor reacts in the next few days. Meanwhile, he's staying in metal form to control the effects of what happened with Raja.

I can understand why. I feel like I just bench pressed a truck without gravity manipulation. My whole body feels stretched and sore. I am tired from all the time zone changes of the past few weeks and the stress of what happened with Jay, and I'd be lying if I said I wasn't thinking about what happened with Raja. Stratagem has us all checked out in the medical bay. Camo is in the worst shape of all of us and he'll be out of commission for at least a week for recovery. We were lucky that a badly sprained ankle was the worst injury the team suffered. Glacier got a lot of bruises but that was about the worst for him. I get a clean bill of health for the long term but the badger suggests I take things easy for a while.

Now gathered in the meeting room, I look about. We don't often have the entire team assembled around the meeting table. We all have lives to deal with as well as other concerns. Besides, there were not that many threats that called for the entire Extraordinary team to be in one place. The large roster allows for time off, coordination, and for mission specialization. Lady Leopard and Blitzkreig can't be everywhere, even with their phenomenal speed, and they aren't always needed to take down a threat. We do have bimonthly large gatherings to compare notes and trade information, as well as some socialization, but it's rare that everyone makes it. Still, seeing everyone here tonight is intimidating.

The Extraordinairies have slowly increased the size of the meeting table and it now seats all ten members with room for extra chairs if we need to call anyone in or want to increase our membership again. Those are unlabeled, while our seats are assigned. It is a circular table; Stratagem suggested it that so we can avoid thinking of any member as truly better than the others. Still, we do defer to the founders. On my right is Glacier, then Stratagem who sits next to Solarcoon followed by Lady Leopard then Force Vixen. Titan Tomcat sits next to Force Vixen, and he's back to his normal height now. Metalyena is sitting next followed by Camo and on his right, my left, is Blitzkrieg.

The layout is a bit of an artifact of membership. Titan Tomcat was the first hero to join the team after the founders. It made a splash when the team had announced they were expanding their ranks. Blitzkrieg joined just after Swiftwolf fell against the Living Code. That was about the time Marvelous Malamute premiered and she soon joined. Metalyena and Camo joined after her, just before The Stranger fell saving the world. It was after Marvelous Malamute died in Vancouver that they had another membership drive and asked Glacier and I to join three years ago.

I know it might be a side effect of Raja's powers, but a part of me has to wonder why I was even here. Raja Raksha had singled me out to go first for this little session. He had purposely gone after me, was it because I was the weakest member? Because of my secret? I hadn't even done anything to try and fight him. It didn't make sense, not when you considered all Force Vixen had done trying to rally us and fight him off. I glance at Force, she seems so drained and ragged, her fur all mussed and she looks more tired than I had ever seen her before.

I sip some orange juice as we wait. Stratagem claims the Vitamin C would help overcome the side effects of Raja's abilities. That is hard for me to believe though, so maybe Stratagem is trying to give us a placebo. All I know is that Raja said a lot of things that struck very close to home.—things I didn't want to admit but which were there. Was I really a good enough hero to be sitting here, at this table? Was I capable enough? Was I doing this for the right reasons?

Sitting beside me, Glacier looks as shell shocked as I feel as he drinks his own glass of juice. He had gotten thrown around a lot in the fight. I should have stepped in sooner and helped my friend. Shouldn't I? Why didn't I?

"Alright, everyone. I realize it is getting late but I felt we should discuss what happened," Solarcoon says standing up from his chair and looking about our assemblage. "Now you've all filed reports but I felt we should cover what has been said to the authorities in St. Paul, Washington, DC and the UN, as well as cover what happened."

"We want to stress that no one is in trouble," Lady Leopard says, her British accent rounding off any edge that could be there. She has perfect elocution. A lot of people call her perfect but she demurs from that claiming she is just like anyone else. Except that she has punched missiles out of the air and has saved millions all while being polite and approachable. "Everyone performed well under the circumstances you were placed in."

"There are things that need to be said," Stratagem chimes in. "I'm glad to say that overall the state of Minnesota and the US Government did not lose much in this attack. There are dents in some armored cars but beyond that very little long term damage. There will be individual insurance claims issues and some storefronts were damaged but happily Force Vixen kept it contained. The criminal conspiracy that had formed got away with nothing and we rounded up all the members except for Ms. Q and Raja. I'm just sorry that Raja Raksha showed up. I truly had no idea he would be there, no evidence pointed to it and none of my statistical models gave any indication."

"You had to make an error eventually, your track record was too perfect anyway," Metalyena says reassuringly as he rubs the temples on his forehead. The shine from his metallic skin looks a little tarnished and the sound of metal on metal sets my teeth on edge. That doesn't usually happen when the hyena's in metal form. Metalyena must be really banged up. "I didn't even know Raja Raksha could enslave people like that."

"You've only faced him twice before this, Metal," Solarcoon says looking around the table. "Raja Raksha has been a persistent foe of the Extraordinaries since our founding. We've only brought him to justice once and he escaped confinement easily. Many times he uses his powers to kill or intimidate by shows of power. His ability to make others puppets takes more time. Time he obviously had with Mishmash."

"I'll be the first to say I don't like Mishmash," Glacier says looking around the table. Glacier has taken on Mishmash more than anyone else, I think, so that is probably true. "But no one deserves to be a slave to that freak."

"Agreed," Force Vixen says. Then sighing she adds, "I'm not sure there is anything we can do about it though."

"There is a psychologist, Doctor Brian Connely, in Sydney, Australia, who has showed a lot of promise. I believe we all remember Charlotte Banning from our second Raja Raksha case so many years ago. She is under his care and has shown remarkable progress to reasserting her personality and overcoming Raja's brainwashing. I think there might be the chance that Mishmash could respond to the therapy."

"That is very good news to hear," Lady Leopard says with a half smile. "Perhaps some of his other victims can be helped as well."

"That is all well and good," Titan Tomcat breaks in standing up from his chair and drawing to his full normal height of five feet, which would be funny if he didn't sound so authoritative and tough when he talks. "But am I the only one who see the obvious problems here? While he is being treated, assuming the Yankee authorities even let him go to Oz, Raja Raksha has access to a superbeing who apparently still has the powers of heroes he has touched. How many of our abilities has he gotten over the years? I thought they faded over time. Good grief, he has The Stranger's powers. Stranger could teleport anywhere in the world or teleport anyone else if he knew where they were, not to mention the time manipulation abilities he developed before he died. If Mishmash is truly Raja's thrall, that means Raja Raksha has access to dangerous abilities. Charlotte was admitted into an asylum nearly eight years ago. I should know, I was the one that took her to Sydney. How long do we have before Raja asserts himself over Mishmash again to commit some act of terrorism? For that matter, Mishmash was hardly stable to begin with; will this Doctor Connely even have the ability to help him?"

"All valid concerns," Stratagem says, and he's obviously thinking as he talks, "It is true Banning was a stable young woman before Raja got his claws into her while Mishmash was never truly stable."

"He was never crazy, just petty and vindictive," Glacier says. "I mean he was never a quivering crazy like Schmetterling or an anarchist nutbar like Atomic Lion. He's just a petty thug with a lot of power."

"He wasn't always that way. He used to be more stable, Glacier. His transformation left him unhinged. Titan Tomcat," Solarcoon begins. Then, his voice softening he says Titan's civilian name, something he does when he wants us to start thinking like people and not just costumed heroes, "Alan, are you suggesting something more drastic?"

Titan sighs leaning against the table a bit before addressing Solarcoon directly. "Nothing I'm comfortable with, Bill. Mishmash was never a good guy but he's a much larger threat now. Not a petty criminal we can take down by ourselves or contain. You saw him out there on the streets; he was a wild animal, feral, and on the leash to a guy who wants to make his own slave kingdom out of India. Maybe we should consider the collateral damage in this case and think about more, well, definitive ends."

"Oh that is horrible," Lady Leopard gasps. "Titan we can't entertain such an idea. We aren't killers, we protect people and Mishmash is a victim in all this."

"I agree with ponytail," Force Vixen says with a flinty bite in her voice. "I'm all for playing rough when needed but Mishmash is a prisoner and can't even articulate how to defend himself."

"I suggest," Stratagem breaks into the conversation, "that before we talk about euthanasia and the moral implications of such an act, that we attempt to learn more. Mishmash's mind might still be salvageable. At the very least we should study the situation more and see if there aren't other alternatives."

"Like a power blocker?" Metalyena suggests.

"We've been trying that for years," Camo pipes in, his voice sounds cracked and slightly pained as he grimaces to Metal's right, "and we're no closer to figuring out how to make one than we were when we started."

"I'm hesitant to end his life until I know more," Stratagem says, his goggles glowing slightly from the TV screens around the room, "although I admit the options right now are very bleak. I would like to try and see if I can find something to help him."

"I agree with Stratagem," Solarcoon says. "We'll take necessary steps when we learn more about the situation. Until then let's table this discussion."

Solarcoon says it with that usual definitive tone in his voice. We all know that for now we won't be discussing it officially. We'll come back to it and it will probably come up in the locker room but for now the question of Mishmash is over.

"The authorities have all been given a complete report as has the local media and some television networks. Some of the cable news shows were irritated that we didn't alert them before hand so they could film the fight," Metalyena says.

"Shock and awe there," Camo says rubbing his paws with a pained look on his face. "They're still sending in requests for a reality TV spot with a hero."

"I assume you've been handling it?" asks Stratagem quirking an eyebrow at the jaguar.

"Party line is that we don't endorse one network, or group, and that we don't wish to be filmed in such a manner," Camo says with a dismissive wave of his paw. His irritation with the idea of a reality TV show is well known. "Though they are getting testy. The To Catch a Supervillain idea is gaining some steam and somebody is going to try it eventually."

"Let them get testy," Titan Tomcat says with a roll of his eyes. "We don't do this for public recognition."

"I assume Agent Jon Crick of the Supernormal Affairs Division has been fully briefed as well," Solarcoon says breaking that train of thought. We've gone over the exploitative TV shows before as well. Nothing we can do to stop them, even if they are taking some big risks. We just try not to encourage them.

"I did it myself," Stratagem says. "Along with the foreign offices of Kazhakstan. I believe that Delhi should also be alerted that we faced Raja Raksha. They like to be kept abreast of his location and actions as he has made it clear he wants to turn Hyderabad into the capitol of his so called Demonic Empire."

"Soundz fair," Blitzkreig says. "Vhen we are done here I vill alert the German Chancellor as to what happened, ya? As vell as the EU?"

Stratagem starts to speak German discussing what I assume are the talking points and official team line. It was discovered early on that a clear and concise message that the entire team shared worked very well for assuring support for the Extraordinaries. Unfortunately it is a little hard to create a party line when not everyone speaks the same language fluently. Stratagem just happens to know German fluently, but then he knows a lot of languages fluently.

Solarcoon nods along. He's picked up a little German over the years working with Blitzkrieg. I've gotten a little as well but I'm not fluent like Stratagem.

We go over the basic story. It is basically what happened, but streamlined and without any personal details. No mention of names, nothing about how we particularly took down specificvillains. You never know what detail can be used against us, so we like to keep it barebones as much as possible. I think that reticence is another reason the TV and news folk have gotten so much more irritable in the past year. They keep looking for some hook, some scandal to sink their teeth into.

"I suggest we adjourn and clean up," says Lady Leopard as we finish going over the story and make sure all details are clear. "I don't know about anyone else but a transcontinental battle always feels better after a warm shower."

"I second the motion," says Metalyena with a tired smile.

We all start standing up and stretching. It has been a long night but it is good to be with my costumed allies. Are they really my friends though? Would they be my friends still if they knew? I look over at Camo as he limps to the locker room; is he an indication of what could happen when the rest of the team finds out?

"Star, may I see you?" asks Solarcoon. I nearly jump into the air. I didn't hear the large raccoon approaching until he was right behind me. How can someone so big be so quiet?

I turn and look up at him. He's wearing his usual sunglasses mask and I can't really read his expression. I can see Glacier out of the corner of my eye looking at me worriedly but I just nod and say, "Yeah. Of course, Solarcoon."

Everyone else is chatting or moving off to different parts of the base. I see Blitzkrieg zoom away in a blur of motion, probably to the teleporter to get back to Germany. Or to the bunker's extra generator, and then a quick run across the Atlantic. Unlike Swiftwolf, Blitzkrieg needs electrical energy to use his powers. I've never been clear on the details but somehow Blitzkrieg can take ambient electrical energy, or in some cases draw upon electrical energy directly, and then utilize it to augment his mental and physical speed. He has never been as fast as Swiftwolf, but compared to most of us he's amazingly fast. After Swiftwolf died, Blitzkrieg became the fastest runner in the world. It wasn't a title the German ever wanted to hold, though. He had been friends with Swiftwolf before he died. It was a close friendship, Force Vixen once mentioned a truly epic pub crawl between the two of them.

Solarcoon leads me through a side door and down a hallway towards the residential section of the Bunker. This is where we keep the apartments and beds for when we have to stay over night, or for more long term issues. Solarcoon opens a door and we go into one of the apartments. Glancing about I see a rumpled bed, some magazines on the floor, dishes in the sink, a photograph of Solarcoon without his mask next to his wife and children. The apartment is a little more lived in than many of the others, obviously. Solarcoon has never really been the best at picking up after himself. He uses this as a home away from home at times and stays here when he has monitor duty.

Solar motions to a chair next to a table with a stack of news paper spread across it, "Please, Star, sit."

I sit down quietly and wait as Solarcoon putters in the kitchenette for a few minutes. I hear a coffee pot sputtering and soon a mug of joe is set down in front of me as Solarcoon sits down to my left, his large body filling the chair more than I ever could.

"Cream?" he asks pleasantly.

"No, thanks," I say taking a sip of the coffee as he does the same. I like a little sugar in mine but I don't really feel like asking. At least it is warm, and it doesn't taste like more orange juice. We sip our coffee quietly and I'm wondering why we came here. Solarcoon doesn't seem angry at least. That seems like a good sign.

Finally he speaks up, "Star Coyote, Ted, I want to talk to you about what happened in Minneapolis."

"Didn't we just do that?" I ask, looking at Solarcoon. He hasn't used my real name very often when in the Bunker. He likes to be business like when we're in masks.

"We discussed the team relations and events, but this is about you," Solarcoon says his sunglasses glinting slightly. I can't help think how strange it is he wears sunglasses. I learned a while back that Solarcoon has perfect vision at all times. Light is never too bright or dark for him, even with those sunglasses on it is like they aren't there; it is part of his power. I admit my mask does restrict my vision slightly, he's lucky he doesn't have to worry about that.

"You don't have to tell me I messed up. I know I did," I say looking away from Solarcoon just wanting to drink my coffee and for this to be done.

Solarcoon sighs and then says, "I was afraid of this. Ted, you did not fail or mess up. You did your job. Camo was wrong to order you away and take on three supercriminals at once."

"I didn't do anything to help fight Raja Raksha," I say, trying not to think about him again looming over me, those words he was saying, those shadows creeping over me like they were leaching into me.

"You were caught flat-footed," Solarcoon responds looking at me sternly. "Ted, we've all been caught off guard and unsure what to do. That is why we work as a team, because if you're unable or incapable of a fight we'll be there to back you up and defend you. You've never taken Raja Raksha on before, and we have no way to simulate what his power does to a person. You could not possibly be prepared to fight him or resist the mental paralysis he causes. That is why we have team leaders. Experienced heroes who know what they are doing. Look at Force Vixen. She's fought him several times now and even she was caught off guard."

"I could have done more," I say simply and it just feels true.

"Ted," I feel Solarcoon's big hand rest on my shoulder reassuringly and as he speaks his warm voice washes over me. "Whatever you heard, whatever Raja Raksha said to you, it is a lie. You have to know that."

"It didn't feel like a lie," I say. Memories flood back into my mind and I can almost feel tears welling up inside of me. "It felt like a whole lot of truth."

"The memories are true, yes," Solarcoon says nodding along, "and some of what he says is. Part of Raja Raksha's power is that he always knows exactly what to say to cause despair or sadness. He doesn't understand what it means to the person and I doubt he cares. His powers revolve around despair and causing humiliation and sadness."

"Well, if he speaks the truth how can you say he was lying," I ask sitting back in the chair looking up at Solarcoon. "How can you be so sure everything he said wasn't perfectly true?"

"I know it isn't perfectly true because I know Raja Raksha," Solarcoon takes off his sunglasses and looks at me with his deep emerald colored eyes. "Ted, he speaks a truth without context. Yes I am sure your memories are real but they are removed from meaning and place in your life. He blocks out the happy memories and the memories that lessen the impact of what you remembered. The words he speaks are without context. They are things you think about on cold nights alone; insecurities and painful thoughts. Beliefs about yourself that you think are true when you're cold and alone even though they aren't actually true."

"I don't know," is all I can say as I sigh and sip on my coffee.

"Believe me," Solarcoon says nodding his head and holding his coffee while looking at me carefully. "You have to understand, Ted, he has done this to the entire team at one time or another. He's forced us to confront difficult feelings and beliefs we think we have pushed aside. Force Vixen especially fears what he can do to her. It is why she fought so hard to stop him from doing that to you. He's tried to break all of us."

"He went after me first, though. What does that say?"

"That you were more immune to his effects than the others," Solarcoon responds. "Raja is very easy to predict in that regard."

"I don't understand," I say genuinely confused. "If I'm so immune how come I didn't react in time? How was he able to make me feel that way?"

Solarcoon nods and pats my shoulder with understanding and it feels so reassuring, "Ted, Raja Raksha had effected the others very easily. He incapacitated them quickly and efficiently. You were surprised and didn't react quickly to the events, and by the time you did, he was able to focus on you more and prevent you from reacting. The others though... Well, Ted, many of them have had events in their lives that made them heroes that are very painful to relive."

"It isn't like my life has been a picnic," I say crossing my arms sitting back in my chair a bit annoyed at the presumption of that comment.

"True," Solarcoon nods. "But you've always been one of our more optimistic members. You have a very cheery view of people overall and I suspect that you have things in your life that help you find a kind of center. I know that you are balancing a career you love and heroing, and not every member can do that. In part I believe you can because you are happy."

I think about Jay, and Jay's parents and Gary and Brandon and Mattie and the rest of my friends and my job and I nod, "I guess I am lucky."

"Raja sensed that." Solarcoon says firmly. "You could have overcome him that way, even as he was trying to block your memories off, you could have fought back if you had known how. Force Vixen has had a very hard life but she could fight him to some degree because she knew what to do. I think you will be able to next time."

I shudder thinking about the idea of fighting him again. "I hope that doesn't come soon."

Solarcoon just nods before continuing, "He knew that you had never faced him before, that you were unprepared, and so he decided to focus his full attention on you. That was how you came under his effect. He focused nearly his full psychic ability upon you. Raja knew the others were incapacitated for the moment and he could do that. It is why they were able to recover more quickly; they hadn't been assaulted like you had, even though they were more susceptible."

I think about that for a moment and then ask, my voice cracking slightly as I say, "It isn't like I've had an easy life. My parents disowned me and never want to see me. What if he just sensed that and decided I was an easy mark for his powers?"

Solarcoon's eyes widen in surprise before the burly raccoon squeezes my shoulder tenderly, "Your parents kicked you out, Ted?"

"Yeah," I sigh. "Three years ago. And, well, they didn't really kick me out. I was living on my own by then."

"I can see why Raja had such a dramatic effect upon you then. He took advantage of that part of your life," Solarcoon nods his head. There is a quiet moment, where I expect him to ask why my parents would disown me, but he doesn't.

Then I look up and ask, "How could you fight him? How come he didn't affect you?"

Solarcoon leans back in his chair and looks at me for a moment before saying, "I truly have no idea."

"But you looked like you knew exactly what you were doing," I look at him in surprise.

"I've faced Raja Raksha before. I learned the first time we crossed paths that for whatever reason my sunglow seems to disrupt his effects. I don't know why. Stratagem hasn't figured out why, either. To all scans and studies it's just natural sunlight being released when I do that. It works though."

"That's just it, Bill," I say using Solarcoon's real name for once. I've barely ever done that here in the Bunker; it is hard to call him by his real name when surrounded by the trappings of his heroism. I found it hard enough whenever I visited him at his home. How can you do that to a guy you respect and admire? A guy who has saved so many and helped found and lead the Extraordinaries. I had a poster in my bedroom of him when I was a teen. "How did you beat him without your powers? After your radiance effect you didn't have any, right?"

"You assume," Solarcoon says. "I might have had some internal power left within me. Enough to resist."

"Maybe," I say nodding.

Solarcoon sighs and continues, "But the truth is that Raja Raksha feeds on depression and sadness. He was already feeding on the team and the surrounding population when he arrived, drawing in enough ambient power to make his shadows appear. Those can only manifest after he has drawn in enough strife. When I broke that effect it left him weak and unable to muster a true defense. I was lucky. I was in a position to muscle through his attempts to start a second round of control. I know how to deal with him and fight through his memory distortions."

I sip on my coffee and we're both silent for a while. I take my own mask off and brush at my eyes. My fur feels caked from my tears as I sigh finally, saying, "He just shook me up."

"He does that to everyone. I'll be talking to Glacier as well about this. Metalyena told me what he thinks Glacier might have remembered. I can assure you what he was seeing was probably worse than what you saw, he just wasn't as brutally assaulted with the same force as you were. You both need to learn that what happened was not your fault, that you're not weak for having these feelings, and that feeling that way is not the whole story."

"I know," I nod and say, but it is hard to believe it.

"I'm not sure you do," says Solarcoon looking at me now. "Tell me, Ted, when I got rid of Raja's shadows did you remember anything? Anything important?"

I look up surprised and nod at that. I wonder if I should say what as I remember that rush from remembering Jay.

"Raja Raksha had you forget those memories that give balance and context. His shadows do it unconsciously. He doesn't even truly know what is in your mind he just does it," Solarcoon explains. "If I may ask a personal question, was it your Alpha?"

I blush at that as I worriedly say, "Yeah."

Solarcoon nods, "I thought as much. You know I haven't looked into your file to find out who this is or how they are related to you. I don't want to do that unless it is necessary. As I understand the scuttlebutt you want it to remain private."

"Yeah, I do," I say looking up at Solarcoon. "I really do."

"Whoever this is they made an impression on Holly. She spoke highly of the encounter and I hear this person threw himself over her when Power Puma appeared," Solarcoon says with a smile. Then more seriously, "It is okay to tell us, Ted. Whoever this is sounds like a good addition to your life."

"He did?" I ask surprised looking up.

"He?" Solarcoon quirks an eyebrow. "Odd, Holly never said he. Well yes, I suppose he did."

Oh no, I really can't do anything right. Holly was covering for me and I just blew it. I blush further as I try to move the conversation along, "I, um, didn't know."

Solarcoon nods, "I wish you had told us that he would have been there."

"I thought that the team doesn't approve of these meetings," I say

"We don't, not technically," Solarcoon says with a slight smile. "But I learned a long time ago that if Holly wants to accomplish something she'll find her own way. Elizabeth Clay is the same way and those two wanted to keep the meetings going. They would have found a way and they'd drag everyone else along for the ride. We just take extra precautions. It would have helped to know he was there so we could intervene if needed."

"Why do you keep all that a secret? I mean, I heard about Lizz Clay from Titan Tomcat and he told me that when we were on that mission in Alberta. It was like some sort of rumor. He just mentioned her and the meetings. Then Metalyena brought up the same thing. Why didn't you all just tell me you wanted to know if my Alpha was going? I would have told," I say glaring at Solarcoon. I'm actually not sure about that last part. I'm a little angry at him and I'm not sure why.

"Did anyone tell you how those meetings began?" Solarcoon asks me his voice tinged with regret.

"I don't think so," I say honestly as we look at each other. "Everybody just whispers about them. I don't even know if Paul knows about them."

Solarcoon grunts and nods before taking a sip of his coffee. Thinking for a moment he puts his mug down on the table and then looks at me directly, "They started a while ago. Not when the team formed but a few years later, before we lost Swiftwolf. At the time it was Elizabeth's doing. She enjoyed her investigations and playing herself against Stratagem. They both enjoyed the challenge. He kept snuffing out the meetings and stopping contacts between the Alphas. It was his way of trying to protect our families. She felt differently. It was a game to both of them I think, the brilliant investigator against the super smart strategist."

"How could any meetings occur with Stratagem set against them?" I ask genuinely confused.

"Elizabeth and Holly have their ways. Lizz is a brilliant thinker at times. She has a way of finding ways around problems that others would never think of, not even Stratagem. Holly has her own ways of doing things. Together the two had some luck," Solarcoon explains. With a sigh he continues, "Then The Stranger died."

"Oh," is all I can say. Bill and the other founders don't talk about The Stranger much. I wish I had known Nicolas Clay, but he died before I even put on a mask. Yet, his death has had such a lingering effect on those who were his teammates. Swiftwolf died alone, fighting his arch enemy. Every one of the founders believes if they had gotten there sooner they could have helped him. I know Solarcoon blames himself for the white wolf's death. He's said as much in the past. It's why there are rules about warning the team when you go up against a supervillain, so the rest of us can come to the person in danger's aid. With The Stranger it was different. The team had all been there, only, Dr. Schmetterling had ensured every team member was incapacitated. When The Stranger died, his teammates had watched helplessly.

"It was a dark time for the Extraordinaries, but it was much worse for Elizabeth." Solarcoon continues, his voice very quiet, "Lizz nearly fell apart from it. Suddenly those meetings became a lot more important. Adam, Brian, Diane, Stuart, they were all shoulders for her to cry upon." Solarcoon is pensive, obviously thinking about the months after Stranger's death. "Holly though, she rose above anything anyone else did. She was there for Lizz in ways… well, I don't want to go into it in full but the two became a lot closer. I think it helped pull Elizabeth back from the brink after seeing the man she loved die, helped her focus on her children again."

"But what does that have to do with the meetings?" I ask a little confused. "She knew all of them personally, didn't she?"

"Stratagem was still dead set against them you see, Ted," Solarcoon says. "Despite the obvious help they were giving Lizz he felt they were too much of a security risk. In fact he became even more adamant after Stranger's death. More interested in protection."

"But what changed his mind?" I ask.

"Nothing. He just doesn't know they happen."

"What? The master of strategy doesn't know about that?" I feel my eyes widen at the very idea. The implications are mind boggling to say the least.

"After Stranger died we took a vote and decided to allow these meetings despite his protests. After all, what if Holly needed the same kind of help one day? I couldn't remove that kind of support."

"Yeah," I nod thinking back to what Jay said about the meetings. When Bill says it the value starts becoming more apparent. I'm starting to feel a little shame for not apologizing to Jay and making up after the fight. "My Alpha said the same thing."

"We decided then to keep it a secret. To redirect Stratagem away from the truth," Solarcoon says with some distaste. He never did like conspiracies or lies. "Support the meetings to some extent and organize a more secret defense ourselves."

"You don't seem to like it much," I say at last, sipping my coffee.

"I don't but the vote was final," Solarcoon says. "And I don't want to deprive Holly of support if something were to happen to me."

All I can do is nod at that.

"It would have been good for you to trust us with that information," Solarcoon says at last. "That your mysterious Alpha would be there, I mean. You'll have to forgive me not telling you sooner about that aspect. I didn't know Lizz would work so quickly and you're the first hero to have a new Alpha since we decided to allow these meetings under the table."

"Camo said the same thing," I comment nodding my head slowly. "Well, I mean about telling you."

"Ah," Solarcoon grunts and then his eyes light up with recognition. "Is this the reason you two have been having trouble?"

"Mostly," I mumble.

"I'll talk to him, Star Coyote. I think you've learned your lesson."

"I'm sorry, Solarcoon. I swear I am," I say pleadingly looking up at him. "But you don't have to do that; Camo and I need to work this out ourselves. We can't have you solving our problems"

Solarcoon just nods, "Alright. I understand that, Star Coyote."

I smile at him and it feels good to sit there and talk to him as we sip coffee. I ask him then with a smile, "How are the kids?"

"Well, the boys are little terrors," Solarcoon says with a smile. "But all boys are at that age. They keep getting into things, last week they tried to make a trashcan soap box racer, and they're climbing about looking for their next adventure. I'm just glad we have that park nearby and the school offers sports teams. Holly and I will probably lose our minds keeping them under control. I shudder to think what they'll be like as teenagers."

I chuckle at that. I remember when I was assigned to watch them. The triplets are a pretty big handful and they know how to gang up on their parents a bit, even if one of their parents has superpowers. It is even worse when they get their bracelets off and can use their own powers.

"Jenny, though," Solarcoon shakes his head with some mirth. "Well, she's just shooting up. I remember when she was still playing with dolls and now she wants to get her ears pierced and wear makeup. She keeps bringing up boys now, too."

I laugh at that and grin, "Get used to it. Little Daydream is going to be an adult one day soon."

"Not sure I approve of that," Solarcoon says with a wider smile as he thinks of his children. He always looks so proud when he talks about them. I get the feeling that when he dresses up in his uniform he's doing it for them. "Heaven help me if she ever wants to put a costume on."

"Would that be so bad?" I ask quirking an ear.

"Would you want to see your daughter gallivanting abut in a costume like Force Vixen's and putting herself in danger? Or leered at by men twice her age? What father wants that?" Solarcoon asks with a calm logical tone. "Tell me something, Ted. You know my family so well, why don't you want me to know more about your friend?"

I look up at the big raccoon and sigh trying to think of an answer. I don't want to tell him and I don't know why. No, that is a lie. I know why, Raja Raksha proved that fact. I still feel what I used to feel before I met Jay, like I'm broken and wrong. I never stopped believing that. Is that why I've tried so hard to keep it a secret? Shame? Am I actually ashamed of my collie? Am I ashamed of loving my amazing Jay? I shudder and look up at Solarcoon, and a wave of all those emotions I felt when my Dad found out comes over me, threatening to overwhelm me. "I just don't right now," is all I can manage to say.

Solarcoon looks at me, his face concerned and the dark band of fur over his eyes making him look stern. "Star, you know you can trust me, trust this team, with your life. You've saved our lives—my life, before and I've saved yours, we've saved yours. You were the one who led us to victory in Sao Paulo when we fought Veneo only a short time ago."

I know he is right, but I just rest my face in my right paw and lean on the table refusing to look at him, "This isn't the right time, Solarcoon, sir. I just can't explain it now."

"You're still feeling the effects of Raja Raksha aren't you?" he asks carefully.

"Maybe I am," I say avoiding his gaze, "Or maybe he just underlined something for me."

Solarcoon doesn't say anything as he looks at me while we sit there silently sipping our coffee. He finally says, "Ted, be very careful how you think about all this. Raja can warp perceptions. His point of view isn't the only way to look at the world, but if you let him he can make you think it is."

"Yeah," I nod and then drink the last dregs of my coffee. I get up from the table, "I'm going to head back to Portland, okay?"

"Of course," Solarcoon says putting on his sunglasses. "Going to get cleaned up before hand?"

"Yeah," I nod with an attempt at a smile. "I will. A hot shower sounds great and it will be late when I get back to Portland at this rate. Better to do it now and then take a nice leisurely flight back."

Solarcoon laughs, "Still hate the teleporter then?"

"Don't tell Stratagem," I say with a smile as I leave the apartment and walk down the smooth hallways. My boots hitting the metallic floor making soft tap taps as I walk. I feel like a coward for not telling Solarcoon right then and there. He was asking and he already knew so much. I feel ashamed of myself for chickening out, angry for feeling anything bad about Jay. Why hadn't Jay told me about him trying to protect Holly? Have we really been drifting that much in the past few days that he couldn't tell me something so important?

The locker room is like it always is, and I can hear a shower going and see the steam wafting about the room just as much as I feel it. I hear someone humming a catchy pop tune. Metalyena always sings in the shower and his deep voice carries, even though the shower makes him sound like some teeny bopper. The big hyena does love his pop rock. I'm probably going to need a full dose of Joni Mitchell soon to get the tune out of my head.

Glacier is pulling some boxers up as I enter the room. He turns and nods as I walk over to my locker. He's already taken a shower and his fur look even fluffier, if that's possible, from the fur driers. He looks tense and distracted. I open up my locker and pull off my mask, blinking my eyes. The lights feel so bright right now.

"Hey, Ted?" Glacier asks and I turn around. He really shouldn't stand around in only his boxers. He's always been so confident about this stuff and unperturbed even though he knows about me now, he still acts the same. He was uncomfortable before but now, after he met Jay, I guess he's okay enough with everything.

"Yeah, Paul?" I ask pulling my uniform off a bit and looking at my toiletries kit.

"We were on the roof earlier. You said something about Camo knowing," he says as I look in the locker now. I had forgotten about all that it seemed so long ago.

"Yeah," I say after a pause as I turn and look at Paul, my top off but leggings still on. "He, well, he saw me kiss Jay."

"Oh shoot," Paul's eyes widen. "Not good at all. How did he react?"

I hear a shower turn off but with quirk of my ear I know another one is running and I can hear that hum from Metalyena so I know he is still in there. I guess someone else is cleaning up as well.

"Not very well," I say truthfully. "There was a lot of yelling."

"Oh dude that sucks," he says his face looking more than a little forlorn. "I never thought he'd react badly. Was this at the latest Alpha meeting?"

"Heard about them then? Well, yeah, Camo didn't react positively," I nod my head and sigh. "He threatened me with a file for suspension."

"He what!" shouts Paul angrily, his eyes glowing now and I feel a wave of cold hit me the temperature dropping like a rock as the steam in the air disappears. Glacier is drawing heat in from his lack of control. Before I can respond or clarify, the muscular husky turns and heads towards the shower room door. I turn to stop him and as bad luck would have it Camo is leaving the shower room at that moment, a towel draped around his waist. The jaguar is still limping and he doesn't even see Paul rushing him.

Camo doesn't have time to react as suddenly, and very forcefully, Glacier grabs him and slams him against the lockers with one paw. The husky's muscled body is taut with anger as he growls at Camo roughly pinning the jaguar.

"You arrogant jerk!" Paul yells loudly, his free hand balling into a fist.

"Glacier! What the hell are you doing?" Camo gasps struggling in Paul's grip, both paws on the husky's arm, pushing at him impotently.

"What the fuck is wrong with you?" Glacier growls slamming a fist through the locker next to Camo's head. "No really; what the fuck is wrong with you?"

"I have no idea what you're talking about!" Camo gasps in pain. "Let go!"

I'm already running at Glacier, warming up to pull him off the jaguar as I shout, "Paul, let him go!"

Before I get there Metalyena, sans mask and anything else, is beside them both, his fur dripping wet as he grab's the husky's arm, stopping him from hitting the pinned jaguar, "Glacier! Stop it! Camo isn't super strong. Let him go!"

"That would be the point," Glacier says his eyes flashing and glowing as he glares at Camo. "How dare you threaten, Star Coyote. I should freeze that perfect pearly white smile right off your face."

"Threaten Star?" Metalyena asks confusedly, looking between all of us. "Threaten him with what?"

"Suspension," Camo growls struggling in Glacier's grip. The word makes the husky growl louder and I can see his hand twitching, his hold getting tighter, "Is that what this is about, you big slushball?"

"Glacier, stop it!" I say worriedly, pulling at Paul's arm, but unless I use my power I can't budge the dog. "You'll kill him! Let him go!"

"No, Ted! No one else gets threatened on my watch," Glacier says with another growl. "No one else uses their authority against a friend of mine without me having a say so. Not anymore. Not like Kevin."

"Paul!" Metalyena says angrily as he shifts his position and uses his other arm to push against the muscled sled dog. Metalyena might be amazingly strong in his metal form but even when flesh and fur he's stronger than most of us, and he uses that super strength now to his advantage. The effect is enough to push Paul back a few steps. As he stumbles, Glacier lets go of the jaguar, who falls to his feet and then knees as Camo's leg gives out from under him. Metalyena stands between the two of them as I move from behind Glacier to do the same. I can't believe he just attacked Camo. I didn't do anything again. I start to say something, but Metalyena is already talking over me, stopping my train of thought, "I know you're angry and I know that Raja Raksha messed with you. He got all of us. But someone had better explain to me what just happened. Right now!"

"It is because of me," I explain. "I was telling Paul about what happened a few weeks ago and why Camo and I were on shaky ground."

"A few weeks ago?" Metalyena quirks and eye and looks between all of us. The big hyena's presence is having a calming effect on the room. "A few weeks ago was, what? Nothing. Okay we have a few pop ups of supervillany but nothing major. Outside of the incident with Power Puma and the Alphas... Wait. Ted, did your Alpha go there?"

"Yes, he did," Camo growls threateningly, but I think that's just because he's scared. The jaguar is crouched defensively away from Glacier behind the big hyena as he shakily stands back up.

"Why would you threaten suspension over that, Wally?" Metalyena says using Camo's real name. "What could Star and his boyfriend possibly do to warrant that?"

"Wait, what?" Glacier voices my surprise as we all stare at Metalyena. Even Camo seems surprised at that.

Metalyena looks between all of us, "Sorry, I assumed everyone here knew." The big hyena's face betrays nothing but confusion.

"Um, I guess we all did," I say surprised at how incredibly casual Metalyena is being. "I told Glacier a while back and Camo saw us together. How did you know?"

"Oh I looked in the records when Stratagem entered him into the files. I mean it is open to all of us and he does note the relationship right?" Metalyena says, and he really looks as confused as I feel. "Titan Tomcat and I both feel that it is important to know who the Alphas are before something happens that requires us to defend them. Besides, I don't like that sort of thing being secret."

"You've known all this time," I say in utter surprise looking at Metalyena. He never let on for even a moment, "Titan knows too?"

"Yeah," Metal nods looking between all of us, not at all shocked or surprised, perfectly nonchalant about it. "I just figured it was your business to bring it up when you felt comfortable with it. Titan said the same thing. Okay, it was a little annoying that you didn't feel you could trust us with this information but it isn't a big deal. It isn't like you aren't the same hero I've known for years. Who saved my shiny furry butt from the Technowitches? You. I figure you earned some leeway."

"Not a big deal?" Camo grouses. "Tell that to some international groups that will have problems with it, Kyle."

"What? You really did threaten him with suspension over this?" Metalyena turns and looks at Camo angrily. "Really? Over this? Wally, what the hell? You've always been fine with gay guys. Hell you know for a fact your posters and calendars sell more in The Castro and Greenwich than anywhere else. You work in a publishing company and head a popular fashion magazine."

"It isn't that," snorts Camo angrily. "Damn it, will everyone just stop assuming I'm some sort of homophobe? Yeah, okay it irritates me when people assume I'm gay because of my powers or my costume, and yes, a gay team member will only add to the stupid rumors. I'm angry because he didn't tell us so we could prepare. Good press on this sort of thing has to be planned out well in advance and our team is already on thin ice with half a dozen nations, none of which are exactly enlightened on this matter. It wasn't over the fact he's gay that I threatened suspension, it was over the damn stupid fact that he was kissing his boyfriend in the open on a rooftop in New York with his frickin' mask on!"

"You were what?" Glacier says surprised looking at me. "Damn, Ted, I thought you were better than that!"

"Look it was just a momentary lapse. I've never done something like that before. It just fit the moment okay, I wasn't thinking," I try to defend myself but really there isn't much of a defense. I can feel my face growing hot as Metalyena and Glacier look at me.

"Clearly," Camo says acidly.

"Alright everyone calm down," Metalyena says. "Now we're going to talk this out calmly and no one is going to punch a hole in anything else. Am I clear?"

"Yes, though perhaps you should put some pants on," says voice from the front of the locker room I turn with everyone else and standing there is Solarcoon and Stratagem. The raccoon and badger look seriously angry.

"What?" Metalyena asks and then looking down I think he suddenly realizes he's been naked and soaking wet this entire time. To be fair, I hadn't really registered that he was giving us all a show either. Metalyena rolls his eyes, "Sorry, sir. I'll get dressed."

"Good," says Stratagem. "Perhaps then one of you can explain why there is a hole in my locker and what this commotion was about."

"I'll do that," Metalyena says as he opens up his locker after grabbing a towel.

"Yes, I think that would be best," Solarcoon folds his arms and glares at Glacier, Camo, and I. "Obviously you were the one to break up whatever was going on."

"Yes he was, Solarcoon," Glacier says. "And, um, sorry if I broke anything in your locker, Stratagem."

"We will talk in the meeting room," Stratagem says coolly. "The three of you should get dressed as well. We will send someone to get you."

Metalyena gets dressed quickly and is out the door with Solarcoon and Stratagem, and I've forgotten completely about getting a shower at this point. Everyone is quiet as we sit on the benches away from each other. Camo stewing and glaring at the both of us. Glacier seems lost in his thoughts as I sit down. It feels like some weird combination of waiting for the principal and for my Dad to come home.

Titan Tomcat comes for us over an hour later and glares at all three of us without saying anything before leading us to the meeting room. Lady Leopard, Solarcoon, and Stratagem are sitting on one side the table with the burly raccoon in the middle, and all the other chairs have been removed. Metalyena is standing off to the side and Titan does the same thing. The setup makes the meeting room look less like a conference room and more like a judge's panel.

"Force Vixen had already headed back to Los Angeles before the altercation in the locker room otherwise she would be here as well," Lady Leopard says, her voice perfectly calm, "as it is very rare for us to have to take a disciplinary action against team mates."

"Though in this case it seems warranted," says Solarcoon, his expression hard to read. As the three of us stand there he continues, "Obviously Raja Raksha's attack has left us all on edge. Glacier, I realize that Raja brought up painful memories but lashing out at your teammates is highly irresponsible and completely unacceptable as an Extraordinary."

"Yes, sir," Glacier says as he stands there, staring back at the three founders.

"Attacking a teammate and threatening his life, especially when that teammate does not have super strength or an adequate method of self defense is deplorable and against every rules of our organization," Stratagem says. "Even if you felt it was reasonable, such an altercation is highly dangerous."

"You must understand." Lady Leopard is calm and her voice is less harsh than the others but there is an edge to it. "If we begin to fight amongst ourselves we endanger much more than the team. The only true defense we have against the myriad of threats we face and the pressures to accomplish good and help others is our ability to work as a team."

"Which is why team cohesiveness and unity are so important to us," Solarcoon says. "We can not have fighting within our ranks. Glacier, you are an excellent member of the team and you've often risen to challenges far above what is expected of you. We can not ignore what has happened, mind altering effects of Raja included. If you ever attack another team mate or threaten a team mate's life you will be removed from the team."

Glacier gasps and grimaces looking at the three members then nods, "Yes, sirs, ma'am." I'm just as shocked by the idea as he is; no one has ever actually been kicked off the team. Not even Omni was when she crippled Baron Xanadu; she retired on her own.

"Camo," Lady Leopard continues looking at the jaguar, "Metalyena gave us the basic facts of the situation. Your behavior in this is as much to blame as Glacier's is."

"He was hesitant to speak about the details of why you and Star were arguing or what could have caused you to threaten him with suspension." Stratagem continues for her. "I do wonder at any situation that would cause Star Coyote to come to New York without him alerting you, and Power Puma would certainly warrant such a warning. Unless of course his…" Stratagem trails off mid sentence, his fingers twitching slightly. We're all used to Stratagem being about twelve steps ahead of everyone it is disconcerting seeing him sitting there thinking. He's glances at me for a moment, but he seems to realize he's stopped mid-sentence and continues, "However, Lady Leopard's super hearing confirmed everything Metalyena said about the altercation."

Lady Leopard twitches an ear and the snow leopardess gives me a look. She knows everything. The woman can hear a pin drop a mile away, and we were shouting just down the hall. She had to have heard it all. Solarcoon continues where Stratagem left off. "She has stated that the details do not matter to the case. Camo, I'm surprised at you and more than a little angry. Threatening another teammate with suspension is not good behavior or leadership. Further, it is not even within your rights or privileges as an Extraordinary. You can file a complaint but you do not have the right to suspend any member. That is left to the group to decide."

"Threatening a teammate in that way is deplorable," Lady Leopard lectures her words chosen carefully as she looks at the jaguar with the full force of her personality. "No matter what he has done or how irresponsibly he behaves. We have methods to deal with infractions. As a more senior member you set an example for your teammates." She continues to calmly lecture the jaguar about how he should have handled the situation, but I don't really hear what she says. My attention has been drawn to Stratagem.

Stratagem doesn't seem to be paying attention to her either. He's leaned forward now obviously lost in thought while everyone else is looking at Camo and Lady Leopard. I don't think they have noticed. I, however, can't look away from Stratagem. He seems lost and confused, his normally steely controlled expression caught in a strange look. The badger even turns his chair slightly away from the group. Then he does something I never thought I'd see him do. He takes off his goggles. Just takes them off and rubs the bridge of his nose.

I'm flabbergasted. I've never seen him without his goggles. I hear a gasp from behind me. I think Titan Tomcat has spotted what's happened, but Stratagem just seems to be thinking, as if no one else was even there. I watch as he takes out a blue hankie and starts to rub the lenses. I had a professor in my environmental studies class who did the same thing. Stratagem looks just like that, like a professor lost in thought. He glances at me, again, staring at me with those oddly golden eyes before putting goggles back on. When the badger turns back to the group his steely composure is back, as much like a mask as his goggles are.

"And we mete out those methods as a group," Solarcoon is saying, drawing me back to the conversation at hand. "We watch each other's back, but we do not act as the keepers of each other. Consider yourself lucky that you are on medical leave for the next week to heal from the fight. Otherwise, I'd personally take more drastic actions regarding this."

"Medical leave for damage that was incurred upon yourself for reckless behavior I might add," Stratagem says tapping a claw on the table with a hint of irritation in his voice. "Three supervillains at once because of personal issues with another teammate is a ridiculous reason to get hurt and a fine way to get yourself killed or worse."

"We do not want another incident like Omni," Solarcoon says, missing what Stratagem is doing or how strangely he is suddenly acting. "We do not go after supervillains alone when we can have teammates at our side. I realize we often defend our home towns and surrounding areas by ourselves but there is no reason to take such risks when a teammate is on hand to handle a situation. The two of you could have handled Therma, Lux and Ms. Q and then easily dealt with Slipstream afterwards. You are the more experienced member between you and Star Coyote; he looks to you for guidance and leadership and you set a very poor example"

"Yes, sir," Camo says looking deeply chagrined and embarrassed.

"As for you, Star Coyote," Solarcoon says looking directly at me now. "I can honestly say I am surprised. When the two of us talked earlier I thought we had come to good conclusion on the situation. You planned to apologize to Camo and work the situation out without my help or official team mediation."

"Yes, sir, I know," I nod.

"No, apparently you don't," Solarcoon says angrily. "Instead of apologizing you instead gossip with Glacier."

"Sir, that really isn't fair. Ted didn't," Glacier begins to say but Solarcoon gives him a withering stare and Glacier shuts up.

He turns and looks at me again, "Star, we can not balkanize ourselves into factions. We must be a team. I have said this before, but I do not think you understood me. One of the worst things for our team dynamics is for our members to become split along lines of gossip. You're lucky nothing worse happened."

"Yes, sir," is all I can say, his stare boring into me.

Solarcoon's face softens a bit as he looks at all of us, "I think we've all had a very long day. I suggest we truly adjourn for now, I have monitor duty tonight. Everyone return to your homes and rest. Try and not go out for a day or two in uniform if possible. We've all been stretched the past month, tonight more than ever."

I look up surprised at what the raccoon is saying. I'm not getting punished? I have to say something, "Solarcoon, wait." I nearly shout, "What are you doing?"

"Calling this meeting to an end," Solarcoon says calmly. "Punishment has been meted out and we need to move on so we can work as a team."

"But I caused all of this," I say plaintively.

"Star, that isn't true," begins Lady Leopard but I stop paying attention to her as I look about the room. All my teammates are looking at me.

My best friend, Glacier is staring at me with an open mouth now. I've gotten him in so much trouble. He nearly killed Camo because of what I told him. He'll be thrown off the team if something like this happens again. What the hell is wrong with me? I betrayed his trust.

I glance at Stratagem and I realize what he was thinking when he became so distracted. He put the pieces together about the meetings and the Alphas; there was no way he couldn't have. It's the only reason I would have been in New York. I just revealed a secret Solarcoon trusted me with less than an hour ago. I've caused Stratagem to learn about it. I've hurt the team. I've betrayed Solarcoon's trust. I've hurt Stratagem's trust in the team. Camo doesn't trust me now. Even Metalyena's trust in Camo has been shaken by this. I'm threatening everything. All by being who and what I am, all by kissing Jay.

"No, it is true," I say looking back at the table. "I caused all of this." Looking up at everyone, "I'm responsible and I'm hurting the team because of who I am."

"Ted," Glacier says resting a paw on my shoulder, "Calm down man."

"No," I say shaking my head, brushing away the big husky's paw. "Don't you all see? I've screwed up. I'm screwed up. I'm hurting all of us by being here. I'm causing secrets to get revealed, and I'm breaking promises."

"Ted, that isn't true," Metalyena says, his voice trying to soothe me. "You can't believe that."

"Why can't I? Look at the evidence. Camo is hurt, Glacier is nearly kicked off the team and we're all here, doing this." I say almost desperately, "I can't even fight back against the Maharaja of Madness." I watch Stratagem's face. I don't want to bring up what I've done to the badger's trust as I continue, "I'm not right for the team."

Solarcoon's paws curl, and he looks at me with a hard stare, "Star Coyote, what are you saying exactly."

"I'm saying that I'm the screw up here. You should be punishing me, not them. That I shouldn't be on the team." There, I said it. I was honest. Despite every secret I've been keeping, this I can say. I've always wondered if I was right for the team and tonight proved I'm not cut out for this.

"Are you tending your resignation?" Stratagem asks coolly, and everyone looks startled at that. I hear Titan Tomcat cuss and Metalyena's face looks really worried now.

"Yes," I say, looking from the badger to Solarcoon. "Yes, I want to resign."

Solarcoon looks at me as everyone gets quiet, his face impossible to read. He's the team leader when you get down to it, what he says goes. His face has gone very still. He takes a few deep breaths, his sunglasses glinting until he finally says, "I'm not accepting resignations today, Ted. Nor will I accept yours any time in the foreseeable future."

"But," I begin to say but Solarcoon waves his hand.

"No. It is obvious you're under a lot of stress and the effects of Raja Raksha have only exacerbated it. I refuse to accept your resignation when you are under obvious mental duress"

"I'm inclined to agree," Lady Leopard says softly. "I do not believe your resignation is appropriate to the situation."

"I concur," Titan Tomcat says from the back. "We won't let you leave like this, Ted. You're our friend and our teammate."

"Yeah." Glacier says, "C'mon buddy calm down." He looks really worried now, and I can just imagine why. I must look a mess right now, but somehow that fits. I've messed up so much tonight resigning in a tattered costume seems appropriate.

"No, you don't understand," I say firmly looking at all of them. "I always promised myself if I caused trouble in the locker room, or with the team cohesion I would leave." I can see the look in Glacier and Metalyena's eyes as they realize why I would take this so seriously. "I am causing trouble. Everything that happened tonight is my fault. I can't stay."

Solarcoon stands up to his full height and looks at me. "Alright, Ted, I hear what you're saying. It seems obvious to me, though, that you are making a rash decision." The burly raccoon looks really upset now. I know he has trouble accepting when someone quits something, and he doesn't understand why I'm doing this. "I am not going to see you resign but you can't function on the team feeling this way."

"Bill," Lady Leopard says her voice soft as she looks up, "Star Coyote is obviously having a rough time dealing with Raja's after effects. Let's all try and remain calm."

"Of course, my Lady," Solarcoon says easily, and he visibly calms himself before looking at me. "Star, I'm going to grant you a leave of absence. I want you to take some time off. No Extraordinary business. Keep your communicator, you are still a member of this team, but I urge you to take a true break from being a hero and think about things and regain your composure. Contact us when you feel ready to resume active duty."

I jerk my head in a nod and turn to leave the room. I can feel everyone's eyes on me. I feel Glacier's paw tighten on my shoulder for a moment and then let go as I walk away. I leave the bunker quickly, I don't even return to my locker to change out of my ruined uniform. I just need to get out. I'm at the hatch to the outside world in moments. I take off down the tunnel that leads underground for a few miles away from the base and then I'm flying in the night air. Tonight not even the cool night air and flying can make things better.

Chapter 9
Homefront

It isn't that late when the phone rings. I glance up from my dinner and I quickly grab the phone. A part of me wants it to be Ted calling, telling me he'll be home soon—that he got delayed by something, like he used to before the incident in New York City. He's barely talked to me for the past three weeks. Another part of me wants to not answer the phone to spite him, to go out on the town with Gary and Brandon and forget about him and just let it ring.

I answer the phone on the second ring and the voice says, "Jay?" but it's not Ted.

It's Adam Fairchild, the fiancé of Force Vixen. He seems like a nice guy and he's called once or twice since the meeting. He's sort of my official contact since we're in the same time zone. He's how I let the rest of the family members know about the confrontation with Camo.

"Adam," I try to sound congenial but I think a hint of disappointment slips into my voice, "How are you?"

"Doing well, just concerned about what is going on in Minneapolis," he says. "Thought I'd check in with you and see what you knew."

"Minneapolis?" I turn and quickly turn on the TV. Did my coyote not even tell me? I thought he would at least tell me if he was leaving the state for Extraordinary business.

"Yes," Adam's voice slows slightly and I hear a hint of concern. "He didn't tell you, did he?"

I look at the TV and see a breaking news report about the supervillains attack. An armored convoy or something is being targeted, but the Extraordinaires were on the scene immediately. I answer Adam a bit more resigned than anything else, "No."

The fox sighs a bit, and I can tell he tried to do it in a way I couldn't hear over the phone. "Turn on channel seven." We sit in silence for a moment as I turn to the channel he's watching, and then we watch the news together for a while, separated by a thousand miles but connected by our secrets and this television stations overly perky anchorwoman. "This fight is insane you realize. So he got found out, this isn't a big deal," Adam says irritably. "I wish you'd just let me talk to Emma or Bill. Let us try and work this out."

"You guys have already done enough," I say, and it's true. The other family members have done a lot to help. I know that Diane said something to Camo or did something to ensure he wouldn't talk about me to the rest of the team. I sit down in front of the TV, the worry welling up inside of me. Is Ted going to be okay? Who is he fighting? "I messed up though and we need to work this out ourselves"

"I suppose so," Adam says. "Well look, this thing in the twin cities, it isn't anything. They'll be fine. It's just jitters on my part."

I see gouts of green flame leap up over some buildings. The news crews cannot get close enough to view what is exactly going on because the police are keeping them a safe distance away. This means I can't even see if Ted is in trouble. I finally force my voice to sound calming as I say, "Yeah I know. If it was, Ted would have told me he was going even if we are fighting. Besides, he has Emma there and she's more than capable."

"Don't I know it," Adam states but I can hear it in his voice; concern for the vixen. "She'll be okay, I hope."

"I know she will," I say with a smile, forcing myself to be cheerful. "She is forceful after all."

"Yeah," Adam sighs with worry, and I have to admit I am worried too. At least now I can talk over the phone with some else like this. That makes the watching easier than before. The news team is talking about how several of the Extraordinaries who had coordinated things with the authorities beforehand were not on scene, and the graphic of Solarcoon and Stratagem's masked faces with question marks over their faces seems unnecessarily dramatic to me. I wonder out loud, "Where are Bill and Samuel?"

"Khazakstan," Adam says, calmly "along with Jane, David and Karl. The news channels aren't covering that as much but there's some giant robot attacking there. Wally and Kyle are with Ted though."

I see a blue energy blast into the sky, "Paul too, I suppose."

"Yep," Adam says. The camera angles change and we're watching two figures flying through the sky. They're moving very quickly but I know one of them. I recognize the blue costume and the outline easily enough. I watch as Ted chases the other figure across the city skyline, and the camera man has trouble keeping them in the shot. The news quickly identifies both of them. The villain is Slipstream, and the reporters downplay him as Star Coyote snags him. Okay, not a dangerous guy, just a thief who can fly. Ted has him well in hand. At least he wasn't in the fight where green flames are shooting up. Adam says over the phone, "Nice catch, I'm surprised he didn't rip his leg off. These super strong guys always seem to know how much force to put behind their grabs."

I don't comment on that outside of a grunt and a nod as I watch Ted drag the hare back to the fight. I may like Adam a lot, but there is no reason to explain Ted's actual powers if the fox doesn't already know them. I'll keep Ted's secrets even if I might not like being one of them. I see Ted land back where the others obviously are with the jack rabbit in tow. The media is saying it is all clear and the criminal contingent has been fully defeated.

Adam sighs happily when they make that announcement, "Okay, that wasn't too bad. At least it wasn't a big badinskie."

I chuckle and sigh relieved as well, "Yeah. Ted looked like he did a good job, too."

"He's a pretty capable guy, you know," Adam says. "One of the best on the team if you give him a few years."

I have to laugh at that, "If he ever learns to think out what he's doing."

Adam guffaws and then says more seriously, "Look, Jay, I'm sorry the meetings caused trouble with you two."

"They didn't," I answer. "This has been trouble brewing between us for a while over this. He's still unsure what he wants and I'm still not used to this stuff. Worrying over him, watching him fight on the television, and keeping secrets like this? It isn't easy."

"Doesn't get any easier," Adam says with an air of truth. "Trust me. I wish it did."

"That is just it. I'm not sure how I can adjust to this, it makes me edgy. As much as I've been trying to accept it all this, it is a lot to take in. It doesn't help that Ted doesn't want to be honest with the team about me. That just complicates the entire thing. Wally's reaction did not help either."

"Wally is an ass," Adam says dismissively. "He's a spoiled rich guy who thinks he is always right."

"Well, yeah," I nod. "Even Diane says that. But it doesn't help that he was sort of right to criticize us. We shouldn't have been so open while he was in costume, especially if Ted wants to keep this all a secret."

"I don't think he even realizes the trouble he has caused you," Adam says and then I hear him click out for a moment. "Aw shoot, someone is calling through. Probably a client from the Center needing hand holding. I'll be back in a jiff."

I hold the phone to my ear as I watch the TV. There is some chatter about how the criminals will be locked up in a state penitentiary. How prisons in Minnesota aren't really prepared for super criminals. Some talk about extradition to a more secure holding system in Illinois. The same old talk. A lot of states have very low rates of super crime and the special prisons to hold some of these guys cost a lot of money. Yet normal prisons can't really contain the likes of, say, Rigger. I remember hearing about how that otter broke out of a prison in South Carolina using nothing but paper clips and a mop. The DA in Minnesota is being interviewed right now and is commenting that as the crimes were in Minnesota they'd like to prosecute the group. I don't think they'll be able to keep them. Maybe that's why these freaks attacked Minneapolis. If they tried to in Oregon I know for a fact they'd be going to the Portland Penitentiary with its specialized cells and trained guards ready for supercriminals.

It is odd we haven't seen the team yet though. They haven't sent someone to talk to the media about the attack yet. Where are they? They're normally commenting by now to stop speculation. Instead, no one is coming out and the magenta force fields aren't coming down. Just as I'm starting to get antsy Adam is back on the line.

"Jay?" I feel a flutter of relief that he's back, and then I catch the tone of his voice. Adam sounds worried, truly worried, and a little frightened.

"Adam, what is it?" I ask. Oh no, please let Ted be okay. Don't let some moron have gotten him with a lucky shot.

"Jay, that was Holly," Adam's voice trembles, and I can hear the fear he's trying to conceal. "I, I don't know what to say."

"Adam, you're scaring me," I say now looking at the TV. Why are the lights going off in the city?

"Holly says she just got a call from Bill. Raja Raksha has crashed the party," Adam explains.

"Who is that?" I ask. The name sounds familiar but there are a lot of supervillains out there. I don't know all their names. I'm not sure I am supposed to really know them all encyclopedically. I'm not Gary.

"I keep forgetting you're new to this. You act like an old hand. Raja Raksha is bad news. Very bad news."

"Oh," I say worriedly, and I can tell I'm not the only one freaked out by the way the lights in Minneapolis are going out. The news team is scrambling to find out what is happening.

"He killed Marvelous Malamute," Adam says, and my chest tightens. "He's responsible for a lot of terrible things and he hates the Extraordinaries."

"Shit," I say at last, watching the TV and the growing area of shadow over the battle field. The on site news crews aren't even responding now. "Is there anything we can do?"

Adam just sighs, "No. God I hate this. I truly hate this. Holly says Bill and the rest of team are rallying to get there but the others are pinned down for now."

I try not to hyperventilate. I try not to panic. Oh, Ted, why were we fighting? I remember what I was feeling only a short time ago, how if it had been Ted calling I might not have picked up, and I feel ashamed more than anything else. I just want him back here. I want to apologize. I want to hug him tight. Why were we fighting like that over something so stupid? He could die. I could lose my Ted and the last thing I thought about him was a cross spiteful thing. The last thing I said to him was, "I packed you a chicken sandwich."

"Listen," Adam says. "I think they'll get there in time, but it is going to be a photo finish."

"Glad they have a speedster then," I say. Watching the TV, I see a flash of color streaking into the city. Lady Leopard? A trick of the light? The blackness has completely blotted out everything in Minneapolis now.

"Listen, Jay," Adam says, "every time they face Raja, well, it's never good. He's a telepath. A dirty, stinking telepath, he's one of the worst."

"Oh god," I whisper, thinking of the world's most powerful telepath El Esclavador and how he enslaved all of Guadalajara only two years ago. If El Gato Cibernetico hadn't gotten involved when he did it would have been worse. What that same telepath did to San Diego just recently. I remember a few days ago some teenager in Boston was abusing his powers. Stratagem stopped that one but not before the creep defiled some of his classmates. A feeling of fear creeping into me as I consider the horror Ted might be going through right now.

"What he does," Adam seems to shudder over the phone before he continues, "It always messes with the team. I've had Emma come home a wreck and be that way for days."

"What do you do? What does he do?" I ask the very idea of Force Vixen being an emotional wreck scares me more than anything else. She always seems to have it together. She always seems to be ready and in charge. It is the reason I am always happy when she's leading a group that Ted is on.

"There isn't much but to be there for her," Adam says his voice filled with a deep sadness. "Raja digs up personal stuff for her. Stuff dealing with her uncle and her family. He uses people's nightmares against them, Jay."

I look at the TV, fear pouring into my world. Ted's nightmares are what we have been fighting about. If Raja uses them against a person, I've made things so much worse for Ted. My heart starts racing, and I feel sick, when suddenly the feed from Minneapolis changes and the sky becomes bright on the TV, night seeming to turn into day as a glow floods out over the buildings from the battle.

"Bill's there," Adam breathes out. "Thank God."

I watch the screen as the light seems to fade. The building's lights seem to turn up as well. Then I see a glowing green figure fly into the sky and another fly up after him. Whoever it is gets caught easily by Lady Leopard before he starts falling to the ground again. I see a large cat towering suddenly over the buildings in his red and white costume. Titan Tomcat must have felt the need to grow a few stories into the air.

Soon, it is really all over, or at least the news casters claim so. Titan has shrunk out of sight. Lady Leopard appears briefly to state that the supercriminals have all been caught except for two. That Raja Raksha escaped, as did Ms. Q, causes some commentators like Alisa Madden to yammer for a while about Extraordinary failures and how the superheroes let supervillains escape so they can stay in business. Lady Leopard has to leave and get back to their base so she can't answer questions and that only causes me to worry. I wish I knew more. My communicator flashing green is less than reassuring right now.

Adam clicks off the phone. He says something about getting the house ready for Emma coming home; needing to make it better for her when she gets home. He's dedicated, I can say that about him. I stare at the TV for another half hour, clicking around channels but there isn't much else going on. I'm not hungry anymore so I put the leftovers away and just sit watching the TV as it gets progressively darker and darker outside. No news really. No real information about what is going on besides speculation. A lot of talk about how this is only the second time Raja Raksha has been in North America. They bring up his attack eight years ago in Pakistan, his movements in Bangladesh and Australia, and sightings in Africa. It is a lot of hokum and rumor. Nothing is substantiated. The tiger is a mystery, his powers shrouded in the darkness he conjures. The worst part is when they show pictures of that poor woman in Australia. Her dead eyes just stare unseeing at the camera as they talk about how she tried to kill the Prime Minister while she was under Raja's control. Will Ted look that way? Like there wasn't anything behind his eyes anymore? Like there had never been a happy day in his life, and there never would be again? A kangaroo doctor claims she is doing much better, but he won't let them see her so I don't know what she looks like now. Those eyes bore into me from the photos.

Waiting is the worst part. I wish Ted would call me. Why is he so angry at me? Why can't he just call and say he is okay? I jump when the phone rings and leap to get it.

"Hello?" I pant worriedly.

"Jay?" It's Diane on the other end. "Sorry, I meant to dial Brian."

"It's okay," I say. "Do you know what is going on?"

"Not much," she says irritably. "God, I hate when this happens. I'm trying to plan out Wally's day tomorrow."

"You seem less than worried," I say and the fact that she's worried about a schedule is reassuring at least.

"Yeah, well, Raja is bad news sure," Diane says flippantly, "but I know everyone made it out. They would have said otherwise by now."

"Oh," I say nodding my head, and that does make some sense. If someone was really hurt, they would call their Alpha right? I mean, the team has a teleporter, don't they? If Ted was hurt they'd bring me to the bunker to be with him, wouldn't they?

"Yeah. When they're this quiet it means they're working out details and exchanging notes. Trust me, nothing major is going on now. I've gone through this before. They never call if everyone is okay," Diane says. "All I got was an automated call from Samuel. Wally has a sprained ankle and a black eye, but I've got a cover story for that sort of thing. If Samuel didn't call you then it means Ted is fine."

I sigh in relief, "You have no idea how good that is to hear."

"Yeah, sorry. I guess you're still new to this," Diane says. "We've all been on edge, a Raja Raksha attack is never fun."

"I got that idea," I say glancing at TV. They're showing that woman again. "Adam sounds freaked."

"Emma never handles these encounters well. He'll be quiet for the next few days." And then with a lot more empathy in her voice the lioness says, "Jay, it will be okay."

"I hope so," is all I can say.

We chat about this and that for a while longer and then Diane says she has to hang up and get back to creating the cover story and tomorrow's schedule for Wally. It sounds like a long night for her. I briefly consider calling Lizz, but it is a school night and she needs to make sure the kids are in bed. Michelle didn't give me her phone number yet, she said she doesn't want Titan knowing she comes to the meetings since she's only a Beta. I could look it up I guess, but I don't want to interfere with her privacy or blow her cover just because I'm nervous. There is Holly, she was really nice, but it is a school night and she has to handle four kids tonight alone. Stuart is on the other side of the globe and I'm not at all sure what the time zone changes would be.

I think about calling Gary or Brandon, but how do I explain a call to them? They know Ted and I had a fight but they don't know about what. How could I explain to them why I am so worried? Why I'm pacing the room? I've known them longer than I have known Ted. Ted is my boyfriend and in some ways a great friend but he's not here. I glance at my phone and think of my parents. God I wish I could talk to them. We've always talked about everything, but I can't talk to them about this. How can I explain all the details Dad will ask for, and how can I explain these feelings to Mom, when I can't tell them the real reasons behind anything? I hate this waiting so much. This is worse than when Ted was fighting Etenoir. At least then I knew what the conclusion was to that encounter. I knew he was okay.

I'm about to call Holly when the phone rings, and I am so eager to talk with Ted I answer it before looking who is calling.

"Hey, Jay," Gary says happily, and the wolf's voice is filled with his usual cheerful tone.

I hesitate before saying anything. I need to play this cool. I need to not sound at all worried so I force myself to smile and say, "Hey, Gary," in the happiest tone I can.

"We're all going out for some late night drinks. Do you and Ted want to go in for that?" he asks.

"Ted isn't, uh, at home," I say truthfully, a hint of my real mood creeping into my tone.

"Aw, dude, you two still having trouble?" Gary asks, his own voice filling with worry now.

"A bit," I say as noncommittally as possible, "we'll be okay." I try fervently to keep my real fear from leaking through, but it does anyway.

"Hope so," Gary says and I can almost see that tail wagging. "If you two can't get it right then what hope do I have?"

I laugh at that and smile for real, thinking of the big muscled wolf, "Look, have some margaritas for me okay?"

"Sure, sure," he says and then he pauses and says more seriously, "Hey, want me to come over? We can do drinks and try to think up ways to tell Ted he's being a doof."

"Nah, its fine," I say and I really wish Gary could come over. I want him here, so I won't feel alone in my own home, but I know Ted will be coming home soon and if what Adam and Diane said is true he won't be in good shape, and that will open up way too many questions if Gary is here. "You guys have fun."

Gary doesn't say anything for a bit and then asks, "Jay, are you sure you're okay?"

"Yes, no need to worry, Gary." My voice is cracking now, but it doesn't matter. I'm allowed to be upset that Ted and I have been fighting.

"Alright," he says. "But look, call me tomorrow if you and Ted are still in trouble. You need to work this out. I'll be glad to be the intermediary guy."

I nod agreeing with him over the phone and he hangs up. I curl back up on the couch and keep watching the TV. I need to be home when Ted comes back. I can just feel it. We need to be there for each other. That's part of the reason you're with someone, to be there with them on dark nights.

The TV starts to talk about the attack in Kazakhstan finally and I can see why part of the team was there dealing with it. That robot just looks insane. Even Lady Leopard was having trouble taking it down alone as the others were evacuating people and getting them to safety. I think I can see Stratagem running up the arm of the thing to reach the head. I have no idea what he did but the robot got shut down. Then they had to zoom off to deal with Raja. The news reporters continue with a quick world tour of the day's super activities. They talk about how Wavefront and the new hero of Sydney, Caduceus, had teamed up to deal with some guy called Marty Mist. There is a brief mention of that black fox in Rome, Sfumato, stopping a daring art theft from St. Peters. There's nothing new about Minneapolis, and it is getting late. I yawn and sigh. I wish Ted was home.

I'm drifting off to sleep on the couch when I hear a knock at the back door, the one leading into our yard from the kitchen. I rush to the door quickly and push the curtains aside to outside as I unlock it. Star Coyote is standing there in his full costume, and it looks like he's forgotten his keys. I open the door for him as fast as I can. How could he wear the costume home? That is really, seriously, dangerous.

"Jay," Ted says looking at me for a moment as he comes in, and then he falls into my arms. I barely have time to brace myself and hold him. He's shaking as he wraps his costumed arms around me. I slide the door shut as best I can as we collapse on the kitchen floor, my back to the closed door.

"Ted," I whisper hugging him tight. "Ted, Snuffles, what's the matter?"

"I'm so sorry," he gasps at last looking up at me looking out from behind his mask. "I'm so sorry, Jay, for everything. Everything is my fault, and I'm so sorry." I reach a paw up and remove that blue mask from his face, looking at him. Ted looks ragged and sad, and a claw mark run the length of his chest, right through his symbol. I can tell he's been crying and he looks so tired. I've never seen him so badly shaken.

"Snuffles," I say nuzzling his nose, "you shouldn't apologize. I was the idiot who insisted on going."

"No," he whimpers, "please, I just, I just hate this. I hate this fight." Ted's eyes are pleading with me as he holds me. I can feel his strength, augmented by his power as if he were trying to hold me down and keep me close. "Can we just be done? I'm sorry. Can't we just forget what happened?"

I sigh looking into his pleading eyes. My coyote is so desperate, and I can feel his muscled furry body under his costume as we cuddle on the linoleum of the kitchen floor. He's shaking, physically trembling in my arms. "Sweetie, a lot of things happened we can't just forget," I say carefully, not wanting to make things worse for him.

"I really want to, though," Ted says, his words coming out in a gush. His voice is weak and he looks so lost.

I smile at him and kiss his nose, "I missed talking to you."

"I missed cuddling you," Ted says nuzzling my neck. "I missed being with you."

"I know," I say at last as we hold each other, "But we still need to talk."

We sit there for a while as he sadly hugs against me, sniffing my fur and trying to hold me as close as he can. As if he's been away for months and just wants to remember every little bit of me. He finally says, "Yeah."

"I'm sorry it happened. I'm sorry that things spun out of control and that Camo found out," I say quietly.

"He didn't say anything to anyone," Ted says. I have to say I'm impressed that Diane was able to keep him quiet as he continues, "Not that it matters."

"What do you mean?" I ask surprised and concerned by the way he said that. "Snuffles, you were so worried about everyone finding out."

"It doesn't matter anymore," Ted sighs. "I resigned."

"WHAT?!?" I shout in surprise. "Ted, why would you do that? You love being an Extraordinary. They're your friends." My paws squeeze his shoulders, as he shakes his head, his muzzle pressed against my chest.

"I'm just so tired," Ted says closing his eyes and shuddering. I think he's near tears again when he finally says, "I'm tired of being ashamed of myself and feeling like I have to keep it all a secret."

"Then why not just tell them?" I ask as I hold him.

"I'm scared," he says at last. "I'm scared of what Solarcoon will say. I'm scared of what people will do. What will it do to the team when people know the full story?"

"You shouldn't be," I say hugging him. "You know I'm here."

"Still scares me," he says. "I just, I just needed some time off. I needed to get away. I was causing too much trouble. I'm wrecking things. I'm making the team fight and I'm wrecking their trust."

I pet his ears softly and sigh. "Sounds like there is a story behind that comment."

"There is." Ted's silent after saying that and we just stay on the floor as I pet his head and hold him close. Ted shudders and nuzzles me once in a while, sniffing me and slowly nuzzling my chest.

"I forgot you," he says suddenly breaking the silence.

"Pardon?" I ask confused.

"I forgot you, Oreo. I forgot all about you, and your parents, and about us," he says, and the words sound dragged out of him.

"I'm not sure I follow, love," I say rubbing between his ears.

"Raja Raksha made me forget about you, let me forget about you," Ted says earnestly. "I forgot about you and remembered everything my parents said, everything that happened at their house, about Alex and it was…" the coyote in my arms shudders, "I didn't like it."

"I hear he did a number on everyone," I say as I pet him. "He messed with you, dear, but that's okay, we're together now. You remember me now right?"

"Yeah," Ted finally smiles at me. "And I remembered why I fight again."

We smile at each other finally and I can feel all that coiled emotion in my coyote and all his worries as I hug him and the comfort he's finding in me right now. I just say what comes to mind, "Hearth and home?"

"Our hearth and home," Ted says. "I was an idiot to be mad at you, Jay. You need the super family. They're good people. I was just so scared about the team knowing. I'm scared about the world knowing."

"I know," I nod along, my muzzle rubbing his gently. "I guess I can see why, Ted. I just wish you could be honest about it. I'm proud of you and I love you. They're proud of you too."

"I was mad at myself for being careless, too," he says. "I hate the idea of you being in danger because I did something stupid. That is why what Camo said hurt so much. You should have hit the panic button, though."

"I know. But I was worried about revealing you." While I want to try and explain what happened, I don't think Ted can handle an argument right now, so I lie by omission. I just don't want to try and explain it all and I know he's right.

Ted smiles at me and sighs, "Well I know what is important now. You."

We kiss, our lips meeting, and I feel his need, his want and fear all mixed together as he pushes into me and holds me. I feel his hunger for closure and his trembling as he holds me to reassure himself.

Our lips break and I look into his eyes. They're filled with tears and I can tell he so desperately wants this to be over. I wish I could let it just be over, but I say, "You can't quit the team though."

"I want to," Ted says, and the resignation and pain in his voice is hard to hear. "Maybe I'd be better as just a hero by myself here in Portland. Stop the gallivanting around the world. Be with you, be safer, and not have to worry."

"They're still your friends. And I doubt they'll just leave you alone."

"I know," he sighs at last and hugs me again. "Solarcoon wouldn't let me resign. He said I was on leave of absence if I really needed it."

"Maybe that will help," I hug my coyote close. "I think you're just stressed by the attack."

Ted nods a bit and presses his face against my neck, "I just don't like how being on the team is making me fight with you."

I know I could answer that the team isn't what is causing that—he is doing that by trying to keep secrets. That he's stressing himself out for no good reason, but I can't—not right now. Right now I just want to hold him. Ted's safe. He's going to be okay. I was so scared before and I have him back in my arms, and that's all that matters. Everything else can wait.

"Well, you can take a break for a while before going back," I say nuzzling him again. "I think you should."

"I'll see," Ted says sadly, "I really screwed things up though."

"I'm just glad you're home," is all I can say to that as I pet his head again. We stay on the floor for I don't know how long. Finally, Ted feels all right enough to stand back up and we head towards the bedroom as he strips his costume off. I don't want to say anything, but the torn costume frightens me when he leaves it littered on the floor as we walk. A tear across the chest like that and a shallow wound the length of his chest means someone got very close to him. He came so close to being really badly hurt or killed. We go back to the bedroom and get into bed, and tonight he's holding me like before, and my mind spins as we just lie together feeling each other breathing. This used to be all I wanted. A while ago I just wanted to be reassured by Ted's arms around me. Now though, as I feel him shivering next to me, I can't help but think that I want more for my coyote. I can't let him leave the Extraodinaries. He needs them and their support like they need him. I kiss his nose and smile. I have him for now and that makes me happy, and he smiles a me.

"I missed you," he says as we drift off to sleep. It has been a very hard night. Tomorrow is another day and another chance to try and fix things.

Chapter 10
A Night Out With Friends

I really do love a good bagel. They're hard to find in Portland. You can get bad ones everywhere but I've only found one spot in the civic square that sells truly good bagels. This is why I'm crouching behind this green park bench right now; hiding a half eaten bagel in one paw and a bag of a half dozen bagels I just bought clutched in the other.

KA-KROOM!

Well, that and a crazed supervillain has decided that today would make a smashing time to make an appearance. A bolt of lightning crackles in the air as the wind whips up around me. I can hear other people screaming and running but I'm not getting up from cover. This moron is shooting at everything and anything with lightning bolts and it's pure luck he hasn't actually hit anyone yet.

The civic square is littered with rubble from the explosion in the mayor's office. Glass shards are everywhere. A tree has been blown apart and bits of wood litter the ground. This bench has a rock on one side but I doubt even that would protect me. The only reason I'm not running down the street directly away from the floating ringtail is the fact that this guy is obviously unstable and I don't want to draw attention to myself.

I glance through the slats of the bench and spot the guy. He's hard to miss, floating in midair and with all that electricity crackling around his paw. Who ever heard of a floating red panda before superbeings started showing up? He's in a purple and yellow jumper, with a cape and a pair of big goggles on his face. Electricity is crackling around him as he laughs in amusement. He looks like a big nerd in a mad scientist Halloween costume, if that makes any sense. He's kind of portly with a slight paunch; the costume hugs his body showing off his rounded, soft looking frame. He'd be cuddly if not for the maniacal laughter. His long tail twitches in amusement at the chaos he is causing.

I glance down at my communicator and smirk at the red light blinking back at me. I hit it myself, so I know what will be coming. The wind is whipping about, causing my fur to fluff out and whip about as well. I think it's because of the temperature change his lightning causes, either that or somehow his floating is doing this. I'm not a science expert, so maybe Ted can explain it to me later. Little shards of glass and wood chips are being tossed about as the red panda holds the square hostage. I can hear rescue vehicles and emergencies service sirens blaring as they rush to get here.

This sort of thing really shouldn't happen. I was just buying a bagel as a mid-morning snack. I work out, I figure I can handle a few extra calories, when suddenly Mr. Show-Off showed up between me and any reasonable exits with his itchy trigger fingers. He blasted out of the mayor's offices and then started taking pot shots at anything moving in the square. It sent everybody into an instant panic. We don't get this level of destruction here in Portland very often. We also don't get quite as much maniacal laughter and petty grandstanding. I'm nearly in the center of the square and I can hear him perfectly well above the wind and lightning. Some buildings windows are rattling about and a car turns over as the wind picks up. I see some people hunkering down in the square, cowering in fear.

People are panicking and I think he's enjoying that fact. I can see someone struggling in one of his arms as he rotates some more to face me. Oh shoot, is that Mayor Richards? I just figured it was a bag of loot he was holding. Did this guy really just kidnap the mayor? Portland's mayor is a young beaver and he's struggling to get free, but it is obvious that the red panda criminal has him well in hand and won't be letting go anytime soon.

"Run fools! Run from Doctor Orgon! No one can stop me!" the red panda cackles with glee. I smile, watching him through the slats of the bench. He doesn't see Star Coyote approaching from overhead until he feels a tap on his shoulder.

The red panda turns in time to get a fist in the face as Star Coyote quips, "I'd beg to differ."

"Star Coyote," Doctor Orgon howls. The punch sends him reeling back a few feet in the air as he drops Mayor Richards. The beaver reaches out as he falls, and Star Coyote catches his paw easily. I'm impressed at how quickly Ted lowers him to the ground and is suddenly back up in the air facing the red panda, who has his attention now firmly focused on Star Coyote. The panda shouts, "I don't know how you got here so quick but I'll gladly deal with you!"

I can feel the tension lessening around the square. People can see our stalwart hero has arrived to help protect us. He's here to confront Dr. Orgon and he's floating slightly above the red panda, arms akimbo. Star Coyote just gives Dr. Orgon a confident smile as the red panda grouses in anger. "We'll see about that, Zappy," he says, his ears flicking with amusement

On the ground, the mayor is staggering to his feet, and I motion for him take cover with me. He makes a bee-line for the bench and rock. I motion for him to hurry up, but the mayor is surprisingly nimble for a beaver. You'd expect him to have problems running, most beaver's do with their short legs and big tail, but he's soon beside me, whiskers twitching and thick scaly tail slapping the ground with irritation. I'll hand it to him, he doesn't look scared. Obviously, he trusts Star Coyote to handle the dweeb. I do too, actually. Neither of us talk, we just watch the events unfold. In normal circumstances I'd be excited to be near the guy. I've been trying to get a meeting with him for months over a new proposed commercial zone, but now is not really the time. I take a bite of my bagel, and for a moment he watches me eating calmly. I offer one to him, and the mayor sort of shrugs and takes it without speaking as we turn back to the floating superbeings.

Dr. Orgon is distracted for now as he circles Star Coyote. The panda doesn't seem too maneuverable in the air, like he has to really concentrate to control his flight. My coyote, meanwhile, is levitating with ease and circling above the red panda smoothly, a confident look on his muzzle as he plays with the villain. I know Star Coyote can see me over the red panda villain's shoulder. All I can do is shrug as the Mayor and I keep behind cover. Star Coyote can't worry about me right now though; he has a villain to deal with. My being so close is a hindrance, but Star gives his full attention to the lightning bolt throwing panda. He has to, the guy is dangerous despite his nebbish looks and his obviously unstable mental state. I know I'll get a firm talking to later for being stuck out here in the line of fire, but I don't care as I watch the fight that is about to happen.

"So, want to tell me what you're doing?" Star Coyote asks looking over the guy. "Or better yet who are you? I don't think we've run into each other before."

"There is a reason for that, I'm making my debut today," the red panda smirks with a flashy display of electricity erupting around his paws.

"How is that going?" Star Coyote asks easily. He's distracting the guy, taking his measure, looking for an opening. He wants to keep the collateral damage down. Meanwhile, the police are encircling the block; getting people out of the way. They've got this down to a science. I can see a female coyote with grey fur and black hair directing some cops to get to a woman curled up on the ground. They're too far away to get to us safely, but I'm not worried. Star Coyote is here to protect me. I still have confidence in him. He's bantering with the lightning throwing moron and that means he's in control. Letting him talk and monologue himself into a bad position, all the while letting the emergency responders do their job.

"Can't complain so far," the red panda says his tail flicking. "I think my overall plan is going well. Though I figured you'd be off with the Extraordinaires in Detroit right now."

"Not all of us serve on the same missions," Star Coyote says. He's being coy there because it's not public knowledge he's on a leave of absence right now. It has been three weeks since that night in the kitchen and he's still being evasive about the whole thing. That tells me more than enough about how he really feels about the situation, that he wants to be with the team. If he were honest about resigning, he would have said something to me or the media by now. Once he's made a decision, Ted doesn't dither around. It's just getting him to make up his mind that's the problem.

"It doesn't matter though. I, Dr. Orgon, shall easily defeat you!" the panda exclaims with glee.

"Wait," Star Coyote stops him with a raised paw. "You're calling yourself Dr. Orgon?" The look of shocked affront on Star Coyote's face is priceless.

Lightning crackles between the panda's paws as he sneers, "Of course!"

"But," Star Coyote quirks his head raising an eyebrow, "Orgon was discredited decades ago."

"Huh?" the red panda stops circling, and he seems confused by that. I know this isn't Star Coyote making a brilliant plan to distract the villain, this is just him being, well, Ted. It obviously has thrown the red panda for a loop though. He's confused by this change in tactics, "Hey, this is a valid name for my electricity powered abilities."

"That is just ridiculous. Orgon hasn't been an accepted theory for energy in decades. Why would you even use that?" Star asks crossing his arms and tapping his foot in the air. "At least with my name there is a certain level of thematic sense."

"Now, wait, I just…" the panda stammers, and I can tell he's flummoxed. I close my eyes for a moment and sigh. What, he didn't think he'd get questions about this? Star Coyote has more than once proved himself to be a big science nerd. What about this could be a surprise?

"You're not really a doctor are you?" Star Coyote deadpans the question looking at the panda. "I mean what self respecting doctor would name themself after a discredited and laughable theory? I don't care if you can solve the city's energy problems, people would laugh at you for using that name."

"Hey, I worked hard on this name," the panda says shyly with a slight whine.

"Nice dodge of the question. Wouldn't Energy Panda have made more sense? Or, I don't know, CrackleZaps, or how about Electron if you want to go the pseudo-science route?" Star Coyote asks. "That doesn't even touch upon why you would do this. Why even go about attacking the mayor or messing up the city knowing that a superhero might intervene? And who ever heard of purple and yellow as a color combination? Those colors just clash."

The red panda stamps his foot, and the movement makes him wobble in midair as he looks up at Star, electricity leaping about his paws. "Aww, stop it. I worked hard at cooking this up. This was plenty scientific. I worked hard on this costume too!"

"Yeah," Star Coyote rolls his eyes, "look, why not just surrender. I'm sure the DA can work out some sort of deal and just use your actual name in court documents. No need for anyone to know about this alter-ego. Maybe the press will even be quiet."

"Shut up!" the red panda shouts, his tail flicking as he sends out a lightning bolt. Star Coyote easily dodges that, though, and quickly zips behind him. Before Dr. Orgon can do anything Star has punched him again and sent him flying. Whatever has been keeping the panda in the air gives out as he tumbles to the ground. Star used a high gravity punch there. Now that the mayor is freed, Star Coyote can stop holding back and hit harder so the guy will go down. The panda is shaking his head in surprise as he gets to his knees on the ground. Dr. Orgon is not even paying attention as the masked coyote lands on the ground and runs towards him. I wince a bit as Star kicks the red panda in the solar plexus. Ted only fights on the ground to get some traction behind his kicks. Why make heavy gravity kicks and punches when a regular punch or kick will do?

The panda folds up on the ground gasping as Star Coyote grabs his paws and wrestles them behind his back. Star might have increased gravity to hold him down or maybe not. Dr. Orgon is struggling but he's not in great shape. He's winded and obviously unable to marshal any response as Star Coyote strips the heavy gloves he's wearing off of him.

Star Coyote has him down for the count as the panda struggles and wriggles under him. That's my Ted, taking down supervillains through mockery and strategic uses of sarcasm; I can't help but smile proudly. The cops are everywhere now, and they've got specialized insulation manacles to contain the guy's lightning bolts. We've had our share of electricity based villainy and crime in the past. They happily cuff him and shake paws with Star Coyote in thanks for his service. They even box up the guy's gloves in special metal containers.

The officers lead the red panda out of the plaza, cameras flashing as he is walks to the paddy wagon and lock up. I hear Star Coyote mention something about how his gloves are probably what allowed him to command electricity and that he probably isn't the brains behind them. Most likely they were created by Anderson Labs and this guy just stole them. That happens once in a while. The nation's laboratories and universities invent some new piece of science and someone with a grudge sees it and gets an idea. It has gotten worse since super science has gotten into the nation's laboratories. That is where I think that freak job that nearly destroyed the world's computer systems, Living Code, came from. I'm honestly surprised Anderson hasn't gone out of business after everything that's happened.

Mayor Richards claps me on the back saying, "That's our boy. Thank you for the cover, and the bagel, sir." Then standing up, he straightens his tie and walks over to Star as reporters start flashing pictures and calling for interviews. The mayor is after all the big story. I'm just one of the innocent civilians sitting outside when the attack occurs. Not a victim, just a person there, and that is the way it should be.

"Excellent work today, Star Coyote!" The mayor congratulates him happily as he stands beside the coyote and shakes Star's paw. "I don't know what we would do without you watching out for Portland. I don't know what I could have done without you protecting me."

"Just doing my duty, Mr. Mayor," Star Coyote says with a smile and then a jaunty salute and he's in the air again. "Always happy to help Portland."

I smile happily and walk back to my office, my bagels in paw and thankfully not at all grimy from the attack. I make sure not to wave at Star Coyote. I can't draw too much attention to myself, but I do have a wide smile on my muzzle anyway. Most people are gathered around the windows, watching the end of the scene outside. Star Coyote has taken off into the sky by now.

He'll be back at work in plenty of time I suspect. I sit down at my desk and eat one of my bagels happily. It looks like a good day ahead. My communicator beeps and I look down. 'Incoming call' flashes on the panel. I smile and pick up my cell phone tapping in a few numbers. Stratagem altered my phone so it can pick up the communicator inconspicuously. I could use my communicator as a phone, but that would make its unique nature far too obvious and I want to be discreet.

"Hi there," I say with a chuckle.

"Hey yourself," I hear Ted's voice, the wind is whipping about audibly so he must be in flight right now. "Any reason you weren't far away from that thing?"

"He was shooting erratically. Besides, you saw where I was. Not a lot of cover," I explain munching on my bagel.

"Just be careful, dear," I hear him say. "Guys like that aren't known for common sense."

"Says the guy in tights," I chuckle.

"Purely for aerodynamic reasons," he counters with his own chuckle. "Besides, the guy was wearing a cape. Obviously not a stable individual."

"I'm sure Lady Leopard would disagree with you. The fun part was you critiquing his fashion sense," I laugh.

"You saw the same outfit I did. I mean, geeze, who walks around in that much purple?" Ted grouses with mirth. "He's lucky I didn't start in on his boots. He did not have the thighs to pull those off."

"Why is it that you can say that stuff and yet everyone assumes a certain slushball husky is gayer than you?" I ask with a roll of my eyes.

"Dumb luck?" Ted asks. "Oops, have to land, dear. Hey have a good day, okay? See you later tonight at the coffee shop."

"Sure," I say with a smile. Getting back to work is easy enough. Unlike some people in the office, I'm not still floored by the events that happened outside. The new guy, Lee Wallberg from Salem, isn't used to this at all. He keeps staring out the window. I wonder if I am becoming blasé to superheroics. Soon it is late afternoon, a good day's work near fully behind me. I glance at the photo on my desk of Ted and me at the State Fair last year and smile.

Ted really is a sweetie. That picture was before I knew his big secret. It is amazing how I can now divide our life into those two parts of before secret and after. It was also the day that Star Coyote saved all those people when that faulty ferris wheel broke. He certainly is dedicated and filled with energy to help protect people. That's probably how he was able to be a member of the Extraordinaries, patrol Portland, keep a steady job, and still date me without any major impairment on any side, other than his tardiness of course. I'll admit, since he went on leave I have seen him a lot more. He's still on patrol but he has made more time for me and our friends.

We have plans with friends tonight, which I'm looking forward to. The gay coffee bar we're meeting at has been the unofficial hang out of our group for years. I'm looking forward to it and so is Ted, so it should go well. In my opinion, a night out with friends is just what the doctor ordered. Assuming there isn't some super crime event in the city that stops or intrudes upon Star Coyote. Still, with the take down of Dr. Orgon maybe I can hope they'll lay low.

I don't even notice my communicator beeping at first, I'm so lost in my thoughts. Glancing down I see it isn't an emergency, just an incoming call.

After quickly getting my phone ready I say, "Hello, Snuffles."

"Snuffles?" says a voice on the other end with a chuckle. A much deeper voice than my coyote's and one I recognize instantly.

"Hi, Paul," I say in surprise. "How are you?"

"I'm good," the husky says with a jovial chuckle. "Hey look, can you do me a favor?"

"What?" I ask. I always want to know what favors are before I agree to do them.

"Can you go to the roof of your building?" he asks.

"Why?" I ask standing up from my chair and looking out my window. The roof? Looking outside I don't see anything odd except the cleaning crews and sanitation getting to work repairing the damage from this morning's attack.

"Can you just do it," Paul says testily.

I roll my eyes and walk out of my office opening the door to the stairwell saying back, "Ever heard of please?"

"Sorry, just in a bad spot," his voice is a bit muffled. "Please hurry?"

I take the steps two at a time and easily reach the roof access door. I got a key to the door after Ted told me his secret, in case he ever needed to do a rooftop pickup for me. Walking out onto the roof, I look about and talk into my phone, "Okay. I'm here, now what? Where are you?"

"See anything out of place?" he asks cryptically. I look about and then I see it over on the corner of the roof

"Yeah," I say walking over to it. "Who leaves a duffle bag up on the roof of a building?"

"Well I didn't leave it up there," Paul says and I can just make out his voice over the edge of the building. I peek down and I see him; the husky waves up at me. He's got his mask on and most of his costume. I say most because his pants seem to be gone and I can see his boxer shorts.

"Nice little hearts there," I say with a smile waving down at him.

"Laundry day," he deadpans. "Stop looking at my shorts. The teleporter nicked my pants and for some reason landed my bag on the roof. Can you toss it down here?"

"Is there anything breakable in here?" I ask as I lift up the bag.

"My cell phone maybe," Glacier says. "Look, I'll catch it. Just chuck it down here. I'm getting a draft and I really don't want someone to take a picture of me in my boxers."

"Let me just get your phone out," I say opening the bag up. Digging around I find it and a watch. I also grab his wallet. "I really don't want to let this stuff get broken."

"Fine," Paul grouses.

"And expect to get jokes about this," I say with a smile as I toss the bag over the edge towards the husky. He easily catches it and waves up at me

"Sure, sure, but if I do, expect me to tell everyone what your nickname is for Ted," says the husky as he opens up the bag and slips on a pair of jeans.

"Our little secret then?" I ask as I open the door to the roof access and start walking down the stairwell. The phone's signal is weaker in here but I can hear him grunt as I skip down to the bottom floor quickly. I slip out the front door and walk into the alley beside the building. Paul is behind a dumpster. I hand him his things and my brush.

"Thanks," Paul says with a smile as he finishes stuffing his costume into his duffle and then does a once over on his fur.

"No problem. So why are you in town?"

"Thought I would stop in and visit a collie?" he offers lamely.

I tap my foot on the ground and quirk an eyebrow at him. It is a look Ted knows well and its one that Paul falls for easily.

"Okay, okay" he says irritably. "I came here because Ted won't return any of my calls."

"Oh?" I'm surprised. "I didn't even know you were calling him."

"Yeah, well," Paul pauses as we leave the alley. His rock band t-shirt looks wrinkled but overall he seems fine. I think he's looking to see if anyone saw anything they weren't supposed to. As we leave the alley, we turn right and start walking away from the civic center and out into Portland. He continues, "That doesn't surprise me. He hasn't talked to any of us since his attempt to leave the team."

"Yeah, he told me about that part at least," I say shaking my head. "By the way, thanks for trying to stick up for him. I know I wanted to do the same thing to, well, you know. I have to admit doing it in the locker room was impressive."

"It was kind of stupid of me," Paul says rubbing the back of his neck. "Fighting between … friends … is strictly prohibited. I can be a hot head at times."

"Ironic," I intone with amusement. "So you came to talk to Ted?"

"Well…" he pauses and then nods, "Yeah, pretty much. I mean I know I'm over what Raja did to us, at least a bit, and I thought he'd be feeling better too and might want to come back."

I think back over the past few nights. The shivering and whimpering in his sleep, the tightening of his arm around me as we slept. I have a hard time believing Ted is truly over what Raja said and did. Looking at Paul, at the way the husky is fidgeting, I'm just as skeptical about him being truly over it. I haven't even heard from Adam in the past few weeks and I know he's busy with Emma because of Raja's appearance. I have chatted with some of the others though, so I know I'm not unfounded in this. Still, I don't bring that up. There is something else that needs to be said. "Do you really think he left over Raja Raksha?"

"Yeah," Paul nods at that. "Why do you ask?"

"Ted is made of sterner stuff than that, Paul," I say coolly as we walk down the street with the late afternoon sun on our backs. "I know Raja did a number on all of you but do you really think that alone was enough to push Ted like that."

"Well," Paul seems to think for short while as we walk down the street. I'm not sure where we are going but I'm not too worried. I've got all my deadlines for the day met. The husky then continues, "Yeah, I guess not. I mean he's done a lot and he's a tough little guy."

"That he is," I nod and smile at that. "What happened might have pushed his buttons and made him a bit more negative, sure, but maybe there was other stuff going on?"

"Do you know something?" Paul asks, stopping and looking at me now.

"No more than what he's told me and what some other folks have said," I reply with a shrug of my shoulders.

"Ah yeah, the family," Paul says. "Still, I can't see what exactly beyond Raja has changed."

"For one thing, how many people now know about me and thus Ted's supposed secret?" I ask.

"Um, pretty much everyone," Glacier says evasively his eyes flicking about and his ears flopping down on his head.

"Right, and Ted has never been comfortable being out. Look at how long it took him to tell you."

"It was way too long," Paul says, his voice dipping.

"Paul," I look up at the husky, "you have to understand that Ted has some issues when it comes to this stuff. Trust me. I've beaten my head against the wall more than once over this. Some of them aren't unfounded; they're personal, though—I don't think I have a right to relate. This is a place he hates to be in. He hates to have confrontations and he hates coming out. Don't you think that the idea of more people knowing would make him uncomfortable?"

"Well, sure. But I don't think that is all of it. I mean Vixen and Blitz and Solar don't know."

"Sure it isn't," I say as we turn and walk down another sidewalk. "There was your discipline hearing which he feels responsible for, the entire Camo thing, and something about Stratagem he's only vaguely alluded to with me."

"Stratagem has a problem?" Paul says surprised. "I didn't think he cared Ted was gay."

"I doubt he does," I say. "Something else is going on that Ted is really unhappy about there, and I can't get a word out of him about it."

"Still, most of us know. So wouldn't it be okay for him to comeback?" Paul seems to almost plead. "I miss my buddy."

"Sure you do," I say patting his shoulder, "but you're forgetting that one very important person doesn't know."

"Who?"

"Who else?" I say it perhaps a bit too loudly, nodding my head as I verbalize for the first time, "The guy Ted idolizes, his hero with the mask."

"Bill?" Paul says with a great deal of surprise, "So what if Bill doesn't know?"

"That is a lot of tension with everyone else knowing, he is your leader after all," I explain gesturing with my paw a bit. "And there is a lot of emotion tied up around him. Bill was the one who invited Ted to join the team; he's the guy Ted has idolized since even before putting on the mask, not to mention how welcoming he has been. The family dinners every once in a while have added a nice touch to Ted's issues. He really does not want Bill to know. It reminds him too much of his family finding out."

"Oh," Paul nods. "I guess I never thought about it that way. I didn't know there was trouble with his family. So you think that is the reason?"

"Part of it," I nod too and wag my tail. "And he's worried about me, and wants more time, and a lot of small stuff besides all of that. There is never one reason—just a lot of reasons building up together."

"So it was kind of stupid for me to come here right after work?" Paul asks.

I pat his shoulder and smile, "Nope. I think it was very good of you to come. You're a good friend, Paul, and maybe together we can get him to rethink this leave of absence and get back where he belongs. Besides, it is nice to get a visit in with you. I liked our little dinner and maybe some more time hanging out wouldn't be a bad thing."

Paul blushes and his Texas twang gets a little stronger, "Well I just thought maybe he'd feel better now is all."

"He is," I say with a smile. "He's just being stubborn and trying to prove to himself that it wasn't stupid to try and resign. I think seeing his friend will go a long way to getting him back on track." "So wait…" Paul looks at me questioningly, "Why are you backing me up here?"

"You mean why am I supporting this when it puts Ted at greater risk and takes him way from me?" I ask nonchalantly and Paul nods. Good to know he isn't afraid to ask the obvious question. I've been wondering it too, off and on. "I'm not sure. A part of me does want him here, safer, and with me. I have to share him with the world when he's on team business and that's hard. I mean he's famous and I know guys and girls are looking at him. I've seen some of the things people put in magazine and online. Not to mention the crazies out there and his life being at risk."

"Well I know you can trust Ted not to cheat," Paul says. "He isn't the type."

"No, he isn't. I've known that for a while. He's proven that to me. It just took me a while to return the favor." "Oh," Paul seems surprised by that. "I, uh, never would have guessed."

I chuckle at the look on his face, "Do you really think it would come up around you? I regret the stupid things I did but we worked it out. The risks he takes as a, um, person in your line of work, more than anything else, that scares me."

"Yeah," Paul nods.

"But they scare a lot of good people I've met and talked too," I explain. "He's safer with you then he would be alone. Really when you get down to it, being on the team, Ted belongs there. He can do a lot of good and he's an asset to the team as well. Not to mention I think it is good for him to interact with other people with powers."

"It does help make it feel like I'm not alone," Paul says. "I bet Ted feels the same way."

"Camaraderie," I grin. "Speaking of which, how about you hang out with us tonight? Maybe we can talk to Ted about all this. At the very least he'll get to see a good friend I know he misses. The only problem is, we have some previous plans but I bet it would be fine to bring you along if you don't mind a more exotic location."

"Oh boy," Paul says worriedly, a weak smile on his face. "Do I want to know?"

"I'll tell you everything when we get back to my office. I have to spend a couple more hours at work." I turn back and lead the husky after me.

"You're lucky San Antonio has been so quiet lately," Paul says trotting along, "and that I brought a book."

"Assuming the teleporter didn't move it somewhere else," I say evenly, "like Mozambique."

"Don't even joke about that," Paul says with more than a little exacerbation and some slight fear. "This is a library book and the school librarian would kill me if I didn't return it. The lady looks like she can kill with a stare and she won't care about matter coils or directional positioners or whatever."

I admit having the husky sitting in my office for two hours as I go over paperwork and fill out documents is a little taxing. Paul likes to fidget apparently. What is it with superheroes and boundless energy? Still, I get done with what needs to be done. There are some models that need to be reviewed before the weekend and we get some strange looks from the folks stopping by. How could I not get stares? A big muscular husky sitting in my office reading a book is going to attract attention. The work day wraps up eventually and the two of us head out to the bus stop.

My car is in the shop for repairs, and I take a guilty pleasure in pointing out all the upgrades the city has made to the bus system lately. It's something I know drives my friends crazy, because I just can't help commenting on the city's infrastructure. At least Paul is an out-of-towner and hasn't heard it all before, and the husky does seem interested. The bus lets us off a couple blocks from where we need to be, but we get there quickly. Seriously, for a guy with the moniker Glacier, he does move with amazing speed. We stop a dozen or so feet away from the entrance when Paul looks up.

"Somewhere Over the Java," Paul says reading the sign and quirking an eyebrow as he looks up at the store's facade. It has the usual wood and steel coffee bar look with large picture windows and accents, and looks like a completely normal downtown Portland commercial edifice. I think the prominently displayed rainbow pride triangle on the door is the thing that is making him truly incredulous, because outside of the name that is the only thing that marks it as a GLBT hang out. He looks at me over his broad shoulder, "You're kidding right?"

"Oh hush," I chide as I begin to push him inside, my paws sinking into his shirt and thick fluffy fur and meeting hard muscle. He barely budges at all as I push against him. Ah yes, super strong, I forgot about that. I don't even think Paul feels me pushing him. Having just plain old normal strength will do that I suppose. Still, it does underline how odd the entire situation is. I guess I better be careful what I do with him unless I want to reveal his super status.

Paul sighs and moves towards the door, and I nearly fall to the ground as he moves away. I was leaning against him so hard I nearly lost my balance completely. Thankfully Paul doesn't notice as he says with an almost audible eye roll, "Oh, fine," and makes his way to the door.

Righting myself in the hopes of regaining some of my dignity, and very glad he didn't really see or feel me just then, I walk up and open the door.

Somewhere Over the Java is a pretty low key spot. Warm lighting, wood accents, thick puffy chairs and sofas, and a carpet that just seems to absorb sound it's so thick. In the middle of winter they even have a fire in the fireplace in back, something I've always enjoyed for cuddling. I see a couple I know playing a game of chess in the corner and wave at them. Neither of them really looks up. If not for the triangle on the front of the door some people wouldn't even realize this was a hang out for the gay population of Portland, though if you know how to look you'd see the other signs. The chess players are playing footsie and, with a little time, you can see the couples that form up among the patrons, the more intimate touches, the cuddling, and the odd kiss. The place has a sweet, subdued atmosphere, and I know Ted and I have shared some very nice moments here. Remembering them would make me blush, but my mind is more on Paul right now as he glances about and grins.

"Hey, not bad," the husky says easily with a wag of his curled tail.

I smile, a bit relieved. I know I shouldn't have worried, after all he's been cool with Ted and I, but he does have that frat guy sensibility around him. I'm just glad that no one is all over their partner right now. I've see that here before too. I don't care how accepting you are, that can be a bit much if you're not expecting it. We head to the counter and get our drinks.

"Jay! Over here!" shouts an exuberant voice. I glance over near the impromptu stage that has been set up for poetry reading and musical events. It got set up years ago and has never really been taken apart. I'm not sure if the owners just don't want to put one in, or if they want to lend the stage a temporary feel. A very large wolf in a red t-shirt that is far too small for his big body is waving us over to a group of chairs and couches in the corner. Gary, as always, seems excited to see me, and I have to chuckle a little at his enthusiasm.

"Oh my and look who it is," Gary says with unrestrained glee as he sees Paul following me over, "Paul Valdimos, right?"

"Uh, hi," the husky nods his head in surprise. I think he's a little shocked Gary remembers him. I'm not surprised. Gary has always had a head for faces and names, and a real thing for huskies, so of course he remembers Paul. "Yeah and you're Gary, right?"

"Oh goody, you remember," Gary says with a flutter of a paw against his powerful muscled chest. "What a compliment!"

"Few people are ever going to forget you, Gary," says a voice from the couch. I grin as I see who else is here. The speaker, an otter in a purple gray vest suit and wine red shirt, sips his coffee. He wears spectacles and has a very erudite air about him, something he intentionally cultivates.

"Oh hush, Brandon," Gary says with a grin motioning for Paul to sit down. I take up a position on a love seat so Ted can sit next to me when he gets here while Paul sits down in one of the oversized arm chairs.

Brandon just rolls his eyes and sighs as Gary sits on the arm of the chair, one paw on the chair back as he leans over Paul slightly. This of course causes Paul to blush a little bit, and Brandon sighs at the wolf. I suppress my grin, knowing that this was inevitable, but when you're wearing an old heavy metal rock band t-shirt that hugs your torso so much it shows off your musculature despite your fluffy fur I think you're just asking for a Gary gush. Especially since I know that it is one of Gary's favorite bands. Brandon has always been a little irritated by Gary's outward flamey behavior, so his sigh is just as expected.

Brandon has always been more sedate and subtle about his affections. I still remember our string of failed dates caused by his distaste for showing affection. It makes him a hard otter to read. Still, I can tell he's having a good time just relaxing here. We're a small group with a wide range of acquaintances, but somehow Gary and Brandon have gotten along well, and the two of them are Ted and my closest friends. Well, except for one person, who is not here right now.

"Where is Mattie?" I ask looking about for the raccoon.

"She couldn't make it tonight," Brandon says and again it is hard to say how he feels about that. Mattie is our little group's resident lesbian. Nice girl, a very sweet secretary, she has helped Brandon out a lot with editorial work on his poetry. She and Brandon have what I could charitably call a rocky relationship, and it is never easy to say where they are from day to day.

"I promised to give her a full report," Gary says with a smile as he leans back on the chair's arm.

"Ah," I nod and grin. "Well I hope you don't mind that I brought Paul along."

"I sure don't mind," says Gary with a giggle. Paul rolls his eyes a bit at that and Brandon sips his coffee remaining conspicuously quiet.

"It's fine," the otter says putting down his coffee cup. "I assume Ted will be here soon?"

"Oh, he's going to be a while. He's got your car this week right, Jay?" says Gary, and I nod slightly, smiling at him. Since finding out Ted's secret, that is the cover story I've been telling people whenever the car went in for repairs. Gary waves a paw at me smiling. "Well then Ted's going to be later than usual then. I heard on the traffic report as I was coming over here that Star Coyote was taking on Rigger over on the west side." I smile slightly at that. I've complained about my car a lot over the years because it's so unreliable, who knew it would pay off eventually?

"What?" asks Paul leaning forward, his ears perking up as he glances between Brandon and Gary in surprise.

"Oh, yeah," Brandon says. "That makes sense. What does that weird science major see in Portland anyway? He always seems to show up here." I grin slightly, settling in as the two of them shift into gear. They will talk about supers for hours if you let them.

"You know he treats this stuff like a game," Gary says with a wag. "I expect he just finds the city more fun."

"I still say he's here too much. I think he just likes fighting Star Coyote." Brandon says with a sniff as he sipped his coffee.

Gary grins, "You just don't like him because he's not a serious otter like you are. But hey, we got Star Coyote, so it's not like he can do too much."

Paul looks about between all of us and then asks, "But what does, um, that have to do with Ted?"

"Oh," Gary giggles, "That's right. You're not from Portland. Ted works over on the west side of town. They've got a huge traffic jam up there because of this thing. Something about a Chevy gremlin with a play-doh cannon making a mess of the freeway. If Ted was stuck behind that he'll be late. Even for him"

Paul slumps back in the chair looking relieved. I think he thought Brandon and Gary knew about Ted's secret identity. I just grin at him as he glances at me.

"Yeah, you get used to the traffic reports and Star Coyote," Brandon says with another eye roll. "Honestly, all these superbeings make such a mess. Do you know how much the city spends on its supercrimes division, civil service, and cleanup after one of their fights?" The otter grins as he points at me, "And don't answer that, you know it is a rhetorical question." I shut my mouth, chuckling a bit.

"Better than what happened in poor Minneapolis," Gary says with a woof. "Did you hear about that prison bust out last week? Ms. Q staged some sort of grand jail break for all her accomplices. The only one that didn't escape was Mishmash because he'd already been moved somewhere else. I hear the Extraordinaries and Feds were combing the state for days."

"Well I think we all saw that coming. Personally I think we're better off having a hero in town, even if it attracts folks like Rigger." I comment with a smirk, looking at Brandon. "I mean, without the heroes we could be spending a lot more money on repairs. And who else would protect us from some of the worst of the worst, like that telepath El Esclavador?"

"Besides, you just have to love the fashion!" says Gary with glee. "How many guys can pull of such tight fitting fine clothes. Especially Glacier, mmm, mighty fine look he pulls off there."

"You and Glacier," Brandon says sardonically with an eye roll. "Honestly, why don't you just write him a letter and put a nude shot in it." I glance at Paul, who quickly takes a drink of his coffee to cover his embarrassment.

"Oh you mean like you did with Swiftwolf when you were in college?" Gary says with a grin. "And because of that comment, I think I will. He might just like it."

This causes Paul to sputter and cough violently. Gary pats him on the back and at last the husky says, "I uh, I need another drink. Jay, can I get you anything?"

"Black coffee," I say with a nod, "Thanks."

"Ooo! Get me a caramel espresso with extra milk!" Gary says with a wag, handing the husky a five.

Paul gets up and walks over to the barista at the long wooden counter bar. As he does, Brandon glares at Gary and says, "You know far too much about me."

"Only what you tell me," Gary says with a wag and a confident grin. Then even more happily, he flops over the back of the chair, his large body laying heavily on the back as he looks at me upside down, his big paws clasped together as he says rapidly, "Thank you, thank you, thank you."

I wuff in surprise and look at the big wolf, flicking my ears, "Um, for what, Gary?" The big muscled wolf looks like a puppy, and his tail is wagging so hard the chair is shaking.

"For bringing the cutie husky with you," says Gary unashamedly as he sighs happily rolling over so he's kneeling on the chair Paul was just sitting in and grinning. He flexes and grins with a pleased growl, "Mmm, what a mighty fine fellow he is too. Big, fluffy, sweet tempered."

"Straight," I say cutting in, hoping to head things off right now. Gary and his crushes. I really hope this won't be like some of the other times. "He's here for a visit to hang out with Ted. He is not Questioning, or Queer, or Bisexual. He's just Straight."

"As far as you know," says Gary with a grin. "C'mon. With a butt like that, how could he be straight? It would be a travesty."

I do have to agree on some level, still I just say, "Be nice, Gary. He's been very supportive of Ted."

"Still coming out?" asks Brandon. "How deep in that closet did Ted go? I mean after what happened with his folks I can understand him being gun shy, but still."

"Deep," I say with a nod not wanting give any more details on how deep it really was. "But he's getting out slowly and Paul is helping."

"Fine. I shall admire from afar," Gary has a wide grin as he gets up and goes back to just sitting on the arm of the chair. "But I can fantasize, right?"

"Like I could stop you," I say with another chuckle as Brandon gives us both a look of slight irritation before sipping his coffee again.

Paul gets back with the drinks on a tray for all of us. I sip my black coffee, the rich scents soaking into my nose. It is very good coffee. Paul is having a cup as well and Gary happily sips espresso. Paul gives his own little introduction to Brandon, leaving out how he knows Ted and his more extracurricular activities. A young ocelot girl I've seen before starts playing a clarinet slowly and softly on the stage. It is a nice bit of background music but not overpowering. The guys who own this place know how to choose their musical acts. Ted arrives just before the second set. He looked a little windswept, and his ears flick slightly, but his tail is obviously wagging.

"Hey guys," he says happily walking over to us. His shirt is unbuttoned and his tie obviously discarded, he drops his briefcase by my feet. Yep, he just came from work, both types.

"Hi, Ted," Paul says with a wide grin. Ted does a double take at the big husky being here, but he recovers quick enough to take the husky's appearance in stride and not let Brandon and Gary onto how odd it is that Paul is here. After all, we need people to believe he's visiting us and that this isn't the huge surprise it is

"Paul," Ted says with what looks like a genuine grin. "Enjoying Portland?"

"You make better coffee here," says Paul with a sip.

"Maybe that can be a reason for us to keep you," Gary chimes in.

Ted laughs at that and flops into the loveseat next to me and wraps his arm around my shoulder. I cuddle comfortably into the crook of his arm and grin saying, "Hi there, coyote."

"Hello there, collie," he says with a smile and nuzzle, giving me a soft peck on my nose. "Showing Paul the sites?"

"Well he got in only a few hours ago," I say with a wag of my tail. I can feel Ted's warm body against me and it makes me smile. Being next to him always feels good. He chuckles at that and I think he's putting together what happened.

"So you take him to our coffee hang out?" Ted asks with a grin pressing against me. I think I've hit his sense of amusement. I think he likes the idea of having Paul here. At least that is what I gather from his tail thumping the love seat.

"Seemed right," I say with a chuckle.

"Well it is good coffee," Paul nods at his cup as he leans back, Gary's body looming over him. "Nice music too."

"And good company," says Gary as he grins and wags his tail behind the husky.

"So were you held up because of that fight Rigger and Star Coyote had?" Brandon asks.

"Yeah," Ted nods with a smile, though he absentmindedly rubs his left shoulder slightly. That might be a sore point physically we'll have to deal with later. At least it gives a good excuse for me to give him a back rub, but he continues speaking, drawing my thoughts away from his shoulder. "That did take up some of my time, though the otter got away. Whoever heard of slinky spring loaded fists and soda pop booster shoes?"

"Wow, you must have been close to the fight!" Gary says excitedly. "Two fights in one day. That is pretty rare. Usually the supercriminals get quiet for a day or two after Star lays the smack down."

"Yeah, normally supercriminals go underground after one of'em gets taken down," Paul says with a more solemn nod. "Surprised Star Coyote didn't call for help."

"Oh, Star Coyote doesn't need that much help," Gary says with a smile. "He's a great hero and he always catches them in the end. I bet he is out looking for Riggy right now."

"No one can be that dedicated," says Brandon with an acidic quirk of his eyebrow.

"Awww, I'm sure he can be," Gary says and Ted blushes slightly at the level of loyalty the wolf is showing his alter ego.

"Well, whatever the case, Rigger got stopped. That was the important part," I interrupt the two. "And everyone is here safe and sound."

"Still, from what I hear there might be a reason he didn't call for help," Gary says conspiratorially. "Well, besides the fact that he's good hero and probably didn't need it."

I glance at Gary, Ted, and Paul and then ask with forced ease, "Oh?"

"Now, this is just an internet rumor so who knows how true it is but," Gary pauses and looks at us, drawing out the tension of his little secret, "I hear Star Coyote quit the Extraordinairies. Or worse they kicked him out for some reason."

"Now, uh, why would people be saying that?" Paul asks, and I can tell the big husky is trying not to let his surprise show.

"He hasn't been seen at any of the fights the team has been involved since that big rumble in Minneapolis," Gary explains, "and they're saying he hasn't answered the question every time it gets asked."

"Maybe he felt that he was being a drag on the team and felt that he was causing trouble," says Ted, pointedly looking at Paul.

"That would be a silly reason," Paul sips his coffee. "Considering all he's done for the team."

"Well I don't know why myself." Gary gives a wave of his paw. "All I know is that it has been commented that in every gathering of the Extraordinairies lately he hasn't been there. A couple of times they were easily close enough to Portland for him to get there, too. Course, it is the internet, so who knows. For all I know it's a meme that the Technowitches planted to cause trouble. Or maybe El Esclavador for all I know."

Brandon shudders at the mention of that name, "Ugh, don't bring that freak up. Talk about scary. Telepathy is just disgusting. I mean you couldn't even tell if he was messing with your mind they say."

"I think that is a rumor," Ted says trying to reassure the otter. Brandon, like a lot of people, finds telepathy very frightening. He's a big fan of superheroes and superpowers but, like a lot of people, if you bring up El Esclavador or guys like him, he changes his tune. Ted continues, "And I don't think it would be silly for him to leave if he was worried about the team."

"Well it would still be a shame," I say leaning back from Ted slightly. "After all, he's done some good things on that team, stopped some bad people, and they've helped him to be a better hero even as he helped them."

"Or maybe it means he'll get more time in Portland," Brandon chides adjusting his glasses. "Maybe some more time from our resident hero would be a good thing. You guys are always going on about how great it is for him to be here. It would mean more time for him to be in the Rose City."

"That would depend a lot on why he left," says Paul. "If he left for a bad reason, or if maybe an overly emotional reason, or for something that wasn't his fault, then maybe leaving was a bad idea."

"Unless he was at fault for putting things into position to fly out of control," Ted says with flinty irritation now.

"Wow, a lot of guesses there," Gary says patting Paul's head even as the coyote and husky glare at each other a bit. No one else seems to have picked up the subtext in that conversation, though they have caught on to the tension in the air. Paul's light grey furred ear flicks as the big wolf's paw begins rubbing his scalp. Like all of us canines he seems to enjoy it.

"Well he's a good hero," Paul says, and then he half closes his eyes and smiles. Seems someone found a soft spot on the husky there. He blinks and continues after Gary withdraws his paw, "I'd just hate to see Star Coyote break away from his friends and team for a bad reason."

"Really think they're friends?" Gary asks with a smile. "I like the idea of superheroes being friends. I never thought about it before, but I can just imagine them all going out for drinks after saving a city. Or watching a movie together in their base. Oh, or having coffee just like we are!"

Gary seems taken by the idea and Brandon chuckles at the way the wolf wags his tail, "Nah. I bet it is all business for them. I mean when would they find the time to be friends?"

"You can always find time for that. I suspect they'd feel a lot less lonely being with people with similar interest and skills," I rub Ted's shoulder slightly.

Ted turns and looks at me. He obvious doesn't want this to continue much further as he says, "I think most heroes would already have some very good friends and don't want to sacrifice them needlessly for the idea of not being alone."

"Who says they can't have both?" I ask resting a paw on Ted's knee.

Before he can respond Gary says, "So, Brandon, how is your poetry going?" Ted looks away from me, and I know that is an end to the conversation for now.

Paul glances away from Ted to Brandon, saying, "You do poetry?"

"A bit," Brandon says humbly glancing at his notebook. "I'm putting an anthology together."

"Slowly," Gary says languidly. As if to under line his point, he leans against Paul's shoulder and seems to snooze a bit theatrically before continuing, "C'mon. Pick up the pace, Brandon. I want to be able to read your work for once."

"Yeah," Ted says with a wag his mood changing as the topic changes. "You've got some great stuff. You have to get it done and share it with the world."

"Any chance I can hear some," Paul asks motioning to the stage with his thumb. The ocelot left the stage during our conversation and it is empty now, so Brandon could conceivably recite something. He won't though; that isn't his way.

Brandon scrunches up on his chair, "Ugh. No thanks. I don't like to recite my stuff in public."

"That is why you need to finish the book. You have some good stuff in there," I say with a nod. "Mattie let me see the latest draft."

"Feh." Brandon flicks his tail and shakes his head, "It isn't ready yet."

"You really do need to finish it." I finish my coffee.

"Leave him be, Jay," Gary says lounging back on the chair. "He'll never really finish it. He's too much of a perfectionist."

"And you always get things done shoddily and too quickly," Brandon retorts irritably. "What is this? Question Brandon's artistic choices night at the coffee house?" The otter frowns, his tail tapping the floor gently.

"I only put out things I am proud of," Gary says with an easy wag resting his hands on his legs as he balances on the arm of the chair. How a big wolf like that can have such good balance and appear comfortable on that perch I'll never know.

"Oh like the entire Silas thing?" Brandon asks his voice dripping with irritation.

"Low blow, Brandon," Ted says glaring at the otter. None of us want to see the wolf break down from thinking about Silas. We all agreed not to bring him up anymore. Gary is always rushing into his romantic interests, which is true, but Silas was a very long term relationship for the wolf and it had ended for other reasons than the wolf rushing things. Obviously Brandon is in no mood to be reasonable though. Gary probably shouldn't have teased him about his poetry.

Oddly enough Gary doesn't react to it the way I'd expect him too. "Oh hush. That is different from actual artistic products."

Brandon sits back in his seat and sighs, "I bet you wouldn't say that if you weren't leaning on a big meaty husky man."

"Hey, now," Paul grouses, "Leave me out of this thing."

"Aww, c'mon. Like you wouldn't know what he is doing." Brandon's sour mood is palpable. "He's laying all over you. He is practically throwing himself at you."

"Spoil sport," Gary says sticking his tongue out at Brandon and getting up from the chair arm. He walks over to another group of chairs and easily lifts an arm chair up from the ground and walks it over to us. Setting the deep blue chair down between Brandon and Paul, Gary makes our group a circle as he sits in the chair. "Better now?" he says with a smile at the otter.

"Look, I don't care," Paul says. "I'm just here to hang out with my friends."

"And get stares from every guy here," Brandon says, giving the husky his attention now.

"I doubt that," Paul says innocently. Ted and I look about, and there are a lot of guys glancing this way. Now that Gary has taken his own seat they're looking a lot more interested. Ted gives me an uncomfortable look and I just roll my eyes.

"Well yeah, everyone is looking," Gary says with a smile at Paul, "but seriously, who wouldn't stare?"

"And with that I think I need another cup of coffee," Paul says standing up and walking over to the bar. I get up and follow, for support reasons, as Ted crosses his arms and glares at our friends. I know he'll be giving them a talk. I think I'll get one later for bringing the husky here.

Paul is already ordering another cup of coffee for himself, decaf, and I do the same.

"Hey, look," I say leaning on the bar as the lynx behind the bar works on filling orders, "if you feel uncomfortable we can leave. Maybe it was stupid of me to bring you along. I just thought Ted would feel more comfortable talking here."

"Oh c'mon. That Brandon guy was just being a dick because you all called him on being lazy, or scared, or whatever it is that's holding him back," Paul says. "I've pushed buddies before over the same things. It happens."

"I'm just saying if you're feeling that this isn't your scene," I begin to say, but I'm interrupted when a lanky fox with stylish glasses walks up to us interrupting me.

"Hey," the fox says with a bashful smile his thick fluffy tail flicking about nervously as he looks up at the big husky. "I, uh, saw that wolf get out of his chair. My name is Larry. I, um, gee, I…"

"Yes?" Paul asks quirking an eyebrow and glancing towards the fox, obviously a little confused.

The fox blushes further and then says very quickly, "Well, if you're ever free, feel free to call me okay?"

The fox slips a phone number on a piece of note book paper into Paul's hand and then rushes back to his seat, blushing furiously. A few people are watching him walk away and glancing at Paul, then back to the fox who is now curled up in a chair blushing and trying not to look at the husky. The fox looks like a kid almost. He has to be early twenties at the latest. Did I ever ask people out like that? Was I ever that scared and nervous about asking someone I found hot out?

Paul looks down at his paw in surprise and then back up at the fox. He looks over at me blinking in surprise, "Uh, that is a first. Should I go over and tell him?"

I hold up my paw stopping that train of thought. "Trust me, Paul, there is nothing you can say. Well, nothing you can say that won't embarrass him more. Just walk away. The kid obviously was just trying to work his courage up to ask a hot guy out."

"Yeah but I'm not into guys," Paul says looking down at the phone number, "and, uh, should I be complimented?"

"He doesn't know that," I say crossing my arms and hoping Paul doesn't see our barista's shoulders slump a bit. "Take it as a compliment for now and move on with your life. Let the kid feel good about asking a guy out. Didn't you ever feel embarrassed asking someone out?"

"Oh yeah," Paul says with a slight blush. "Man, back in middle school, right in the middle of the lunch room. I got laughed at by all my buddies and by her. That was just embarrassing." The big husky grins a bit, his face red from the remembered shame. "Although I did start working out a lot more after that."

"Well I bet he's in the same spot. You might as well let him think he got a little close," I explain easily.

"Oh, c'mon I bet he could handle it," Paul says dismissively. "This isn't middle school."

"Trust me, a lot of gay guys are late bloomers," I say with a smile. "Ted had to spill a slushy on me as an excuse to talk to me and he was in his late twenties at the time."

"Now that sounds like a story," Paul says with a smile and a waggle of his ears. "So you're saying the guy might not take it well?"

"When you're just learning how to fit into these things, it's a bit hard to feel comfortable," I say with a shrug as I tap my paw absentmindedly on the counter. "He'd probably take it fine in the end, but it would be embarrassing, so why do that to him?"

Paul nods and wags his tail, "Okay, fair enough I guess. Still, I mean, it can't be all that bad."

"Excuse me?" an older looking labrador walks up and looks at Paul. "I saw that young thing approach you. My name is Lyle."

"Uh, hello," Paul says perplexed, and I almost want the ground to open up underneath me. Cripes, again already? I've been coming here for years and even I didn't get this kind of turn around when I was single. I guess Gary being all over Paul was acting like a ward against this kind of thing from happening; he does have a reputation for being possessive of his flings. I sigh and watch the train wreck unfold.

The labrador smiles, his tail lazily wagging back and forth, "I'm sure a discerning young man like yourself doesn't want to deal with a less experienced young fellow like that."

"Uh," Paul says with all his remarkable command of the English language.

"You're obviously new around town as well," the lab says as he takes out a business card. "Feel free to call me some time when the muscle head or little boys aren't all over you. I'm sure smart fellows like you and I will have plenty to talk about and I can show you some very interesting things in town."

The labrador walks off, tail raised high, as Paul glances at that phone number now in his paw. Then looking at me he says, "He's kidding right?"

"No," I say easily.

"Geeze, whatever happened to gaydar?" Paul says putting the lab's number on the bar, though he does make a flourished gesture of putting the fox's number in his pocket. Larry the fox blushes at that, but I can see the smile on his muzzle from here. The barista seems to smile at that as well. I think he's been hearing our entire exchange, and I know he's been through something similar in the past. Everybody who works at Somewhere Over the Java gets hit on like Paul is now.

"It is a bit overblown," I say looking at the husky. "Yeah, sure there are times you can tell, but people have different levels of skill and really it is all about reading people and the clues people want to present."

"Yeah, but aren't all of you good at it?" Paul asks a bit crudely.

I sigh and give the husky a look, "Only after lots of practice. Once you put yourself out there, ask someone out, and have them shoot you down because you don't fit that person's orientation you learn to start reading signs. At least I did. Ted just learned to hide it as much as he could and keep his eyes open. Gary just throws himself at people from sheer friendliness." I grin at Paul, who grins back. "I'd say Gary's the most successful of us, since he always seems to stick."

"Yeah but then shouldn't folks figure it out?" Paul asks looking around and I think finally noting some of the guys glancing his way or whispering to each other. He continues to blush slightly. "I mean from practice."

"Two things, Paul," I say holding up one finger, "First of all. Your clothes aren't exactly sending the straight laced heterosexual message." Paul glances down at his clothes but before he responds I continue, holding up a second finger. "Secondly, you're in this coffee bar. Here everyone just assumes the default is gay."

"Not sure I understand that," Paul says ignoring the clothing comment as he quirks his head at me.

Okay. Obviously our frat boy husky is a little thick on this point, so I might as well explain it to him. I point at the door to the coffee house and say, "Out there everyone assumes we're straight unless we tell them through symbols, words, or actions that we aren't. Straight is the default."

Paul seems to come to the realization before I have to say it, and the big husky says, "But in places like this everyone just assumes you're at least interested in the same gender."

"Right," I nod. "Clubs, hang outs, coffee places, they're all about community, sure, but it helps give us the feeling of not being alone and maybe not worrying so much about asking someone out."

"Oh," Paul nods and oddly enough grins, "So everyone is checking me out?"

"Well, except for maybe the girls," I nod at him.

"Surreal," Paul says as our coffee comes up. It looks like the barista is using the nice coffee mugs for us. "I never thought about a room of guys checking me out."

"You, um…" I pause and then just ask, "Are you okay with that?"

"Well I'd be lying if I said I was," Paul says with a smile and a wag. "But hey, if people want to check me out, that is cool. It is different from what I'm used to, but maybe other guys have looked before too, I dunno. Just as long as no one does anything inappropriate I'm good and its fun seeing Ted relaxing a bit with you. He acts different here, and it is nice to see him happy. Besides, I don't know how to really say this, but you two are pretty cute together."

I can't help but blush at that comment as we head back to the gang. Gary and Brandon both look a little chagrined from what Ted said to them while we were up. I do quickly state before we rejoin them, "But if you want to head out of here, I can understand that."

"Nah," Paul says, "in for an inch in for a mile, as my Ma always said."

We sit back down, and Gary his ears slung back and looking very sorry says, "Hey, Paul, look, I'm sorry if I was too forward. I'm just silly sometimes. Maybe I'm just too excitable. I really don't want you to feel uncomfortable."

Paul waves his big paw, "No worries, Gary. You knew the score and so did I. If I had felt really uncomfortable I'd say something."

Gary's ears perk up and he smiles happily his tail thumping into the chair as he wuffs with a wide smile, "Oh, good!"

"Well that's a relief," Ted says with a smile. "So, anything else going on, Paul?"

"Hey now, this isn't 'all about Paul' night you know," Paul says as the clarinet ocelot from before starts playing again.

"You're new to the bunch of us, so you might as well provide new conversation," Brandon says with a smirk.

"Wow," Paul asks with a smile. "You're all that boring then?"

"Oh hush," Ted smiles. "So what is going on with you?"

"Not much," Paul says earnestly. "I mean besides the usual stuff of work, hobbies and general things around the old Mission City."

"What about, oh what is her name," Ted asks thoughtfully, "Cindy?"

"Eh, we ended it," Paul says with disarming honesty. "She said I wasn't being committed enough."

"Aww man, I'm sorry," Ted says flicking his ears in empathy with the husky. I have no idea who Cindy is but the husky doesn't exactly look distraught, more relieved.

"Yeah. The girl obviously doesn't know what she is missing," Gary says nodding his head and patting Paul's back. "I mean you seem like a pretty committed guy to me. Visiting friends in other cities when they're down and being all supportive, that is pretty heavy commitment."

"Or at least you should be committed for putting up with Gary," Brandon says.

"Thanks, Brandon," I say with an eye roll. "Truly helpful."

"Hey," Paul's voice cracks slightly, "it happens. Not every girl works out."

"I guess so," Ted says with a sigh. "Still stinks."

"I'm sure I'll find someone eventually," Paul says. Then with a grin at Ted and me he says, "After all, if you two can find each other how hard can it be?"

"You have no idea," says Gary with a dramatic sigh. "These two have been broken up and gotten back together more times than I can count. They're just lucky."

"Lucky is one word for it," Brandon says with a rare smile. "But Ted and Jay are both pretty loyal people."

"Speaking of loyalty, the ol' gang misses you," says Paul pointedly looking at Ted. "You know they don't blame you for anything. They'd just like contact."

Ted sighs with exacerbation, "Look, I screwed up, okay, and I really don't want to get into it."

"Emma is really messed up about this," Paul continues looking at Ted. "I mean you didn't even call and tell her. She had to find out from Bill."

"Oh, geeze," Ted rests a hand over one eye, obviously a little distressed by that thought. Emma has been training him for years. They're a lot closer than his irritation at her rough edges might convey to outsiders. "I didn't think of that."

"You didn't even call?" Gary says quirking and ear and looking at Ted with some annoyance.

"Gary you don't even know what this is about," I say reprovingly though I have to admit his opinion might be helpful here.

"I don't have to. This sounds like typical Ted," Gary says folding his arms, "Captain Martyr Complex, as if he can save the world by taking responsibility for other's actions."

"Gary, you really don't want to get into this," says Ted with some irritation as he looks at the big wolf. I think Gary actually hit a nerve there. Good, Ted should see he's being a bit obtuse and maybe an outsider can knock some sense into him.

"I think Gary is right," Paul says. "No one blames you for the stuff that happened that night. We were all stressed out and there was some stuff that had to be said and let out in the open. Hell, I think we still need to talk about some of the secrets people are keeping. No one is angry you kept yours. They really aren't a big deal. "

"They're a big deal to me," Ted snaps a bit, his left paw clenching into a fist as he glares at the husky and then at the wolf. "This is not an easy thing for me and I don't see why I have to put it out there." Gary and Brandon share a meaningful look, and then turn their glares to me. I just sort of flick my ears. I know they both realize that Paul is talking about Ted's issues with coming out.

"But the guys don't care. We like you around, Ted, you have to know that. I like having you around," Paul says plaintively. "You're my best friend."

That seems to shock Ted a bit because he looks at Paul in surprise, the big husky looking at him sweetly, calmly, and above all, earnestly. Ted shakes his head in surprise. "Paul, now you know that isn't true, you have plenty of friends besides me."

"Oh please," Brandon grouses. "You're kidding right? Ted you've been an emotional roller coaster for weeks now. Up and down, up and down, like an damn yo-yo. This guy literally crossed the country to see you and visit with you. He didn't come for our coffee or to be flirted with, he came to be with his friend. What part of that doesn't sound like a best friend?"

Ted actually blushes, his ears bright red at that, and fingers his coffee cup sighing a bit as his tail wags indecisively. He's complimented at being called a best friend, but chagrined by being told this way. Conflicted over who knows what else, but the delivery was perfect. Gary stands up and stretches. "You know I love these heart-to-hearts but I think we're getting too emotional and soap opera like. Next thing you know some clone, or twin, or masked crime fighter or whatever will walk through that door and declare their devotion to me. Hopefully Glacier."

"Oh please," Ted rolls his eyes. "As if that is plausible."

Paul almost looks like he has a response to that but Brandon breaks in, "Ugh, you and plausibility. That reminds me of that Doctor Orgon character earlier today."

Paul and Ted both tense up at that, and I nearly do as well. I didn't see the point of relating the fact that I was there. I didn't see Brandon anywhere, so what does he know?

"What about him," asks Gary, "besides his abysmal fashion sense?"

"See!" Ted turns to me and grins as he points at Gary, "Just like I said on the phone."

"You are so gay," Paul says resting his head in his paw and Brandon and I chuckle at that one.

"Guilty as charged," Gary says with a very satisfied grin.

"They had audio of it on the radio. Well, technically I suppose it was Jay who complained about Orgon in that science fiction movie a few years ago," Brandon says, "but that take down today reminded me of our resident science duo."

"Now what does that mean?" I ask crossly.

"Just that we don't watch science fiction movies with you two anymore for a very good reason," Brandon says.

"You both tend to be very literal," Gary says, "and not very fanciful."

"Tell me about it," Paul says with an eye roll. Sticking a thumb out at Ted, "You should see him sometimes. I'd hate to think of these two together."

"We have," Gary says flopping back into his chair floridly. "They're both like that. They are bookends of irritating responses at the TV when they disagree with some event on a show or a movie. They do not suspend disbelief."

"Hence my reminder of this morning," Brandon says. "I mean honestly, Star Coyote was making fun of the guy's name and how it related to science. Ted and Jay have done that more times than I can count."

"Too true," Gary says with a grin. Then tapping his foot on the carpet he says, "Hey look, I'm thinking of getting out of here."

"I thought we were having fun," I say with a wag of my tail looking at Gary.

"Yeah, but Flambé ` is doing a thing tonight," Gary says. "And I really want to hit it. Hey why don't you all come along?"

"Flambé?" Paul asks in confusion.

"A local club," I begin to explain.

"It's only one of the hottest, most active clubs in town," Gary says. "Really awesome to hang out in."

"If you don't mind a constant repetition of thumping techno," Brandon says. "No thanks. I'd like to stay here and relax tonight."

"Actually, going out for some dancing does sound fun," says Ted but then he looks at Paul. "But I don't think we can."

"Aww come on, Ted," Paul says with a smile. "I haven't been out to a club in a while. I think I'd like to go. Besides, I've never seen you clubbing. I think it would be hilarious."

"Um, Paul..." I hesitate to point this out because he looks excited, but I'd be a bad dog if I didn't, "Flambé is a gay club and bar."

Paul to his credit doesn't show much of a reaction besides his tail wagging a bit slower. All he says is, "Well I guess I should have expected that."

"Oh you'll have fun," says Gary with a grin. "Never been to one?"

"Well." Paul thinks for a moment and then answers, "No, never."

"Oh we have to go now!" Gary exclaims with glee his tail wagging happily. "C'mon, Ted, Jay, don't deprive the poor boy of an experience."

"Yeah, guys, lets go," says Paul with a grin. "You might as well show me the club you hang out at."

Well, my night is about to get surreal. Taking a straight guy to a gay bar has never been high on my list of fun things. Still, it would be fun to go there and I admit the sight of Paul there is intriguing, so I shrug my shoulders and smile, "Oh, why not?"

"I'm not exactly in club wear," Ted says tugging at his shirt. "And, Paul, are you sure about wanting to go?"

"I haven't gone out in a long while. I might as well check it out," says Paul. "The San Antonio club scene is dead."

Gary puts a big muscled arm over the husky's shoulder, "Right! Though you can't go in that shirt."

"Um—" Paul looks down at his shirt, "Why?"

"It would be a crime not to show off those abs," Gary says with a smile. "Don't worry. I have a top in my car!"

"What about me," Ted asks with a chuckle as he stands up. I join him as we gather up our things to leave.

"Well I don't have something for you," Gary says indicating his muscled frame and then Paul's similarly thickly muscled torso. "Unlike the hunky husky here, we are not the same size."

"Oh right," Paul says with a knowing grin. "You know, I bet changing my shirt isn't just for the club."

Gary mockingly puts a paw on his own chest and says breathlessly, "You wound me, sir!"

"Not mortally I hope," I say with a chuckle. "Alright, why not head out. I think it would be a nice change of pace. I'm sure you and I are dressed alright, Ted. It isn't like we're out cruising. We can take Gary's car, parking is murder around there anyway."

"Well, true," he says with a laugh. Then looking at Brandon, "Are you sure?"

"Nah. I want to relax and sip my coffee," the otter says.

Leaving Somewhere Over the Java is easy enough. Brandon waves us off as we exit and head over to Gary's car. I'm amazed at how outgoing Paul is being. Ted finally looks to be in a better mood after weeks of being unsure about everything. Having the husky here is truly helping him. Paul is just another good argument for him rejoining the team. I think he's finally getting the idea that the Extraordinaries are his friends. Paul seems excited to try something new. Gary is gleeful at showing the husky a selection of tops, and maybe seeing him shirtless. Well, to be honest, I suspect he really wants to see that husky shirtless.

Chapter 11
Flambé

I look over at Jay as we walk up to the front of Flambé. I cannot believe we are doing this. Today I've already faced down a play-doh cannon and a disgruntled nerd with lightning gauntlets—why does this seem like the most intimidating thing I could be doing? It is only Flambé. I've been here tons of times with Jay, without Jay, and everything in between.

"I can't believe you got me to wear this," a voice says and I turn and see exactly what is bothering me. Paul is here. The same Paul who just now called me a best friend, and who I have to admit I feel much the same way about. He's wearing jeans from earlier when we met up at Somewhere Over the Java, but he has changed into a very tight fitting mesh shirt that leaves very little of his torso to the imagination. He adds, "I look ridiculous."

Gary is wagging his tail excitedly, "No, no, you look great!"

I do have to agree with Gary. The black mesh shirt does look good on Paul. Really good on him. It causes his white fur to really stick out just a bit and it frames his muscular pecs fantastically. Jay is grinning next to me and nuzzling my neck. Seeing Gary pulling out a couple shirts earlier and holding them up to the husky, I was skeptical of him finding something that would look good in his car. I don't care how well the wolf can accessorize, I doubted he was toting around a good shirt for Paul. Yet he somehow came through. It looks fantastic on him and pretty sexy. Not that I ever want him to know that.

266

Which brings me back to the central issue: I'm about to take my very straight friend into a Gay Club. This seems like a terrible idea on paper, and yet oddly exciting. A little illicit almost, and it has been nice hanging out with my friend. Well at least we'll be able to leave if things get bad.

Jay just grabs my paw and opens the door, leading me inside. He's always taking charge when he knows I'm being too contemplative. Flambé is a nice big open dance club. Two floors, but the second always reminds me of the Bunker meeting room with its cat walks instead of an actual floor. Thick, powerful music is resonating around the room. Thumping and pounding making my heart skip a bit. It's dark in here with mood lighting and flashing lights to fit the music. Colored lights are glowing and flashing all over the room adding to the ambiance. The four of us move over to the side as people dance in the middle for everyone to see. I see couples making out, groping each other and a scent of heady sweat, arousal, and action permeates the room. Paul's eyes look like dinner plates as he looks about, his eyes catch women making out with women. What is it with straight guys and lesbians making out? Talk about unattainable. Jay just squeezes my paw and I smile at him. When you get down to it though, a part of me will always be mystified why most men aren't falling over themselves to be with Jay.

Gary is grinning and already his powerful muscled hips are swaying to the beat. "Ooo, feels like a good night here," he says loudly over the music.

"Yep," says Jay with a grin nuzzling my neck again. "They have a competent DJ for once it seems."

"I'm just amazed how much this is like every other club I've been in," Paul says. After I quirk an eye brow at him he continues, "Well, other than all the guys kissing, it looks pretty much like any club I've been to since I got my first fake ID."

"Oh, I remember mine," Gary says with a grin. "I snuck into this really cool one called Throb."

"And there the story ends," Jay says easily reaching up and patting Gary's head. The music is playing and bodies are gyrating out on the floor, and I just have to join in. It seems like too much fun. I grab Jay's paw and we're out on the floor. I glance back in time to see Gary almost pulling Paul out onto the floor. The light on his white furry chest making it glow as he starts to dance and sway to the music with Gary egging him on. The two big muscled canines are flexing and swaying, moving with the music. Who knew Paul could dance? I knew he was nimble, but he's actually a good dancer too. A tail sliding over my crotch draws my attention back to Jay. My collie smiles innocently, coyly, and leads me deeper into the throng of people and we began to dance, throwing ourselves into the music, orbiting each other, feeling each other. I let go, just getting into the swaying beat with my collie. People glance at me but all I can look at is Jay as he sways his thick fluffy furred tail, his ears wobbling, his pert snout smiling, moving to the beat. He draws my eyes as he dances close to me, our bodies meeting, moving to the tune. It feels good just to throw myself into it all. We're both sticks in the mud sometimes, we don't get overly involved with stuff like this, but sometimes cutting loose just feels right.

Jay teases a button open on my shirt as we dance and he grins at me. He's enjoying this too. Finally the song ends, the music dipping down as the DJ transitions to a new song. Panting the two of us move off the dance floor and grab a table before getting some drinks. I get a normal beer for Paul, Jay orders schnapps and a fruity mixed drink for Gary; we know him well by this point. I get water. I'm driving tonight, and by driving I mean flying, and if I'm carrying two people I want to be as clear headed as possible. Gary can handle one fruity drink. I know he will be here a while and he's a big guy. He's got amazing alcohol tolerance.

I look at Jay and smile as we rest, but we've both had a long day so I doubt we'll stay long. "So why bring Paul?"

"I thought it would be nice for you two to do friend stuff outside of work," the collie says with a grin and a pat between my ears. "And he came to me. He wanted to talk to you."

"I'm still not sure about all of this," I glance out onto the floor. Gary and Paul are already starting to dance again as the music starts back up. Looking back at Jay, "I mean taking him to a gay coffee bar and now here?"

"He seems to be doing okay," Jay says indicating the floor and I look back. Paul's hips are swaying, his body tense and firm, flexing and stretching, getting into the beat as he dances besides Gary. The two seem to match each other's movements. Their big muscled furry bodies moving to the song, Paul's eyes are closed and he's smiling obviously enjoying the entire thing. I can see some guys are staring at him and Gary, watching them both dancing. Gary is obviously looking at the husky, watching him dance with a far away look on the wolf's face. Their bodies get close together, and then draw apart, and then together again as they dance.

"I had no idea he could dance," I say in surprise.

"For a straight guy he does have moves," Jay says sipping his drink and I hear an audible groan from someone nearby as he looks away from the dance. My collie looks up at me, "Are you sure Paul's straight?"

"Painfully sure," I say with a chuckle remembering all of the very intimate details the husky has told me over the years of dates he's been on. Still, looking at him out there in that mesh shirt his with his curled tail wagging over his round ass, it is hard to believe.

"Well at least he's into it," I say watching as Gary slides around the husky, never touching him but matching the moves, the two big guys acting like counter weights on a seesaw. Guys seem to approach moving closer to Paul but Gary always seems to intercept them. A look, a flick of his tail, every signal seems to be part of his dancing and yet is directed at anyone getting too close, and the approaching party veers away. Gary is a known entity in these clubs and he's got Paul's back. He doesn't stop a panther woman with far too many piercings from dancing with the husky though, something Paul seems to really enjoy as her ears flick and her tail bats his legs suggestively.

"He's a good guy, you know," Jay says resting a paw on my shoulder drawing my attention from the floor. "The others sound like good people too."

"They are," I nod my head thinking about the team. "I'm scared is all, Jay."

"You've been brave before," he responds easily.

"Do you really think I should go back?" I ask looking into his eyes and he smiles.

"Yes," he says smiling at me with a look of confidence I've seen a hundred times before. "Just think about it, okay, Ted? I know you'd be happier if you did."

I'm about to pursue it further when Gary and Paul lumber back to the table. The big wolf is leaning against Paul a bit and they're panting from the effort but grinning.

"Nice to see someone able to keep up with me," Gary says as they get to the table.

"Hah, more like you keeping up with me," Paul says keeping up his usual brinksmanship. "Oh hey, beer!"

The two scoot over to the table as we stand and sip our drinks, talking. I can't help but notice the glances from guys walking by. They're all looking at Gary and Paul, watching them carefully. A couple guys look pointedly at Paul, trying to catch his eye, but they wander off when Jay or Gary gives them a look.

"Fun times," Paul says with a grin as he wags his tail and looks around the table. "I might have to come back here sometime."

"That panther flirts with anything that moves," Gary says with mock jealousy. "Don't make that your reason."

"Nah, not that, I'm just having a good time," Paul grins.

"We'd be happy to have you back," Jay says easily and leaning over the table. "Especially if you wear shirts like that."

"I'll admit it does seem to work for this crowd," says Paul as he sees someone staring at his chest. "Who knew?"

"Me," Gary grins. "I know what guys like."

"You should only use that power for good," I laugh.

"Hey, Gary, want to go another round out there?" Paul asks with another grin.

"You know it," Paul says. With very wide grins the two canines turn back to the dance floor and the crowd parts to let them in. They are getting impressive amounts of attention.

"Well, that's Paul," I say with a grin to my collie.

"And Gary," Jay says as he watches the two. I turn and watch too. It does draw your attention seeing the two big canines dance out there; pumping their muscular bodies to the music as they move about rhythmically.

"He's a good friend; they both are," I say while I watch an impressive twirl around a less coordinated goat. "I'm worried about hurting him."

"I think Paul is an adult. He's responsible for his own actions just like you are. He's done a lot as a…" Jay pauses to try and find the right word to cover up 'hero'. Finally he just says, "He's a responsible guy and can make his own choices. Like the choice of coming here with you. Showing you what a friend he is and hanging out with you in a place like this. Getting leered at by horny guys for you, and making it clear he cares about you."

I have to laugh at that and nod, "He is special."

The two dancing have an avid audience by this time as they sway and dance about. Paul grabs Gary's hand and they dance close, smirking at the crowd around them. They're doing a little bit of Dirty Dancing as they slide over the floor, playing with everyone's attention. Paul twirls the wolf and they slide close and continue to dance.

"He's also a big tease," Jay says. "Hope he doesn't hurt Gary."

"Gary is an adult too, you know," I grin, "Mr. Double Standard."

"You know how he can be with his crushes," Jay responds. The music ends and the two come back to the table panting again.

"Hah that was fun," Paul says patting Gary on his shoulder. "Thanks for going along with that hand grab."

"Oh no, thank you," said Gary with a wide grin and very happy wag of his tail. "What inspired that?"

"Eh," Paul shrugs his shoulders, "I figured I'd give some of the watchers a show."

"Works for me," I say with a wide grin, "I certainly enjoyed the view."

"You've seen plenty before," Paul retorts

Gary giggles and grins leaning over the table and looking at me, "Oh has he?"

"Yep, in a locker room," I say with a grin. Seeing how Gary has to realize what that would entail he opens his mouth almost begging to know more but I cut him off saying, "Though I won't be telling."

"Oh, you horrible teases, the both of you, making a poor little wolf like me all interested," Gary says.

Before we can say anything else a very large black wolf walks up to our table. I've seen him before. He always wears thick silver chains and leather straps that are far too revealing. He's got pierced ears. Trailing behind him is a mouse in a collar. I've never seen the mouse before, but I know the wolf by reputation. He's pretty much a creep, but he's never gone near me or Jay before.

"I liked the dance you just did," the big wolf says to my husky friend. He's pretty much Paul and Gary's size, but he has an air of intimidation they don't have, and he's flexed it to show off his powerful build. "Very nice dance there, pup," he says.

Paul isn't really fazed by him at all. No one like this guy could do that. Paul has taken on a lot of people far more imposing than this poser. The husky just smirks and says, "Thanks."

"Come with me, pup." The wolf rests a paw on the table and drapes his arm over Paul's shoulder boxing him in a bit. "Leave the fruit and the fairies and let a real man show you a good time."

Paul easily slides out of the arm and looks at the wolf, "No thanks. I'm with some actual men."

"Not a request, pup," the black wolf says, a menacing growl in his voice. "No one says no to me."

"Really?" Paul says looking the wolf in the eye now. "Because I just did."

The wolf growls and a big hand rests on the back of Paul's neck as he flexes his powerful arm. "Let me make it clear. You're coming with me."

I'm glaring at him now. The mouse is panting a bit watching the show. I clench a fist. This guy needs a beat down. Jay is looking worriedly between me, Paul, and the wolf. Paul is now looking at the wolf angrily and I can feel a slight chill waft over me. No one tells Paul what to do and if he thinks he can force the husky he's sorely mistaken.

Before either of us can say anything though, Gary pipes in, "Really, Zach, no one says no? I seem to recall Rick saying no."

The wolf turns his head and looks at Gary. Gary is standing up proud and tall, his hands on his hips. Gary quirks his head sweetly and gives a coy smile back to the other wolf. The wolf growls, "Name's Leather and you know it fruit."

"Sure," Gary waves his paw dismissively, I think making his wrist go limp to exaggerate the motion. "But do you really think you have a chance here? After last week with Dylan, or that time with Rick, or with what Frankie has been saying?"

The mouse is staring, surprised, glancing between the two wolves as Gary confidently talks to the wolf looking at him. The wolf flexes his shoulders as he growls, "Shut your yap."

"Right," Gary yawns at that. "Or you'll hit me, and get yourself kicked out of yet another club. Good move there by the way, genius."

The wolf clenches his paws as he glares at Gary who just wags his tail lazily and smiles, "Now shoo. Away with you, find some airhead to hit on like a graceless 18-wheeler, the adults are talking."

The wolf turns and stomps away obviously flustered. I stare amazed at Gary. Actually, all of us are, including the mouse, who just stares at Gary until the retreating wolf barks at him to follow.

Paul finally asks, "So was that the gay equivalent of defending my honor?" as Gary sits back down with us.

"More like putting your coat over a puddle," Jay says with a wag of his tail. "I was seriously worried you two would need to beat the snot out of that guy."

"Oh he's all talk," Gary says with an eye roll. "No big deal."

"Does he actually force people," Paul began to say glancing about the room. Some people are giving thumbs up at Gary for chasing the wolf off.

"No," I say shaking my head. "I've checked. Every time has been consensual; he's just a rude, overbearing jerk. Some people like that but he takes it to a pretty big extreme."

"Well let's all be happy Gary has such a fine command of gossip," Jay says with a wag.

"And the dance floor," I say raising my glass. The four of us chuckle and grin.

"Want to go back out there? Really tweak that loser?" asks Gary with a mischievous grin offering his elbow to Paul. Paul laced his arm through the wolf's and smiles at him.

"Sure," Paul said the two large canines walking back out to the floor.

A good hour of dancing and talking later and we finally leave. It was a good night and I'm still shocked that Paul has done all of this. He's smiling though. He's had a good time. Gary drops us off at the coffee bar to collect our "car".

"I still can't believe neither of you have been caught for public indecency," Jay says as he plays lookout in front of the alleyway.

"We're careful," Paul says. "Aw, shoot. I forgot to change shirts back with Gary."

"I'll get it from him," I say with a grin. "I see him pretty regularly."

"Nah, I'll just get it next time we go out to Flambé," Paul says easily.

"You want to go back?" I say surprised as the husky tucks the mesh shirt in his bag.

"Well I had fun," he says with an easy wag and a smile as he slides on his mask. "What can I say? It was a good time and I'd like to come back."

"Wow," is all I can say as I finish putting on my own costume.

"You both ready?" Jay asks.

"Almost," I say pulling out a black opera mask from my brief case. "Here put this on so we don't have a repeat of that photo Lizz got you with."

Jay smirks at me, "So now I'm the Crusader Collie?"

"Maybe," I say with laugh. Jay puts it on with a smile. I grab him in one arm hefting him up easily and he nuzzles my neck. I grab Paul's arm and I lessen gravity around all three of us. We soon fly above the city heading back home. The three of us masked, amused, and having fun.

I take one side trip to stop an armed robbery of a convenience store. Glacier doesn't need to help, but he does freeze the tires of the get away vehicle.

Getting back to our neighborhood, I am again thankful that there is a small wooded area and a lake nearby. I've used it as a changing spot many times before, and it is in easy walking distance to home so it's perfect for the three of us. We switch out of costume and walk the rest of the way. Paul will use the teleporter early in the morning to get home. I stretch and sigh as we reach our door.

"Well that was fun," I pant happily as we enter our home. Paul looks about, taking in the place. It is his first time here. Jay and I head into the kitchen and prepare some cocoa, our own little ritual to wind down after clubbing. Paul seems to take it in stride as we sit down at the kitchen table and start to relax.

"I'll be feeling this all tomorrow," Paul says with a groan. "I haven't danced that much in years."

"I'm honestly surprised how much you cut loose," Jay says with a pat on Paul's shoulder. "Most straight guys act reserved in a gay bar."

"Hah," Paul chuckles, "their loss. Actually it was something you said earlier to me that convinced me to go all out."

"Oh?" Jay says in surprise. "What magic words were those? Maybe I can use them on some of my more uptight coworkers."

"Just that everyone assumed I was gay," Paul says with a wag. "I'm not, but it was oddly freeing to think other people considered me that way."

"I'm not sure I follow, Paul," I say flicking a big ear.

"Well," Paul sighs, "after I got my powers, being with people got a bit harder. Temperatures drop if I'm surprised or in a foul mood. I'm super strong so it can be dangerous to be around me. I need to be careful. It was easier going out when I was just a powerless frat dog."

"I think I see," Jay leans back in his chair. "There wasn't any pressure to perform in the club. You weren't expecting to go home with anyone. No plans to be with someone. Instead it was just cutting loose a bit."

"And let's face it, if I had clipped anyone it would have been Gary and he looks like he could handle an accidental tap from me," Paul says with a chuckle. "Hell, I haven't had this much to drink around non-superheroes in, well, wow, since I got my abilities. I was always afraid if I got too tipsy I'd hurt someone."

"You're a happy drunk," I say remembering the time he got drunk with me. We were out in the middle of nowhere Texas on a stakeout that culminated in nothing more than a fight with Whirlwinder, and afterward we had split a bottle of rum.

"Right," Paul nods a knowing grin on his face. "And what if I go to be a happy drunk and broke someone's arm giving them a playful slap? I have enough on my conscience as it is, thanks."

"I guess I never would have thought about it that way," Jay considers the husky for a moment. "I mean Ted has to actively turn on his power most times and when he doesn't he's just floating most times."

"Well, it is a lot of fun to float," I grin. I levitate to make my point, the chair holding me rising off of the ground slightly.

Paul genuinely laughs at that, "Lucky. Yeah, I'm scared sometimes about what I could do. I'm not even the strongest person on the team but I still have these powers, I'm still stronger than most people. Don't even get me started on sex."

"Well now I have to ask," Jay said quirking an eyebrow and with a little prodding the husky sighs and continues.

"I'm always worried when I'm with a woman that I'll accidentally freeze them or drop the temperature too low," Paul says with a blush. "I mean, can you imagine some of those parts getting frozen? Not to mention if I held on too tight or gripped the wrong way."

I shudder at the thought, "Lovely mental image there."

"See!" Paul exclaims with a smile as his paw rests on the table. "But hey, if a bunch of guys want me that is cool. I won't be sleeping with them. I don't have to worry about freezing them."

"Has that ever happened?" Jay asks.

"No, though rooms have gotten colder and ruined the mood before. I just worry. I mean, girls aren't built like, say, Gary is."

"A little chauvinistic there," I eye him, "I mean Emma is no shrinking violet."

Paul nods at that and rolls his eyes, "Okay, true there. Look, I never said it was reasonable, just a fear. All I'm saying is at the club I didn't need to worry as much, so I cut loose a bit, and it felt good to finally do that."

"Fascinating," Jay says with a smile as he gets up from the table. "Now I better get your things so you can sleep tonight. It is getting far too late. Sadly, you need to sleep on the couch"

We do have a guest room in our house, but Jay is right, Paul can't sleep in there right now. We've just been using it for storage lately, and it is not clean. It would be easier for Paul to sleep on the couch, even if his big body might have trouble fitting on it. Jay goes to get some blankets and a pillow while the two of us sit in the kitchen and talk.

"So," Paul pauses and looks at me. "Anything I can do, Ted?"

"What do you mean?" I ask looking at the husky.

"Is there anything I can do to bring you back," he asks. "To make you happy, get you to come back to us?"

I smile at my friend and pat his big hand, "You've already done a lot."

It is true. I mean if Paul can be this comfortable with Jay and I together, really put up with who I am and even enjoy being around me, why am I so afraid the rest of the team won't do the same? It underlines how irrational I am being. Maybe I can do this. Maybe I can tell the team. Be on the team and function there while being out of the closet. I'd like to see my friends again. Work with them again.

"So you'll come back?" Paul asks excitedly, sitting up and wagging his tail.

"Maybe," I say noncommittally as we look at each other across the table. "Though if you start wearing mesh shirts as part of your uniform I'll be there in a second."

"Har har," Paul chuckles, stripping off the mesh shirt in question. He smiles at me, sitting back and glancing round our kitchen his eyes rest on a photo of Jay and I cuddling on the beach. He smiles while looking at it, "You know, you and Jay are a really cute couple."

I blink in surprise, "Cute?"

"I mean you look good together," Paul says with a sigh. "Happy, like you have something worthwhile in each other. The way you two hold each other, talk to each other. It's, well, cute. Reassuring, you know? It makes me feel like these things can work out."

I blush heavily at that, "I'm glad you approve, Paul."

"Like you needed that," Paul says with a smile. "Who knows. Maybe one day I'll find a girl like Jay. I doubt it though."

I laugh and smile at the big husky, "Heh, thanks. But you know it isn't always perfect and we're still adjusting to our lives together with me being a mask wearing superhero."

"Something tells me that you always have to adjust to things," Paul says sagely. "I mean people in general have to when in a relationship."

"Yeah," I nod along. "He needs some more time. I mean, look at what happened in New York with Power Puma. What if he doesn't hit his panic button again? That was insane. He should have called for help immediately."

Paul seems shocked by that and he quirks his head looking at me, "But, Ted, he did try to hit his panic button."

"Huh?" I ask confused looking at the dog.

"At least that's what Metalyena told me," Paul says with a nod. "His brother Brian told him that Holly stopped him from hitting the button."

"That," I pause trying to parse the idea and I can't, "Paul, that makes no sense."

"Hey," Paul says holding up his paws, "it's just what I heard. Brian was there though, and Metalyena gave him a hard time about not hitting his own button."

"Well why didn't Jay tell me that?" I ask angrily. We could have avoided a lot of fighting and nights alone, a lot of tension, if I had known this weeks ago.

"Because I didn't think it was important," says Jay from the doorway into the living room and I know he's put the blankets on the couch.

"What?" I say testily, "That is crazy! That is a huge deal, Jay."

Jay steps into the kitchen, looks at me, searching my eyes for a moment, and then sighs, "Ted, it was a really hard night for us already. I didn't want to complicate things even more."

"Complicate things?" I ask glaring at him. "I'd say that was pretty damn important!"

"No, it wasn't," he says with that infuriating calm precision when he is sure he is right. "Ted, it doesn't matter because at the end of the day I didn't hit the button. I did a stupid thing not calling for help."

"Yeah, but it was because someone else told you not to," Paul interjects. I glare at my collie irritably as he looks between Paul and me.

"But I still didn't use my own judgment," Jay says. "I went with hers and it was wrong. I knew it was wrong, too. We're not in the military and she didn't outrank me. I should have done it. It was dangerous, and what if Camo hadn't beaten him? Then what? If I am going to be in love with a superhero I should trust my judgment and try and protect myself."

"No one else called though," says Paul. "They didn't want to overload the response and make Power Puma realize just how close he was to family members."

"Well we should have," Jay says earnestly. "It was stupid for me not to call. I don't have super abilities. None of us did. We got lucky."

"This isn't a reason not to tell me," I say pleadingly looking at Jay. "Jay, I've been around Holly a lot. She's a very nice, but she can be quite commanding when she wants to be. She's a mother of four. Who wouldn't respond to that? She told you not to do it. I would have understood. I wouldn't have been angry or confused like I have been. I mean, this is Holly. I've watched over her kids and she keeps them in line with little more than a word."

"That's just it. I didn't want to get her in trouble," Jay says firmly. "I was responsible for my own actions. And besides, she shouldn't get in trouble because of me."

"Like Bill doesn't already know," I stand up and looking at my border collie. "Look, Holly is a good person but I don't want you thinking that way. You're being too hard on yourself."

"Well you do know all about that," Jay retorts.

"What is that supposed to mean?" I ask in surprise.

"Ted, you always act like a martyr," Jay says, his tail fluffing out. "Brandon was right at the coffee house when he said that. Case in point: this asinine leave of absence."

"Now hold on. That is not the same thing," I start to say.

"Sure it is," he says looking at me directly and unflinchingly. "You're taking other people's actions for your own. You blame yourself, and you're trying to avoid it. Maybe I should have told you what Holly did. I didn't want to complicate things, but it is the same general idea."

"It isn't the same," I respond. "I hurt the team. I let Stratagem know about how the others were lying to him. I caused Glacier to get in a fight. Not to mention everything about Camo."

Paul's face twists a bit in confusion. "Wait, who was lying to Stratagem?"

"He didn't know about the meetings." I say quietly. "The other founders cut him out of the loop because he tried to stop them."

"Oh." Paul says quietly, his gaze looking off into the distance for a moment. "That explains why he's been so distant then. Look, I can't speak for why the others are keeping secrets from Stratagem," Paul says earnestly, "But I was the one who got angry in the locker room. I attacked Camo. Not you. You didn't ask me to attack him for you, you didn't tackle him, and you didn't slam him into a locker. I did."

"I…" I pause and sigh heavily, "Look, I just…"

"You just don't want everyone to know that you sleep with men," Jay says crossing his arms. "And every misfortune, every problem with the team, you find a way to blame on yourself over that fact."

"Hey, now," I respond, tail raised and ears flicking. "That isn't it at all."

"Yeah it is," nods Jay. "Never mind that you're good for the team, that they're your friends, or that they are all responsible adults who dedicated their lives to helping people. Nope, because you bugger men, specifically me, you think they'll all act like immature morons."

"He has a point," says Paul looking at me now with his piercing eyes. "You are acting like people are going to turn on you, as if you don't trust us. It isn't a big deal, Ted it really isn't. Come on, Ted, most of the team already knows. Just make it official."

"What?" I sigh, my ears falling against my head and I feel tears welling up in my eyes, as I put words around my true fear. As I think about our fishing trips, training, meals together and everything else, as I finally say it, "What if Solarcoon wants me gone?"

"He won't," Paul says.

"What if he does?" I ask, my voice breaking as I look between them, my heart pounding in fear.

"He won't, Snuffles," says Jay coming over and hugging me tightly.

I don't even respond to him using my nickname, I just hug him back tightly. "You said the same thing about my parents," I gasp as last.

Jay pauses, and then says at last, "I was wrong. But I don't think I am here."

"Bill is too good a man for that, Ted," Paul says resting a big paw on my shoulder. My lover is hugging me tightly and I feel my best friend's presence and it's comforting. I don't think he even knows what happened with my family but he still seems confident.

"I'm scared," I say at last as we stand in our kitchen, the inky black of night outside reminding me of what started all this.

"You're not alone," Paul says. "I got your back, buddy." The big husky smiles at me, his paw gripping my shoulder firmly.

"You won't be alone on this end either," Jay says kissing my nose. "We're in this together."

"I'm sorry," I say finally the hugs breaking as I glance around at my friend and boyfriend. "I've been an idiot."

"Not something unexpected," Jay says with a wag of his tail. "I was too. I should have said something about Holly."

"Now what?" Paul asks looking at the two of us as I wipe my eyes.

"Now?" I nod my head, thinking. "Now I need to talk to someone, and I need to think, but you are right. I'm not leaving the team for the right reasons. I'm scared, but I can't let that rule my life."

"You'll go back," Jay doesn't say it like a question. It is a statement of fact for him.

"I need to check some things. I need to talk to Stratagem," I say now as I think about the badger in the meeting room and the first time I've seen his face without the goggles. "And this is a good break to figure some stuff out and to spend time with you."

"You can tell the team, you know," Paul says with a smile.

"I will," I nod my head. "I have to, I guess. I just need to figure out how to do it in a controlled circumstance so it goes the right way."

"Well when you do," Paul nods, "I got your back, just like I said."

We finish our cocoa and adjourn for the night. Paul flops heavily on our couch and curls up going to sleep. For the first time in weeks I feel truly relaxed and able to sleep. I dream as if there are no weights on me.

No worries. Jay cuddles against me once more. Raja Raksha no longer haunts my dreams. My friends are with me. Now I just need to figure out how to be who I am with the team and with Solarcoon.

Chapter 12
Boston Bravado

Flying at night can be a lot of fun: the chill in the air, the stars above, the moon light shining over you illuminating your way. Flying across country into the night is fascinating when you can move faster than most jets, watching the night race up upon me from the horizon. I'm still not sure how I can do it. I'm in Boston now, flying above the spires and glass towers, flitting between them, slowing down so I don't break or rattle anything, searching for my destination.

I'm looking for a meeting hall. Unfortunately I'm a little lost. Navigating around a city can be difficult from the air. I know what I'm looking for though. It started in Seattle. Then the same crime happened again a week later in Oakland. Last week the same thing occurred in Portland, which is how it got my attention.

A room filled with rich business men, all tied up and cuffed, and then placed in embarrassing poses. Their pockets were looted, millions taken from bank accounts, and yet every last one of them clammed up, unwilling to say what had happened specifically. Only that they were robbed and did not want to press charges.

Belinda Ramerez was the one who saw the connection between all the crimes, or more accurately, that the cases were likely perpetrated by the same person or persons. She was the one who asked me to look into them because while she could tell the MO in each case was the same, she couldn't figure out who was behind it. I spent a solid three hours pouring over case notes with her until I saw the connection. I was never a detective but I had something they didn't, personal information. Namely that three of the victims, one in each case, were members of an infamous fraternity of a college in Oregon. One I knew because I had attended that school. They weren't in my year, but they were close enough. Each one an up-and-coming banker or businessman, and each one also a certifiable self-involved twit with far more money than common sense. It says something for me to comment on their common sense—after all, I'm a man who flies around wearing tights.

None of them had made the connection either, of course. Patterns aren't always easily recognizable. I only saw it from dumb luck and because I can take a very easy guess who is behind this. I turn left and I know I am on the right track. Boston is tricky to navigate. I'm also not just here for the case. I know there is another opportunity in Flagstaff, AZ, that seems just as likely. I came in part to talk to Stratagem.

If they hit Flagstaff I'll be sure, and I know Boston will be next. If they hit here, then I can hopefully catch them mid-crime and wrap this up, ideally with the badger at my side. He just hasn't returned any of my calls. I finally broke down and called Glacier over it to ask him if he knew what was going on. That is when I found out the whole story.

Stratagem had been downright taciturn to the team. Electing to not go on missions, barking orders at people, and generally obsessively directing them. He normally just gives polite yet firm suggestions. Now he was rarely staying for meetings and almost never talking to anyone beyond a shouted order. It wasn't a surprise that he wasn't responding to calls. There were also rumors of some very vicious captures in the city. Several crime bosses and gang members had been taken down with greater than usual force. Especially for Stratagem, who prides himself on using only the minimum force needed to accomplish a goal.

I needed to see him, to talk with him, to apologize for my part in events. I'd also like us to handle this together, just in case. Hopefully he knows I am in town right now and he'll come. I did just get lost after all and someone has to have seen me flying all about the city and called someone. Stratagem would hear about it.

I'm over the warehouse cum dance club on the wharf, lately a popular spot for the city's elite. According to the internet, there are a lot of rumors of illegal activities surrounding the place, with prostitution and drugs being just the tip of the iceberg. Just like the other spots that were hit. Tonight, the club has been rented out for a party by some financial group. I float above the roof and look in the skylight and my theory is confirmed. Looking inside I can see high priced electronic and sound systems, a table lined with food, caviar, ice sculptures, a thick velvety red carpet, and a crime in progress.

I don't bother to break through the glass. Dramatic as that would be, the shards could hit the innocent bystanders down there. Besides, why do that when the skylight provides a very nice hatch? I easily open that and float down to the ground, interrupting the festivities.

All the men have been tied up with leather straps and some of them have been gagged, probably for making too much noise. I smirk at who I see at the center of the room filling up a very large canvas bag with loot. They've both stopped and are staring at me in surprise. The dollar sign on the front of the bag is a nice touch for them. They do love the touch of absurd to help mock their victims.

"Cinnamon," I say and then turning my head to her sister, "Spice."

"Well, well, sister dear, it seems we've been found out," says Cinnamon. The russet colored fox smiles at me. She has a deep burnt brown-red fur coloring with the usual black socks on her feet and hands, and the creamy white fur on her neck trails down her chest. The thick fluffy tail has been immaculately groomed and the black tip flicks with little concern for my arrival.

"Oh indeed, sister," says a slightly higher, sweeter voice. It's Spice, her more apple-red fur glowing in the light. Her white accents are much more like snow trailing up under her chin and tipping her tail. She's similarly well groomed, they always are. "This should be fun!"

The two are siblings and as close as twins; partners in crime and viciously capable opponents. They've become a constant thorn in my side in Portland. They're both dressed in their usual get ups, skimpy lace and leather. Biker hats on their heads, and clothes cut to show off their tails, legs, and cleavage.

"I have to say this is one of your more interesting schemes. A lot less flamboyant than usual as well," I say making no sudden movements, waiting for them to make the next step. "Let me guess. You play yourselves up as an escort service or strippers with very loose morals. You get your mark to invite you and ensure no other women are coming."

"Oh," purrs Spice with amusement, "he's guessed a great deal."

"I know," Cinnamon says coyly tapping her muzzle. "So very charming, Starry. Handsome smart coyotes like you are so intriguing."

I try not to roll my eyes. They always hit on me during these exchanges. Instead, I continue, "You then proceed to titillate the wealthy young men until you get them all locked up and then you rob them blind; including delving into their bank accounts and grabbing their credit cards. Have I got it so far?"

"Oh you always were so smart, Starzy," Spice coos with glee, bouncing a bit on her feet as she smiles at me. It's a predatorily confident smile belying her innocent air. Cinnamon gives me the same look.

"Of course the marks have no idea. No idea what even connects this case to the three others I know about. It wouldn't surprise me if there were more," I say as the two start to circle me, breaking off in different directions. I don't move. I wait for it, continuing on as if their movement doesn't concern me, knowing that for now they are distracted by my banter. They enjoy this part of a crime too much to interrupt me, and I smirk at them because I know I've got one thing to break their cool.

Cinnamon giggles, "They're so willing to part with their money why not play them for it?"

"I know. I mean they fall for it so easily, Starzy," says Spice she and her sister are fingering their whips now, moving in perfect harmony. They both carry heavy bull whips and they are experts at using them. The tricks they can do with them are astounding and death defying. Even worse, they've been altered by Rigger, who trained them years ago, and they have all sorts of odd tricks to them. The second they unhook them the fight will begin for real. They're too nimble and quick to rush. They have unnatural balance and grace and even with my gravity defying abilities I couldn't get them while they work as a pair. They know how to work as a team, and that's why I hoped to have a teammate of my own to back me up tonight.

"I'm just surprised you held a grudge this long, Cinnamon," I say looking at her now directly with a smile on my muzzle. "Most women who put themselves through college by stripping don't get this worked up."

Cinnamon sputters angrily, "I have no idea what you're talking about!"

"Come, come, Star. That isn't a nice thing to say to my sister," says Spice with a bit of annoyance. Do I detect a hint of worry in her voice? Yes, I think I do.

"Oh but I know it's true. See that tiger over there," I point off to a corner and a tiger who has been gagged, wiggles and squirms and blushes tremendously as I point him out. "He happened to belong to a fraternity that three of your other victims went to. They lived there at the same time you attended the school, Cinnamon."

Cinnamon is glowering at me now, her face dark with anger. Spice is trying to calm her and keep them on their better ground but I have her angry and when one of the vixens gets angry I find they make mistakes, a common situation in superbeing fights.

"Let me guess," I say tapping my muzzle confidently. "One of them tried to cop a feel? Told the campus what you were doing? Humiliated you?"

"Yes," Cinnamon growls angrily at me. "Yes, damn it, they humiliated me in front of everyone. Him and his spoiled rich friends, they never had to work for school. Never had to sweat for it, never earned it. Instead they wasted what they had and then got cushy jobs. I got loans. I got kicked out because of entitled twits like him."

"So we're getting our revenge," says Spice matter-of-factly with a curt nod of her sweet little head. Not exactly a shock there, a lot of their crimes are about getting revenge.

"I won't let you do that," I say simply. "I bet what they did was wrong, but this is wrong too. Most of these guys have never met you."

"They're all the same," Cinnamon growls, unfurling her whip. Spice is following suit but she's slower about it. Obviously I have them off their game now.

"I don't think you have the right to make that choice," I say, starting to float above the ground. "I don't think you have the right to punish them, either. There is such a thing as the law after all."

That does it. Cinnamon hates it when someone invokes the law when it comes to what she sees as an injustice. Her whip cracks outwards, but I'm already moving, grabbing it with one paw and using it to change the gravity around her. She's nimble and quick, but changewhich way is down and she trips up.

That is exactly what she does now. Cinnamon tries to tug the whip back and instead she flies up into the air. I'm already altering the gravity around us, oscillating it up and down quickly, the rapid changes making her dizzy as she keeps a tight hold on the whip.

Now this would be a problem if Spice had struck at the same time, I couldn't do this to both of them at once. Normally they have great timing, but I got Cinnamon to strike early and Spice wasn't ready for it. I'm fighting them one at a time and I can handle that. Cinnamon is already discombobulated as she lands heavily, and I rush around her, tying the whip around her quickly, using it as an impromptu rope. It won't hold her but it will distract her long enough for me to handle Spice. I turn to face her now, grinning.

The vixen has her whip at the ready, her face hardened with concentration as she flips easily up into the air. Using her whip she grabs a beam and uses it as leverage pulling her self into the air for a flying kick. I dodge it, barely, but she wasn't trying to hit me. The kick was a fake out; she was getting over to the bag of cash again where the sisters obviously had some other tools. That was stupid of me; I shouldn't have let her get near their gear. A pair of bolos flies at me, twisting around me and tying up my legs and my left paw. Shoot. I wasn't expecting that. Spice does a cartwheel, flipping up onto the table covered with food, smirking.

"Have to hand it to you, Starzy," she says it with far less sugar this time, a sign of respect from her. "I wasn't expecting you to get Cinnamon like that."

I struggle with the bonds around my feet and hand, "Have to be me, Spice."

"Oh you do indeed. Throwing stars for a Star Coyote?" Spice fondles some shuriken in her paw and my eyes widen. They're not playing around this time. I doubt they'd kill me but I suspect I might have gone further than usual pushing Cinnamon like that. Before she can throw the shurikens though, her paw is grabbed very tightly. She yelps in pain as the points cut her badly, dropping the stars.

Stratagem glowers at her but doesn't say anything as he smacks a paw into her stomach and then flips her over his head. Spice and Cinnamon are not physically strong, they're better at thrown weapons and dodging attacks. Land a good solid blow and the fight becomes a lot easier. She flies against the table, a punch bowl cracking, shards of glass and rivulets of red drink splashing over the table and the vixen. I'm struggling to get the bolo off me, and I'm nearly there.

Stratagem advances on her and she is up on her feet. Her whip cracks out but Stratagem just intercepts it with a paw and growls at her. He tugs on the whip hard, sending her stumbling forward as his fist connects with her jaw. Ouch! A little rough there, Stratagem. She's staggering now as he punches her once more, and I frown. That blow was definitely excessive. I get the bolo off finally and I'm standing up as Spice is gasping in pain. She's down for the count, but Stratagem has her arm and the badger does another flip throw, though this one is against a wall. She slams into it with a sickening smack. He's advancing on her prone unconscious form. I think he's planning on hitting her again from the look of his stance. Then, with a barely audible click, I watch as a metallic staff lances out in his paws.

Oh, God, no. I've seen that staff before. Stratagem doesn't go around unarmed and seeing as he doesn't technically have superpowers he's mastered concealing weapons on his person. Many of them are based on miniaturization and being easily folded up. His staff is one of his most dangerous, if simple looking, weapons. It is made of a lightweight super tensile metallic alloy. He tried explaining the chemical composition to me but it gave me a headache. Supposedly he was inspired by the same super strong metal that Metalyena becomes when he goes into his metal form. Stratagem only uses it against extremely dangerous or super strong foes who can handle it, like the Iron Ravers or Nth Knight. He can't seriously be thinking about using that on an unconscious supercriminal like Spice. Her body looks limp. She has cuts oozing blood and mixing with the punch. He's going to kill her with that thing. This isn't about disarming and incapacitating a foe, this is much more. He looks ready to kill, and I won't let him. I'm up in the air and flying faster than he is walking.

"Going my way?" I ask easily as I grab him by the scruff of his neck and we're off into the sky, sailing out of the skylight in moments. The cold night air hits my face as we zoom out of the warmer warehouse. He doesn't struggle much but I can see his clawed paws tightening on the staff. I land us on a roof of a building nearby. We need to talk but obviously we have to stay near the action.

He turns to face me, and for the first time I get a look at him. I notice now that we're out of the fight that his fur looks disheveled. Has he not brushed lately? His costume looks dirty, rumpled and out of place on him. Stratagem is usually a lot more put together. His goggles shine from ambient light but I can see is face well enough to realize he is tired. He looks like a bit of a wreck. He just stands there, paws twisting on his staff, watching me.

I'm the first to say something, "What the fuck is wrong with you?"

"I have no idea what you mean, Star Coyote." His voice is hard, precise, and cutting.

"That was excessive and you know it, Stratagem," I say angrily, looking at him.

"She was the one with throwing stars," he answers back coldly.

"You know for a fact that Cinnamon and Spice are nonlethal. They would have hurt me, maybe, or maybe she would have used them in one of their overly grandiose exits they like to do, but they wouldn't have killed me, much less crippled me or hurt bystanders." I'm angry. "Unlike what you were doing. She was down even before you did that throw and you know it."

"I'm sorry if I don't trust my teammate's reports as much anymore," he says coldly. "It has come to my attention that they might not always be filled with the truth."

"You know I give good reports, Stratagem," I answer, fuming at him. I've grown to respect Cinnamon and Spice over the years. I might not like them but neither of them deserved that kind of rough treatment. I growl at him, "I called you multiple times. Why didn't you respond? We could have coordinated and avoided this."

"I can hardly trust your reports and the idea of a coordinated effort seems laughable to me," he says flexing his fingers. "Are we done?"

"No, we're not done," I retort. "You can not just pass this off as alright."

"Pass off? You mean like you and my so called friends tried to pass off all those meetings," says Stratagem angrily, his eyebrow raised as he stares me down, his eyes hidden behind his goggles. "Lying to me and bald facedly taking advantage of my trust?"

"Damn it, Stratagem, you were going to kill her!" I growl at the badger. "You've never killed someone, let alone crippled them, and all you can talk about is trust? You never use that damn staff except in emergencies. You've told me that multiple times. Yet you lanced that thing out with her on the ground."

Stratagem stares at me for a moment and I think I've gotten through his thick skull. He finally responds, "Sometimes trust is all you have to rely on. It is something very important to me."

"More important than someone's life?" I ask glaring at the badger.

"I…" he pauses for a moment and seems unable to come up with a response. He collapses his staff and tucks it away. Is he actually shocked at what he has done?

"Why are you acting this way?" I ask, tail raised, my fingers flexing. "You've always been the hero with your head screwed on right. Always had the ideas, been the thinker, helped all of us act better."

"Well I'm sorry if I have weak moments as well," Stratagem retorts. "It is not easy discovering that all the trust you put into your friends hasn't been repaid in kind."

"It is not exactly easy to trust you in return, Stratagem," I say tail fluffing out at his seemingly callous reaction. It is like he's trying to step back from what he has done, trying to rationalize it when he really shouldn't.

"I have no idea what you mean, Star," he glares at me.

"Oh? You wear those goggles everywhere. I wouldn't know your face at all if you hadn't taken them off when you were distracted. I don't even know your name, yet we're all supposed to trust you with our identities—our family's identities."

"And how is that different from you, Star?" the badger snaps, the light flashing off his goggles as he growls at me. The growl is full of so much anger it makes me take a step back. Why is it that I find angry badgers so scary? "How long would you have kept Star Coyote from Jay, the man you supposedly love? And how long would Jay have stayed a secret from the rest of us if he hadn't forced the issue? I have never researched you or the others Star. Finding Jay would have been trivially easy if I had. The team wanted to keep secrets, and I kept my own. I have only researched those people that the team has brought to me. Once I knew them, I trusted them with my identity in return. I thought that I could trust them, and I trusted the team that what you kept secret would not threaten the rest of us. Now? The only person I can trust is Jay because he had no idea he was betraying me."

I took a step back, shocked at how angry the badger sounds, but I can smell the hint of fear in the air. Stratagem sounds almost unhinged. Still, I won't let him sidestep the issue. I glare through my mask at the badger and growl low, my voice rumbling, "You always have to be right, don't you? You always have to know everything. I have a damn doctorate and you make me feel like a stupid child."

Stratagem glowers at me, the wind ruffling his trenchcoat, "That was never my intention."

"Well then maybe you should get off of your pedestal and stop acting like some imperious leader," I retort angrily. "Maybe you should trust us so we can trust you back. And I mean actually trust us for once, instead of making people fear you with your cloak and dagger routine."

"You want me to trust you? You have no idea how much I have trusted you, you arrogant pup." the badger growls. "You weren't there at the beginning. You haven't seen the fear in people's eyes." His paws are twisted into fists now, and he's practically spitting his words. "The fear people have of our powers, of who we are. You were a child when this began. You have no idea what it is like to be me and be around all you powerful men and women. So grandiose, so amazing, so loved for your abilities and actions, when if people knew what I was they would hate me for it. Do not talk to me about trust."

"What are you talking about?" I bark back angrily. "A regular guy who is smart? I think people know that already, and if they have a problem with that then they're just like those petulant little kids who call others Brainiacs for being smart. Get over yourself, Stratagem."

"No. I'm not a regular man," the badger huffs angrily and then, whether from anger or a need to win, I'll never know, but he says it anyway. "I'm a telepath, Ted."

"You're what?" I ask taken aback, staring at the badger. This was a shock, I never expected him to say that. There also wasn't so much of a hint of that on the horizon. He's a telepath? That is more than a little scary when you think about it. Has he been in my head then?

"You heard me," Stratagem shouts. Then his shoulders slump as he sighs heavily, his voice getting softer, "That is my big secret. Only Bill knows, god only knows how I can even trust you or him with knowing what I am—the monster in the team's midst."

"Monster?" I'm surprised that the badger could even think that about himself. He isn't a monster. I've seen him save people. I remember all the times we've fought side by side. He's always looking out for the civilians, always finding ways to help and protect. When we're zipping through the air dealing with giant robots he's on the ground. I remember him saving a little girl in Quebec that no one else even knew was there. I would never think of him as a monster. But I just did, didn't I? The first thought I had was if he had read my mind. How could I not trust him to stay out of my mind? Of course he hasn't done that. This is Stratagem and I don't care how unhinged he might be behaving, he wouldn't do that. I begin to say just that but he interrupts me.

"And for a long time now I have fought to keep from becoming that monster," he continues, almost ignoring me. "If I wanted to, I could know everything about everyone. I have kept my personal word though, when I discovered my abilities, I swore I would never use them. I have never looked at more than your surface thoughts, which I can never block entirely, but the temptation is so great. I could do research though. I can use my natural talents to find information and investigate. I can avoid the easy path. If I could find something another way, then I didn't need to look. Even if I hadn't done the investigation, I could if I needed to. Now do you understand why my research matters so much to me? Why trust matters? To find out the whole team no longer trusts me..." the badger's shoulders heave and he shakes his head, trying to clear it.

"But then how could you not know about Jay before I told you?" I ask confused. "I know I would have to have thought about him at least once."

"I try not to concentrate on one mind. If I don't concentrate it becomes white noise for me. I pick up every mind within miles of me, Star. It becomes a pleasant sound, like the waves of the ocean, or perhaps a better analogy would be a choir of distant voices. But that is where my power truly become insidious, truly frightening." The badger raises his paws, as if trying to hold his thoughts, and I can see the very real fear in his face. "I network the minds around me, borrowing an imperceptible fraction of thought from everyone. Allowing me to think, calculate and make intuitive leaps before others can even process what is going on. I can't turn it off or stop it," he says his voice cracking from pathos.

"That doesn't make you a monster," I say strongly and I believe it too.

"Yes, it does. Invading the minds of thousands of people? Using their minds without permission and against their will? All for my own benefit? I can't think of anything more evil. I've tried to force my power to stop, Star. I built dozens of telepathic inhibitors, all of which failed." The badger sits down heavily on the roof's ledge, pulling off his goggles once more and I see his face for the second time ever, but his eyes are closed in sadness. "But the telepathy is always on, always working, always making my mind faster as I come to new leaps, new thoughts. Once I nearly drove myself mad by actively preventing myself from using it. You say it doesn't make me a monster, but what of El Esclavador? What about what Raja Raksha did to you? Even Power Puma, he's a low level telepath. He uses it to charm people to his way of thinking. Look at my peers and tell me this isn't evil."

I stand there surprised, looking down at the slumped badger. He looks ready to break apart from telling me this, from revealing all of these secrets. The badger rubs his eyes and I can see tears welling up in them. "When I started this career, I didn't even realize what I was. I didn't even know what I was doing. I just wanted to help, to teach and spread knowledge. Help lessen fear so people could learn freely. I did this so people could think freely, and I don't know whether that is ironic or just sad. I didn't understand my power until years later when I built a telepathic detector to help the team against threats like El Esclavador. Then I realized why everything came so easily, why I could make jumps in logic so quickly and why everyone saw things my way. If I wanted to, I could probably control the thoughts of several million or more people, Star Coyote. That makes me far worse than even someone like Raja."

"But you don't," I say with conviction as I sit down beside him removing my own mask and looking at him. "You don't. You're my hero. You and Bill and Emma and Jane and Swift and Stranger, you all stood up to the darkness, to the temptation to abuse your powers. You said there was a better way. You showed me, showed the world we could be something more. You're someone I've always tried to be. You and the others showed us a better way. Protection, service, never killing, those were the values you gave us. You're my hero. You are the reason I put this mask on. Why I go out there and use my powers for good."

Stratagem's face is twisted in anguish as he says, "What if I can't stop, Star? When I began doing it I could only pick up a couple blocks around me. I estimate a hundred people at most. Now? I touch the entire city of Boston, the whole state without thinking. Thousands. Millions! What if I can't stop." He trembles with obvious fear from the thought of millions upon millions of minds linking into his network.

"Then we'll help you find a way to cope," I say wrapping an arm around his shoulder looking into those golden eyes of his. "At least I understand why you're so paranoid now. Why you make such a big deal about what is and isn't a secret."

"You know the same could be said of you, Ted. To a lesser extent," Stratagem says looking at me.

My brow furrows at the comment, "What do you mean?"

"Star, you're frightened of what people think of you. That people will think you're a monster because you're trying to follow that most basic of wishes: finding someone to love and respect. You shouldn't be afraid at all, not in the slightest. You worry because there are small minded people out there who will irrationally hate you for who you are. People actually have a reason to fear me, but not you. You're too good a hero for that and too good a man."

I feel a pit open in my stomach. The badger is right of course, but still, it hit close to home. I looked at the badger with a slight smile, "You always know just what to say. Are you sure you don't read peoples thoughts?"

I smile and playfully punch his shoulder to underline the fact that it was a joke. The badger stares at me for a moment in horror, golden eyes wide, and then he smiles broadly and laughs richly.

"Yes, I'm sure." Stratagem shakes his head. "That the team could hide something as important as the civilian meetings should prove that.

But when your unconscious mind picks up the thoughts of an entire state, you learn how people think, even if you don't read their thoughts directly and don't intend it."

I smile at him and stick out my paw, "Hi, my name is Ted. I'm a superhero and in love with my amazing boyfriend."

Stratagem looks at me for a moment and then smiles weakly at me, sticking out his paw and, giving me a firm handshake, "Hello, Ted. My name is Samuel. I'm a professor and a superhero. I can read minds but all I want is to keep people free and safe. Though I think I've gone a bit mad in the last few days." I feel his paw trembling a bit in my grip.

I cough slightly, not wanting to push that idea. Stratagem does look much calmer now. More in control, less feral, but he is still a mess. "So, Samuel, besides a degree in psychology, what else have you picked up in your sleep by reading thoughts?" I force my voice to stay bright and cheerful.

He laughs a bit, almost like it was a relief to talk about this with someone. "The violin? How to knit? Almost any language there is. Anything really. Conceivably I could push my telepathy out to contact many more minds and with concentration link into them much more fully than I do now. I've never wanted to push that part of myself.   I like using my own acquired skills and abilities. I feel like a thief when I push myself like that, Ted. I didn't earn that knowledge. Now, I am a professor of mathematics. I do theorize that even without my telepathy, if I put the busy work in, I would have gotten my doctorates in a number of fields. However, my first love has always been math."

"Wow. I guess I can't even imagine the implications of all of that," I say with a nod as my tail thumps the ground a bit. "Having all of that available to you must be pretty intense."

The haunted look on Samuel's face tells me it must be pretty bad. "There is one respite," he says with a nod. "I can not read the minds of my sister or mother."

"Well that is some relief at least. Any idea why?" I ask genuinely curious. I know I'd be glad not to see into my family's heads.

"They are very likely low level telepaths. Not enough to do anything like I can but enough to stop me. It's terribly hard to read another telepath, and I have never wanted to try. And our powers are hereditary. Just look at Bill's kids or Lizz's children," Stratagem says looking out across the cityscape.

"Oh," I nod my head at that thought, again reminded about a good reason I won't have kids. "So they can't read minds?"

"No. They remain, thankfully, ignorant of their abilities. That is the reason I never want them to know about my masked crime fighting, but I monitor them around the clock. If something ever changes I want to be there for them."

"You're a good man, Samuel," I say with a nod thinking of that kind of dedication to his family. Then a thought occurs to me. "Wait. Telepathy can block out other telepaths? That would mean in Minneapolis when we fought Raja Raksha, you were the one who blocked out Raja! That is why you weren't in hand to hand combat with anyone, you were blocking him."

Samuel's face twists again, a look of uncomfortable concern on his muzzle. "Not quite. Solarcoon's glow does create a positive emotional reaction. A warm fuzzy feeling if you will. He dispelled Raja's shadows. I just created a bulwark defense for everyone so they would recover and he couldn't reassert himself." The badger's face hardens for a moment and he looks very serious. "Never reveal that, Ted. We must ensure Raja Raksha never understands our tactics, lest he overwhelm us," Stratagem says emphatically.

"Okay, but I don't see how. You sound like a strong telepath," I say. "Unless you think he actually could be stronger."

"Together, Bill and I can stop him—disrupt his foul talents. He never even realizes there's another telepath working against him. That's why the plan was for Bill to pretend to be immune; he's already resistant because he is a happy man. Because his powers are based on the sun and Raja gets his powers from the shadows, the tiger assumed that dichotomy was why he could not affect our leader." The badger looks down at his gloved paws and sighs. "It was during one of Raja's first attacks that I came up with that plan. After what he did to Emma, I told Bill what I was. I couldn't let that happen again. We needed a way to fight him, a concrete tactical plan, and I doubt I could stop him if he was actually focused on me."

"But I think you could take him if you tried," I say confidently patting his shoulder.

The badger shakes his head solemnly. "Raja awakens your own demons, your own thoughts about yourself that can hurt you. I know myself well enough to know that my own fears would overwhelm me if Bill wasn't the target of Raja's attack. He's made of sterner stuff than most people." The badger rubs his forehead, and now he looks a bit sheepish. "Look at what I did to myself without the Mad Maharaja's help."

I have to agree with him there, he's really done a number on himself. "You nearly killed Spice you know," I say after a pause as we look over the skyline, listening to the sirens below us. The police have arrived and are escorting people out of the building. Some of them look very angry. At a guess I'd say Cinnamon escaped with the loot. I'm less sure about her sister.

"Yes, well," Samuel stops, watching the street bellow as Spice is loaded into an ambulance. She does not look good. "Do you," he pauses again for a moment, "think I should apologize to them? They've never been the kind of villains to hurt people on purpose. I'd hate to be what pushed them to that point."

"Do you really think an apology, however nicely worded, will ever make up for the fact that you hospitalized, and possibly crippled her?" I ask frankly as I watch as Samuel put his goggles back on.

"No," he says quietly. He watches them finish loading the vixen into the ambulance, and his face sets into a stern look. Then he nods once and then reaches into his trench coat, "However, perhaps this will help."

The item he holds looks like some sort of compact mirror. Of course, it came from Stratagem's pockets, so its function probably has little to do with what it looks like. He hoards super science and makes his own. It has a silvery sheen to it and looks innocuous as he peers at it.

"What is it?" I finally ask.

"A cellular regenerator," he says. As I quirk my eye brow at that, he nods and smiles. "A healing device. It dramatically increases cellular repair, knits bones in an instant, it can even regrow limbs if programmed properly."

"That," my eyes widen looking at the little item, "that is really powerful."

"Yes," Stratagem nods, "very powerful. I wish I could understand the way it truly works. Sadly, I did not make it. It is something I took from Ms. Q, which means the specifics elude me. She has her henchmen carry them so they can be healed quickly in order to get her jobs done."

"Well I guess that means there won't be scar tissue," I chuckle thinking about the fennec fox and her fixation on her men looking pretty.

"One of many questions I have about it," Stratagem nods. "They also only work once, which is deeply infuriating. I've only been able to grab three over the years. I used one on myself once, and another is in my lab at the bunker, disassembled."

"So this is your only working one?" I ask staring at it now. "Samuel, that is a huge deal. What if you need that thing later?"

"Always a risk," Stratagem puts it back in his pocket. Standing up he continues, "However, when seeking forgiveness, one should be willing to pay the price. My mother taught me that and I need forgiveness at least for myself, and I have transgressed one of my most deeply held beliefs tonight. Besides I seem to recall you telling me I was a hero."

I chuckle at that and stand up myself, "Well, wherever Spice is going Cinnamon can't be far behind. Maybe we can get two birds with one stone."

"Assuredly," Stratagem says with a smile. "Do you want to come along, Ted?"

"I've got nothing else planned tonight," I say with a laugh. "Should we just head for the penitentiary?"

"They're taking her to Mercy first. At least that is what the police reports are saying. They'll stabilize her and then move her to a more secure location."

I stretch, grinning slightly as I put my mask back on. "Well here I thought we'd need to teleport inside, but getting into a hospital sounds easy enough."

"We will let the doctors stabilize her. One of the flaws with this thing is that an improperly set bone heals improperly, and I broke her arm in the fight as well as cracking a few ribs," Stratagem says clinically, but I notice a twitch of remorse all the same.

We take off into the air quickly. Who knows what might get in our way at the hospital. For instance, what if a crowd of media shows up wanting to talk about the capture of Spice and her hospitalization? Stratagem doesn't want to make a public statement on this or that he'll use this healing device on her. He wants to do it quietly and I can respect that. However, it does mean we have to approach quietly and slowly.

The media doesn't show up. At a guess I'd say someone at the party has been pulling favors to keep their name out of the press for a while and it has given us the cover we need to avoid a circus over the first real capture of Spice. Those two have a nasty tendency of escaping lock up. So all that really needs to happen is for us to wait for the doctors to finish their work. Stratagem finds us an old solarium for us to wait in for the time being. It's dark and cold at night, but we won't be in here for too long. The two of us sit together without speaking, and I can tell it means a lot to Samuel that I'm staying.

Hours later, the hospital is turning off lights and people are turning in. It's late but worth the wait I suspect. We creep downstairs watching out for orderlies and guards. Stratagem has the schedule for the guards that have been placed on the floor to watch Spice and make sure she won't escape. We avoid them easily and are on the floor in moments. The closest we come to getting caught is when a guard sneaks out to get a smoke.

"Why no guard outside her door?" I ask as we creep down the hallway.

"Her injuries are severe enough that the doctors have told them she won't be much of a threat for at least a week, if...if ever again. The police aren't concerned she'll get away. They should be taking Cinnamon into account but the assumption they are working on, I believe, is that she has already left the state with the loot. That and I hacked the files and changed their roster around. No one has been assigned and no one thought to look into why. In two hours someone will be here, but for now we are alone," Stratagems says. We stop in front of the door to her room. "Now I need something from the supply closet at the end of the hall. Can you go in and watch Spice? I need to move quickly by myself."

"Understood," I nod at the badger as he stalks down the hallways, moving very quietly. He does have a knack for moving quietly and quickly.

I open the door and slip inside. Spice is on the hospital bed, her costume removed, bereft of her normal clothes and other items. She looks small and weak there. Asleep she looks oddly innocent, as if she needs protecting. Her breath is reedy and quick. Damn she looks like a mess.

"Come to finish the job?" a female voice asks coldly. Cinnamon gets up from a chair and glares at me from under that hat.

"Cinnamon, you know I wouldn't want this to happen to Spice," I say looking at her. "I assumed you knew me better than that."

She looks at me for a while, searching my face. As she stands there with her tail flicking she finally relaxes and says, "You're right. That was unfair of me, Star."

"How is she doing?" I ask looking down at her. "She looks, um, fragile."

Cinnamon sighs and looks down at the bed, "She's always been the weak one, the one that needed to be protected. First from our uncle, then at school, and even now. I always watched out for my little sister. I've tried to give her what she needed."

"She always seemed happy to me," I say with a twitch of my ear. "You've been a good sister to her. Well, besides the crime thing, but I don't know which of you two cooked that up first."

Cinnamon looking at her sister smiles weakly, "It was a team effort. This seemed like such a good plan too. I figured we'd make a couple cool million easily. Maybe hit Monte Carlo this time. Spice really enjoyed Monte Carlo. Plenty of boys to play with there."

I smile at her comfortingly, "You two do enjoy messing with men's heads."

"It is a shame you are so hard to mess with," Cinnamon says with a smile at me. "God, Jenny, you have to get better. I can't stand having a heart to heart with this guy."

"Oh gee, thanks," I grouse in mockery.

"Thanks," Cinnamon says after a long quiet pause. "You pulled that psycho off of her, got him away at least. I appreciate that. I know this sounds odd, Star Coyote, but you've been one of the better guys in our life."

I flick an ear in surprise, "Not sure I understand."

"You respect us; you're a nice guy even during a fight. A gentleman. I haven't met many guys like you," she says to me.

I blush a bit and smile at her, "That is very sweet of you to say."

"Hey we might be enemies, but I understand why you do what you do," she says with a smile. "I think you're too concerned with the law and protecting people who don't deserve protection. You think I should work within the law."

"True," I nod. "I also think the both of you are a bit hedonistic in your robberies."

"You and Rigger," Cinnamon sighs with a grin. "You know he helped train us to be better fighters? And better criminals. We still tithe him a bit from each heist, but it was worth it. He's another good man."

"He can be," I say with a smile. "If a little annoying with his inventions."

"Part of his charm," Cinnamon says. "You know, Star, you're going to make some woman very happy."

I don't respond to that part. I know Stratagem will be here soon and I need to try and get her to remain calm for that. "Stratagem wasn't in his right mind. He needed some sense knocked into him."

Cinnamon balls a fist and slams it into her paw, "Oh please, let me be the one to do it."

"Sorry, I beat you to it. He is better now. He's very sorry."

"Spice might never walk again," Cinnamon says angrily. "Sorry is not going to cut it, hero."

"I know," says a deep voice from the door. Cinnamon and I turn, and Stratagem is standing there. He looks ominous in that door way like that, the light making just a silhouette.

"Oh fuck," says Cinnamon tensing up immediately. "I should have seen it, a double cross."

"Hardly," Stratagem says. "Star, please restrain Ms. Barclay; I doubt she'll listen to me yet."

It takes me a moment to realize that he means Cinnamon, I'm not used to thinking of her as Ally Barclay. She's already unfurled her whip. The room is far too small for her to really use it effectively, but she's ready to try. I grab her before she can lash out, intensifying my gravity as I hold her, making myself very heavy. She struggles in my grip.

"Damn it!" she yelps pulling at me. "I should have known it. Damn it! Never, ever trust people like you!"

Stratagem approaches Spice as I wrestle Cinnamon to the side. He takes a moment to look at her, taking his own sweet time as I hold the struggling vixen in my grip. He looks over Spice's chart and nods his head. Then he approaches the IV running into Spice and takes out a syringe. A very big syringe.

"Get away from her, you bastard!" Cinnamon yells struggling and pulling at me, trying to get to her sister. "Don't you touch Jenny."

"What are you doing?" I ask as the syringe approaches the i.v. "I thought you were using that cellular device on her. You said nothing about drugs."

"Ms. Q's cellular regeneration device is a cruel thing, Star," Stratagem states as he inspects the syringe for a moment. "It does not take into account the feelings of the person it is being used upon. It is very painful, the kind of pain that haunts a person. I would like to spare Spice that pain, so I am going to inject her with this very potent synthetic opiate. On top of the other medications in her bloodstream it should forestall most of the pain."

"What are you talking about," Cinnamon gasps looking between us.

"Cinnamon, I am truly sorry for what I did," says the badger calmly. "I am attempting to make amends."

"Or you're attempting to kill her," Cinnamon growls angrily. "Star, you couldn't possibly trust this monster. You saw what he did to her. What he could have done to her."

She states it as a fact, not a question. She is so sure of me, trusting me in this regard. I have to admit she is right; a part of me is scared. I don't know if Stratagem is truly better. If letting his secrets out and talking to me has truly calmed him down, gotten him back from that precipice of the abyss. I'm taking a chance. I don't truly know him, but if I try to stop this now, everything that happened tonight, the deep and important talk we had would be for naught. I have to take a leap of faith and trust him. All I can say is, "He's my teammate."

"So what?" Cinnamon says trying to stamp on my foot. Her relative gravity is lot lighter than mine so I don't really feel it. She's right. I'm gambling on Spice's life. How can I risk that on the nebulous concerns of a teammate and friendship?

Before I can say anything to stop Stratagem he has already injected her with the pain killer. He then takes out the compact and starts working very quickly, "Cinnamon, this cellular regenerator will repair what I did to her physically. In fact, her appendix will be regrown. It will be that exacting."

"See," I whisper. "Cinnamon, he's trying to apologize."

"No, that's worse, you don't understand!" Cinnamon cries struggling even more furiously, enough that I'm actually rocking.

"Oh I do, Cinnamon," the badger says frankly his goggles flashing in the low light of the room. "I know what you're concerned about. You need not worry, Spice's operation will not be undone."

"Operation?" I ask perplexed.

"But you said…" Cinnamon stops struggling and looks at Stratagem in surprise, "If it regrows her appendix, what about, well, all that?"

"The device has few settings, but I have programmed it so it will ignore that at least. In fact, it might smooth out any lingering issues," he says with a nod. I get the feeling neither of them are going to tell me what they are talking about. "Though, yes, that could have been a complication if I hadn't found the records on my computer while I was retrieving these drugs. As a side note, they will be burned out of her system while the device does the major work."

He sets the compact on her chest and steps back. For a moment the thing just sits there and beeps, giving off a soft hum. It seems far too quiet in here. Then Spice begins to thrash on the bed, convulsions gripping her as she bounces as if a doll in some maniac child's hands. The heart monitors and everything else start to beep and twitter violently. She spasms and jerks for what feel like hours but I know it's only a few minutes. Cinnamon is staring agog and horrified. Then as suddenly as it began, it stops. The monitors all return to normal beeping. The room is quiet for a moment longer.

Then Spice's eyes flutter open and she groans, "What happened?"

Cinnamon pulls at me and I let her go as she rushes to Spice's side eyes full of tears, "Jenny?"

The two on the bed hug tenderly for a moment and Spice says, "Ally? What? We were at the club. What happened?"

"You got caught," I say with a grin, wagging my tail.

"Yeah. I remember I was fighting that badger and he," Spice pauses. "Why don't my legs hurt? I got cut up and I think I sprained my shoulder, but when he threw me I felt..."

"Yes," Stratagem says, "I did put you unnecessarily through the wringer."

Spice stares wide eyed at him and then back at her sister saying with a smile, "There is a story here."

"Nothing to worry about," says Stratagem. "Star Coyote saved you from me and stopped me from doing something I'd regret for my entire life. I hope what I have done here will help repay you for my mistake, at least in some small part."

Cinnamon looks at me and then at Stratagem and then at me again. She says, "Well, Star, it seems you have a good friend."

"One of the best," I say wagging my tail more furiously. Happily I think I see Stratagem blush.

"Thanks," she says looking at Stratagem.

"My sister saying thanks. This sounds like one crazy story," says Spice lying back on the bed. "Can you tell it to me in the morning after I get some sleep?"

"Of course," Stratagem says and then he fluidly snaps a handcuff on her wrist and then onto the bed. "Now I realize you might normally be able to pick through that but you don't have your tools on you, you're dazed and tired from the rigors your body went through, and ideally, you're still confused from everything that has happened."

"Hey, now," Spice says tugging at the cuffs.

I grab Cinnamon while she is distracted. "You two are wanted for a couple dozen robberies and assaults you know. Just for this case alone I might add," I say holding the fox. "How about we end this for tonight?"

Cinnamon smirks at me, "Oh, you super boys and your rules."

"At least we're consistent," I say with a smile.

"Fine you caught us," Cinnamon says, relaxing in my grip. "At least Jen is okay."

"Oh my," Spice says with a smile at Cinnamon. "Yep, a nice story that I'm going to get to hear soon."

"In five to twelve ideally," I intone with a smile. "C'mon, Cinnamon. I'll fly you to the police station."

"The police guards will be here soon. Spice, I left detailed notes for the attending doctor. Make sure he sees them and gives you a check up. These cellular regeneration devices can be finicky at times," Stratagem says paternally.

"Yeah," nods Spice. "Fair enough."

Neither Cinnamon nor Spice seems worried about being locked up. I suspect they believe they'll be able to escape. They might, but Boston has a long history with supers. I suspect these cops might be a bit more careful than in most towns.

As I fly Cinnamon and Stratagem to the police station to drop the vixen off, I ask, "Any chance you'll tell me where the loot is?"

"Hardly," she says with a smirk.

"The DA might be more lenient if you turn over the stolen goods now," says Stratagem.

"Or they'll be a good bargaining chip later," she says with a flick of her tail against my body as we land in front of the station that Stratagem directed me to. Some of the boys in blue are pointing at us. We drop her off at the station with a minor report to check on Spice. A couple cops back away from Stratagem. They look frightened. Stratagem tries not to convey emotion, giving them his calculating thinking face. I suspect though that he might be bothered by it. After dropping off Cinnamon and making sure she is in a very secure cell I fly Stratagem into the air again.

We drift for a while gazing over the city looking for any other trouble. Heading towards a drop point he requested we are silent until he says, "Thank you."

"For what?" I ask.

"For stopping me. For getting me back to my right mind. I have work to do to restore some trust but I think you saved me from making a truly horrible mistake," he says.

We set down on the roof he indicates and I nod, "You'd do the same for me."

"Ted, come back to the team," he claps a paw on my shoulder. "I'd like to have you there as a friend. I know the others want you back as well."

"I will," I say with a smile. "At the very least, knowing your secret ensures that I want to work with you."

"How? I would think it would frighten you away" he asks surprised.

"You trust me," I say with a smile, "and that feels special."

"Perhaps you can trust our other members with the truth about you and Jay?" he asks.

"I'll try," I say with a sigh and a blush. "It isn't simple."

"I know," he grins. "Perhaps I should also tell everyone my secret."

"I'll be right beside you when you do," I say.

"As will I when you tell yours," says the badger. Then I am shocked to find the badger hugging me tightly and whispering, "Thank you, my friend."

Chapter 13
Showdown over Salt Lake City

"Good morning, Snuffles," Jay says as he hands me a mug of coffee. "I didn't have the heart to wake you up this morning. You looked so sweet, snoring as you slept."

"I do not snore," I say taking my mug. I grin at him as I brush down the last of my fur. I'm still in my bathrobe, a Christmas present from Jay's parents. "I just breathe deeply."

"When did you get back from Boston?" he asks as we wander back into the living room. Sunlight streams in the front window as a lazy Saturday begins.

"Late. Samuel and I ran into each other and we had a talk." I take a sip from my mug.

"So it's Samuel now, hmm?" says Jay with a grin.

"We had a lot to talk about," I say noncommittally and then a kiss on his nose. "Sorry about the past few weeks."

"You really have to stop apologizing. We've both been a bit of a wreck."

"Yeah," I nod and blush a bit at that. "Still, I think I can make up for it."

"Oh? How?" My collie quirks his head cutely.

"I'm taking the day off," I say with a grin. "I already arranged it with the cops and the mayor's office. Today there will be no calls for me unless a doomsday device is about to go off."

"Hmmm, that sounds nice," Jay says with a smile. "We could do some projects around the house."

"Unh-uh" I grunt with a grin as I put down my coffee cup and hold my collie. "We're going to take a real break. Go somewhere nice and relax. This is a day off for both of us."

Jay smiles conspiratorially at me and wraps his arms round my neck drawing me close. "So where are we going, hero?"

"We'll figure it out," I say wagging my tail. "But I want to spend the day with just you."

"Sounds great," Jay breaks our embrace and grabs the TV remote. "Let's check out the weather and we'll figure out where to go."

My eyes widen as I see him turning the TV on and I shout, "No! Not the TV!"

Jay quirks an eyebrow at me, "Is something wrong with the boob tube?"

"Knowing my luck it will show some police stand off or something I need to get involved in." I say.

Jay just rolls his eyes and turns on the TV anyway, "You're being paranoid, dear."

Of course last night it was on CNN when he turned it off and that is what turns on and the TV blares, "I repeat a state of emergency has been declared."

"See," I grouse looking at Jay

"That proves nothing," says Jay watching the TV. "It could be anywhere!"

"The state of Utah is in a panic today," the news reporter states.

"There," Jay smiles. "Utah isn't your turf usually. Heck, they hate costumed crime fighters there. Not your problem."

I keep watching the TV staring as they show footage of people running and screaming down the streets; cars piled up in a city gripped by fear.

"The Governor of Utah has declared a state of emergency today, where only half an hour ago Salt Lake City came under assault from a strange machine," the TV newswoman announces. Clips start to flash showing a craft on tank treads rumbling down the street. Cars are being crushed underneath as it continues to advance. Police officers are shooting at the thing, but their bullets bounce harmlessly off a force field which flickers every time something hit it. "The large machine is nearly at the city center and government and militias have been unable to prevent its advance."

"Um, is it just me or is that a hot pink death ray mounted on that thing," Jay says looking at the TV. "With lavender highlights?"

"It is not just you," I say as the TV shows a full shot of a gigantic ray gun mounted atop the tank. The bright purple tank. "Someone really needs to go back to fashion school. There is a reason gun metal and camouflage work so well for military devices."

"I doubt fashion sense is the primary concern of whoever is doing this," Jay says as gunshots continue to hit the force field impotently.

"The machine, with what super science experts at Stanford are now confirming has a death ray mounted on top, has apparently stopped in Temple Square. While it has not broken the wall around the Temple grounds, it is extremely close to the Salt Lake Temple at the heart of the city," the announcer continues. "The governor has announced that they are asking for all assistance. Federal forces are attempting to muster an intervention. It has also been confirmed that the mayor and governor have both called Phoenix, AZ."

"Okay," Jay says. "They have this in hand."

"Yeah," I say as the camera picks up a flash of golden light zooming forward. It's Solarcoon running up from Arizona. He's probably been waiting for the OK. This is good timing, Solarcoon is at his strongest in daylight. The sun fuels his full power and he can run amazingly fast with it in the sky. Solarcoon is not the strongest, fastest or most durable super-being on earth. He is actually fairly mid-level powerwise, and besides his glow ability he has very vanilla powers. But he is faster and stronger than normal people, and more durable as well, being able to heal himself at an accelerated rate. It all depends on how he channels his solar energy. With his tactical skills, experience, and training, he's become one of the best heroes in the world. He knows how to utilize his abilities to their fullest, unlike a lot of us. I know I've benefited from his training a lot. The one-on-one sessions he gave me when I first joined the team really taught me how to be a better hero. I owe him just for that.

Solarcoon stops in front of the tank and his sunglasses glint in the morning light as he looks up at the thing unafraid. We can hear him state, "Alright. Whoever you are, this stops now. Whatever your reasons for this attack on Salt Lake City, they aren't worth pointless violence. Stop this, let's try and not escalate any further."

"Escalate!" A voice screeches, "These cultists are the ones who escalated things!"

A figure comes out of a hatch and walks out on onto the front of the tank like it was a stage. A bright pink cape flows behind him, and he's wearing a pink mask and purple go-go boots. With that big nose and big ears he is obviously a koala bear.

"Is that koala wearing a pink cape?" Jay asks.

"Yep," I say as the TV zooms in on him.

"With a purple gay pride triangle clasp?" Jay asks again.

"Yep," I say nonchalantly.

"And is he wearing..." Jay stops, quirking his head, his face looking halfway between bemused and annoyed as he stops speaking mid-sentence.

"Yes, love, those are pink boots, a gold thong, and the pink cape," I say watching the TV with amusement.

"This is going to be painful to watch," Jay say resting his face in his hands. "I can just tell."

The koala beings to speak, "And I, Doctor Fabulous, have come to seek redress for wrongs committed!"

"Doctor..." Jay freezes, head still buried in his paws as he asks, "Doctor Fabulous?"

I have to laugh at that. I mean c'mon, Doctor Fabulous? I have to give Solarcoon credit. He doesn't seem to react to it. He has always been diplomatic that way.

Doctor Fabulous continues, "For too long these fools and ignorant people of Salt Lake City have supported hate legislation and oppression! No longer, I say! I, Doctor Fabulous, will strike back for all the gay people who they have hurt and oppressed! Salt Lake City and the Mormon church will know my wrath!"

"In a thong," Jay crosses his arms. Looking deadpan now, he says, "Why do I have the feeling he is not going to be advancing gay rights very far?"

"I think the death ray is a good indication," I say quirking an eyebrow.

"You fools have impinged on our right to marry and our right to freedom of expression for the last time! Those who support the beatings and bashings and abuse, you will all pay!" Doctor Fabulous says as he begins typing on a computer.

"I don't think so," Solarcoon says firmly, rounding back and slamming the force field around the machine with his fist. The entire thing flashes and sparkles. Solarcoon rears back and strikes again, using his full strength with the bright sunshine fueling his power. Doctor Fabulous looks up from his work and glowers at Solarcoon.

"Oh and don't get me started on you so called heroes! Where were you Extraordinaries when they took our rights away? When they sent money and boots to other states to fuel oppression? Where were you to defend the rights of gay people and justice! Nowhere! No defense for gay people being attacked either! Well today I strike at you so called heroes as well even as I bring true justice to Salt Lake City for their crimes! MWAHAHAHAHAHA!"

"He just maniacally laughed," Jay notes sipping his coffee. "Solarcoon better kick his ass now."

"You're taking this well," I glance at him.

"This Doctor Fabulous looks like a joke and c'mon, this is Solarcoon we're talking about," Jay says with a smile. "I've seen Solarcoon fight before and with the way you talk about him, I get the feeling there is nothing he can't do."

Solarcoon hits the force field again and backs off a few steps. "Look, I understand a level of political anger but this is obviously dangerous. You will hurt innocent people."

"Shut up!" Doctor Fabulous screams. "These so called innocents had their chance. Just like you did!"

Doctor Fabulous pulls a bright purple ray gun from his cape. Where did he hide that thing before? Thongs don't exactly have pockets or holsters. It's just there in his paw and before Solarcoon can say anything else, the ray gun fires a bright angry-looking red ray.

Now Solarcoon is fast, strong and capable, but his power has its limits. To reach the extreme speed that allowed him to run from Arizona to Utah in a few minutes he needs to sacrifice his super strength and pur all his energy into speed. I can tell that he did the same thing to increase his strength when he hit that force field, but in reverse. He slowed himself to the speed of a normal person and that means his reaction time is slower as well. He doesn't have time to dodge the ray. Who expects a koala in a thong to have a gun?

It strikes Solarcoon right in the chest. The news cameras are zoomed in close, so we can see it hit him on the TV. Solarcoon falls to his knees gritting his teeth, shocks of red energy lancing over his body. We can all see his face contorted in pain, until he begins to scream in agony.

I hear Jay say something, but I'm already in the air. My robe falls to the ground as I zip into the bedroom. I'm naked underneath that, and if

I hadn't been I would have ruined anything I was wearing by tearing it off. I'm moving quicker than I ever have before, zipping to my closet and grabbing my costume. I can still hear that scream of pain from Solarcoon echoing through the TV. I've never heard him utter such a noise. I know I shouted, "I have to help," as I fly out of the bedroom. My costume is already partially on when I slam open the backdoor, and I launch myself into the sky with as much speed as possible.

I'm already well above Portland by the time I affix my mask and finish zipping up my costume fully. My tail twitches as I begin to race across the sky more quickly now that I have my suit on, no longer distracted by putting it on mid-flight. I hate doing that, it slows me down terribly. Zooming forward, adjusting my costume and increasing my speed, I swoop over the landscape as fast as I can. I'm nearly all the way across Oregon when I get my communicator into my ear and call the bunker.

"Bunker, this is Star Coyote," I shout as the wind whips across my ears. "I'm nearly at the Idaho border, what is the situation?"

"Star?" I hear Metalyena's voice on the other side. I can hear background noise, "You're in the air?"

"Yes!" I shout, "Now what is going on? Who else is incoming on this?"

I know they're looking at Salt Lake City. I know they have to be seeing this and they have to be reacting already. We have to have a team assembling to head there. I can still hear that bellow of pain from Solarcoon. I can't let him feel that way. I have to save him!

"No one," Metalyena says over my communicator.

"What?" I shout nearly stopping mid air but I push on, "But Solarcoon just got hit!"

"I know, Star Coyote. I know," Metalyena says. "The problem is that the teleporter is down for maintenance. Stratagem scheduled today for a retooling. It is completely shut down."

"It will take me at least another half hour, maybe more to have it back up," I hear Stratagem say. "I'm sorry, Star. I had no idea this would happen. These damn new villains are too hard to predict." He sounds worried, and that only makes me push myself harder.

"So who is on the way?" I shout streaking over into what I think is Idaho.

"Force Vixen is in the air but she isn't that fast a flyer. She won't be there for a while still. Blitzkrieg and Lady Leopard are our best bet,"

Metalyena says and I can hear him tapping at a computer. I know what he is doing, tasking the Extraordinary satellites and computers on Salt Lake City, focusing all our attention there.

"The problem is that they were both in the middle of something when this came up," Stratagem says. "I estimate they won't be there for at least another fifteen minutes."

"So I'm the only one then," I growl. "Got it."

"No, Star," Metalyena says. "This is way too dangerous. You should hold back, move in with Lady and Blitz when they get here. Get some muscle and experience behind you."

"I can't just hold back," I shout. I'm flying as fast as I can, so fast it almost hurts now. Please don't let me be too late. "Solarcoon is in danger. That monster will kill him. Salt Lake City is in danger."

"Ted," Metlayena shouts my name, I think to shock me. "Think about what you're doing. Solarcoon wouldn't want you to risk your life point-lessly. This is a new threat; we don't know what other tools and weapons this guy has. He's already hit Solarcoon. You cannot just rush in there."

"I have to stop him," I say. "I'm almost there. I think I'm over Utah now."

"You crossed the border 12 seconds ago," Stratagem says. "I hate to break in here, but we have another problem."

"What?" I hear Metalyena ask.

"This Doctor Fabulous has a very standard looking death ray from the satellite photos and scans, well besides the coloration. Humph, this wire should be over here. Anyway, despite an odd energy variance I can't place, it is obviously powering up to fire."

"Oh that is just peachy," Metlayena grouses. "How soon will it go off?"

"Well before Lady Leopard and Blitzkrieg can get there," Stratagem says matter of factly. "It is aimed directly at the Salt Lake Temple."

"Oh that is just perfect," I say rolling my eyes and growling slightly. "This guy is going to make some very angry Mormons. Just what the gay rights movement needs."

"The temple has well over five hundred and thirty people inside of it," says Stratagem now and my mind switches from irritation to concern. "I can't be exact on that count. There is interference from the death ray."

"They haven't evacuated it yet?" shouts Metalyena. "What are they thinking? I'll call the police directly; they have to get those people out of there."

"The city has no experience with this sort of event," Stratagem says. "People were taking refuge inside the temple as the attack occurred. They thought they would stop it before it reached the square. The tank just rolled down Temple Street, the city's main thoroughfare. The rest of the streets are clogged with cars, detritus, and people. They don't have time to get people out."

"Oh God," Metalyena states with obvious concern. I try to pick up the pace again, straining myself to move as quickly as I can.

"From the scans, I am looking at an estimated 68% structural damage to the temple at minimum. There will be casualties," Stratagem says. "More than likely the building will be destroyed."

"No!" shouts Metalyena. "We're the Extraordinairies. We do not fail like this. There has to be something we can do!"

I can see the city on the horizon right now. I know what Stratagem is already suggesting even before he says it, "Ted, you're close. At the speed you're going you'll be in the city and at the Temple just before the cannon fires."

"What will that do," begins Metalyena but he stops and I think he realizes the conclusion I've already come to. What I know Stratagem was leading up too. There aren't many options.

"Tell Jay I love him," I say thinking of him standing there with his coffee mug watching the TV, of our now ruined plans for the day, ruined plans for the years to come.

"No! Ted! NO!" I hear Metalyena shout as I turn off my communicator. Streaking into the city, I follow the trail of destruction. I'm moving too quickly for this setting, I know some windows are shaking and breaking in my wake, that the collateral damage is being increased by my passage, but that doesn't matter. What matters is ahead of me. I can see it now. Bright pink and glowing now, I can see the ray is preparing to fire. I can feel the energy and heat coming off of it.

Death ray lasers are odd devices. The blasts can be blocked because they, for whatever reason, seem to focus onto the first thing they strike. They were first designed to destroy a target without damaging the surrounding area. Stratagem and I are hoping that a coyote sized block will take the full force of the blast and buy time for the others to get here before it recharges.

I wish I could claim that in the last second as I streak in front of the ray as it fires, my back to the temple, that I thought of Jay. That I was thinking of Solarcoon and all he had done for me and everyone else, inspiring me to do this. That I thought of Paul and my friends on the team, or Gary and the gang, or even that I forgave my parents. No, the thing I thought as the death ray blasted me was, "I can't believe I am about to be killed by a pink death ray."

CHAPTER 14
REACTIONS

I don't feel anything. I know I should feel something, but there's nothing beyond an odd hint of ozone in my nose and a crackling over my fur. I had shut my eyes expecting there to be pain, but instead I just feel nothing. I open them, blinking into the sunny day. The area is quiet. I glance behind me. The temple is standing; I can see people in the windows looking at me, watching the events outside. The idiots should be getting out of there.

I look down at the ground. Guardsmen and police are staring at me. Solarcoon is on the ground unconscious. No one had come to his aid. No one has gone out there, no one is risking themselves for him, and after all he has done. What is wrong with these people?

"NO! Impossible!" screams a voice. Ah yes, that's why no one has helped him. I doubt I'd want to get close to the mad scientist either unless I had superpowers.

I stretch my body out. I had reflexively tucked in a bit, but I think it is an understandable reflex since I was expecting the blast to kill me. Now is not the time for reflex or acting like a normal person. Now I have to be brave, I have to be strong. Bill would want me to be strong. Jay expects me to be strong. These people need me to be strong. I flex my fingers and float above the city glowering at Dr. Fabulous, giving him a confident smirk.

"Alright, Fabby," I try to mock him a bit, but there aren't many nicknames I can queue up on the fly more ridiculous than Dr. Fabulous. "Why don't you pack it in now. Your death ray is about as potent as Luxembourg is a power player in world politics."

"This can not be!" shouts the koala while tapping at his computer in frustration. "I must not have calibrated correctly! Well, no matter. I can recharge it, and then nothing can stop me."

"I think we will," I say with far more confidence than I feel at the moment.

Dr. Fabulous raises his ray gun, "Lets see what Mr. Agony-ray has to say about that!"

He starts shooting at me. I'm ready for him though; I dodge and twirl around the blasts. He's a pretty good shot, but he's not good enough against someone who is moving. He got lucky with Solarcoon, a one in a million hit. For me though, I'm ready and I'm quick. I loop around one blast, pirouette around another, and then dodge a third.

"Keep it up, Fabby. I can do this all day," I quip with ease. Those angry red blasts of energy are coming close to me, but not close enough for me to worry much. I just have to stay up high so his missed shots don't hit any bystanders.

"Freakin' Breeder!" the koala grouses at me. Then he points the gun at the crowd and smirks. "Let's see them dodge like that."

I hate when the newbies figure out the 'attack the innocent bystanders' routine. As he fires, I'm already there, swooping in to quickly grab a door that had cracked off a wrecked car and swinging it as a shield to block the blast. The door shudders in my paws, but is unaffected. Okay, it was a gamble. I had hoped this thing worked on biological nerve endings and it seems I was right. It could get under clothes but the door was thick enough to block it. Tossing it aside I state, "This isn't about these people, Dr. Fabulous. Leave them out of it."

"This has everything to do with them!" he shouts with grandiose ease as he starts fiddling with his agony ray. "You have no idea what it is like to live in a world with people like this."

I glower at him. His attitude is irritating. Understandable, but really irritating. I fly in closer, hoping that if I hit that force field with a heavy gravity punch I can crack it while he's distracted. Unfortunately he's finished fiddling before I get there. I try and veer out of the way but he's changed the way the gun fires, and instead of just firing a beam it comes out in a wide cone. The angry red energy washes over me, and I flinch a second time, expecting pain. The searing unbelievable pain Solarcoon had been in, but at most I feel an odd tickle. I quirk an ear and look up at the koala. Not to minimize Solarcoon's suffering but my only response can be, "That all you got?"

"Not possible!" the koala shouts looking at his gun. "I was so sure I had calibrated it correctly. That and my death ray. How can they be failing like this?"

"Dumb luck," I suggest with a shrug as I float up again looking at him. I have to add, "Look. Obviously you're not very good at this. You got lucky once, but that's over now. Why not just surrender?"

"No," the koala gripes as he feverishly adjusts the gun, now obviously lost in his own thoughts. "This should not be possible. The only weakness I gave my weapons is that they don't work on gay people."

"Wait. What?" I bark in surprise.

"You heard me, you breeder freak," the koala says, a manic grin on his face. "I made it so my inventions won't work on gay people. The force field, the death ray, even my agony ray, none of them would affect gays, lesbians or bisexuals. I haven't figured out a defense for the transgender but I'm sure one day I will." He thrusts a finger into the air, literally posing as he brags. "Genius, don't you think?"

I'm equal parts horrified, mystified, and irritated by that comment. "So wait, are you saying all those bullets hitting your force field had a sexual preference? That the stone work in the temple has a preferred partner? What about gay people inside of that building?"

"No, of course not, don't be ridiculous. The protections only affect living things." The koala taps at his computer for a few moments. I'm just flying there in front of him, dumbfounded and feeling the wind around me. I can hear whispers in the crowd, and it looks like the cops are finally getting people out of the temple. I hear cameras flashing as I look at the koala. He continues ranting as he types furiously, "I specifically made it so gay people would be exempt! Theoretically the clothes they were wearing would be unaffected as well, though I haven't tried to see. Besides any gays in that cult's temple are obviously traitors!"

There can be only one response for that. Only one possible thing I could say to something with that kind of ridiculousness, "That. Is. So. GAY!"

"ARGH! I hate when you breeders say stuff like that," Fabulous blasts at me with his agony ray again. I don't even bother dodging it this

time. In fact I get in the way of it so no one can get hurt, floating back and forth intercepting the blasts. I give a mock yawn while I do it too. This guy needs to be put in his place.

"Because you're doing such a good job of working against that perception," I say irritably. "You know, what with rolling a giant tank through a city while presenting yourself as the most toxic stereotype possible."

"Shut up!" he shouts at me now. "You can't possibly understand what it is like being a minority in the world. Being attracted to the same gender can get you killed. Having imperious straight people tell you that you have the right to marry, as long as it is someone from the opposite gender. You have no idea what it is like to get treated like this. For people to treat you like you're a freak for no fucking good reason!"

I have to admit I can understand, even agree with what he is saying, but this really isn't the time to have a political discussion. Besides, he's obviously taking real grievances and contorting them into an excuse for his behavior, for his violence. I look down and again I see Solarcoon's prone body.

I glare at the koala and ask angrily, my tail bristling, "Oh, I have no idea, huh?"

"No, Star Coyote! You couldn't possibly! No straight ever could!" Dr. Fabulous shouts at me.

"Right. So because I'm straight I couldn't possibly understand your feelings and problems huh?" I shout now angrily. Where does this guy get off making insinuations like that?

"No, of course not! You heterosexuals never could understand it! Not until I punish all of you and show you how strong we gays are!" he hollers at me. The ridiculous nature of a claim like that coming from short koala in nothing but a thong and cape would make me double over laughing. If, you know, the guy didn't have a giant pink tank.

"So you're saying I'm a straight guy who couldn't possibly understand what it is like to suffer the stigma of being gay. Wow, my boyfriend will be shocked, shocked I tell you, to learn that!" I shout, the retort spilling forth from my muzzle without me even thinking.

Finally that stops him. Dr. Fabulous stops his ranting and raving and he just stares at me agog. I fly forward and I feel a slight rush of energy pass over me as I pass through the force field without even slowing down.

"You know what really pisses me off? You just forced my boyfriend to watch me die on live TV," I say with a growl as I land on the tank, glaring down at him. "I'll never forgive you for that, you giant fruitcake."

I grab him by the collar of his cape and lift him up so we are eye to eye. He's not a big guy, rather short and dumpy when you get close up to him. I glower at him and whisper under my breath, "How dare you threaten people like this? How dare you act like this and claim to speak for gay people? How dare you threaten Solarcoon's life, you arrogant jerk."

He looks at me with real fear in his eyes. He raises his agony ray up, not even pointing it at me; he's planning to fire once more into the crowd. Not a chance. My paw flies up quickly and I grab the muzzle of the gun and make my hand heavy. Very, very heavy. I easily crush the weapon in my paw.

"Nope," I say, "you're not hurting anyone else in that crowd."

"Actually, Star, I think he was aiming at me," says a woman with a British accent. I turn and see Lady Leopard, who is hovering above us now. I wave up at her with my free paw, some of the anger draining from my face. She waves back, and then rearing back smacks her fist into the force field. The entire thing shimmers and flickers. Obviously that was a lot of pressure on it, but it holds. Lady Leopard shakes her head, her long braid waving in the wind. "Well, isn't that a fine mess. It appears his force field is a little stronger than I expected. Good thing it doesn't affect you, Star Coyote."

Blitzkrieg zooms in and looks between the two of us, "I see I vas not needed."

"You're needed now, Blitz," I say to him. I look back at the koala with an evil grin as I lift him off his feet, clenching a fist, "Any requests?"

"Not the face?" Dr. Fabulous asks, scrunching up his face and dangling from my paw.

"Fair enough," I slam my fist into his stomach, winding him and tossing him out of the force field. Lady Leopard easily grabs him as he flies out.

"Was that truly necessary, Star Coyote?" she asks raising an eyebrow slightly.

"Maybe not, but it felt right," I say flying out as she lands next to Blitzkreig. She's holding Fabulous by his collar so he doesn't try anything and Blitzkrieg is still taking in everything. He glares at the koala and growls. Solarcoon is only a few feet away. I land next to him and lean down taking off my glove I check his pulse. He's breathing and his pulse feels fairly regular. I haven't felt this relieved before in my life. I stand up and look at the two of them. Senior members, yes, but I know what has to be done.

"Blitzkrieg, grab Solarcoon. You're the fastest person here. Run him back to base and get him checked out. He needs medical attention," I order. I look at the polite snow leopard nodding her head and looking expectantly at me, "Lady Leopard, you take Dr. Fabulous into custody. Make sure he gets booked."

I walk through the force field up to the attack tank and survey it. Looking over it I reach my paws down to get some purchase.

I hear Lady Leopard asking, "And what will you do, Star Coyote?"

I lessen the gravity on the machine, making it lighter and lighter, lifting it upwards I move underneath it. I smile mischievously to Lady Leopard, "Oh, not much. I'll just be taking this back to base. It would make sense for you to do it, sure, but Dr. Fabby might have put in booby traps. And well, seeing as I don't like boobies I think I'll be immune to anything he tosses out."

"Hold it right there," a cocker spaniel in riot gear strides forward. "Where are you taking that thing?"

"Into custody," I say, lifting myself up into the air.

"That is evidence and property of the State of Utah," he growls at me.

"I am sorry to say that that is hardly true," Lady Leopard says as she looks at the spaniel. "The UN and US government have both signed agreements saying we can take this sort of thing into custody for the safety of the general public. They will be surrendered when we are finished disengaging any traps or dangers as well as taking it apart."

"The UN has no authority here, missy," the spaniel says arrogantly. "And you Extraordinaries have no right to mess with state evidence."

Dr. Fabulous is struggling in Lady Leopard's one handed grip but he can't get away. She doesn't even seem to notice him whipping about. Blitzkrieg has already picked Solarcoon up and zoomed away with him.

"Oh, whatever. Try and stop me." I say irritably and I launch myself into the air. I really do not want to have a long protracted legal fight over a pink death ray, the entire idea is absurd. I hear the spaniel bark some orders and someone actually shoots at me, but the force field is still working and the bullets bounce off harmlessly.

I'm half way across Utah and nearly at the Bunker's Large Object Storage door when I realize what I've done. I just barreled out of the closet completely and utterly. I just outed myself to the entire state of Utah, to the whole world in fact. For the sake of shutting a guy down with a smart quip, I just came out of the closet. How many reporters and TV stations were broadcasting live, world wide, at that moment? I had even joked about it later, literally stating I didn't like boobies. My breathing gets more rapid and my chest feels tight as I fly.

At the very least, all those cops heard me. There's no way this is going to stay quiet. I'm nearly in a panic as I approach the hidden door to the bunker, which slides open automatically upon detecting my communicator. I fly in and look for a spot to put this garish thing down. The ceilings are vaulted and the hanger is littered with mechanized battle suits, power devices, giant rocks of unknown origin, along with strange aircrafts and other devices, including a blimp that is submersible courtesy of Rigger. Stratagem comes in here when he wants to figure out how one of the huge devices work, but he's pretty much the only one who does.

I find a spot for it and gently place the thing on the floor. I walk away from the bright pink death ray tank and try not to think about how badly my legs are shaking. What have I just done? I hear the door into the bunker proper open but I'm too lost in thought. I shudder. It feels like that tank is sitting on my chest.

Then powerful muscled arms encircled me, and the crushing sensation is real now, which throws me for a loop until I realized that Metalyena had grabbed me in a tight hug as he says happily, "Ted! That was amazing!"

I gasped for breath and grinned up at the hyena as he holds me for a moment and then cough out, "Thanks, but could you, well, let me down?"

Metalyena blushes and sets me down on the ground and then says, "Its just, wow. That was an amazing take down. I mean you shut him up and then you shut him down. It was amazing!"

"I'll say," Force Vixen said, sauntering into the room with a confident smile. "You know, Ted, I've worked for years to find the right phrases to shut pompous morons like that up. I didn't think you had it in you."

"Uh," I blush at that before saying, "Thanks."

"And I take it you knew, hmm," Force Vixen said giving Metalyena a sly grin, making the hyena blush a bit. "I figured as much. Honestly, Ted, it would have been nice to know about this beforehand. Well, I suppose this was why Adam was so evasive about the entire dinner in New York."

Before I or Metal could say anything she motioned for us to come with her as we leave the storage area and started walking towards the central meeting room. Force Vixen continues, "I mean this isn't even a big deal. Why would you keep something like this from us? I'd be more annoyed at Metalyena and Glacier for not telling me but I suppose they figured this was your secret. Whatever, the talking heads will chew on it for a few days and then we'll be done with this nonsense. At least you got to take an arrogant idiot with a death ray down."

"It was the heat of the moment," I say evasively. Why did she have to keep talking about it so casually? Today has been bad enough already. I don't have the chance to ask her to stop talking about before we get to the meeting room. The room is shrouded in darkness, it often is when there's an emergency like this, and before my eyes adjust to the gloom I hear a voice shout, "TED!"

Suddenly, another pair of arms is around me in another hug. A very tight, strong hug, as Stratagem grabs me around the neck saying, "I meant for you to hurl a car or a trash can in front of the death ray, not your body! You had plenty of time to find one!"

"It all happened too fast, Stratagem," I say, half shocked by this display of emotion. Stratagem has never done something like this before. He never grabbed me in a hug like this after a mission. No one ever did that. "I mean I just did what I thought I could. I didn't think I had time to pick anything up."

"You had 1.3 seconds, you insanely naïve, stupid, brave, wonderful hero," says Stratagem with a broad smile while breaking the hug and looking me in the eye. "Don't ever do one of my half-baked plans again. Think about what you're doing, okay?"

"Of course," I blush amazed at the amount of pathos Stratagem had put into that as he looked at me. Then he reaches up and removes his goggles to brush at his eyes.

I don't know who was more surprised at seeing Stratagem remove his goggles, me, Force Vixen, or Metlayena. I don't think I ever will get over the shock of seeing him do that. Stratagem brushes the tears out of his eyes for a moment, composes himself and smiles, "I'm glad we stopped that madman and you've decided to be more honest with yourself. Now, I'm going to check on Solarcoon in the infirmary and then finish repairing the teleporter. Force Vixen, I am amazed you were able to increase your flight speed by 19.5% this time."

"Well, panic for Bill's life will do that," Force Vixen says with a winning smile. "I flew as fast as I could. Not that I was needed"

"It iz lucky that Doctor Fabulous was not very smart ya?" says Blitzkireg with a smile as he enters the meeting room. The big German comes over and claps a paw on my shoulder saying, "Bill vill be fine. You came at the right time for him. I ran him here and he vill recover soon. And you even saved the city. Gutt work!"

"Thanks, Kai," I blush feeling his strong paw on my shoulder giving me a reassuring squeeze. I'll admit Blitzkrieg and I are not that close. I've had trouble connecting with him. He came into heroing much older than many of us and he's hard to read at times because of the language thing, but the reassuring squeeze on my shoulder feels nice.

"I must return to Nuremburg," Blitzkrieg says. "I left my daughter Frida alone und I rarely zee her. Gutt job, Star Coyote."

With that, and a crackling sound followed by a hint of ozone, the speedster wolf was gone. He's one of the few people who can run around the world, so it made sense for him to come all the way here but with the time zone changes his personal life could suffer needlessly if he stays too long. He's already having trouble managing things. Just getting to see his daughter Frida after losing the custody case is a huge deal for him.

"I should head back to England as well," Lady Leopard says with concern. "I just wish to make sure Solarcoon is alright before leaving. I believe Holly should be here when he wakes up. If no one would mind, I'll go collect her and hopefully he will be awake very soon."

Stratagem nodded his head in agreement. "I'll check our instruments and look him over. I am confident that he will make a full recovery. It would have been nice to get the agony ray to study. Next time, Star Coyote, don't crush the entire device, please?" The badger gives me a wan smile. He then says, "Force Vixen, if you could accompany me, your experience in medicine will be helpful."

"I was a girl scout who took some first aid classes," says Force Vixen rolling her eyes as she follows the badger.

"You still have the most experience in medicine of anyone here," says Stratagem matter-of-factly. "Now, Ted, I want you to come to the medical bay with us. I know he claimed you were immune, but I want to make sure Fabulous' devices have truly had no effect on you."

The medical lab, I think frantically, where Solarcoon is right now. "No, I'm fine, really," I say weakly, and for a moment, my eyes meet Samuel's through his goggles, and I know he can see the fear welling up in me.

"Alright," Stratagem says smoothly as he turns to Metalyena. "Metalyena, I'm ready to reconnect the teleporter to the power systems. Could you please do that? I know it is a long walk but your invulnerability should help you if there is an over charge like there was last time."

"You got it," Metalyena chuckles as he heads out another door and down the hall. Force Vixen follows after him, with Stratagem lingering only a moment before leaving me alone. "Star, if you could please stay here at the Bunker for a while longer. You're the only one on the team immune to this death ray and I'd like to study that and have you on hand in case there are traps inside the tank."

I nod weakly at him and he heads for the medical lab. Yeah, remind everyone that I'm different, about what I did to stop that thing. I take a deep breath and sigh heavily, collapsing into my chair, just staring into the darkness of the central meeting room. I can almost hear Jay celebrating their reactions. Even Force Vixen is okay with who I am. They didn't even make a big deal about me coming out to the world. They're still my friends, I'm still a hero, but I can feel myself beginning to panic.

I peel my mask off, clutching my head as I think about what just happened. Screens around the room are flashing information, and I can see news reports of the attack on Salt Lake City even now. I can't quite hear them, they're turned down too low, but their collective voices make the room seem like it's filled with whispering people. One station is playing footage of me taking the death ray head on, and I see myself on the TV, my body curling up reflexively as I wait to die. What must Jay be thinking right now? He saw me nearly kill myself to stop some madman. There is the nightmare the two of us had talked about time and again since I revealed my costumed identity, right on the screen, happening over and over again. He watched it happen, and he's probably watching it again right now, my poor collie. I want to call him, but I keep thinking about the fact that I've never called him from inside the Bunker before. I was too worried someone would overhear me. Lady Leopard would have for sure, so I never called him. I never wanted this secret to get out. There was a time once, after I was first approached for membership, that I considered telling the team. I had been a hero for two years by then. Solarcoon himself had shown up in Portland and asked me to join the team.

Bill said they had been watching me, that they were impressed with my skills and my attitude. They wanted me to join the the only superhero team on Earth. These were people I had respected and idolized for years, the people who had inspired me to become a superhero and they thought I was good enough to join them. I wanted to come out, to tell them the truth so they would know who they were really dealing with. I had put it off to train and learn with them first, to see if I really could be a hero in the Extraordinaries.

The room was still dark, the whispering of the TV screens filling the room as my gaze drifts over to Solarcoon's chair. The empty chair even now feels filled with his presence. His yellow symbol glints in the light of the monitors as I look at it. Then after I had joined, Solarcoon started inviting me to meet his family. We started going on fishing trips together, something Dad and I used to do with my brother. Holly treated me just like a son, and I still remember how wonderful the Thanksgiving dinner she made me one year was. Bill talked to me as a friend, a mentor, even though I was starstruck just being around him. He taught me better combat techniques, helped me make my costume safer, and helped me build alliances in the Portland police department. He helped me be a better hero. I had wanted to tell him back then. Jay was always pushing me to be open about being gay, and while I was scared, I agreed with him. I wanted to tell everyone everything. I wanted Jay to know years ago that I was Portland's hero. I didn't want to keep this all bottled up. It felt like I was being crushed by my secrets, just like I feel right now.

So I decided to do it. I would tell Jay and my parents the truth of who I was, what I was doing, and then I'd tell the team about Jay. So I took Jay to meet my parents. Even if my brother hadn't found out and threatened me with exposure, I would have done it anyway. Jay had introduced me to his own parents months before. I liked them a lot and they were very welcoming. I had thought my parents would be just as welcoming, and I wanted Jay there when I told them I was gay. Then I was going to tell them all about what I could do, that I was Star Coyote, and that the Extraordinaries had asked me to join them.

Looking at Solarcoon's chair I can't help but flinch at the memory of what happened next. The feeling of my father's fist connecting with my face, causing me to stumble, my father shouting at me after I told him I was gay. We stood in the backyard and I told him what Jay meant to me and he listened without saying a word. I glanced away for a moment, back to the house where Jay and my mom were talking, and when I looked back he just hit me as hard as he could. I saw the second fist before it hit me. I could have done something, I could have fought back. But who wants to fight their father? I had training, I had superpowers, it wouldn't have been anywhere near a fair fight, but I couldn't do it. The second blow knocked me over, but he didn't stop there, he just kept attacking me. Finally Jay pulled him off of me. He fought back for me.

Tears run down my face as I remember that night, staring at Solarcoon's seat, at his symbol. We left after that, and I tried calling my parents every day for a month after that night, but they never wanted to talk to me again. They hung up the phone, they didn't return my calls, and eventually I just stopped calling. Eventually I let Jay back into my life but it was a hard month for me, just trying to be alone and wishing I could have my parents back. I couldn't, so I spent more time in costume with Solarcoon—with the team, I mean.

Standing up I walk around the table and rest my paws on Solarcoon's chair, thinking how I betrayed his trust by not telling him. I should have told him, but he's so much like my dad was. So stoic and calm, the burly raccoon is always smiling in a quiet way. I can still see the look of revulsion on my father's face through the haze as he held me down and hit me. The thought of Solarcoon reacting like that frightens me to the bone.

"Yeah, well, I think he's a freak," a quiet voice whispers behind me. Turning in shock, I look for the source of the voice and find it's one of the TV's, tuned into a news channel. The caption reads 'Reactions from Portland', and the volume is down so low I couldn't hear it from the other side of the table. Another coyote is speaking to the reporter, "I mean, who wants that kind of thing to be a superhero? We have kids in this city. What is he doing even telling people what he does in the bedroom? What's next? Is he going to wear a skirt like that vixen in LA? No way man, that queer should just get out of our city!"

I can see a whole crowd of people behind him nodding their heads, and my heart just breaks. My own city doesn't want me? The people I've protected for so long, the people of Portland want me gone? Before I can even react or think about that any further, I hear a door open off to one side.

"Ted?" I see Holly Jefferson standing there, looking at me worriedly. Her motherly face is a mask of concern, the dark band of black fur rumpled slightly as she looks at my ashen face. Lady Leopard is right behind her, her own face filled with concern. This is just too much. I can't be here. I don't want to hear Solarcoon say what my father said. I don't want to make Holly cry like I made my mother cry. I don't want this to happen again. Before I even realize what I am doing, I'm gone. I've run out the door opposite from Holly, barreling down the corridor and as far away from her as I can get. I run for the Bunker's exit, and I'm in the air flying back to Portland as fast as I can.

Today was supposed to be a day just for Jay and me. It seems so unfair that it had to come to this. I don't even bother stopping in the woods to take my costume off, I just rush inside the house. Jay turns around as I come in. He's been staring at the TV and obviously crying. Oh my collie, not you too. We don't speak we just grab each other and hug each other tightly.

As I feel Jay shudder with worry, his arms holding me desperately, he whispers, "I thought I had lost you."

I can only shut my eyes and hold him tight. He's worth so much to me, but right now it hurts. It hurts so much to think that everyone in the world knows I'm gay, and soon Solarcoon will know too. We hold each other tightly and I know that things will never be the same again.

Chapter 15
Phone Punt
Punditry

I glance down at my phone as it rings and sigh. Not again. I pick it up to my ear, "Hello, Adam."

"Jay," he says and then pauses. I don't think he is sure what to say.

I answer the question I know he is trying to formulate, "No, Adam, he hasn't gotten off the couch. Yes, he's still in a mood. No, he doesn't want to talk to any one."

"Have I gotten that predictable?" Adam asks congenially as I sigh and pour myself another cup of coffee.

"Well, you've called every day for three days after what happened," I say glancing out the backyard window at the steely gray clouds high in the sky. Looks like it might rain today. "You and everyone else in the family."

Adam chuckles at that and says, "I guess we have been a bit zealous."

"Only because you care," I sigh walking out to the living room. Ted is on the couch staring at the TV in his bathrobe. His fur is mussed and he looks disheveled. He keeps clicking between news channels, either hunting for or avoiding the stories about him, I can't tell.

"How is he though?" Adam asks.

"Well I'm going stir crazy," I say and Ted glances up at me sighs and looks back to the TV.

I hear the TV report, "This follows Iran's announcement that the Extraordinaries are banned from their country for moral depravity, with the threat of death and the threat that any incursion will be seen as a hostile action upon their borders by NATO. That makes ten nations, including Russia, Zimbabwe, and now Kenya, which have banned the team from entering their borders. The new hero of Nairobi, and the only hero in Africa, Kilimanjaro, was approached for comment but the meerkat declined the interview stating he was needed elsewhere. These total diplomatic breaks with the superhero team followed the events in what is now being called the Assault of Salt Lake City, where the superhero Star Coyote revealed his homosexual orientation."

"Emma really wants to talk with him," Adam says slowly. "Would he take the phone now?"

"No," Ted says as I motion the phone towards him. He turns back to the TV changing the channel with a sad sigh.

I sigh and say, "Sorry."

"He really needs to talk to the team," the fox says on the other line with a hint of exacerbation. "This is just nuts. He should be out there fighting this crap. He should be letting us help him."

"Preaching to the choir, Adam," I say turning back to the kitchen. It has become my haven the past few days as Ted has essentially set up camp in the living room and refuses to leave the spot unless necessity moves him.

"Look, could you maybe..." Adam begins but I hear a beep on the other line.

"Sorry, Adam, can you call me back? I think someone is calling through," I say with only minor irritation. Honestly I'd just like this conversation to be over.

"Sure," he hangs up and I click to the next caller.

"Jay?" Michele's voice asks questioningly.

"Hi, Michele. I was just talking to Adam," I say with a roll of my eyes.

"Oh," I think the tabby is pausing to think of a good response. She finally says, "You know my husband really wants to talk to him right?"

"I know," I sigh, tail fluffing out. "He's been refusing to talk to anyone. I had to turn Glacier away yesterday and he was on my front door step."

"He turned Glacier away?" says Michelle shocked. "Why did you let that happen?"

"Ted just point blank refused to talk to him," I say thinking how crushed the husky looked at that. We had talked for a little while outside. I had thought for sure that Paul of all people could talk him down.

"It isn't fair," Michelle says irritably. "Yeah okay, some people are being jerks but others aren't. The mayor of Vancouver said he'd be happy to have Star Coyote in his city. Denmark had a pro-Star Coyote rally yesterday. Not everyone is being crazy."

"Ted is being myopic, Michelle, what else do you want me to say?" I comment rubbing the bridge of my muzzle.

"You're his boyfriend—try and knock some sense into him," she says.

"I've been trying," I say then the phone beeps. "Call me back?"

"Of course," she says

"Ted?" asks a man I don't recognize as I flip over.

"Sorry, this is Jay," I say trying to sound upbeat to the unknown man. I really don't want a stranger detecting irritation from me right now.

"Hi, Jay," the man says. "This is, um, Kyle and I was just calling to see if Ted wanted to talk. He isn't picking up his other, uh, phone."

Oh, Metalyena. I nod my head, I always liked him. He's the first hero outside of Paul to call our land line. I sit at the kitchen table and glance out the window to the backyard. The bleeding heart flowers are in bloom. I always liked those. "Sorry, Kyle, you and everyone else. He isn't picking up."

"Oh, um," Kyle stops, and it's clear he isn't sure what to say to me.

"It is nice to talk to you," I say easily. "And I appreciate the call. Look, he just needs time, I guess. He'll get back in touch."

"I know," Kyle says and I can just imagine the big hyena talking on the phone to me. I'll admit that despite the strained nerves and tiredness of the past few days I am getting a nerdy little thrill talking to the hero. I hear a clanging klaxon and the hyena sighs, "Damn, that's my cue. I'll call back later.

He hangs up but I know that I'm going to get a phone call any second. Turns out, I'm wrong. I get a luxurious full minute before the phone rings again.

"Jay? This is Holly." I sit up in my chair as she says that over the phone.

"Hi, Holly," I quickly get up and move to the living room. She hasn't called us before now. I have no idea if Solarcoon tried to contact Ted directly; he won't let me look at his communicator.

"Now, I'm not saying anything, but c'mon isn't it a little suspect that this gay hero was the one to 'Stop' the gay supervillain?" says some woman on the TV.

"C'mon, Denise, that is hardly a fair," a man retorts. Oh joy, another pundit roundtable. I'm really learning to hate these things.

"No you come on, Tyler. What's to say this guy hasn't been playing hero and just setting all of these things up."

"I'm getting sick of this screed about heroes setting up these fights. Evidence is lacking," the man retorts.

"It's far too pat," the woman responds. "I mean, suddenly you have all these gay rights groups pointing to Star Coyote as an example of supposedly virtuous behavior. It looks staged if you ask me. Never mind that a gay koala tried to use a death ray on Salt Lake City."

"Which Star Coyote stopped," the man, an ocelot, growls.

"Funny how no one has seen Star Coyote recently. Especially after the break out of that same koala from his holding cell in Nevada, another clear violation by the Extraordinaries forcing themselves on state government and law enforcement."

"I suppose you'll blame him for the escape of Cinnamon and Spice yesterday from their cells in Auburn, Massachusetts?"

"You said, it not me" the woman gives a venomous smile. "For all we know, he's working with those two degenerates and splitting their ill-gotten gains and he helps them avoid getting caught. I hear that badger in Boston was finally giving them the defeat they deserved but he stopped him. He intervened and they got away with millions."

Ted whimpers on the couch and takes a bite of ice cream off a spoon. I really hate it when he eats from the carton. I sigh a bit, looking between him and the TV. These round tables are getting worse. Next thing you know they'll accuse him of making some insidious virus or causing lame reality TV shows.

"I hate that woman," Holly says. "Sorry, I can hear it from here. You know she said horrible things about my husband. Hmmph and they all seem to forget that Bill was the first responder and nearly died trying to protect them. Thank God that Ted got there."

"Would you like to talk to him, Holly?"

Ted looks up his eyes the size of dinner plates at that very suggestion of talking to Holly and he shakes his head frantically.

"Yes," she sighs sadly before adding, "but from what I understand he isn't talking to anyone."

"No," I shake my head as well. I really thought maybe Holly would get him snapped out of his funk. "He isn't."

"Jay…" she sighs again, "Just tell him, please tell him, thank you from the bottom of my heart. He saved my husband's life and many others.

He's a good man. We…" she pauses once more and I hear her sniff a bit. She sounds like she's holding back tears. She says, "We love him. Jay, make sure he knows that."

"I will," I say surprised at the emotion coming from Holly on the other side of the phone. "I promise."

"Thank you," she hangs up and I feel a hollowness inside. I can't help but think 'Damn it, Ted, stop making me your shield from the outside word'.

I look at him as he watches the TV. He's clicked the channel again and someone else is yammering now. "You never know with superfreaks. The whole degenerate lot of them should be locked up."

"Are you really claiming then that Star Coyote is only one of many gay superheroes?"

"Probably the whole lot of them are," a mole says angrily. "All of them dirty unstable homosexuals. Gay is just their term to escape righteous persecution."

Ted flips the channel. Camo is on screen behind a podium, flashes are clicking and shining off of his sunglasses as he stands before a room of reporters. Most of them look agitated and the room is very crowded, "No, Maggie Toulver, I will not respond to that question."

"Why not?" an angry looking shitzu calls out.

"It is inappropriate, crass, and stupid, Ms. Wong," Camo says his tail flicking angrily. "Asking for a list of other gay superheroes is not appropriate. People who think that any group or organization should disclose the sexual orientation of their members are scum for asking. Please feel free to tell that to your readers in Rapture Magazine by the way, Ms. Toulver, and yours in Politics Review, Ms. Wong."

Oh wow. Camo does look stressed. I wonder how long he's been up there. He looks tense, irritable, and angry. The press agent that works for the Extraordinaries looks truly frazzled and that comment seems to have just added to her stress. Ted just sighs heavily. Is he actually feeling responsible for THAT? Maybe he should be out on stage taking these damn questions and not leaving a friend to take the fire for him.

"So the Extraordianries will still not give an official response on the recent coming out of Star Coyote?" calls a lion.

"The team's response remains the same. Star Coyote is a member of the team in good standing and he's done a lot to help protect people, especially the people of Salt Lake," Camo says irritably. "Now, if that is all the questions you have about recent events we actually called this conference for, I need to get back to my duties."

"Camo, what about the rumors and accusations of impropriety!"

"The recent signs of manipulation?"

"...Cover ups..."

"Gay agenda..."

"Response to the Family United Rights statement earlier today in relation to superheroes?"

Camo ignores their calls and just walks out of the room. I've never seen the jaguar do that before on TV. Ted whimpers and clicks the channel again. I look at him and I spy what he is eating.

"Is that my pistachio ice cream?" I ask in surprise.

"Yes," Ted takes a big spoonful and sticks it in his muzzle.

"You hate pistachio," I raise my eyebrows and feel a much larger tremor of annoyance. I know it is petty, but damn it, I love pistachio ice cream and he hates it. It feels like a huge waste.

"It is all we had left," he says.

"That doesn't..." I begin to respond but my phone is ringing again. I cuss under my breath and answer the call with a little more bite in my voice, "Yes?"

"Hey, Jay," Elizabeth Clay says and I detect an oddly exuberant air to her voice. "Look I know you're on the end of your rope. Everyone is calling you too much and I'm trying to get them to quit, but Ted's silence is maddening. I'm just calling because I had an idea."

"Oh?" I ask surprised tail wagging slightly. Any plan of Lizz's sounds better than what we're doing right now. "What?"

"You've seen the press response," Lizz says and I can just see her leaning back in her chair legs propped onto the desk. "I don't know if you saw Camo's press conference, just now. It was supposed to be about the recent attack by El Esclavador and Dr. Schmetterling in Madrid but it degenerated into a huge mess. Heck, they didn't even ask if Sfumato was going to join the team and he was spotted there. You know how much the press loves to ask about the roster of membership."

"Yes, I saw," I glance back at Ted.

My coyote is watching another news show now. The TV says, "... Protests in Salt Lake City which has stated it will not allow superbeings in its city limits under threat of immediate imprisonment, an even harsher ban than the one that state currently has for uninvited superbeing activity in their borders. They have stated unless a formal apology is given, there will be other repercussions. Many speculate the much publicized outing of Star Coyote is behind some of these reactions as well as the removal of the new villain Dr. Fabulous and his death ray from the state. The governor has disavowed such claims but the mayor of Salt Lake City has commented that the depravity of the superheroes has been evident for some time..."

Lizz talks over the TV in my ear, "Well, a lot of this is just that there is a media frenzy for information. Sure there has been positive news and support but it is getting drowned out by a lot of nattering and arguments." She continues, "I think this could be cut off if Ted got out there and made some statement or appeared somewhere. Answered some questions and push the public past this initial shock.."

"Don't I know it," I say glaring at Ted, who is pretty much ignoring my looks at this point.

"I mean, Camo is essentially fighting with his hands tied behind his back. He can't give a truly official declaration until he talks to Star Coyote. He needs to get in on this and start playing ball," Lizz continues.

"I know," I nod. "He's sort of in a holding pattern right now."

"Well he needs to break out of it, Jay," she says sternly. "This thing is swinging out of control."

"What do you suggest?" I ask pleasantly. I really hope her plan is a good one.

"An interview, a real in-depth interview with a popular syndicated reporter," says Lizz matter-of-factly.

"You?" I ask with a smile.

"Well, I won't lie and say it wouldn't help me out. My editor is always looking for another big story and it would sell very nicely. Besides, it would scoop every rival I have. I'm always looking for a way to tweak Madeline Lee," Lizz admits and I can almost see the sly smile on her muzzle. "But it would help him, too. People need information. The media needs its pound of flesh or this is just going to get worse. The general public needs to see that Star Coyote is no worse a hero for being gay. That he is the same celebrated hero he was before coming out."

"I agree with that," I say with a nod.

"I know there is a lot to his story, a lot that can be said," Lizz says. "He's a compelling younger hero. People liked him because he was charming, funny, and sweet. Let me see if I can bring that back. That sentiment isn't gone, just obscured behind a media furor. You know there are people trying to defend him. This needs to get away from the general anti-supers feelings of some people and vague homophobic thoughts. We can start him down that road."

"I believe you," I say holding the phone in the crook of my shoulder as I look at the disheveled coyote on the couch. "And that is pretty much where I stand too, Lizz. Hell, I'm about ready to call a news channel and tell them I'm the boyfriend they keep bringing up."

Lizz laughs at that but Ted puts down his spoon and stares at me wide-eyed, looking even more fearful. At least that got an actual response

Lizz continues, "Look, Jay, just talk to him. We're on the same side here and I can help."

"I know," I say again with a wag of my tail.

"Alright. I need to get back to work," Lizz says. "I have a lovely story about gun running gangs and a pipeline up to Toronto going right through the city of brotherly love to get finished off here."

"Good luck," I say with another smile. We hang up and I look at Ted, "That was Lizz."

"I guessed," Ted says with a sigh.

"She wants you to do an interview," I say sitting down on the couch and look right at Ted.

"No."

"Look, will you just listen to her? She wants to do an interview with Star Coyote and…" I begin to explain but he cuts me off.

"No." He says it definitively.

"She just thinks, and I do too, that maybe you should make an official statement," I explain.

"Later."

"Define later." My eyes narrow as he eats the last bite of ice cream and sets the carton down. Yep, I'm at my breaking point. Keep pushing, coyote, keep pushing.

"Later as in not now," Ted says, flipping to another channel, pointedly not looking at me.

I grab the remote and turn off the TV, "You mean never."

Ted looks at me and licks his nose for a moment, sees my reaction to that movement, and thinks better of what he was going to say. "Yes."

"So what is the plan? Sit on the couch and feel sorry for yourself for the rest of your life?" I ask determined to have this out.

"Maybe it is," he says to me. "Do you see what they're saying about me, Jay?"

"There have always been people saying crap about superheroes and gay people," I retort angrily. "Hasn't stopped you before now. You know this is because you wanted to have one part of yourself that was still a little straight."

"What?" Ted growls at me in surprise. "No it isn't. I'm gay. I've told you I'm gay, we have a gay relationship. I told my parents. Remember? You had to pull my dad off of me before he punched my skull in. We have a damn house together!"

"Yeah and then you promptly used your masked identity to ensure that some people would always think you were straight. You've been using Star Coyote as a mask of respectability because you're ashamed of being gay."

"I have not," Ted says angrily. "Stop being an arm chair psychologist. I never told anyone to avoid all of this," he waves at the now silent TV.

My nostrils flare in irritation. "Maybe. Or maybe what you were really afraid of was Bill and Holly Jefferson finding out."

Ted gives me a hurt look and says, "I don't want to talk about them."

"After all, they invited you into their family. Had family meals with you. You've take their kids to baseball games and helped out around the house. You and Bill went on fishing trips together. Odd how you never once mentioned to me you were doing all that, that Holly had to tell me how much time you'd spent with them. Odd that you never invited them up to Portland. Oh right, then they'd find out about you and me," I say glaring at Ted, continuing to talk about it just to spite him at this point.

I soften a bit when he looks at me, his paws trembling slightly as I continue, "But Holly just called. She was calling to thank you for saving Solarcoon's life. You saved one of the greatest heroes in the world, Ted. You saved a good man, and a lot of innocent people. I get the fact that you're freaked, Ted. This came out in the worst possible way. I don't like how this happened."

"Me neither," says Ted sadly, tail thumping the couch. My own tail wags listlessly in response. "But it hurts so much having them say all these lies."

"You dropped the ball. You can pick it back up," I say confidently, reaching out and taking his paw. "We can fight back against them."

"You don't know that for sure," he says turning away from me. "Maybe I've just been an idiot thinking I could do all of this."

I glare at Ted. I am getting sick of his sad sorry-for-himself-act. It is getting on my last nerves. "Damn it, Ted, Lizz can help. The team can help. You don't have to do this alone. I'm right here to help, too. Let us in."

"It might be too late," he says looking at his paws.

"Only if you let it be too late."

My phone rings at that exact second breaking the conversation and I'm fuming as I answer, "What? What now?"

"Geeze, bite my ear off, why don't you," Gary responds. "I'm just calling to say I'll be at your door in a few minutes."

I nod my head, forcing my voice to be calm as I say, "Thanks, Gary."

I turn off my phone and look at Ted, "That was Gary. I'm going to be going now."

"Going?" Ted asks surprised. He looks at me as I stand up and I think he's finally noticed that I've put some nice clothes on. "Going where?"

"Flambé," I respond easily.

"In the middle of the day?" Ted says looking at the clock.

"Its one of the meeting points for the rally," I respond standing up and brushing my fur a bit.

Ted quirks his head confused, "Rally?"

"The Pro-Star Coyote rally that the Portland GLBT, PFLAG, and Rainbow Alliance are helping to organize, which you would know about if you had paid attention to me for the past two days. All of Portland's gay people and supporters of gay rights show up and we march to show support for Star Coyote, our hero."

"What?" Ted seems surprised by this.

"Well, we want to counter those stupid people on TV and those people who have camped outside of the mayor's office," I respond honestly as I glance at him feeling a tremor of conviction up my spine. "Though considering how Star Coyote is acting right now, I have a hard time believing he is a hero."

"That isn't fair, Jay," Ted says standing up and looking me right in the eye.

"Isn't it?" I say with a bite in my voice as I stare at my boyfriend. "You can't sit by and let this happen. We won't let you, Star. We'll fight for you even if you don't want to show up."

"Jay," Ted begins to try and talk me down but I'm too angry right now to be reasonable.

I cut him off with a wave of my paw, "Ted, you're a brave man. You nearly sacrificed your life for thousands of innocent people, a lot of whom are now calling for your head. You've fought hard, but if you won't fight back for yourself, fight back for us, I'm not sure we should even be together."

"Oreo," Ted begins to say, his voice hollow, but a knock at the door resounds through the house and I'm heading to the foyer, pointedly ignoring him.

"I want my hero back, Ted," I say calmly. I let my anger flow out as I breathe deeply and open the door. "And I better have a full carton of pistachio ice cream back in my freezer when I come home, too."

I slam the door before he responds and walk out tail held high, even if my face is halfway to crying. Gary gives me a look as I stalk past him, but we just head to the car silently. Getting into the little car I wonder if I did the right thing.

"Isn't Ted coming?" asks Gary as we start to drive away.

"No," I say irritably.

"What is his problem?" Gary asks. "I mean Star Coyote has saved my life. I owe the guy huge just for that. And he saved Mattie and Brandon from that fire. He protected all those people at the civic center when Dr. Orgon attacked. He stopped that horrible gay basher last year. I can't even count all the times he's saved you, Jay!"

"Look, Gary, I'm not going to try and fathom Ted's issues," I say looking out the widow.

"Okay, I admit Ted himself has never been saved by Star Coyote, but that's no reason to resent him." Gary stops for a moment, thinking. "Actually, now that I think of it, Ted and Star Coyote are never in the same place. I mean I've never seen them together. They're the same age too I bet, and they're coyotes who are gay..."

Well obviously I need to stop this line of thought, quickly. I look at the big wolf rolling my eyes, "Gary, there are how many coyotes in this city? I'm sure there are plenty of gay male coyotes who fit the same description."

"I'm just saying it's odd," says Gary. "I mean, you never see them together."

"That's absurd," I say with a false chuckle. "How many people in this city haven't been seen near Star Coyote? Trust me, Gary, if he was a hero, I'd know."

Gary chuckles as well. "Yeah. I guess it is kind of silly. Ted is too wishy-washy to be a superhero anyway. Can you imagine? That would be funny to see. Then I suppose Paul would have to be Glacier. If that was the case I'd like to think I'd know."

"Paul?" I ask easily trying not to take a deep breath. That is a connective leap I did not see coming.

"Well he is a husky," Gary says tapping his muzzle with one finger as he turns the car with the other. "It would make sense. Hey, how do they know each other anyway?"

"College," I say easily. Damn it. Gary is too much of a superhero geek and too smart for this, we need a topic change. "Ted isn't coming because he is having issues."

"Again?" Gary rolls his eyes irritably, "I swear that puppy has more issues than Vogue."

"What can I say," I comment with a shrug, "it's just who he is. By the way, don't steal other people's jokes."

"How do you put up with it, Jay?" Gary asks after a long pause. "I mean, he was a closet case when you started dating. He gets beaten up by his dad when he found out. You've both had some pretty serious fights. I don't get how you're able to handle it all, how you can even still be together after all that."

"I'm not sure myself," I say, glancing at the wolf. "Sometimes I wonder why I even bother."

"Oh," Gary is quiet for a long while as we drive into the city proper, away from our little suburban home, getting closer and closer to Flambé. As we stop at a red light near our destination he then says, "Jay, I know I sounded like I don't understand you two but it was really because, well, I'm jealous. You and Ted have something I wish I could have—a relationship I find amazing. You're both so happy together a lot of the time. He's really grown, thanks to you. You settled down too, and it has worked for you. You're a better man for being with him. I—I wish I could have that. Hell, there was a time I thought you and I could have that."

I pat the wolf's arm and smile up at my oldest friend. We've been good friends for years. I always knew he felt a little of that. We never were very good together as partners, we are much better as friends, but I do know one thing, "You'll find it someday, Gary. Sometimes you have to wait."

"I'm not so sure," he says, a bit of a dopey smile on the big wolf's muzzle.

"I am," I say with a smile. "You're too good a guy not to find someone. Just make sure it is someone as good as you. Being in one of these long term relationships can be wonderful as long as you can respect the guy."

"I've read Jane Austen too, you literary queen," he says punching my arm playfully and we smile at each other. The light turns green and we zoom onwards. Soon we've parked and we have to walk to Flambé. I've never seen so many cars in front of the club. Walking in that sunlight I can't help but smile. The day feels good despite arguing with Ted. Maybe, just maybe, he'll get up off the damn couch and get out here. Maybe we can prove how much he means to all of us, how much he means to me.

It takes us a while in the crowd, but eventually we find our friends. Mattie and Brandon have made signs and are happily brandishing them as they wave us over. I never thought I would see the day when Brandon would be holding a big protest sign.

"Finally, you're here," the bespeckled raccoon says with a grin.

"I'm amazed how many people are here," Brandon says with a wide grin. "Can you believe it?"

"No," I say with a smile. The club is filled with people holding signs or banners. Everyone is talking excitedly. A lot of people are wearing rainbow striped four point stars or "Portland's Hero" or "Proud of Portland" or "Star Coyote Saves" t-shirts and I can't help but smile as I look at everyone. They're excited. They're proud of my Ted. I wish he could understand what having a gay hero would mean to the community.

"We won't let them drag our hero through the mud," Gary says nodding his head. "He doesn't deserve this."

"I'll say," says Brandon. Mattie chimes in. "You should hear people. It puts everything he's done in a different light, sure, but it doesn't change the fact that he's a hero."

"I wonder who his boyfriend is," says Gary with a conspiratorial grin.

"Could be anyone," Brandon says glancing about. "I mean if he isn't a speciesist kind of guy, he might be just about anyone here."

"With a body like that he could have his pick," a goat nearby says with a wide grin. "I spent all yesterday calling all my old coyote boyfriends and asking if they were Star."

"How did that go, Charlie?" Gary obviously knows the goat, which is not a surprise.

"None of them owned up to it but it was fun to reconnect. One of them asked me out again. Who knows, maybe I'll be dating a superhero," the goat says and then seeing a coyote at the door he waves. "Oh hey, it's Byron. Excuse me."

He wanders off and I grin. Ah, the anonymity of the crowd. I grin mischievously as I say, "He has a point though. It could be anyone. For all we know, his boyfriend is here right now."

"Hah. I hope he is," says Brandon. "Who ever it is deserves a medal for putting up with what people are saying."

"Not to mention congratulation for bagging a sweetie like Star Coyote," says Gary with a wide grin and a flick of his wolfish tail. "And he'd deserve to see our support, too."

"Oh, Gary, hush," Mattie says with a flick of her wrist. "Oh hey, my new girlfriend will be here too by the way. She's a little late."

"The hyena?" asks Brandon, and I realize how out of the loop I've been recently. I didn't even know Mattie had broken it off with Chessie. "The one who looks like a thug?"

"She does not," Mattie says rolling her eyes. "She's coming to support Star Coyote. She'll just be a bit late. I can't wait for you all to meet her."

"Hey, where is Ted?" asks Brandon glancing about.

Before I can answer Mattie responds, "Knowing him, he's probably late or distracted by some pretty sparkly stuff."

We all chuckle at that, but Gary gives me a sidelong look. I shrug and sigh. Well at least seeing Mattie's latest flame will be interesting; she's had a long string of bad ones. What is it with her and mean girls?

My phone rings and I sigh answering it, "Hello?"

"Hey, Jay, this is Diane," says a voice and I hear her clicking at a computer keyboard.

"Hi, D," I respond with her initial so she knows I am in public and I can't be too detailed. "What is it?"

"I'm just curious if Ted is going to, well, make a statement or anything," Diane asks and I note a hint of desperation in her voice as well as irritation.

"I'm working on it," I say tapping the bar feeling frustrated. I had been letting myself forget the problems with Ted. Brandon and Mattie are looking at me, but Gary is talking to someone else.

"Try and get him to get out there," Diane pleads with me. "The boss is on the warpath at this point. I don't know who he is going to claw apart first: the reporters or your boyfriend. Someone is going down. He's on his last nerve."

"I gathered," I say and then thinking of a way to mention the news conference I add, "I saw him."

"I bet," she said with what can only be described as a teleological eye roll. "He's been getting slammed with this and the others are all avoiding the media like a plague. You should have heard some of the crap someone said about Force Vixen to her face."

"Yeah," I nod and then my phone beeps. "Hey, D, look I'll talk to you later. I am trying, but someone else is calling through."

"Got it," she says and hangs up.

I answer the phone again with a sigh and Brandon chuckles, "Ah, the old digital manacle."

Mattie smirks and punches Brandon in the arm, "Quiet, luddite."

"Jay!" I hear a very worried voice respond on my phone.

My eyes widen as I answer in confusion, "Sam?"

"Jay, you have to get away from Flambé immediately! I just found out that..." the phone cuts off in a crackle of static.

The big front doors to the club slam shut with a loud bang, and I can just hear them locking, and everyone turns and stares at them. Some of the patrons try and push them open. My paw drifts to my pocket. That is when the sky light caves in and glass shards rain down on to the dance floor. People scatter screaming to the sides as a feline figure falls to the ground with easy grace.

A very familiar feline figure, one I've seen before in person. The red, black and white costume, the tawny fur, the flicking tail as he stands up confidently, his perfect muscular form flexes as he growls an insidious grin on his muzzle, "Well, well what do we have here? Some support for the faggot hero? I don't think we can have that."

I've clicked the button sending out the code red distress signal even as everyone stares wide eyed in fear. Gary whimpers the name everyone is afraid to say, "Power Puma."

CHAPTER 16
ENEMIES AND ALLIES

I sit back down on the couch as Jay slams the door, leaving me to my thoughts. How can he understand where I am coming from? He hasn't gone through what I have. Sure he's gay, but his parents love him. He has friends. He has respect. He isn't going out there saving the world only to have people turn on him and start saying things like I've planned these attacks and that I would do horrible things to people. The very idea that I would have anything to do with helping Dr. Fabulous offends me.

The thing is, as angry as I am, I get the feeling Jay is right. That he has every right to say what he did to me. I think if positions were reversed and he was the superhero, he would have behaved differently. I think he'd have told me earlier. I think he would have been more honest. He would have told the team sooner. I know, despite what he says, that he would be a hero, maybe a better one.

That makes me think of the others on the team. I ran away. I ran away from Solarcoon, from my friends. They all know now. The world knows, and I ran away. I turn the TV back on to drown the thoughts out. It is easier to have other people talking than to think about it myself.

It flips on to a news commentary show, this one with Carl Tanner, a rather famous reporter. The big bear is saying, "... and joining us is Mayor Richards of Portland."

"Pleasure to be here, Mr. Tanner," the mayor says evenhandedly, and the beaver straightened his tie slightly.

"As well as Mayor Ryans of Salt Lake City," says Carl Tanner with an insipid smirk.

Mayor Richards seems surprised by the other guest. The two are on split screen. The beaver looks from Tanner to the ground squirrel that has just appeared on the screen. He actually seems genuinely surprised. I don't know why. I've caught the Carl Tanner show before and Tanner likes to ambush his guests with their rivals.

"We're talking today about the recent revelation of Star Coyote being a homosexual," said Carl Tanner, the bear's muzzle breaking into a gotcha smile.

Mayor Richards coughs, his webbed paw over his buck teeth, "I was under the impression that this interview was about Portland's bike services."

"Well that isn't how we roll on the Carl Tanner show," said the older bear tapping some papers on his desk with a smirk at the split screen. "You've been very quiet on the controversy, Mr. Mayor. We here at the show felt you should give your opinion."

"You know what mine is, Mr. Tanner," the mayor of Salt Lake City says, his nose twitching. "What the opinion of all right thinking people is, that this attack on our city was proof of the inherent evil of these homosexuals, and of superbeings in general. Our city was assaulted, homes destroyed, lives threatened, all by the Gay Agenda. Well, no more I say. Toss these perverts out. Get rid of them."

"You're response, Mr. Mayor?" Tanner says and the screen is filling with Mayor Richards' face.

The beaver closes his eyes for a moment opens them and then says, "Well, Mr. Tanner, my staff would advise me—has advised me—not to make a formal statement on this issue."

"Fear of these freaks calling him a bigot most likely," the ground squirrel says triumphantly. "I can tell you this, we'll be making sure that they know exactly how far that flies in our city. Have a spine, Mayor Richards. Stand up to that freak Star Coyote and tell him what you really think."

"What I really think?" the beaver questions, flicking an ear. "Well if you hadn't interrupted, I would have given some pat response, but I'm done with that. Freak? How dare you, Mayor Ryan. How Dare You! Star Coyote was willing to die to save your precious temple, to save your city. He dove in front of that blast and took it essentially point blank. You can see it on every video closeup, he's honestly surprised to have survived."

"Good acting," the Salt Lake City mayor dismisses. "Their kind is good at that."

"Their kind? I wasn't aware I had traveled back to the 1860's," Richards says sardonically as he sits up. "Portland's superhero was willing to die to protect your city and it's citizens. Yet you repay him with slander, lies and a laughable stereotype. I can see his near sacrifice was worth it for such an example of American culture."

"So Portland wants to be represented by a gay freak?" the mayor of Salt Lake shouts back.

"You mean a hero willing to sacrifice his life even for people who repay him with hatred, distrust, and lies?" I sit up, transfixed by the mayor. I didn't even vote for the man. I never campaigned for him, in or out of costume. I'm paying attention now. He looks at the screen for a moment and then says, "You're damn right we want him in Portland. We at least know that good examples for our children, good examples of our people, should be celebrated."

"Are you claiming that Star Coyote is a good example for children?" Tanner breaks in and he actually looks surprised by this.

"Yes," says Mayor Richards with a smile. "He's a great example for all of us. Here we have a man willing to serve and help people. He shows a dedication and service I've rarely seen in anyone. I've met the young man and he is truly a good example for all of us. He has tremendous power but instead of abusing it he uses it to help people. He's polite, just, and intelligent. Isn't that we want all our children to aspire to? We in Portland don't forget the help he's given. The lives he has saved. He's helped the city on building projects and clean up, he's saved cops' and firemen's lives, and he's protected children. I've seen him volunteer at youth centers. The man isn't just a hero. He's a Portlander and we're happy to have him!"

"So you'd like him to expose your children to the perversion of what he is? Tell people how great his lifestyle is?" shouts Ryan. "What of your own son, Richards. Do you want Star Coyote getting anywhere close to him?"

"My son? Are you implying something, Mr. Ryan? If my son was gay it would be a surprise yes, but I would like to think he respects me enough to talk to me. I'd like to think I'd respect him for who he was. As for Star Coyote campaigning for gay rights? I've never seen that coyote campaign for any issue outside of more money and time for our brave servicemen, cops, and firemen. Unless you're calling policemen gay, Mr. Ryan, I have no clue what you are babbling about."

Ryan sputters, unsure how to respond to that, and even Tanner seems a bit shocked. I'm standing up though and staring. The mayor just stood up to defend me. What is wrong with me? Why am I just sitting here when the mayor, when Jay, when Camo, when everyone else I know is going out to fight for me?

"Mr. Richards, you realize you're going against your party on this and against the campaigners in front of your own office?" asks Tanner firmly. "Probably against the will of the people, at that."

"I'm never going to please everyone," Richards says with a smile on his bucktoothed face that makes him look, well, as if a weight has been lifted from him. "I've seen those people outside. I've also seen the letters in my office asking me to save our hero. A woman wrote to say how he saved her entire family and how she hopes I will do the right thing. The chief of police visited me today to beg me to help protect our hero. Special interest groups are always going to give their point of view, and they do it from both sides. There is even going to be a very large march today of people in support of Star Coyote. I've seen that too. Something your network seems to have glossed over completely."

"Nonsense," shouts Ryan. "We wouldn't have that here in Salt Lake City."

"Well it is a damn good thing I don't live in Salt Lake City then," Richards comments. He continues, "If the voters have a problem with me supporting Star Coyote and they want to make that the only issue they care about then they can vote me out of office. I invite them to take part in the democratic process, and if they want to ignore what I've done for this city and what Star Coyote has done for this city than they can do that. They'd be myopic idiots but I invite them to try and get rid of me over it. If they dislike our gay superhero they can move to Salt Lake City. I'm sure Ryan would be happy to have them."

"I'd expect this from you toadies to the Extraordinaries," Ryan screams, obviously getting flustered now, his face turning an ugly color of puce under his fur.

"Yes. How dare I support people who work tirelessly to protect people's lives," Richards says acidly. Then turning to the screen, he states, "I'll be going now, Mr. Tanner. Next time you setup an interview like this, you'd better make sure you aren't going up against a publicist the likes of Polly Paulson, who will use it to demonstrate why you shouldn't be on the air.." Tanner goes to commercial, but it doesn't matter. The mayor just defended me on national TV.

I stand there, staring at the TV, amazed. I can't just sit here anymore, not after that. I slip off my bathrobe and run into the bathroom. I quickly clean up, brush my teeth, and then run into the bedroom. I grab my costume and slide it on. I stand in front of the mirror and smile. It feels good on me. It feels right. I wag my tail as I put my mask on.

"Well, time to get out there," I say with a smile. It's time to be with my friends. I'll go to the march, and then Jay and I will contact Lizz. I'm just opening the back door when my communicator starts buzzing. I pull it out and glance down, and my eyes widen. Code Red. I lift it up, and the screen says 'Portland'. Jay!

I rocket into the air. I hear the window in back of the house shatter from the burst of speed I gave off. I don't need to use the tracking device or call the base, I know where he is. I fly to Flambé quickly. By the time I get there I see some police cars have already pulled up into defensive positions.

I see Belinda and I land next to her asking quickly, "What's going on?"

"Oh, you finally show up," Belinda says sardonically with a wink.

I just sigh, "Look is there a supervillain in there or not?"

"Power Puma," O'Bannon, the sheepdog says quickly, pointing at the building. "He's somehow barricaded himself in there with a boatload of hostages."

"Damn it," I mutter fluttering an ear. Not good at all. Jay is in there, I can just tell.

"We're going to try and seal the place off but we don't have an easy entrance for after that," Belinda continues.

"There is a skylight," I say glancing up at the roof. "I can make it in there. Draw his fire. Maybe get the doors open and keep the civvies inside safe."

"How do you know about that?" Belinda asks.

I force a grin on my muzzle and say, "Well, I have been there before."

"When," Belinda starts to ask but she stops and tilts her head slightly. "So it is true then?"

I feel sheepish as I nod, "Yeah, it is."

Belinda snaps her fingers, "Drat, well there goes my hopes for dating a nice coyote."

I blush and wag my tail, "We can always talk about boys."

She chuckles at that and I get the feeling she actually wasn't kidding about that dating thing. Has Belinda had a crush on me all this time? Before I can continue that line of thought though, Officer Sanchez breaks in.

"As lovely as this moment is," Sanchez comments, "We happen to have a supervillain."

"And we don't have any of those special tranquilizer darts the NYPD created," O'Bannon adds with a slight snort, "Who ever heard of a three million dollar, one dose, specially crafted weapon? How did they even get that kind of cash?"

"Apparently Fredrickson Publishing gave them the money a few years ago when puma started making the Big Apple a stomping ground," Belinda answers adding, "You should read the files I send you O'Bannon."

"Hostages," Sanchez adds once more, "and Power Puma has a short attention span the guy might fly off the handle."

"Right," I say nodding my head, getting serious. My thoughts turn back to Jay, Gary, Brandon, Mattie and everyone else. "Okay, you worry about getting the people out. I'll try and make Puma focus on me."

"I'll call for back up," Belinda says quickly racing to her car. "Sounds like we'll need to come down hard here."

O'Bannon just clicks the safety on his gun, giving me a cocky smirk on his furry muzzle. I smile at them and lift up into the air. I know they have my back

I glide over the roof, land, and walk over to the skylight as quietly as I can. Glancing in, I see the lion pacing with his tail flicking. Everyone is cowering at the sides.

"Well, you fairies, you're about to learn about pain," Puma says with a grin. "Your faggot hero isn't here by now, like the little coward he is. I made sure the police knew I'd be here. I guess I should start killing you. That might get his attention."

I lift up and quietly float down into the room as his back is turned from me. I hear gasps of surprise and whispers. Everyone is watching as my paws hit the ground. "Threatening innocent lives, you're the coward, Power Puma."

Power Puma whirls about and grins maliciously upon seeing me, "Well, well, the fairy shows up."

"There are easier ways to get dates, Power Puma," I say with a smirk. "Personal ads for instance."

The mountain lion growls at me and we circle each other slowly, every eye is upon us. He's strong and fast. If he lands a punch on me I'll really feel it. I just need to avoid that and end this quickly.

"You know, I should have known you were a homosexual freak. I just assumed your genetic purity would protect you from such degenerate thoughts," Power Puma says coldly. "No matter, once I wipe you out that stain will be gone."

"Well I'm sorry that I'm too fabulous to meet your standards, Pitiful Puma. I'm pretty sure I'll overcome my disappointment," I say with a smile and a wag of my tail.

"Pervert," Puma spits, "unashamed pervert. Well, I know how to deal with you."

Power Puma runs at me. I dodge his fists, flitting about, using my flight and gravity to avoid them as I wait for an opening. A left hook grazes my cheek fur and a right hook nearly lands on my solar plexus. He's quick, dangerously quick. It takes all my concentration to avoid him at this speed. I flit and dodge around him, trying to gain an upper paw but he's fast, easily countering my moves even as I dodge his. I see an opening, slam a fist into him with a high gravity punch, but a lighter one than usual. I've never fought him alone before, and I don't want to go over board. Unfortunately, I miscalculated and he shakes off the punch, smirking at me. He growls, leaping forward, and I feel his paws slam into me, smacking me against a wall.

Damn it, I lost track of where we were in the club. I let him fight me into a corner. I shake my head, dazed by the impact, and I feel a paw wrapping around my neck, claws pressing into my flesh as Puma lifts me off the ground.

He growls, "Let's see if you can make smart comments when your face is a bloody stain on the wall."

"HEY!" I hear a voice shout, and suddenly a table, one of the metal ones that the club has all over the place, slams into Power Puma's head. The big cat shakes his head in surprise from the force of the blow. His entire body had shifted with that blow, and the table is bent and misshapen as it hits the floor. Power Puma has a thick skull though, and he still has a grip on my neck, as he turns his head and smirks as the one who hit him with a table demands, "Let our hero go!"

I see a wolf, a very big, white-grey and brown furred wolf standing there in his far too small tank top. It's Gary. Everyone else scattered when

I hit the wall, but he ran forward, grabbed a table and attacked Power Puma. If anyone ever calls him a wilting flower or a little weakling fairy again, I'm bringing this up.

Gary's paw lances out and slams into Power Puma's jaw, "You big jerk!"

The punch slams into Power Puma's muzzle, but the puma's chin doesn't even move. Power Puma just growls at Gary, "Nice try, fruit. You know what, Star Coyote?" The puma smirks at me. "Why don't I tear your little defender limb from limb while you watch. How does that sound?" The puma punches me hard in the stomach before letting me drop to the ground. It was a punch to wind me, not kill me. He wants me to suffer

Gary is holding his right paw in pain. He might even have broken it from trying to punch the durable cougar. It probably felt like hitting a brick wall. Power Puma laughs a bit as he advances on Gary, a grin on his smug face. I shake my head and try and get up. I need to stop him, but, damn it, that hurt. Puma's getting too close to Gary. I might not be in time. Gary is trying to take a defensive stance but he's a lifter, not a fighter, and he looks scared.

KAZOT! KAZOT! Two laser blasts lance thru the space between Power Puma and Gary. Every eye turns to see where they came from, and I stare wide-eyed in fear. Jay is standing a few feet away with his tail raised high, the puma's laser smoking as he glares at Power Puma, "That was a warning. Next ones won't miss." The gun must have been knocked off of Puma's belt when that table hit him.

Power Puma leaps at Jay screaming, "Brave words from someone about to lose his head!"

Jay doesn't have time to even pull the trigger. He's too exacting, he needs time to think and adjust and that could kill him now. I won't let that happen. My friends have bought me the few seconds I need to clear my head, and as Puma attacks, I see my opening. Leaping up, I reach out and grab the cat's tail with my gloved paw. I move with the momentum of the leap, lessening gravity around him and twisting my body. I'm spinning now, literally swinging a cat by his tail. Power Puma yowls in surprise as I swing him around the room, forcing people to duck back, and then I hurl him, letting go of his tail. Yes! I aimed right.

Power Puma slams right into the front doors of the club, his own body breaking them open as he flies out into the street and slams into a car, crumpling it horribly. I fly forward, quickly landing outside of the club, and the crowd inside is cheering and starting to follow me.

I raise my paw to hold them back, "Stay inside! Let me handle this!"
Power Puma smiles menacingly, "Yes, let him handle this," the cat
purrs. "Please, let him handle this."

I'm a bit surprised how smug he sounds. Why would Power Puma
look so confident? He's down on the ground prone; he won't be able to
get up in time to take me out. Cops are all around us. Then I hear a shim-
mering hum, and I look up and realize the extent of Power Puma's trap.

Above me, a crowd of people are floating gently down to the ground
around Power Puma. Leading them is Ms. Q, the fennec fox's emerald
green dress fluttering as she floats downwards, her Q staff glowing with
a sunny yellow aura that surrounds the other people floating around
her. Every one of them is a supervillain. I see the Quebecois fanatic boar
Douleur, the menacing poodle Geweld, Atomic Lion, Interrutorre the
beaver, with his advanced computer costume blinking. There's Raver,
Lux, Thrum, Los Hermanos in his bandit mask and big spurred boots,
Therma, the Iron Ravers, and even Nth Knight is here, grinning madly
with his sword glinting in the sun.

They all land behind Power Puma, forming a semi circle in front of
the club. I feel the wind whipping about and Whirlwinder, Slipstream,
and Dr. Orgon land off to my left, closing off the last gap, the last escape
route. They're all smirking at me menacingly, paws flexing, leering at me.
I think this might be the biggest assemblage of supervillains I have ever
seen, anywhere. I glance behind them at the barricade, where Belinda
is calling out orders frantically. The cops and SWAT team are trying
to rally, but they've been caught off guard just like I am. Who could be
ready for this?

"Did you really think, Star Fool, that I would come alone?" Power
Puma asks rhetorically standing slowly and grinning in evil, malicious
triumph. "No, I found others all too happy to come and destroy the
aberration, the faggot hero trying to defend his friends and city. Today
we shall righteously wipe you from the earth"

I glance back in the bar, where people are at the door staring with
fear. I see Jay and all our friends standing behind him. Oh God, I can
see Jay standing there in shock, and he's lowered the laser pistol in his
paw. He looks horrified and scared.

"Ah, I see you're checking on the precious civilians, hmm?" Power
Puma says his voice dripping with honeyed delight now. Knowing he
has me cornered, he starts to gloat, "You know after we kill you, after
we obliterate you, how about we go in there and kill every single one of
them? All those faggots and supporters of yours will be dead, just to

underscore how much of a failure you are as a hero. After that, perhaps all those cops who have come to try and help you? Why, maybe we'll raze the very city of Portland now that I think of it. Wipe it and its proud mayor and citizens off the map."

"Why?" I whisper angrily looking at the puma.

"All because of you," the puma grins. "It will be your fault little coyote. You will be the reason they all die. Why Portland will be, must be, obliterated."

I glare at Power Puma now, a cold fury blazing in my heart. No, I will not let this happen. I will fight them. I will stand up to them. I clench my fits and growl, "Over my dead body."

"That would be the point," Power Puma says with a malicious grin. "You can't stop us, little coyote. You're just one little fairy, while we are strong, and powerful, and most important, normal. The Extraordinaries have abandoned you. Oh they claim they haven't but they aren't here, are they? And why would they come to your defense? You have no allies or friends to help you. Prepare to die."

I'm about to respond but I flick my ear as I hear a whoosh of air. Turning I see Dr. Orgon flying at me, "Less talking, more fruit bashing!" The red panda flies at me, his paws crackling with electricity and I prepare to fight. Fight for my life and everyone else's, to the death if I have to.

Before I can move though, before anyone else even moves, a loud CRACK CRACK echoes across the street, and two whips wrap around the flying red panda. One grabs an arm, the other his neck, and they grow taut as they pull at him. Dr. Orgon has made the classic flier mistake. He isn't ready to be pulled in a different direction, and he tries to use his speed to escape the tether, but his momentum works against him, making him pivot in a wide circle. Orgon wobbles in the air and slams into a wall, slumping down unconscious.

"Hey, Dr. Orgon, stop making Whirlwinder look good," shouts Slipstream, his jackrabbit ears twitching as the other villains chuckle.

"Hey!" growls Whirlwinder, "I brought him for a good reason."

"Self aggrandizement?" asks the rabbit.

I don't listen to them argue, because my eyes have been drawn to the roof above the club. I stare up at the two grinning vixens perched on the edge of the roof.

"CINNAMON AND SPICE!?!?" shouts Power Puma in actual surprise. I'm surprised they came too, even more so that they just slammed Orgon. The two vixens leap off the roof and land on one of the decorative street lamps in front of Flambé.

"Why, Cinnamon, he actually sounds surprised," Spice says balancing easily on the lamp post.

"Indeed he does, Spice," Cinnamon says with deep amusement as she fondles her whip giving Power Puma a look of confident ease. "I wonder why, after we made it so clear we disapproved of his little plan?"

"Well, he did force us to break out of jail earlier than we had planned to," Spice says, chuckling throatily.

"Though you have to admit, it is worth it just to see his face," Cinnamon says with an amused grin.

"Indeed," Spice says leaping onto the ground on my left and Cinnamon joins her on my right. "After all Portland is our town, too, and as the good Mayor Richards said, Star Coyote is Portland's hero."

"What are you two doing here?" I say, voicing the words I think most of the crowd is thinking.

"We rather like it here," Cinnamon says with a smile at me. "The cops are competent and actually make it a challenge."

"We also like the hero," Spice says, "after all, you did save my life."

"A very gentlemanly thing to do," Cinnamon says as the two of them turn to face the assembled villains, grinning easily. "You see that so rarely these days, don't you agree, Power Puny?"

"That's right, they can't all be good guys like Star Coyote," Spice says to her sister. "But that's why we're here."

"We won't let you hurt Star Coyote or this city," Cinnamon says to the gathered villains. "We'll gladly fight your little coalition."

"It might be fun," Spice says with a smirk and a nod of her head towards the unconscious Dr. Orgon. "You know, I am glad Rigger gave us the heads up about this, aren't you, Puma? He couldn't make it himself. You did after all break his leg when he tried to stop you, Pummy. That is another reason we're here. No one does that to Riggsy"

"Oh, indubitably," says Cinnamon.

"You did what to Rigger?" growls Ms. Q, her hackles up as she glares at Power Puma. I think that has offended her, and even though they've had a rocky history with the otter, Lux and Thrum don't look very happy with the puma. Rigger has a lot of friends, especially among the supercriminals, superbrains, and technology users.

"It doesn't matter, I'll kill all three of you then," Puma growls his claws twitching as he looks between the three of us. "The faggot and the two bitch traitors."

"I'm hardly a traitor for standing with my sister," Cinnamon said with a snooty huff.

"Yes and I'm hardly a traitor for sticking up for GLBT rights. After all, once a transsexual always a transsexual," says Spice with a flirty waggle of her hips, "even post-op."

"What?" Power Puma says in the silence that follows that comment, a horrified look on his face. Some of the other male villains look really weirded out by that too, and I admit I'm also trying to contain my shock as well. Spice is transgender? I had no clue.

Cinnamon smirks with unhindered glee, "Oh yes. Didn't you know? That was what we spent the money from our first caper on."

"It was a delight," says Spice with an amused eyebrow quirked. "Though I suspect, sister dear, that he might be reacting to the fact that he slept with me." She smiled broadly. "Twice."

"Oh my, you might be right," Cinnamon says with mock apologetic inflection, one paw held up to her mouth. "What is it with these species purity fellows and sleeping with vixens?"

"No idea," Spice says with glee. "Illicit thrills?"

Power Puma is twitching with rage and suddenly a thought occurs to me and I can't help it—I have to ask. "Spice, wasn't your first heist the time you stole a couple million dollars from Puma's defense fund?" I ask, pointing at the vixen quizzically.

"THAT WAS YOU!?!" the puma howls in anger flexing his body.

"You didn't know?" Spice says, "My, you are a thick one."

"Well you know what mother always said, no accounting for sense or taste," says Cinnamon and the sisters get their whips ready as they smirk at the puma. The bemused crowd of villains is glancing at each other. It seems they were not ready for that, or the two vixens coming to my aid in general.

"Oh lets just deal with this before it gets irritating. I have better things to do than stand around in a crowd," Douleur the boar says flexing his arms and a series of blades flies from launchers on his wrists. Before Cinnamon, Spice, or I can even begin to dodge the cloud of tiny blades, they jerk to a stop, hanging in the air unsupported a few feet away from the startled boar.

"Stop stealing my fucking act, pig," shouts a voice from the street crowd, and this time my eyes widen in total surprise. Killa Thrilla is hopping over the barricade and stalking towards us with a growl through the line of cops, who can only stare at her. They don't even try and stop her. "I'm already planning to cut ya, ask yourself how deep you want it to be before you steal my moves," the ganger snarls as she walks the cloud of knives twist and turn to point at the villains, hovering in a cloud of sharp edges around the hyena.

"Killa Thrilla!" I exclaim in total surprise as she takes a place beside Cinnamon and fingering one of the floating knives.

"I'm as surprised as you are, Starzy," Cinnamon says.

"Don't act so surprised, ya morons. Power Puma is going after us dykes too," Killa Thrilla says flicking her tail. The cloud of knives shift around her as she eyes up the crowd in front of us, each knife pointing at a different villain. "His little speech made that clear."

"I always knew you degenerate hyenas were full of perversion," Power Puma says glaring at Killa Thrilla, pointing at her like he was in a court room. "Here at least is proof of that!"

The other villains are now looking very uncomfortable. Four supers versus all of them? Sure, they were probably still going to win with that kind of advantage in numbers, but now we've got a certified blood crazed knife throwing hyena on our side. If Killa Thrilla cuts loose on the crowd of them, she's going to live up to her name, and that doesn't sit well with some of them. My mind is till trying to wrap around the idea of her coming to help a superhero. I'm not too surprised by the idea of her being a lesbian, but it is still a shock. This just got interesting.

"TANYA?!?" shouts a very familiar voice and I glance over my shoulder. Mattie, my very good, sweet friend Mattie, is looking flabbergasted at Killa Thrilla.

"Hey, Matts," Killa calls back as she takes out a very large knife from her jacket. "Let me deal with this. Hey, Puma, meet my friend Bowie!"

She hurls the knife hard towards Power Puma. The mountain lion is quicker than I could even give him credit for, much less someone as overconfident as Killa Thrilla. He's up in the air with a jump. He twists and twirls with impossible grace, grabbing the hilt of the bowie knife. Twirling back he throws it, using the force that Killa threw it with and his own moment to hurl it back at her. His boots hit the asphalt as the knife flies towards Killa Thrilla faster than the eye can see.

I don't have time to react, it all happens in the space of a second. Killa Thrilla is shocked too, and she doesn't have time to use her power or training to defender herself as she realizes what is hurling towards her chest. Before the knife reaches her though, a pink energy disc appears in front of her and the knife bounces off it harmlessly, clattering to the ground

"Well, Power Puma, I have to give you credit. You do cause the oddest bedfellows," says an amused voice, and its one I know very well. Force Vixen continues, "You've actually caused me to save Killa Thrilla's life. That is a first."

"Love you too, toots," Killa says with a mock smooch at the vixen floating above us.

Suddenly the illusion that allowed them to gather unnoticed ends, and they're around me. The Extraordinaries, all of them, are here. Stratagem is flexing his gloves, his trench coat flapping in a slight breeze. Lady Leopard lands a few feet from me. Glacier is at my left side, with Camo and Metlayena right behind me and to the side a bit. Bltizkrieg runs up sliding in-between Cinnamon and Spice with a smile. Titan Tomcat is slamming his fist into the palm of his paw with smirk on his muzzle. Force Vixen is on the other side of Glacier, and Solarcoon is at my right hand, glowing in the bright Portland sun. His strong, confident presence fills me up. My teammates are here. They came. My friends are here with me and I can't help but smile broadly.

"You know I always wondered if she was looking up my skirt," Force Vixen mumbles off hand to Glacier in a stage whisper that carries across the street. The husky just rolls his eyes.

"Sorry to tell you this, Puma, but we never kicked Star Coyote out. He is our teammate," Camo says with a growl. "Though I'm not that surprised you'd think that. You are a moron after all."

"You've never gotten this fact, Puma," Titan Tomcat says with a smirk. "We are a team. We always have been and will be. He's come to the defense of Toronto and Canada multiple times. Why would we ever desert a teammate in his time of need?"

"He's also our friend," Glacier says with a smile. "A good friend, too, who has always shown loyalty to us."

"Even if he doesn't return our calls," Metalyena mumbles in my ear with amusement.

"We don't desert our friends either. Especially a friend who judges us not by our flaws but by our strengths," Stratagem says, his paw flexing as a metal staff extends from under his coat. He taps the rod against his palm. "But you'll never understand that, will you, Ezekiel," the badger's face is calm, but Puma snarls when he uses his real name.

"The truth is, Power Puma," says Solarcoon his voice booming as a big paw rests on my shoulder and squeezes it reassuringly. "Star Coyote is many things to all of us. A friend, an ally, a teammate, and, to me, he is family. I won't let you threaten my family or my friends. We won't let any of you threaten this city. You have one chance. Surrender now into our custody."

"Oh crap," says Slipstream waggling his rabbit ears at the wolf in the welder mask beside him. "We are so dead."

"Shut it, we can take them!" says Whirlwinder raising his gloves and a powerful, if small, tornado spins into life in front of him and rushes towards us.

I shout without thinking, "Blitzkrieg! Clockwise!"

All those years of training together as a team have paid off. Blitzkrieg doesn't think, he just zips around the funnel in a clockwise fashion. The team had long ago learned that Blitz could create wind currents by moving fast enough; it was a trick Swiftwolf used to use. The wind blast from Whirlwinder's gloves is countered and stopped by the move and the force of the sudden backlash of the disturbed funnel knocks the unsuspecting Whirlwinder to the ground.

"Well then," Solarcoon mutters, "if that is the way it has to be. Orders, Star Coyote?"

"Me?" I ask looking up at the raccoon. "I've never been in charge before."

"Well this is your city after all," the raccoon says his smile conveying more confidence that I've ever felt. And he says low enough so I and a few others can barely hear it, "And I trust you."

I smile. I know what to do. I shout my orders quickly, "Blitzkrieg, there are civilians in the club pull them back! Force Vixen, counter Ms. Q and make sure she doesn't try to get these yutzes out of here. Camo, take down Raver and run interference. Lady Leopard and Titan Tomcat, the Iron Ravers are all yours. Stratagem, you take out Atomic Lion, Interrutorre, and Nth Knight. Glacier, freeze Therma and deal with Los Hermanos. Cinnamon and Spice, Whirlwinder and Slipstream are yours. Metalyena, you can handle Geweld. Solarcoon, Thrum and Lux are all yours. Thrilla Killa, deal with Douleur and, please, try not to kill him."

"Spoil sport," she says as knives she held earlier fly at Douleur, causing the shocked boar to duck and block his own weapons.

The villains heard my marching orders clearly enough, but they're still caught off guard. They've never truly worked as a team before, not all together like this. I know what I am doing because, outside of Killa Thrilla, I know these people.

"Power Puma is mine," I say advancing on the lion.

"Cocky," the mountain lion lashes his tail. "I'm going to smack that grin off of your muzzle."

"Like to see you try," I say leaping forward in flight as the battle commences, both sides rushing towards each other. Blitzkrieg knows to get Jay first. He probably doesn't know what Jay looks like but as long as my collie has his communicator on him, Blitzkrieg can find him and grab him. I can concentrate on the battle itself and not worry now. I know Jay and the others will be safe.

* * *

I just watched an assemblage of heroes appear around Ted and the three supercriminals who had come to his aid. That's what surprised me the most about the fight; that those three came to his aid, especially one that enjoys pointless violence for its own sake. I heard Ted order Blitzkrieg to do something but before I even heard the rest I find myself being picked up in strong, muscled arms. Wind whips past me as the scenery becomes a blur. In a moment, almost a blink of an eye, I find myself well away from Flambé, at a city park.

"You is Jay, ja?" asks the big wolf with a smile. His uniform is tight on his firm fireplug body as his ear twitches.

"Ya," I answer, shocked to be held in the arms of the muscular wolf. Been a long time since that had happened.

"Gut." He lets me drop, and zooms away. I was just saved by a super fast wolf. Then with only a slight blur and the whipping of the wind other patrons of Flambé appear. Mattie appears beside me, staggered by the sudden change of scenery. Then a deer, a wolf, a mouse, and Brandon, then another otter, and a jackal, and Gary who is grinning madly, and shouting "I just got saved by Blitzkrieg!" Around us, the whole crowd is appearing in a rapidly expanding group of excited people.

"I can't believe I'm dating a supervillain," Mattie says, and I really wish I could respond to that one.

Brandon handles it, "Well it isn't that big a surprise."

"I think it's kinda hot," Mattie says with a smirk, her ringed tail flicking as she glares at the otter.

"Women," Gary says with an eye roll.

* * *

I dodge Power Puma's fist easily, a confidence in my step now. I feel better than I have for days and my punch lands, sending him reeling back. I'm not holding back a second time. He can take it. I also know that if I go down, my friends will come to my aid. They'll protect me and save the city. It is a liberating thought.

I hear growls and groans, and powerful metal fists slamming the ground behind me as the battle starts in earnest. Gears turn and metal squeals in protest, as Lady Leopard and Titan Tomcat force the Iron Ravers away from the rest of us, down the street into a clear spot. The four metallic bears are automata that went horribly wrong. They have the minds of a biker gang controlling them, or what is left of those minds, and those overly masculine bikers are offended by the very idea of a single woman taking them on. Unfortunately for them, Lady Leopard, while demure, is no ordinary woman. She easily ignores their blows and returns each punch, sending Wrought reeling, grabbing Rivet and slamming him into Wrecker with the sound of twisting metal and then pitching them both down the street. Ripper punches her but it doesn't affect the good Lady at all, she just grabs the fist and flings the beast into one of his cohorts. Lady Leopard could unwind and go all out on the machines, use her full strength if she wanted to. They aren't alive after all, and there isn't any real way to destroy them, they just rebuild themselves. She won't though, she always holds back, it is just who she is. The Lady will, however, keep that muscle under control while we deal with the others.

Titan Tomcat meanwhile circles the fighters, keeping them from separating from their fight with Lady Leopard. He's grown larger, expanding upwards so he has the strength to handle the metallic bears. Wrought tries to grab and toss him into the fight, to confuse and make Lady Leopard fight on an uneven footing, but the cat just dodges him. Just because he is big doesn't mean the tomcat isn't fast. Titan doesn't bother hitting the machine; instead the feline shrinks, vanishing from sight and dropping into the bear's interior. Many people forget Titan can shrink as well as grow, and when he does he's still as strong as if he had grown to giant size. Becoming miniscule, he attacks the big bear machine's knee; taking it apart from the inside and sending the bear crashing to the ground, his leg coming off completely. Titan expands suddenly then, becoming nine feet tall, pinning the bear down and slamming a fist into the snout of the disabled metal bear, giving him what would have been a knock out punch for anyone else. Lady Leopard might not be willing to play dirty, but Titan is all too happy to rough these guys up to keep them contained. Wrought just shakes off the blow and pushes him off, stumbling towards the cat, his leg trying to reform under him. Titan just grins and meets him again, continuing to shrink and grow, dodging and parrying and dismantling the metallic bear.

Above them, Force Vixen is already in the air as she engages Ms. Q in a dogfight, sending force fields in front of her to intercept blasts from the fennec's Q staff. Blocking blows, the ostentatiously clad fennec fox is growling as she twirls and spins her staff. It's an aerial ballet, and the two vixens are snapping biting comments back and forth at each other as they try and gain the upper hand.

Power Puma tries to land a punch but I slip around it and grab his arm, hurling him a couple feet before he finds his footing and leaps back at me, charging recklessly. He should have turned and tried to help Lux and Thrum, who are fighting right behind him. Solarcoon has faced both villains before, and he knows their moves well. A bit of speed lets him take Thrum down first with a well placed sweeping kick, getting him off his feet and down to the ground before he can muster a sound wave attack. Solarcoon's speed shifts to strength and he punches the squirrel hard sending him down for the count.

The burly raccoon turns on the mouse, "It doesn't have to be this way, Lux. I know you two are just here for mercenary reasons. Surrender."

"No! I refuse to be defeated by you superheroes again! You aren't masters of light like I am!" she shouts, trying to blind him with her light attacks, colorful blasts shining around him. For anyone else, that attack would have blinded them, maybe even confused them so they couldn't fight, but against the raccoon it is pointless. Solarcoon can't be blinded by any light, or lack thereof, and he just absorbs the light blasts that hit him. He's striding toward her confidently. I knew he could handle Lux's ability, which is why I told him to handle those two. He disarms Lux easily, twisting her arms behind her back and cuffing her. She struggles a bit and then gives up.

Power Puma is in a rage now, an uncontrolled fury aimed at me. Screaming invectives against gay people and hyenas and any other group he can think of as he tries to tear into me. His paws cut through the air but I dodge and duck and weave just as I've practiced countless times before. Power Puma is at his weakest when his plans start to fall apart. He gets stupid, letting his anger take control.

Meanwhile, Camo is confusing Raver. The girl keeps trying to send out scream attacks, but Camo is never in the place she suspects. Add to it flashes of light in her eyes and random figures and the illlusion that her allies are closer than they are, and she's more dangerous to the supervillains than to Camo. The jaguar even tricks her into nearly blasting Ms. Q out of the sky. It is no wonder that a well placed fist sends her flying. Camo smirks and turns to defend the bystanders, using a discarded hubcap from a broken car to intercept an errant blast, saving the lives of several police officers. He runs past me, saluting, calling out, "Hell of a party, Star!" as he starts to create more illusions. He doesn't need to do that for me, or for Cinnamon and Spice who are corralling Whirlwinder and Slipstream handily.

"Well, look what we have here," Cinnamon says advancing on Slipstream and Whirlwinder. Both criminals are positively scared of the two advancing vixens. Cinnamon and Spice are high level girls, famous for their daring do, while Whirlwinder is a joke and Slipstream is far too green to take them on in a fight. Sure, they could just fly away, but how does that look?

"I surrender," Slipstream says quickly. "They are not paying me enough for this."

"Coward!" Whirlwinder tries to fly forward in a shoulder charge, as he yells, "They're only two little girls we can … ERK!"

Spice's whip wraps around him and pulls him like a yo-yo, twirling him out of control, when Cinnamon's whip snakes out and jerks him hard the other direction, sending him careening into a wall. The same wall of Flambé that Dr. Orgon was slammed into, and the ineffectual criminal falls on top of Dr. Orgon, who was just managing to get back up. The two collapse in a heap.

"Silly boy," Spice says as she walks forward and Cinnamon does the same toward Slipstream, and the jack rabbit cringes.

"Aww, man," he whimpers, backing away slowly. He knows they're too close now for him to fly away, they'll just do the same thing to him they did to the other flying twits.

Cinnamon slides up to him and coos, her finger stroking under his chin, "Now are you going to ever attack a gay person again on purpose?"

"No, ma'am," Slipstream mumbles looking into her eyes. "I was going to ask you out sometime, maybe see if you girls wanted to do a heist, but I'll be quiet."

"Oh he's learning, sister," says Spice with a smirk leveled at Cinnamon.

"Well, just to make the point clear, let's underline the lesson," Cinnamon says, and together they punch the rabbit, sending him down to the ground hard. "Goody. Hey, maybe sometime we should team up with him though. Now that he's learned his lesson."

"Could be fun," the two vixens chuckle and then run back into the fight.

I can't see the rest of the team, my eyes are focused on Power Puma. I can hear them though, and I can guess what's going on, my mind flying over the ideas. I know my team. I've watched them take down these villains before.

I know that Stratagem is running up to Nth Knight, Atomic Lion and Interrutorre. Those three were grouped together, and I know that Stratagem can handle them. Even as Nth Knight raises his sword and shouts some nonsense about chivalric honor, Atomic Lion will be flaring up with energy because he knows what is coming, he has to, he's faced the badger enough times before. The thing is, Stratagem knows all that too, and while the radioactive lion is expecting him to use a spray jet that will require the badger to get in close, Stratagem instead stops for a mere moment, and then bounds up into the air using spring loaded shoes, a design he stole from Rigger. The badger sails over the big lion, pellets raining down from his paw. They explode on contact with Atomic Lion, a big cloud of white foam expanding around the green-flamed feline's body.

"Augh! Containment foam!" the lion coughs and sputters, his flames dying under the thick chalky liquid that covers him. Atomic Lion's powers are neutralized under that stuff, making him much weaker, and he's so obsessed with not being weak that instead of using his prodigious normal strength, he'll waste time trying to get it off, giving Stratagem time to get his friends down for the count. The badger doesn't give him a second glance, instead countering the sword swing from Nth Knight with his staff. Stratagem probably even knew I would send him after these three before I said it. Having Interrutorre and Atomic Lion standing together like that, there was no other place he could go. He has the best counter to Atomic Lion with that foam, and sending Stratagem against a tech villain makes perfect sense. The spring loaded shoes have even gotten him close, and the badger's goggles shine in the sunlight as his staff meets Nth Knight's sword, while his other paw flings a collapsed net at Interrutorre almost casually.

The techno computer whiz doesn't even try to dodge it. He thinks he'll be able to cut through it with his energy knife, but as the net drapes around him I hear a crackling zap. The net is a powerful electromagnet. As it closes around him the hyper advanced computer gear on the beaver short circuits, completely failing. As he struggles in the net bereft of all his tools, Stratagem just smirks and turns his full attention to Nth Knight, twirling his staff, blocking blow after blow of his sword.

"You should learn, Interrutorre, that a brilliant mind's tools shouldn't always use circuitry or the same system," he says as he counters Nth Knight easily.

"Witch," yells the knight as he tries to parry and thrust at the badger. I know Stratagem can handle him though. He's dangerously good with that staff.

"Perhaps," Stratagem says, sidestepping the knight's blade and knocking Interrutorre out with a casual smack from the butt of his staff.

Power Puma is furious; his lieutenants are all being thrown around and defeated by our better organization and abilities. "I'll kill you, you diseased scum," he growls at me.

"Considering how you sleep around I'd suspect that you're the diseased one," I quip, twirling around him, using the momentum of his blow to my advantage and kickng him in the small of his back hard with a full heavy gravity blow. It sends him reeling to the ground. "Cute butt. Though honestly, I doubt there is any guy who would want to tap that."

"Star, please try not to make lewd comments to the crazed Nazi. It's just so tacky," Force Vixen says as she flies overhead, her force field countering a golden blast from Ms. Q that was designed to catch me off guard. The fennec and vixen twirl in the air, each propelled by their own particular energy forces. Ms. Q's staff creates force bolts and fields to counter the discs and bubbles that the red fox sends her way. Countering and dodging blasts bodies entwine in the air as they flit and fly above the fight.

Ms. Q is panting and growling by now, she's getting a work out beyond her normal experience. She hasn't fought Force Vixen alone before, and she isn't used to being in a fight with someone who counters everything you do. Force Vixen is cool and calm throughout it all, confident and smirking as she counters blasts of energy from Ms. Q.

"You should be focusing on me," the fennec growls as she creates a shield to counter the vixen's manifesting force fields.

Force Vixen, riding on a disc of pink energy, just smirks as she easily blocks a blast from the staff. "As if I need to give you my full attention."

On the ground below them, Douleur and Killa Thrilla are parrying and thrusting blades, their knives appearing, disappearing, flying through the air, dropping, and sliding under foot as they fight. The boar is refined and careful. He's a master of hundreds of weapons and styles, and his flashy fleur-de-lis costume belies his incredible skill. He is finesse and style incarnate. Killa Thrilla lacks his style, but not his education with blades. Her telekinetic skills are useful, allowing her to attack from any angle, but she is truly proficient with knives and that knowledge is what she is using now. The two are dancing about each other, blades flashing but rarely connecting, their bodies easily dodging around each blow as they snort and huff and slice.

They've never fought each other before but I knew this was how it would go. The boar is a mercenary when not fighting for what he sees as a need for a free Quebec, but he won't hesitate to kill. Killa Thrilla certainly never hesitates to kill. They are two of the most dangerous people on the field because of their ruthlessness, but as long as they are distracted by each other they won't be able to kill or hurt anyone else. If I'm right, they are too evenly matched to seriously hurt each other.

I see a blade flung into the air towards Force Vixen, but instead of hurting her it intercepts a bolt of energy from Ms. Q. "Now we're even," Killa Thrilla shouts to the pink clad superhero.

Force Vixen just smirks and a force field intercepts a blow from Douleur. "Just keep telling your self that."

Therma was frozen long ago by Glacier who has turned to fight Los Hermanos. Hermanos is a tricky guy, he's a talented acrobat and he can teleport in a round about way by turning into a cloud of sand, but he can only has a range of a few feet. He took his name from his circus days before his brother was killed by a corrupt police officer. Unfortunately for him, while Glacier might look like a big muscled meat head, he is far from it. The husky follows his blows easily, and his leaping dodges soon end with him being frozen mid leap. Glacier gives him a salute before turning his full attention to the dwindling crowd of villains.

Even as Therma escapes using her flames, she is met by Solarcoon, Glacier, Spice, and Cinnamon, who all surround the ermine. Her attempts to throw flames at them are countered easily while the vixens tie her up. Meanwhile, Blitzkrieg is nearly done getting the civilians out of the way.

"I am going to curb stomp that smile across the street, you smug mutt," screams Power Puma, his blows barely missing me that time. But he isn't directing his forces and they're crumbing under an organized group like ours, which is the point of me fighting him. I'm just distracting him while our more powerful foes crumble. They're not being marshaled, not being led, they're just distracted and disjointed. They're losing what advantages they had. A lot of windows have been blown out and there are big chunks of the pavement that will need to be repaired, but it doesn't matter. We're containing them.

I smile and a punch connects with Power Puma's face as I say, "Keep dreaming."

Camo is helping Stratagem with Nth Knight now, confusing the big dog as his sword tries to hit false images. It is only a few more moments until Stratagem's fist slams into his face at last and the St. Bernard collapses onto the ground in shock, worn out from swinging his sword about and the force of the blow. Camo and Stratagem turn their attention to help the others.

Atomic Lion has finished cleaning himself off, his fire burning the last of the foam off just before he gets hit by a metallic fist from behind. Metalyena slams the lion down to the ground, right by the unconscious poodle Geweld. It was almost unfair sending the hyena after Geweld. The poodle can shape shift his body into deadly metallic weapons capable of far more damage than people would expect from such a small effeminate poodle, and he's proud of that fact. The destruction he has caused in Spain and France during his crime sprees there is legendary, but Metalyena can take it. His invulnerable metal skin hasn't even been scuffed by the blades of the poodle before Metalyena finally landed a solid blow and punched him out.

Behind Metalyena, Titan Tomcat intercepts Rivet as he tries to break from the fight with Lady Leopard. The Iron Ravers have finally noticed that most of their allies are down for the count. Wrought is struggling to help his metal biker brothers, but he's been seriously damaged fighting Titan, so Titan can easily push Rivet back at Lady Leopard. Titan Tomcat's now huge body is more than a match for the metallic beast which he locks into combat with fervor. Lady Leopard is still countering the other three, who are lost in a rage at fighting a woman who will not bend, will not curse, and will not even mutilate their twisted metal bodies to allow them to reform into a more dangerous configuration. They can't understand her polite carefulness and kindness, and it infuriates them to no end.

Glacier looks into the sky and smirks, his eyes glowing blue as he sends a freeze bolt into the air, hitting Ms. Q's staff. She is too focused on Force Vixen to see the blast coming and the Q staff shatters from the extreme cold. The fennec, powerless, starts to fall to earth before being grabbed by Force Vixen. The pink skirted fox smirks and floats her to the ground where she surrounds her and the other fallen foes in pink force bubbles. She can't create strong enough ones to contain the still fighting foes, containing this many is already a strain for her mentally, but she can keep the ones who are down contained, freeing the rest of us to marshal and combine to take down the rest.

Power Puma growls at me, "You are slime, a degenerate, and a fool if you think you can defeat me."

"No," I reply coldly, factually. "You're the fool, Power Puma. Your forces have crumbled. Your allies are down or didn't you notice?"

Puma looks about surprised and realizes that it is true. They have all been defeated, the only loose one is Douleur and the Ravers, and they can't break free from the supers fighting them. "Impossible."

"Not really," I say taking advantage of his distraction and slamming my fist into him hard, increasing my gravity dramatically. My body quakes with the force, the ground seems to shake under the weight of my feet, but I continue as I advance on the Puma, "Let me make something clear, Power Puma.

"Never, ever, threaten this club or any other gay club again," I say as my fist smacks into his muzzle again, sending him backwards. He stumbles and growls, but I block his counter punch easily and continue to advance on him, pushing him back hard.

"Never threaten my friends again," my blow slams into his chest and he shakes and coughs, badly winded. Shaking, he tries to throw a punch but I block it even as I advance upon him. He's winded and confused. I've worn down even his legendary stamina.

"Never threaten these police officers again!" I shout now as I slam him with a left hook. He's dazed and shocked by the force of the blows as I reel back my fist.

"And never, ever, THREATEN PORTLAND," I yell as my fist connects under his chin sending him high into the air and back down again, the blow finishing him off. "I hope I made myself clear."

The crowd is silent for a moment, as my voice rings across the street. Then an angry shout breaks the silence. "Screw this!" shouts Thrilla Killa angrily, dropping yet another knife, balling up her fist and punching the boar right in his snout. Douleur falls over more in surprise than anything else, and Camo kicks him upside the head and cuffs him as he lays there, dazed.

"You could have done that the entire time, couldn't you?" Camo asks.

"Not as fun as cutting," Thrilla Killa says with a shrug.

"I think I see why there are clubs in New York that emulate you," says Camo with a smirk. "On to more fun?"

The hyena grins and flicks another knife into her paw, "Got that right."

I hear a pounding growing louder behind me. Wrecker, the Raver that looks like a giant grizzly bear, has broken free from the fight with Lady Leopard and is charging at me, intent on at least getting me before he goes down for the count. He isn't moving very fast though; he's taken quite a beating.

Titan Tomcat, Glacier, and Lady Leopard have the other three rounded up but they won't be able to stop him. It doesn't matter now, the four of them might be in a rage, but their allies have been dealt with. The team is joining up and combining their powers now, ready to put them to bed. I ready myself to fight him as he charges towards me. Spice swings in from a lamp post, gleefully joining me now that Therma is defeated. Killa Thrilla comes to my side as well, smirking as she readies a blade and the three of us advance on the huge metal bear.

We all glare at Wrecker as he roars, "Dykes and Faggots! I won't be defeated by you." He's charging like a bull, crashing down the street towards us with a terrible inevitability.

A knife sparks off of his hide and Killa Thrilla growls at him, "You ain't as tough as me, ya metal lout."

Spice cracks her whip, just goading him on by saying, "Just try and stop us." I do wonder what these two plan to do to a city wrecker like this guy, but hey, moral support is nice. I know I can take him by myself. I could just make him ultra light and carry him into the air and toss him into the ground or go the direct approach and gravity punch him into pieces. I don't have to hold back after all.

"Well, all we need now is a Bisexual and we got the entire spectrum," Spice jokes.

Killa Thrilla takes out more of her knives and grins as we prepare for Wreckers' assault. His brothers in arms are finally collapsing into metallic heaps since Lady Leopard only needs to concentrate on one at a time. She politely, but firmly, pushes Wrought onto the ground, mentioning something about always taking a seat in front of a Lady. Titan downs Rivet with a smash, his paws bleeding from being cut from the jagged metal but he's won this one. I'm glad he is up to date on his tetanus shots. Glacier, Solarcoon, Stratagem, Cinnamon, and Camo are surrounding Ripper, while ice, magnets and illusions confuse and weaken him as the foxy Cinnamon climbs agilely across his back, searching for the switch

369

that turns him off. They're hard to find, but with all the distractions he is unprepared to defend it. With Cinnamon's skill and dexterity she locates and uses the switch rapidly.

Wrecker is the last villain standing as he growls at us through his ursine muzzle. We're ready for him as he finally closes the distance. Suddenly I hear a WONG and the twisting of metal, and Wrecker crashes to the ground dazed as Metalyena climbs up his back and smashes his fist into the riveted bear's head. He smiles at us as he stands over the fallen metal bear and says, "Someone order the B for that GLBT sandwich?"

"You know I always suspected," I say with a chuckle.

"No you didn't," Metalyena laughs at me as he comes down hard on the ground beside me, pavement cracking under his metallic paws. His shirt and pants are ripped, but his metal form gleams unhurt in the sunlight.

"Yeah, okay that's true" I say with a shrug. "But it would have been great if I had."

We gather together in the center of the street. The police come forward, their special capture manacles and paddy wagons ready to take them all away, the Special Powers division on of the Portland police being truly useful right now. They really earned their budget today as they help secure and encase every villain.

"That was some show," Belinda says with a grin as she walks up to all of us. "Thank you, Star Coyote. Thank you, Extraordinaries."

"Glad to help," say Spice with a grin and Cinnamon smirks

"You two are not Extraordinaries," Force Vixen says irritably

"Oh but we helped so much," says Cinnamon with a smile, fluttering her eyes at Force Vixen, and delighting in the annoyed reaction it causes.

"Couldn't have done it with out us, you might say," adds Spice devilishly. "Perhaps honorary membership?"

"And we appreciate it," I say with a grin and a wag of my tail. "Don't we?"

"Of course" says Stratagem with a professorial tone. "However, now you two and Tanya," the badger says with a nod towards Killa Thrilla, "have to go and answer for your own crimes."

"You are after all, wanted for a number of felonies and robberies," says Lady Leopard crossing her arms. Force Vixen taps her foot in amusement and Solarcoon just gives them a look.

"Awww, can't we claim extenuating circumstances," says Spice with a mock apologetic smile.

"I'm sure the DA will be very interested if you come quietly," says Belinda as I chuckle.

"Mmm... how about not," says Cinnamon reaching into her pocket. "Hey, where are my smoke bombs?

"Did you really think we wouldn't grab those?" Stratagem asks holding up some spheres

"Screw this. I'm out of here," Killa Thrilla says flicking her wrist in the direction of Belinda. No knife comes out though.

"Looking for theze?" Blitzkrieg asks holding up a frightening number of knives. "I zout perhapz I should remove those, ya?"

"Fucker," Killa growls irritably but she knows she can't get away from all of us, especially disarmed. All three surrender peacefully and I suspect the DA will be a bit more lenient. Or maybe not, all three are wanted for a host of crimes. Still, I might testify on their behalf. They did come to save me after all.

"Now that was a fun time," says Camo with a grin

"I'll say," Metlayena says turning back into his furry form

"Thank you for the help," I say shaking Cinnamon and then Spice's paw before they are cuffed. They both give me a coy smile. I suspect I'll be seeing them soon. I haven't seen many prisons that can hold them.

"Belinda, would you mind if we excused ourselves," I say to the police officer. "I think you have everything in hand."

"Pretty much," says O'Bannon as they load Atomic Lion into a special lead lined paddy wagon. The lion looks forlorn and is still dripping with another application of containment foam.

We fly, float, or grapple hook off into the skyline, racing over the rooftops of the city. In moments we are away from everything that happened. From the battle site, from the cops and, as Stratagem checks for reporters and everything else, we are soon very much alone in my protected city. We stand on an old warehouse's roof. I look at the faces of my team mates, "Will we teleport back to base?"

"No. I think what needs to be said can be said here," says Force Vixen.

I stand there in silence for a while and we look at each other. Everyone is glancing about. It has been a long few days for them too, I think. Finally I say it, "I'm sorry for running. That was wrong of me. I've regretted it every minute since I did it."

"Didn't stop you from leaving us hanging with one of our biggest PR explosions in years," Camo says irritably. "Do you know the crap we've all been dealing with? The reporters alone were infuriating. Damn it, Ted, it would have helped to compare notes, to workout some strategy to deal with this."

"Not to mention how it felt to not have you there when Bill woke up," Force Vixen says. "That wasn't fun at all." Solarcoon looks away for a moment, and he almost seems embarrassed by that comment.

Hanging my head, my chest tightens as I feel more and more ashamed. It was stupid of me, I know that now. I finally say, "I don't have a defense for what I did. I just freaked out. So much had happened. The world knew something about me I was never comfortable sharing. It took me off balance."

"Well now the world knows about some other people," Metalyena responds. "Maybe that will draw some attention. Besides, at least you were brave enough to say it out loud. I never said I was bi until today."

"Oh and there is something we're going to have a nice long talk about too," Camo says looking sidelong at Metalyena.

"Obviously," Stratagem interjects, "we've all been keeping secrets. We claimed we had not been, as a team, but we had. Perhaps because we had not felt as comfortable with each other as we should. Our trust was lessened as the team grew." The badger's goggles gleam in the sun as he looks at us. "We started believing we knew what was best and stopped trusting each other as friends. The more experienced heroes became reclusive," he says indicating himself and Titan, "while the younger heroes become their own group." The team glances at me and Glacier, and then at Camo and Metalyena. Even now, standing in a group together, we have paired off to stand beside each other. "We used to talk more as friends. We need to return to that."

"It will be hard to find a way back to trusting each other," Titan Tomcat says as Force Vixen finishes tying bandages around his lacerated hands. "Maybe I should finally put my wife in the Alpha clearance. It seems she already knows all of the other Alphas as it is."

"We will," Solarcoon says looking at me directly. "I think we can start looking at this series of events as a chance to begin putting us on the right path. To being more honest, to being a better team, and being better people."

"I think that this is my biggest secret," I say blushing slightly.

Solarcoon walks close to me and he smiles down at me, "Star Coyote, Ted, I want you to know I forgive you for what happened. I can understand the reaction. I'm not angry at you for it."

"You're not?" I ask surprised looking up into his sunglasses and he gives me a warm smile.

"No," he says resting a paw on my shoulder. "I can understand it, and I forgive you for it. I'll be honest with you. I had never considered that there might be a gay member of our team. I never thought of homosexuality except in the most abstract of ways. Ted, I'm sorry you ever felt scared about telling me. I meant what I said to Power Puma. I consider you family and I hope you can forgive me for ever making you feel as if you had to fear telling me anything important."

I can't help myself I push forward and wrap my arms around his waist hugging him close. He stands there surprised for a brief moment and then returns the hug saying, "You're the kind of man I hope my children can grow up to be: funny, even tempered, polite, and brave. Never forget that."

I look up and smile at the raccoon, "Thank you, Bill."

He smiles and pats my ears lovingly, like a father. "Anytime, Ted."

"Well this is an interesting sight," says a voice and I turn around quickly. Standing on the roof is Jay. He smiles at me. I run over to him and embrace him tightly. We hug and nuzzle our lips meet and it feels like our first kiss. I finally break that kiss and smile at him, "Jay."

"Ted," he says happily hugging me, "glad you saved the day."

"Heh, I think you did that, Mr. Take Pot Shots at Power Puma."

"Well, I was about to collapse in fear," he says with a nuzzle of my neck. "But like hell I'd let him hurt you or Gary or anyone else. Is it true you punched him out?"

"Sorry you couldn't see it," I say wagging my tail happily.

I nuzzle him and smell his scent happily until I hear a cough and I turn and blush seeing the entire team staring at us. I blush even further realizing I had levitated us a foot off the ground. Returning to the roof I smile and say, "Everyone, this is my boyfriend Jay."

"Well, finally we meet," Force Vixen says coyly with a smile

"I am sorry. I thought perhaps we would like to all meet Jay," Blitzkrieg says, "so I ran and gots him, ya?"

"I was glad to come," Jay says looking at all of us. "I've seen you all on TV. I still can't believe I am actually meeting you."

"Hi, Jay," Metalyena says shaking his paw and Jay happily returns the shake. "Don't worry. It gets easier over time."

"Or not," Titan Tomcat says with a grin also taking Jay's paw. "But it is good to finally meet you."

"Sorry about New York," Camo shakes Jay's paw.

"Forgotten," says Jay with a smile gripping Camo's paw.

"You made an excellent impression on Stuart," Lady Leopard says taking his paw as well.

"Not to mention Adam," Force Vixen adds.

And so it goes, everyone introducing themselves and talking to Jay. Bill takes his paw and removes his sunglasses, looking down at my collie for a moment. Smiling, he says, "I'm glad he's found someone that makes him happy."

"Me too," Jay says shaking Solarcoon's paw. It is right then and there, a moment of clarity, that I know what I truly want in life as I smile and watch the two of them shaking paws. We're all talking now and chatting and Jay is at the center, everyone greeting him and learning about him and I know now that having him here is worth everything that came before.

CHAPTER 17
BUILDING A BRIDGE

When we bought our home I had casually noticed that there was a small wood nearby, which is not uncommon in a Portland suburb. It wasn't until today that I had ever really taken a stroll inside of it. My arm is wrapped around Ted's waist and his around mine and we're walking together slowly, cuddling in the relative privacy of the copse of trees. Ted occasionally points out a spot he had used to change into his costume, as the sunlight dapples our fur and the leaves waft in the breeze.

It's been a two weeks since what the media has dubbed the Battle of Portland. Some pundits are calling it one of the most watched and celebrated super fights in history. It is probably a bit early to proclaim that, but hyperbole has never stopped the media before. Cameramen from pretty much every news organization had gotten in line to see it. Power Puma had called them ahead of time, or one of his servants had, giving them plenty of time to set up and film the event. They hadn't bothered to alert the police or mayor's office. That blew up in Puma's face as well. Everyone heard his little threat of killing Star and then destroying the city. The much publicized smack down has been reported over and over again, of Star Coyote outmaneuvering, out-thinking and out-fighting the monster.

Mayor Richards's approval ratings are some of the highest they have ever been. There are a lot of people who like how he stood up to that Tanner guy and to the mayor of Salt Lake City just before the battle. If he keeps it up he'll win reelection next year in a landslide. It helps that the prison for super criminals that was constructed under his first year in office has contained all the captured people, except for Cinnamon and Spice naturally.

Star Coyote has approval ratings in the high nineties in our city; across the country they're well over seventy percent. Part of that was the fight and part of that was the article Elizabeth wrote. She made it appear that she had gone through official channels, saving Polly Paulson's job apparently, but the end result was the same. She interviewed me as well, for completion's sake, and used what I told her for added emphasis. I wasn't named, and she didn't say she had interviewed Star Coyote's boyfriend, but it's clear when you read it that she did.

The article isn't just a fluff piece, it is some really good investigative material on what Star Coyote has done for the city, both good and bad, as well as a reflection on heroics in general. The research is amazing and something tells me it was work she had been putting together for years and saving for just the right moment. Star came off really well because he was honest and sweet in the interview, just as he is in real life. I clipped the article for the quote he gave about me: "I won't say anything about him except to say he's the guy who gets me to wake up in the morning, put the costume on and fight. If it wasn't for him, I doubt I would be a hero." There is talk that Lizz might get a Pulitzer. It has apparently become one of the most downloaded and read articles in recent years from her paper.

World wide, there are still people who have a problem with Star Coyote being gay, but they've been silenced by a general support or blasé attitude from everyone else. His continued support and work with the Extraordinaries helps there too. The Exraordinaries are glad to have him back and they've countered a lot of the negative press. It does help that Metalyena came out during that fight. That revelation and the fact that three super criminals came to stop Power Puma drew some of the attention from Star and got the world talking about homosexuality and gay heroes in general, not just Star Coyote. Sheleighlie, the superheroine of Dublin, came out as a lesbian soon after the fight and it caused a minor stir, especially with the Catholic Church, which had endorsed her actions, but overall there hasn't been as much of a dust up

Right now though, I can't help but think how great the last few weeks have been. It has been odd. Ted has been amazingly attentive.

Talking to me, hugging, me, leaving small gifts around the house for me—thoughtful and sweet in ways he has never been. I smile at him as we start to walk away from the woods.

"Love you," I say kissing his cheek.

"Ditto," is all he says with a sappy grin. Then more seriously he says, "You were right, Jay."

"Right about what?" I ask, tail wagging slowly as I press against him.

"About things in general. I've been scared and worried about what people think. But it doesn't matter what the general public thinks. What matters is how I feel, and I feel happy with you." He kisses my head gently. "And it is more important for me to act like a hero and help people."

"I'm glad," I say with a nod. "It is good to know you're here with me and that you can listen."

"Yep. You do have an annoying, almost Samuel like, tendency to be right," Ted nods with a smile. "And I figured out something else out."

"Oh?" I wonder looking at him.

"Yeah," Ted grins and stops. Blushing slightly, he breaks our cuddle and takes both my paws, "Jay, you've always been the brave one, the guy who pushed me. Sure I asked you out first, but after that? It was always you pushing me. It was always you pushing me into taking our relationship to the next step. Calling ourselves boyfriends, meeting your parents, getting our house together, all of that was your doing. You've pushed me, forced me to not be static. To change and grow and find a better way, a way to be happier."

"It isn't like you've done nothing for me," I counter with a smile. "You've gotten me to work harder, to dedicate myself to doing better. I've done some of my best stuff since we started dating and it isn't just because of the long hours. It is you. You got me to stop being a party boy and start really growing. Hell, I doubt I ever would have taken a potshot at a crazed super Nazi before I was dating you. "

"So we've done a lot for each other," he says kissing my nose. "I just wanted to be clear."

I smile at my coyote, leaning in close to him as we walk. It has been a good month. The only odd thing is how nervous Ted has been acting today. I just shrug it off though; I mean what else can happen after the past few months. Then we turn a corner on the street, we can see our house from here and that causes me to ask Ted, "Snuffles, why are so many cars in front of our house?"

He just grins slyly and we walk faster to the house, our embrace broken but still holding hands. We fairly jog up to the front door and he smiles at me, "Surprise."

I quirk an eyebrow at him but the door swings open. Gary and Paul are standing there wearing goofy novelty party hats. The two of them fairly stuff the door as they grin at the two of us.

"Welcome home," says Paul with a sly smile.

"We got everything ready like you wanted, Ted," says Gary with undisguised glee. His wrist is still in a splint from punching Power Puma, but that hasn't slowed him down in the slightest.

"What are you planning?" I ask giving my coyote a look.

"You'll see," Gary says happily pulling us both inside. Paul just chuckles and closes the door. Walking into the living room I have to stop and stare.

The living room is full of people I know. Chairs are crowded in and a table has been set up with assorted finger foods. No wonder Ted was cleaning house so vigorously lately. Why didn't he tell me about this?

Gary and Paul are right behind us. The first thing I see is a pair of snow leopards talking to a pair of foxes. I recognize Stuart immediately, his tweed jacket and his glasses are a dead give away. The female leopard's hair is loose and hangs down a bit, a hair clip keeping it clean looking. She's wearing glasses and an outfit that would not be out of place in the 1940's. It suddenly occurs to me who she is: Jane, Lady Leopard's alter ego. They're talking to Adam, who is wearing a polo shirt and a nice pair of pants, his arms wrapped around a very dowdy looking vixen. Her hair is in a loose bun, she's wearing glasses and a long dress. She looks, well, mousy. That can't possibly be Force Vixen's civilian identity. Can it?

Diane the lioness is on the couch talking animatedly with Brian, Metalyena's brother, and the two are laughing and their hands moving at a rapid rate as they talk. Right beside them on the couch, a very stylishly dressed jaguar sips a beer and rolls his eyes adding in his thoughts every once in a while. That has to be Wally; or Camo as I've usually thought of him. I know the other hyena in the room, currently talking to Brandon of all people, has to be Metalyena, or I suppose I should call him Kyle. They're chatting up a storm and I think I hear the name Yeats being thrown around. Kyle is wearing a nice shirt and sweater combination that fairly bulges over his muscled frame, and it plays off of Brandon's usual sweater vest look. The two are certainly into whatever they're talking about, I'll give them that.

I can see Michelle and her husband. Glasses must be popular as a civilian disguise look, I wonder if I should get Ted some horn rimmed ones. They're happily talking to Lizz who is wearing a turtleneck shirt and jeans. She's a lot taller than the two smaller tabby cats. A stout looking wolf is nodding along and twitching his snout a bit. That has to be Blitzkrieg, right?

Three raccoon boys suddenly run past me, yelling loudly as a plump little jackal girl in pig tails runs after them, a doll clutched in one of her paws.

"Jenny, watch your brothers," says Holly from her position near the table.

"Simon, help Jenny," Lizz says almost casually. A young jackal boy and a raccoon girl, the girl looks slightly older but not by much, both give exacerbated sighs and stomp after their siblings.

I look more closely at Holly and I see a big raccoon beside her. He's wearing a simple t-shirt and slacks but its hard not see him in that jacket and sunglasses giving some speech and rallying people. Solarcoon and his wife are just sitting at my kitchen table. They look like an good couple. They look sweet together, warm and inviting and happy. They're talking to two older border collies. Oh God, they're talking to my parents? What in the world are they doing here? They smile as they finally see I'm in the room, actually everyone in the room sees Ted and I now, and they're looking at us and the conversations have all stopped. Do they know something I don't?

"Mom? Dad?" I say in surprise as my parents walk over to us.

"Jay, Ted," my mother says happily enfolding me in a hug and then quickly hugging Ted. Dad chuckles and shakes my paw.

"What are you doing here?" I say blinking in surprise. "What is everyone doing here?"

"We're meeting your friends, Jay," Dad says with a sly smile. "Ted invited us and, I think, everyone else here too. He wouldn't say why."

"I still don't know who half these people are," Gary adds. "How do you know all these folks?"

"College," Ted and I answer in unison and then looking at each other we start to laugh. A round of chuckles breaks out across the room as everyone waves and greets us.

Someone hands me a drink and I start circulating, talking to people happily. I still wonder what is going on. Ted is sticking by my side, grinning very broadly. Before I can ask, I hear a knock at the door. I look at Ted and arch an eyebrow. It seems like everyone is here.

"I have no idea," Ted shrugs in surprise and everyone else seems confused as well.

"Well someone might as well get it," I say walking to the front door.

Opening the door, I see a badger standing on the doorstep wearing a tweed jacket and bowtie. In his paws is an icing laden bunt cake. He smiles at me, his familiar golden eyes twinkling as he says shyly, "I, um, understand bringing dessert is customary."

I smile happily and step aside welcoming Samuel into our home. Ted's face breaks out into a very happy smile as he exclaims "You came!"

"Well isn't he darling looking," I hear Gary whisper to Paul who is staring wide eyed at the badger as he walks in. A lot of the heroes are staring in surprise and it is hard to contain my laughter at how some people here don't even know why his visit is shocking. At least Paul is not the only one here surprised. Metalyena, um Kyle, seems particularly flabbergasted.

He puts the cake down on the table laden with food and Solarcoon, I mean Bill, is at his side shaking his paw and saying, "It is good to see you here, um."

He's obviously not sure what to call the badger and I'm not sure either, honestly But with the room so quiet and all eyes on him, Stratagem covers it with a genuine smile, "Samuel, and I decided I should come. A very smart, very good friend told me recently that I need to trust others as much as I want them to trust me."

Gary looks at me and whispers, "People are acting weird. What is the big deal with him coming?"

"I'll tell you some other time," I whisper back.

"This is truly weird," Wally says from the couch sipping his beer.

"I'll tell you what is weird," I say filling the silence. "Coming home to find the house filled with kith and kin. Not that I mind, but I would have tried to clean up a bit. Care to explain, Ted?"

Ted smiles and takes my paw in his, grinning at me, "Just something I said earlier. You're always the one who makes the big choices and gets us to move to the next steps in our relationship."

Everyone is watching us now as I blush, "Well, maybe so, but it does take two."

"True," Ted blushes as well and I can see he is steeling himself for something. Then suddenly Ted drops to the ground still holding my paws. On bended knee he looks up at me and my eyes widen in surprise, "Well this time I'm the one taking the big step. Jay Carson, you make me happier than anything in the world. Everything I do and everything I've done, I do because you inspire me. You make me happy; you make me strong enough to deal with the craziness of my life. Would you please make me the happiest coyote in the world and be my husband? Will you marry me?"

I stare for a moment looking into his warm brown eyes feeing his fingers on my palms. I can feel every breath I take. Everyone's looking and it has gotten very quiet in the room. I don't know what to do. I feel frozen on the spot, by surprise more than anything else.

Gary finally calls out, "You better dang well say yes!"

"What he said," Emma calls out.

I smile broadly and I can feel tears of joy in my eyes as I say, "Yes! Of course! YES!"

I feel the band of gold slid over my finger and he's standing, smiling at me as I smile at him. His arms wrap around me and mine around his and we are so close I can hear his heart. We kiss, our lips locking, and I hold him so tight. I never want to let him go. Both our tails are wagging so rapidly as we sink into a kiss that just feels perfect. I feel like I should be the one floating. Like I could lift him up and we could fly. I hold him so tight. Finally we break our kiss and smile at each other.

"Ew, gross," says one of the raccoon boys drawing our attention.

"Tell me about it, JJ," say the second who is wearing a baseball cap.

"Right there with ya, Mark!" says the third.

"So let me get this straight," Simon the jackal boy says. "You guys think girls have cooties and yet that is gross too?"

"Well, yah!" says JJ. "They're kissing!"

Simon's sister pokes JJ with her finger and the three boys yell and run off. Simon sighs and runs after them as Jenny stalks after them saying, "Boys."

I giggle and nuzzle my coyote. He nuzzles me back and whispers in my ear, "Love you."

"I love you," I say happily breaking our hug. My parents are right at my side.

Mom is crying happily as she hugs me and Dad shakes Ted's paw saying, "So I suppose you'll finally be calling us Mom and Dad?"

"Yes," Ted says and then with a pause he adds, "Dad."

Holly grabs me in a tight hug whispering in my ear, "Take care of him."

I whisper back, "I will, just like you do with Bill."

She smiles at me and Bill shakes my hand. Lizz smiles happily and hugs me saying, "It's always worth it." I smile at her, and I think I detect a hint of a tear in the steely smiling face.

Everyone shakes my hand or gives me a hug to congratulate me, with Gary even running over happily to lift me up in a bear hug. Paws pat my back and Ted's, and everyone is laughing and hugging us and talking excitedly. I look over at Ted and he smiles at me and I know that we have each other and our family has us.

Epilogue

It's downtown Portland in the summer and the heat of the day begins to warm us as the sun shines down on our heads. It's still morning, but the haze and chill is burning off as I lick my icecream cone. Ted smiles and tries to grab a droplet dripping down his.

"I'm going to have sticky paws by the end of this," he chuckles.

"You always have sticky paws," I retort with a grin, seeing the glint of sunlight off of his ring.

"Tease," he sticks out his tongue and smiles at me. "Hey, you know what today is?"

"What?" I ask with a chuckle

"Today is the day I spilled that slushy," Ted says with a cocky grin, and his tail wags and hits my butt, making me jump.

"Oh is it?" I grin. "You keep track of these things still?"

"Always," Ted says with a smile.

I grin, looking into my coyote's eyes and say, "Thank you, Mr. Carson."

"No thank you, Mr. Rodriguez," he grins and I blush, laughing at him. We haven't really changed our last names. We had a ceremony, and everyone came, it was our way of affirming we have each other.

I'm about to say something when I hear a familiar buzzing sound. Ted quickly grabs his communicator out of his pocket, "Yes?"

"Star, we need you immediately," says a voice I've gotten very familiar with, Belinda. "Cinnamon and Spice have just robbed Councilman Quincy's fundraiser."

I can hear sirens approaching us already. I silently point to a collection of trees nearby and the two of us run under cover as Ted says, "On it."

In moments I'm holding his ice cream as he changes into his costume. Blue mask on, he slips his communicator into his utility belt and smiles at me, "Be back soon, Oreo."

"I know," I say with a chuckle. "Now go save the day, before your ice cream melts."

I watch him fly off into the air, the wind whipping around my fur as I smile. No matter what anyone else may claim or say, I know a simple truth as I watch him fly into the air. He is mine and I am his. We are together and wherever he goes and whatever he does, I'm right beside him. I know this simple fact: my husband will always save the day and I will always save his.

www.ingramcontent.com/pod-product-compliance
Lightning Source LLC
Chambersburg PA
CBHW071151020726
47502CB00002B/370